About the Author

Peter Tallon was a professional geologist who, after a period surveying and prospecting in Kenya and Egypt, joined the construction materials industry rising to the position of managing director of a multi-million-pound company. Married with two children and four grandchildren, he has lived in Suffolk for the last forty-two years where the beautiful coast and countryside form the setting to three of his previous books. 'Michael Shapmire' is his fifth book and is also based in Suffolk. Anno Domini Part 2 is his sixth book.

Peter Tallon

Anno Domini Part 2 - Germania

Olympia Publishers
London

www.olympiapublishers.com
OLYMPIA PAPERBACK EDITION

Copyright © Peter Tallon 2023

The right of Peter Tallon to be identified as author of
this work has been asserted in accordance with sections 77 and 78 of
the Copyright, Designs and Patents Act 1988.

All Rights Reserved

No reproduction, copy or transmission of this publication
may be made without written permission.
No paragraph of this publication may be reproduced,
copied or transmitted save with the written permission of the publisher,
or in accordance with the provisions
of the Copyright Act 1956 (as amended).

Any person who commits any unauthorised act in relation to
this publication may be liable to criminal
prosecution and civil claims for damage.

A CIP catalogue record for this title is
available from the British Library.

ISBN: 978-1-80074-937-5

This is a work of fiction.
Names, characters, places and incidents originate from the writer's
imagination. Any resemblance to actual persons, living or dead, is
purely coincidental.

First Published in 2023

Olympia Publishers
Tallis House
2 Tallis Street
London
EC4Y 0AB

Printed in Great Britain

Dedication

For Neil Amos for his skill and support creating the maps that help bring my novels to life.

Acknowledgements

As always, I thank my son Lawrence for his valuable editing of my work and also Neil Amos as stated in the dedication at the beginning of this book.

My thanks once again goes to Hetty's Little Copy Shop in Halesworth who produced the final draft of this book making it suitable for sending to Olympia Publishers.

I am also grateful for the support of the editorial, production and publicity staff at Olympia Publishers. Finally, for those interested in further reading, I strongly recommend Michael McNally's excellent publication entitled 'TEUTOBERG FOREST A.D 9 The destruction of Varus and his legions' produced by Osprey Publishing, Oxford, 2011, in which he gives a gripping and entirely credible reconstruction of the last days of Varus' ill-fated army as well as a full account of all the facts and main characters involved in this terrible disaster for Rome.

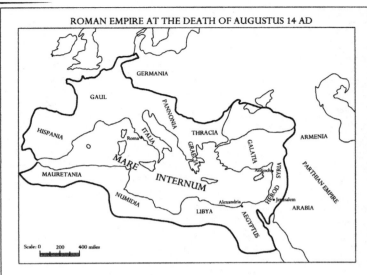

FOREWORD

The assassination of Julius Caesar in 44 B.C initiated a bitter civil war which left no part of the Roman empire untouched. After thirteen chaotic years, Octavian, Caesar's grand-nephew and the future Emperor Augustus, emerged the victor when he finally defeated Marcus Antonius at the Battle of Actium in 31 B.C. During this time the land of the Jews, which had been conquered by Pompey in 64 B.C, began its own civil war giving a young, energetic palace official called Herod the opportunity to form an army and with Roman support, take control of the Jewish states of Judea, Galilee, Samaria and Idumea.

Herod secured the backing of Marcus Antonius and Octavian who, grateful for his loyalty during such uncertain times, awarded him the title of King of the Jews and added some non-Jewish lands to his domain thus making his kingdom almost as large as it was in the halcyon days of David and Solomon.

From a Roman perspective Herod was the ideal client king, paying his taxes into the imperial treasury in full and on time every year and keeping his kingdom in order by ruling with a rod of iron. But the ordinary Jewish people were desperate. Their king, who lived lavishly in the style of a Greek rather than a Jew, had not a drop of royal blood in his veins and taxed his people mercilessly to fund his opulent lifestyle and extravagant building projects, not least the construction of the world famous Second Temple of Jerusalem. Shrewdly, he made sure his soldiers were well paid and the governing elite, which was drawn mainly from the Pharisee and Sadducee sects, was well catered for.

But fundamental social changes were taking place amongst the majority of the population who had descended into abject poverty under Herod's rule. Some joined the third sect, the Essenes, which had values more in line with the aspirations of the common people, but this sect had turned its back on modern life, cutting itself off from mainstream society and dwelling instead in the Judean desert in self-contained, inward-looking isolation. The Essenes had also foresworn all forms of violence.

Sometime in the second half of Herod's thirty-three year reign, a fourth sect appeared; the Zealots. This sect dedicated itself to the liberation from foreign domination of every part of the land promised to the Jews by God. Foreign domination included Herod and his family. The Zealots believed that the only way to achieve this was through violent revolution and although they were as yet few in number, they soon found themselves at the spearhead of a disaffected people. But the Jews had an endemic weakness, a weakness that had destroyed the empire of David and Solomon and reduced a proud people from being an imperial power to a minor entity on the international stage; internal squabbling. The Jews seemed to prefer fighting amongst themselves instead of defending their borders against foreign predators. Even under the tyrannical Herod no united opposition could be achieved until suddenly, in 4 B.C., a rumour began to spread which had the power to unify the people at last.

In Bethlehem, the city of King David, the Messiah who was a direct descendant of David himself, was said to have been born. Everyone knew of the prophecy that the Messiah would restore the Jews to their former greatness, but a counter-rumour that he had been killed by Herod when the king ordered the murder of all the male babies in Bethlehem caused confusion. Consequently, the rebellion that broke out when Herod died a few months later did not have universal support because a rebellion against Herod was a rebellion against Rome too. Even so, Publius Quinctilius Varus, the Roman Governor of Syria, which also included Herod's realm, was obliged to send two of his precious three legions to Jerusalem to support the loyal troops there who were in danger of being overwhelmed. Even then, the rebellion was only crushed after fierce fighting.

Ten years of uncomfortable peace followed during which the Zealot sect, the main focus of anti-Roman feeling, bided its time and quietly built support amongst the poor, who were the vast majority of the Jewish people. Its charismatic young leader, Eli bar Abbas and his inner council, which included Judas Sicariot, the teacher and mentor of the Messiah, knew they would have to wait at least another ten years before challenging the Romans again because only then would the Messiah be old enough to lead his people in person. But they had not reckoned with the behaviour of Herod's eldest son and successor in Judea.

Archelaus, Ethnarch of Judea, inherited all Herod's vices but not his one essential virtue, ruthless efficiency. His rule became so incompetent that some of the leading Jews eventually wrote to Emperor Augustus Caesar begging him to remove the ethnarch as soon as possible, but the response was slow in coming. A Roman legion was obliged to remain in Judea to support Archelaus against his own people, something that was never needed in Herod's time. In the fifth cohort of this legion was a young centurion called Caius Pantera, the true father of the Messiah. At the time, this secret was known only to five people; Caius and Mary of course, Joseph, Mary's husband, and Ruth, Mary's closest friend. The fifth was Lucius Veranius, also a centurion in the fifth cohort and the narrator of this story.

Meanwhile, in far off Germania, a country cloaked in dense forests, mists and powerful rivers where huge, fearsome warriors dwelt, trouble was brewing.

In later years, Lucius Veranius received first-hand accounts of these troublesome times from Caius Pantera and Judas Sicariot. He chose to write their stories in parallel because they were contemporary and often overlapped. He always said they made better reading than his own memoirs would have done. You may judge for yourselves.

CHAPTER ONE

It was a cold, windy, late Thishri (October) evening in the first year of the rule of Archelaus, Ethnarch of Judea. Judas locked up his office in Joseph's house and walked slowly down the hill to his home in Nazareth's lower town wondering how he had yet again failed to secure a construction contract he should have won. The work, in Nazareth itself, was a small extension to the synagogue. He had checked and re-checked the costs and added a very modest profit margin, yet the contract had been won by the bar Micah brothers who already had more work than they could handle. This meant that once more he faced the choice of paying skilled workers with no work or losing them to competitors.

As he approached his house, he saw a figure sitting on the ground with his back leaning on the front door. The figure stood up and walked towards him. Suddenly Judas forgot his business woes as he recognised Joshua the Messenger, the title the young man had been given for his valuable work in the recent rebellion.

"What brings you from the comforts of Jerusalem to the chilly hills of Galilee?" smiled Judas as the two men clasped hands.

"Great news! The Messiah is returning from Egypt."

"On his own?"

Joshua laughed, "He is not yet a year old; with Joseph and the rest of his family of course."

"Come inside and while you wash away the dust from your journey, I will prepare us something to eat."

An hour later, the two men had dined and were relaxing in Judas' reception room in the flickering light of two braziers set into the walls.

"You look well Joshua. Zealot life must suit you."

"Indeed yes. I am helping with the distribution of food to the needy in Jerusalem."

"So, bar Abbas is already winning hearts and minds with good meals?"

"And plenty of wine too."

"Of course. How soon must you return to Jerusalem?"

"I shall leave tomorrow morning."

Judas pondered for a moment. "Could you go using the road through Jericho? It would add half a day to your journey."

"Certainly."

"Thank you, Joshua. Tonight, I shall write two letters for you to deliver to my father's house. One will be for his wife, my step-mother Rachel, asking after my father's health for he has been unwell. The other, the real reason for your visit, is for the house slave Arethus. You remember him from the last time we set foot in the house?"

"Yes."

"You must give him the letter covertly. If it is not possible to do this without Rachel's knowledge, then do not deliver the letter at all."

"I understand. The tension in that household was palpable even to a stranger like me."

"Arethus is a good man but vulnerable. I do not want to give Rachel an excuse to get rid of him. He is too old to survive such a change."

"Rest assured Judas, I will find a way to deliver your letter to Arethus."

Judas had no doubt of that, but he was sad that Joshua would be leaving so soon. He had become fond of the young man but he quickly pushed the uncomfortable implication to the back of his mind.

A week later, a messenger arrived at Judas' office bearing a letter from Jericho. Judas paid the man off, sat down at his desk and broke the seal; it was his father's. But as soon as he unrolled the scroll, his hopes that his father might have recovered were dashed; the writing was in a different hand.

Date: Last day of Thishri, first year of Ethnarch Archelaus.
My Dear Boy,

I am sad to inform you that your father is dead. He never recovered consciousness after you left but his stubborn old body clung to life until the sixteenth of this month when he died peacefully in his sleep. It was opportune that your letter arrived a few days ago.

But there is a problem. Before he had his seizure your father had begun to see Rachel in her true light. He wrote a new will which left his estate equally to you and your young half-brother, Jacob, but with a requirement to care for Rachel for the rest of her life, which could be many years, or until she remarries, which is likely to be much sooner. I delivered a copy of the new will to the temple archives and your father locked away the other copy in a secret drawer in his desk. Well, it turns out that it was not as secret as he thought – Rachel must have known what was happening for she is as cunning as a fox –

because when I went to retrieve the will to send it to you, it had gone.

Therefore, I bid you to make all haste to the temple to secure the other copy otherwise you will lose your inheritance. The previous will was made in the aftermath of your unfortunate visit two years ago. It leaves everything, including me, to Rachel.

May God speed your journey to Jerusalem.

I remain your loyal and affectionate slave,

Arethus.

There was no time to lose. Judas immediately summoned Ehud, Joseph's deputy manager, to cover for him while he went south to the capital. His father's last words to him had been 'She knows.' Now he understood what he meant. Hopefully he would not be too late.

He arrived in Jerusalem three days later. It was early in the afternoon and he first went to the Zealot office, previously the safe house, for he was uncertain how he would be received by the authorities. It was not at all how he remembered it. Instead of the shoddy upstairs room with just a few straw mattresses strewn across the floor, it now occupied the ground floor too, which had been refurbished with well carved wooden tables and chairs, chests and cupboards for storing records and newly whitewashed walls. Two clerks sat at one of the tables busily scratching away with parchment and quills but most surprising of all Isaac, leader of the secret Zealot force known as the Shadows was there supervising the installation of wall brackets for oil lamps to improve the lighting on dull winter days such as this.

When he saw Judas he said, "Welcome Judas Sicariot. It has been too long since we last met."

"Indeed. How goes it with you? From what I see you seem to be prospering."

"There are advantages to being an accredited organisation. Since we abandoned the sword, we work in the open just like any other sect and help the poor, hungry and many others too."

Judas glanced at the two clerks. Isaac immediately understood and said, "Come and see our upper room where we can speak in private." This room had also been refurbished and was designed for conferences, meetings and sleeping quarters for Zealot officials. The two men sat opposite each other separated by a small, Phoenician made, cedar wood table upon which were two goblets and a jug of lime water.

Isaac filled the goblets and handed one to Judas. "You look troubled my friend."

"I am surprised to see the leader of the Shadows here. Hiding in full daylight I suppose?"

"Exactly so, though I do not use my true name."

Judas explained the purpose of his visit to Jerusalem and ended by asking, "So you see, I need to know if I am one of those excluded from the amnesty granted to our freedom fighters after the rebellion was crushed."

Isaac took out a scroll from a drawer in the table. "Varus was well pleased with the victims supplied to him by our craven rulers; there were eleven hundred and forty-three of them, even more than he asked for. All were crucified outside Jerusalem. Because of that, the list of exclusions from the amnesty was short. Most have been caught and now there are only three names left, Eli bar Abbas our leader, Asher bar Antipater Herod's cousin, and the false messiah Judas the Galilean. You are not on the list but be careful when you enter the temple because the religious authorities may take a different view, especially in your case."

"Then I shall come back here as soon as I leave the temple. I do not expect to be there long so if you do not see me again today, you will know something has happened."

With Isaac's warning still ringing in his ears, it was with some trepidation that Judas entered the temple enclosure by the tall, imposing Hulder Gates which formed the eastern entrance to the sacred compound. He saw Ananas, chief secretary to the high priest Joazar ben Boethus, and Caiaphas his ambitious lackey. Both were enemies of Judas and would know all about Judas' part in the rebellion because they had met at bar Abbas' headquarters just before the attack on the Roman camp. But, concluded Judas, that made both of them equally complicit in the uprising so it would be in their interests to remain silent on the matter.

As expected, Judas was challenged as he entered the main temple administration building, but the guard recognised him from his days as a temple student and escorted him to the records office where he was left in the company of the clerk of wills and benefices. The well fed, friendly little man, who sat behind an incongruously large desk, put down his quill.

"Judas, how good to see you again. It must be two years since you left."

"It's good to see you too Abel." Judas glanced round the office which enjoyed a southerly aspect over the city. Despite the cool day, the window shutters were open and he could clearly see the new legionary encampment beyond the city walls which had replaced the much smaller one destroyed in the fighting. "You seem to have cleared all the evidence of the recent conflict from the temple."

"Indeed," smiled Abel, "And there was a great deal to do. Those Roman barbarians had no respect. They even used sacred areas as latrines."

"What about the Holy of Holies?"

"They turned that into the commander's private office and dining room."

"Has it been cleansed and re-dedicated?"

"Not yet. Our high priest, Joazar, has declared that should take place at Hanukkah, which is still a few weeks away."

"Most appropriate; the anniversary of the cleansing of the old temple by my namesake Judas Maccabeus."

"Well Judas, what brings you here?"

"My father died recently. I have come to read his will because the copy at home has been lost or stolen."

The clerk frowned. "Well, that's odd. Only yesterday we had a similar enquiry—"

"Enough!" The stentorian command came from behind Judas. He turned to see Caiaphas standing tall and proud in a side doorway to the office. "Abel," continued the priest, "Has this man shown you any identification?"

"But it's Judas bar Menahem. We both know him well."

"There is a procedure which must be followed. I will deal with this. You may leave us. I shall call you when I'm finished."

The humiliated Abel hurriedly departed. Caiaphas strode into the office and stood behind the clerk's desk, arms folded and eyes full of aggression. "Well Judas bar Menahem, or should I call you Judas Sicariot?"

Judas now realised he had lost the race to the will, but he

would not slink away like the bullied Abel. "I do not care what you call me. I have come to read my father's will."

"I am amazed at your nerve coming here at all. I should have you arrested. You have been proscribed by the high priest for treachery."

"And no doubt blasphemy, sedition, murder and any other trumped-up charge he can come up with. He seems to have forgotten your clandestine visit to bar Abbas' headquarters when it looked like the Zealots would win."

Caiaphas could not deny the meeting took place, there were too many witnesses. He moderated his voice, but only a little. "You may read the will if you wish but then you must leave."

Behind the desk was a large chest from which he took out a scroll and handed it to Judas. Judas checked the seal, it looked freshly waxed, broke it and unrolled the scroll. "You picked up this scroll in less than a heartbeat," he said. "It must have been on top of the pile, so I assume it's been read recently?"

"You can assume what you like but don't take any notice of what Abel said. He can barely remember what day of the week it is."

Judas slowly read the will from beginning to end, then rolled it up again and handed it back to Caiaphas. "Where is the latest will? This one was superseded months ago."

"I know of no later will," answered the priest in a tone that was too neutral to be genuine.

"You are a liar."

"Be careful Judas."

"It is a mere statement of fact. Abel, who is not as stupid as you make out, was about to tell me someone came here for it yesterday. How much were you paid to destroy it?"

Caiaphas slowly turned and closed the window shutters so

they could not be overheard. "Thirty silver shekels."

"You were cheaply bought."

"I would have done it for nothing to see the arrogant Judas bar Menahem brought low."

"You will not get away with this."

"Proud words but meaningless. The word of a priest against a criminal Zealot. What chance do you have?"

"Caiaphas, I promise you upon the grave of my beloved mother I shall find a way."

Such a vow visibly shook Caiaphas. "This meeting is ended." His voice wavered a little as he added, "Leave now!"

***

II

Now that he understood the full extent of Caiaphas' treachery, Judas decided that going to Jericho for a confrontation with Rachel which he could not win was pointless. She had the support of the temple; that was all she needed. The old will would stand in the absence of evidence to the contrary so, disconsolately, he headed back to Nazareth. He arrived three days later, but the sun was already setting so he delayed the return to his office until the next day.

When he arrived for work next morning, there was a surprise waiting for him. He was momentarily disconcerted to find the office door unlocked, but when he walked in there was Joseph himself sitting at his desk. Ehud was sitting at Judas' desk but made no attempt to vacate the chair.

Joseph smiled, "Good morning Judas. It's good to see you again."

"And you too Joseph. When did you get back from Egypt?"

"Two days ago."

"Mary and Jesus are well?"

"In the best of health and Mary is with child again."

"Congratulations. When is the baby due?"

"In five months."

"And Reuben?"

"He stayed in Jerusalem to report back to bar Abbas, so we came with a caravan from there."

"I'm sorry I was not here to meet you."

"So am I, but it must have been a serious matter to take you away from your work."

"It was. My father died and I have been cheated out of my inheritance by his second wife and a corrupt priest."

Joseph frowned, "Can you prove this?"

"The evidence has been destroyed so I cannot."

"What will you do?"

"Carry on with my duties to you and your son."

"Good, good," said Joseph rather awkwardly, "But, well, your work will be a little different from now on."

"How so?" asked Judas, feeling the answer would not please him.

"Jesus is now ten months old. He is very active and will soon be walking. It would be good for both of you to spend as much time together as possible."

"But what about the business? I am your manager."

"I will still need you for that but in a more restricted role. I blame myself for putting too much responsibility on your young shoulders. I should have asked Ephraim to help you."

Ephraim, Joseph's pompous household steward, was the last person Judas would go to for help. "But why?" he asked.

"I have been going through the accounts for the time I was away. They make for unhappy reading."

"I know," agreed Judas. "I do not understand what I have been doing wrong."

For the first time Ehud intervened. He spoke with exaggerated concern to defend Judas. "Sir, I feel you should know that, apart from the first contract, Judas did everything right in my opinion. We went through the costs and margins together on all subsequent contract bids, yet we still lost them."

Joseph answered, "Apart from the two subcontracts you

submitted while Judas was away, both of which you won. They are the only work we have now."

"I cannot explain that sir."

Although Ehud was speaking the truth, there was something in his tone of voice which begged the comment, 'what a fine fellow Ehud must be, for he is loyally supporting his young master even though it's obvious Judas failed the business.' Judas' confidence was at a low ebb and he wondered briefly if he was being unreasonably cynical about Ehud's motives, but Joseph's response removed all doubt.

"Thank you Ehud and I admire your loyalty, but I have decided that from today you shall deputise for me when I am absent from the business, which from now on will only be on rare occasions. You, Judas, will continue your excellent work managing the accounts without the extra work that accompanies the role of business manager. That responsibility will now be taken on by Ehud. The new arrangements will give you more time with Jesus and allow you to offer your financial skills to the Zealot sect, where you are already held in high esteem, as you are here."

Judas was bitterly disappointed. No matter how hard Joseph tried to portray the change as a re-organisation, the plain fact was he had been demoted. He looked at Ehud sitting in what was no longer his chair and knew there was no point in objecting; the decision was made. He could not really be surprised because the business was undoubtedly failing under his management, but if only he had not been away when Joseph came home, he might have been able to counter the poison whispered into Joseph's ear by the pompous steward Ephraim who, Judas felt certain, was the prime mover in all this.

Joseph tried to ameliorate Judas' obvious disappointment.

"Come now Judas, there is much to look forward to. In a moment I shall take you to see Jesus and you can judge for yourself what a fine boy he is. He will soon have a brother or a sister. Ruth and Ehud's wedding will be celebrated next month, and yesterday we heard that Tetrarch Antipas has decided to make Sepphoris his new capital city."

"But the Romans thoroughly destroyed it."

"Exactly! So, imagine how much reconstruction work there'll be. There should be more than enough contracts for every building business for miles around. Now cheer up and come and see Jesus."

They left Ehud in the office and went downstairs into the main house where they met the stalwart matron Deborah just outside the nursery. "Keep your voices down," she whispered as she opened the door, "he's just gone to sleep."

Mary, as always, a picture of cool beauty, was sitting beside the cot. She spoke warmly to Joseph, "I've just fed him and, as you know, he sleeps well, so talk softly and you will not waken him." She did not seem to notice Judas.

"Excellent. I've brought Judas to see how his young pupil is developing."

"So I see. Welcome Judas." Judas thought, I might as well be a delivery man for all she cares, but then he chided himself for being oversensitive because of his disappointment a few minutes before. "I am glad we are meeting in better circumstances than last time," he said.

Mary smiled but there was no friendship in her eyes. "Yes, being the mother of your Messiah is burdensome. At least the child I am now carrying need not fear being murdered in its bed."

"He is every Jew's Messiah my dear," said Joseph gently.

"The risk is for the greater good."

"Really? I don't suppose the mothers and fathers of the murdered babies in Bethlehem would see it that way, or was that for the greater good too?"

Joseph had no answer so Judas responded for him. "No-one could have predicted the depths of evil that Herod would sink to."

This only served to goad Mary's fiery spirit further, "I see, but from what I hear, his successor comes from the same mould. It seems to me that Herod was provoked by the Zealots. Do you consider yourselves free of blame?"

Judas knew full well that this was one of those barren arguments that would not change opinions; he confined himself to saying, "At least we can learn from the errors we made. The Zealots have now forsaken violence and seek to build their support through persuasion and charitable work, but others still pursue violence no matter how futile."

"Well, that's progress of a sort I suppose but what will happen when my son becomes an adult?"

Judas was momentarily surprised by Mary saying 'my son' rather than 'our son' as if Joseph's view did not matter. She was indeed a strong-willed woman, but it was not his place to comment on that. He simply said, "Jesus will take his place as the anointed King of the Jews."

"And do you believe the Romans will permit that?"

"They permitted Herod to be King of the Jews for thirty-three years, so why not Jesus?"

This drew out a wry smile from Mary, "You are a clever one Judas Sicariot. I can understand why you were chosen to tutor my son."

A little cough from the cot warned them they had raised

their voices too much. Deborah glared at the two men and waddled past them to stand possessively beside Mary. "I think you should leave now while we try to get the baby back to sleep again."

Joseph and Judas made a hasty retreat back to the office. Ehud had departed to supervise a small subcontract in Sepphoris so they were alone. "Do not be angry Judas," said Joseph, "Mary has always been wilful."

"I am far from angry. Your wife should be admired for her perception. We Zealots have been too sure of ourselves and only defeat in battle has made us change our ways. If we had listened to people like Mary, many lives might have been saved."

"And what do you think of Jesus?"

"A fine-looking child," though in truth all babies looked alike to Judas.

"He is advanced for his age. You will soon be teaching him business management."

"A skill all kings should have, even anointed ones," acknowledged Judas, smiling for the first time that day.

Judas left the office at noon to write a letter to bar Abbas in the privacy of his own home where he could think without the distraction of others around him. As he walked slowly down the hill to the lower town, he met Ruth returning from the market carrying a basket of bread and cheese. This was the first time he had seen her since she escaped to Egypt with Joseph and his family. She was an attractive woman, but was always overshadowed in Mary's presence.

"Welcome back Ruth, you must be pleased to be home."

"Well Nazareth is certainly different from Alexandria. How goes it with you?"

"Not well I regret to say. I have been demoted and Ehud has taken my job, so your future husband has just been promoted. Ephraim always disapproved of Joseph appointing me to be his business manager and now he has gotten his way."

"I wouldn't be so sure about Ephraim, though I don't doubt he'll be pleased."

"You are probably right Ruth. The truth is I did fail and now I'm looking for someone to blame. I have decided to write to bar Abbas and ask to be relieved of my duties here."

"I am sorry to hear that. When will you leave?"

"Not until after your wedding. I would not want to miss that celebration."

"Celebration?"

"Are you not looking forward to your marriage?"

"I have no objection to marriage in principle."

"But Ehud is a good man, if a bit…"

"Dull?"

"Serious is the word I was looking for. Surely your parents consulted you about this?"

Ruth felt she might have said too much already; she simply replied, "Of course. I had better get back before this bread gets cold. Good day to you Judas."

He watched her walk back up the hill to Joseph's house and wondered. Her demeanour was more that of someone preparing for a funeral than a wedding, but there was something else; she was not so much sad as sullen.

***

III

The reaction to Judas' resignation letter was startling. Within seven days of sending it, a reply came. That was surprising enough but, best of all, it was brought by Judas' old comrade Reuben, who had spent the last ten months with Joseph's family in Egypt. Reuben arrived on the evening before the Sabbath just as Judas was preparing his meal.

"Your timing is perfect," said Judas as he opened the door to the weary traveller, "I am about to sit down for the evening meal; there is plenty for two."

"Thank you, Judas, but a drink first please. I have been walking since dawn. I have brought an urgent letter for you from bar Abbas."

While Reuben settled in and drank his wine, Judas broke the seal. The letter was brief and to the point.

Date: The thirteenth day of Heshvan, Year One of Ethnarch Archelaus.

To Judas Sicariot,

I received your letter today. Do nothing until we have spoken. By the time you read this I will be on my way to see you. This is an order not a request. I have a diversion to make on the way so expect me on the seventeenth.

Eli.

Reuben asked, "Is everything all right? You look very serious."

"I think so. Bar Abbas is coming to Nazareth; he'll be here the day after tomorrow."

"Will he be alone?"

"He does not say. Let us eat now and you can tell me all about Egypt."

Judas had begun to tire of hearing for the fourth time about the great lighthouse in Alexandria, the great city of Memphis with its wide streets lit up at night, the huge pyramids built by the Egyptian gods themselves; he allowed the unintended blasphemy to pass without comment; and the verdant banks along the River Nile, but at last the long day caught up with Reuben and he retired to his room leaving Judas alone with his thoughts. His letter to bar Abbas had certainly created an effect, but of what sort he was none the wiser. He wondered if he should have spoken to Joachim before sending it, which would have been quite easy now that the old warrior was living at home again in Nazareth, but there was no point in worrying; he would find out soon enough.

True to his word, bar Abbas arrived just after sunset on the seventeenth. He was accompanied by Mary's father Joachim, and Asher, brother of General Achiab, commander of the regular Jewish army based in Judea. Judas was greatly relieved when bar Abbas greeted him warmly and embraced him as an old friend, but the Zealot leader would say nothing about the purpose of his visit until they had washed and dined. When the plates had been cleared away and the wine goblets refilled Judas quietly dismissed Reuben but bar Abbas stopped him. "Let Reuben stay for he is involved in what I have to say, but first can we light the fire? Nazareth is colder than Jerusalem."

The tinder quickly flared up shining a warm glow on the

five men. Bar Abbas took a deep breath and said, "We have much to discuss tonight, nothing less than the future of the Zealot sect for the next generation."

"It's strange how we now seem to have all our meetings at night," observed Judas.

"And it is likely to continue that way because Asher and I are being hunted as enemies of the empire, me because I led the rebellion and Asher because he is regarded as a traitor to the Jewish people."

"To the wealthy Jewish establishment," interrupted Asher, "but I am still in covert contact with my brother who secretly supports our cause."

"Varus," continued bar Abbas, "was wise enough to limit Roman retribution to the leaders of the rebellion and carefully avoided offending the governing class in Jerusalem, which now regards him as something of a hero. His demand for a thousand 'rebels' was amply met by those who purport to lead us and, as you know, they were all crucified outside Jerusalem. In the event most of those selected were enemies of the temple rather than of Rome."

"No surprise there," growled Joachim.

"So now only Asher, I and Judas the Galilean remain to be caught. The Galilean is lying low in one of his rat holes on Mount Hermon, but Asher and I must change our identities or live as permanent outlaws. Asher has moved his family to Caesarea Maritima, where the population is more Greek than Jewish and the influence of the temple is weak. I have acquired a small house in Bethlehem, which is near enough to Jerusalem for me to stay in contact with events in the capital, but already I am viewed with suspicion because I have no family connections. A man of marriageable age living alone always raises questions in the minds of his neighbours."

Bar Abbas paused for a moment to take a drink from his goblet. The fire crackled cheerfully in the grate. Eventually it was Judas who broke the silence. "There may be a solution to your lack of a family. Reuben will remember the dramatic events that accompanied the birth of the Messiah last year. Had God not intervened by giving us a benefactor, Jesus would have been murdered along with his family and all the other hapless children of Bethlehem."

Looking at Reuben, bar Abbas said, "You did not speak of this when you reported to the Zealot office in Jerusalem."

"You were not there, nor was Isaac, and I did not know the people in the office. There could have been a temple spy amongst them, in which case our enemies would discover that the Messiah had escaped the Bethlehem massacre, and the life of the man Judas speaks of would have been endangered."

"Reuben, your caution does you credit," acknowledged bar Abbas. "Judas, please continue."

"Our benefactor's name is Ezra. He is a widower and childless. In appearance he is old and wizened and very irritable, but beneath that unprepossessing exterior, he has a heart of gold and firmly believes Jesus is the true Messiah. The weather was bad as we approached Bethlehem and Mary had just gone into labour. Not only did Ezra provide us with food, shelter and warmth ensuring Jesus was born safely, but when we fled he delayed Herod's soldiers, who were just minutes behind us, long enough for us to escape the slaughter that was about to take place."

"Then we have much to thank him for and I shall see he is rewarded, but I don't understand what this has to do with my lack of a family."

"Because I am sure Ezra would claim you as his son if it helps our cause. He has proven himself already and to assist the leader of the Zealots would give him something to live for. He lives alone but if he were to give you his name you would become Eli bar Ezra with your 'father' living just a mile away from you."

Asher shook his head, "But Judas, the temple records will show his wife bore no children."

"Why should anyone take the trouble to check?" countered Joachim.

Judas said, "Even if they do, the temple does not record illegitimate children. I'm afraid Eli, you will have to be the son of Ezra's imaginary mistress, a bastard."

Bar Abbas laughed, "Well it won't be the first time I've been called that, but while it does not matter to me, what about the shame it will bring to Ezra?"

"I have a feeling that will not trouble Ezra either," answered Judas. "He is not the sort of man who heeds the opinions of others. If I write to him and explain everything, he will decide. At worst he can simply say no."

"Then let it be so. Judas write your letter and I shall see it is safely delivered. Eli bar Ezra sounds like a good name to me and I shall be happy to use it until the Messiah declares himself. Now we need to discuss the future organisation of the Zealot sect, as it is now officially known." Bar Abbas put his hand on Joachim's powerful shoulder. "After much persuasion and years of brave service, Joachim has finally agreed to stand down as my second in command and spend more time with his dear wife Anna. I will still come to him when I need advice and it will be good to know that young Jesus will have extra protection in Nazareth with his grandfather living close by. My new deputy will be Asher who, amongst his many accomplishments, was in charge of training Herod's army. He will make sure we will never again go into battle against professional soldiers unless our men our properly trained and equipped and have a reasonable chance of winning. That is the lesson of our past disappointments."

"But Eli," interjected Judas, "Have we not foresworn violence? Is that not the reason we have gained official status?"

"Well, yes and no."

"Spoken like a true politician," observed Asher with a twinkle in his eye.

Bar Abbas explained, "It is true we are now committed to peaceful means to gain our ends but we know that eventually it will come to war, so we must be ready to take on the Romans with or without Parthian help. We have many years to prepare until the Messiah is old enough to lead us, so while the main body of our sect will recruit the hearts and minds of our people for when the great day comes, we will also continue to prepare for war using a covert military arm. This force will train selected volunteers in secret camps well away from towns and cities, who will become the corps of officers in our future army. They will eliminate any who threaten our cause, carry out raids on temple properties and other establishments owned by wealthy Jews and gentiles, and ensure the funds we need continue to flow into our coffers. The Shadows of course will help."

"Are we to become thieves then?" Asked Judas.

"Of course not!" replied bar Abbas with mock horror. "I call it enforced redistribution of wealth from those who stole it back to those who created it in the first place, namely sturdy Jewish farmers, labourers, craftsmen and so on."

"It's still theft."

"Look at it as a tax. Government taxes put the burden on the poor for the benefit of the Romans, Herod's family, the priests and their lackeys. Our tax simply reverses that process. We do this not for ourselves but for our people."

"I understand that, but who will ensure our tax is administered properly and does not corrupt those who take it?"

"You will Judas and I shall speak of that in a few moments. Asher will command our military arm in Galilee and Perea while I do the same in Judea, and Idumea. I shall also remain in command of Isaac and the Shadows."

"What about Philip's domain?" Asked Joachim.

"Gaulantis and Trachontis are gentile lands, hardly any Jews live there, so we will concentrate our efforts on God's Promised Land and leave the rest to itself. We may eventually try our luck in Samaria, but for the present we must not overstretch ourselves. The Samaritans hate the temple hierarchy as much as we do, but they also foster heresies which will need to be corrected before we can rely on them."

Judas said, "These are ambitious plans, but who will be the public leader of our sect while you and Asher are still being hunted?"

"Ariel," replied bar Abbas. "He has what the Romans call 'gravitas' and the character and presence of a leader. He will be based at our headquarters in Jerusalem and build a network of offices in our main towns and cities. From these offices our volunteers will spread our message to all our people, even the most humble toiling in the fields without, of course, revealing the location of the Messiah. Ariel will try and recruit the Essenes, who share our values and may join us now that we have publicly abandoned violence. He will infiltrate the Sanhedrin with our supporters so we can identify those who are the main threats to our progress. Finally, with the backing of our alms-collecting and 'taxation', Ariel will organise assistance to the sick and needy; people listen better when they have food in their stomachs."

"This is indeed a worthy cause," agreed Judas, "But it will require money, and plenty of it."

"And that is where we need you. We will continue to raise funds for the cause, as other sects do, from public donations and wealthy patrons, though most will come from our unofficial taxation, but this inflow of money must be managed properly. I want you to become our financial controller. It will involve many risks but I know that will not deter you. Will you accept?"

The recent demotion by Joseph now seemed a trifling matter. Judas did not hesitate. "I accept."

"Good, then the next decision to be made is where to locate our treasury. I welcome any ideas from you."

Bar Abbas' request was met with silence until Reuben, who was a practical sort of man, suggested, "Why not here? I could dig out a chamber beneath the floor of this room, cover it with wooden boards and replace the matting. I would do this work myself at night and spread the spoil in the courtyard outside, so that only we would know about the existence of the chamber."

"We will do this together," said Judas. "I can work with my hands as well as my brain. We can start tomorrow."

"Well, that's agreed then," affirmed bar Abbas, "And when, Reuben, will you be ready to receive your first delivery?"

"With the two of us working, I should say in about three weeks. The ground in Nazareth is hard and we will have to break up rock in the lower part of the chamber because the soil here is thin."

"I will help too," volunteered Joachim. "The exercise will do me good and we'll be ready in two weeks instead of three."

Bar Abbas said, "Well, now that is resolved we will need your accounting skills too, Judas. Our treasury must be managed as a business, cash in, cash out, costs, payments to our full-time staff, donations to the needy and so on. At present what wealth we still have is scattered around Judea and Galilee in the homes of trusted supporters, but even I have no idea how much we possess except that it's much less than it used to be thanks to the rebellion. You will have total control and we five shall meet once a year at Hanukkah to review your accounts and decide on priorities and investments for the following year. Much of our income will be items of value rather than coinage, which means you will need the services of Samuel bar Ahab."

"I have not heard of him."

"He is one of us, Judas, he will be the sixth and last person to know of the whereabouts of our treasury. He is a jeweller by trade and escaped with his wares from Sepphoris just before it was sacked by the Romans. He has returned now and I will take you to see him tomorrow. Samuel is well connected and was recruited by my father many years ago. He will be able to assess the items of value we acquire and, when needed, change them into coinage, either Jewish shekels or Roman denarii. You will find him both useful and reliable."

"Will he be able to give advice on investment opportunities? It may be worth investing any surplus we have in property or trading ventures."

"I am sure he can, but you can ask him yourself tomorrow. He knows many people in the commercial world and is a successful businessman himself."

Once again, the sun seemed to shine on Judas' world. He was now within the innermost circle of the Zealot sect and trusted with its greatest secrets, yet there was still one more surprise to come. Bar Abbas refilled his goblet but when he next spoke, it was with the chilling softness of a veteran killer.

"I must now turn to the most important matter of all, the safety and well-being of the Messiah. To put it plainly, he must never be alone, nor must he be beyond the protection of the Shadows. Our enemies cannot be certain he succumbed to the Bethlehem massacre, but you can be sure they will not rest until they know one way or the other."

"Jesus was beyond our protection for almost a year in Egypt," observed Judas. The Zealot leader looked at Reuben. "You may speak now."

Reuben cleared his throat and said apologetically, "Judas you are wrong about that; he was always protected. I could not tell you until now, but for the last five years I have been one of Isaac's Shadows. Poor Daniel and I were assigned to you when you first joined us."

"Why was I not told?"

"There was no need for you to know. We may only reveal our identity if either Eli or Isaac permits it."

"Hiding in plain sight again I suppose," shrugged Judas. "That is our way. I am sorry I could not tell you before now."

"And you will understand," added bar Abbas, "Why we were more shocked than you realised when you told us of Daniel's murder by Judas the Galilean. Believe me, we will find that monster; the Shadows will not rest until Daniel is avenged. As for the Messiah, the slightest threat to him must be extinguished without hesitation or debate. Reuben will see to it; he is the Messiah's Shadow as well as yours."

"Well, I confess that tonight's meeting has been full of surprises," said Judas, "But at the end of it all I'm greatly reassured and I now see Reuben in a new light."

Asher chuckled, "Seeing a Shadow in a new light? Is that possible?"

***

IV

Ruth's wedding was arranged for the first day of Shevat (January). On this special day, Joseph lifted his ban forbidding Mary and Ruth to speak to each other and permitted Mary to help Ruth prepare herself for the ceremony. The morning dawned cold and wet; it was midwinter and not a traditional time for a wedding. Mary was laying out the wedding dress on the bed in Ruth's small room at the back of Joseph's house. She looked at the thin, white material.

"You'll need to wear something warm under this or you'll shiver through the ceremony."

"My future husband does not want to waste money on a dress that will be worn only once."

"His father is poor. It is understandable."

"Yet Ehud can afford to buy a house in the upper town almost as large as Joseph's."

"And you are complaining about this? Most brides would be delighted," said Mary.

"How can he afford it?"

"By being frugal I suppose."

"Mary, would you want to marry Ehud?"

"Women seldom get to choose their husbands. You know I did not."

"But Joseph is a kind and considerate man. He has good reason to hate me because I colluded in your affair with Caius, but instead of throwing me out onto the streets he arranged a marriage as a way of removing me from his household. But he is not a good judge of character otherwise he would have found someone else for me. I know I should be grateful but there is something about Ehud, something deep and dark. He frightens me."

"Pre-marital nerves Ruth. You may be pleasantly surprised. He has certainly prepared a fine home for you."

"With furnishings in his mother's awful taste! I was allowed no say at all."

"He is an only son. You cannot be surprised his mother dotes on him."

"And where did all the money come from? Ehud's family could never afford a well-appointed house in the upper town."

"Joseph pays his men well. Ehud must have saved his money or invested it wisely."

"Perhaps," said Ruth, unconvinced. "I suppose I shall know soon enough."

"That's better. Now sit down while I brush your hair."

Ruth did as she was bid and said, "Mary, it's so good to be able to talk to you again. All that time in Egypt, and yet we could not speak to each other."

"I know. It was hard for me too. You are my one true friend. At least as mistress of your own household we will be able to meet and talk together."

"That is the one saving grace about all this. We can meet in the marketplace and chatter to our hearts' content – Ouch!"

"Sorry, there was a knot in your hair but it's out now."

Ruth was silent for a while, relaxing under the soporific effect of Mary's firm, steady brushing. Suddenly she blurted out, "Do you still think of him?"

"Every day."

"Caius was a fine man. Any woman could love him."

"I know I do."

Ruth sighed deeply, "Well he certainly changed our lives and changed my views about Romans."

"I think you liked that centurion he was with?"

"Yes, and I thought Lucius liked me too but perhaps I misread the signals."

"I don't think so. I recall his eyes lighting up whenever he saw you."

"Do you think Caius still loves you Mary?"

"I think so, I pray so. I am certain he would want to see his son."

"How can that be? Legionaries must follow the legion wherever it goes."

"I know, I know. I have no illusion about seeing him again but I have the memory of our time together and I can still dream."

"Do you love Joseph?"

"I try to but every time I see Jesus I think of his father. I can't help it."

"Well at least Joseph accepted Jesus as his son. He didn't have to do that."

"True. He did it because he loves me."

"Does he love Jesus?"

"He is kind and considerate to him but he holds back; any man would under the circumstances. When I give him a son of his own he'll be the happiest man in Galilee." Mary put down the brush and admired her handiwork. "There, your hair is done. It has a natural wave which enhances its beauty. Now it is time to get you ready to go."

It did not take long to dress Ruth in her plain, white

wedding dress and as Mary was carefully placing the veil over her head, Ruth said, "Before I leave this house, there is a question I would like to ask which has always puzzled me."

"Ask it then."

"I know on rare occasions future brides sometimes spend the last part of their betrothal under close supervision in the house of their husband-to-be, but we were in Joseph's house for months. How did that happen?"

"We have the Zealots to thank for that. My father was seldom at home because he was fighting Herod and the Romans with bar Abbas, so my mother returned to her own mother's house instead of living like a widow. Because the Zealots believed I was to be the mother of their precious Messiah, my father decided that in his absence I would be better protected in Joseph's household than in my grandmother's all female house; my grandfather died a few years ago. Of course, I was to be strictly chaperoned by my childhood friend. You know the rest."

"Didn't do very well did I?"

"No and I bless you for it. Come on now, it's time to go."

The wedding ceremony was over. Ehud had spent more time talking to his possessive mother and characterless father than to his new wife. Joseph had done his best to add some merriment to the heavy atmosphere, but it was like trying to light a fire with damp kindling requiring much effort but achieving only a small flame which soon faded. He was the last guest to leave Ruth's new home. She watched Ehud close the door behind his master and nervously waited for him to speak. He had drunk plenty of wine and wobbled slightly as he turned to face his beautiful bride.

"Well?"

"Well, what?" answered Ruth.

"What do you think of your new home?"

"The house is very grand. The home will be what we make of it together."

Ehud frowned, not sure if he liked the answer or not. "Well come and sit with me and I will explain what I expect of you. It is important that we begin life together with no misunderstandings." Ruth sat down opposite him separated by the wedding table, which was littered with the detritus of the feast; half eaten sweet cake, pieces of bread, pools of spilt wine and scattered fragments of cheese and dates.

Ehud paused for a moment, as if coming to a great decision. "First, you will obey me absolutely, no ifs or buts. I realise you are one of those women who think themselves the equal of men but that will not happen in this household."

"Do you not want my advice?"

"If I need advice I have my mother and father. Second, you will not leave this house without my permission."

"What about buying food and provisions for the household?"

"My mother will do that. She will bring all that we need here." While there was no surprise about Ehud's demand for absolute obedience, the ban on leaving the house came as a shock to Ruth. The consolation about married life, so she had thought, was the freedom to see Mary again. Now even that was being taken from her.

"Am I to be a prisoner in my own home? Why are you doing this?"

"You will not question my decisions. Third, only I give orders in this house but when I am away you may instruct the house slave. His name is Hiram and he lives in the shed in the courtyard. I purchased him a few days ago in the slave market in Sepphoris. He is experienced in household duties but a bit frail."

"He was cheap then."

"Yes. He is old but still has a few good years left in him." Ehud picked up a half full goblet and drained the contents. An unpleasant smile, a leer almost, crossed his face. He began to slur as the wine took effect. "Finally, your primary duty is to provide me with sons, many of them, so that my name will continue for generations to come, but you do not look good for childbearing."

"Am I not attractive to you then?"

"Too thin. Your hips are narrow. They should be broader."

"Like your fat mother I suppose." Ruth knew at once she had made a mistake, but she could take no more. Ehud did not answer. His eyes narrowed. He stood up, walked slowly round to her side of the table and glowered down at her. She could not remember exactly what happened next, but suddenly she found herself pitched onto the floor, dazed by a massive slap or punch in the face. Her limbs felt leaden, the ceiling seemed to sway but she was just conscious enough to hear Ehud hiss,

"You will never speak disrespectfully of my mother again."

Ruth tried to get up but was too shaken to do more than prop herself on one elbow. Blood poured from her nose, staining her white wedding dress bright red. She felt too faint to speak. Ehud hauled her to her feet. "As I said, your primary duty is to provide me with sons. We will start now!"

The violence seemed to arouse him. He gripped Ruth's hair and dragged her to the bedchamber. There he stripped her, tearing her wedding dress to pieces as he did so, and violated her like an angry animal. Although she was still only half conscious, the pain seared through her body like fire; she thought she was going to die. When he finished, he slapped her across the face, left her bleeding on the bed and went back to the wedding table to drink himself into oblivion.

Thus, passed poor Ruth's wedding night. Her long nightmare had just begun.

CHAPTER TWO

I awoke during the late afternoon in the Antonia fortress in Jerusalem which housed the Felicifera, the bringers of happiness, known to the coarser elements in the legions as the cats. Sunlight came flooding through the open window casting a golden light on Zenub's perfect brown skin. She was my favourite cat and was still asleep after our lovemaking. I glanced at her Alexandrian water clock and saw it was only half empty which meant there was still an hour left before her next client was due. Life was good. Five years had passed since the great rebellion, five relatively peaceful years during which, through the retirement of our cohort's senior centurion, Titus Cotta, I had progressed to being the centurion of the third century and Caius now commanded the fifth. There were still sporadic attacks inspired by the Zealots, especially in Galilee, but these were easily dealt with by our auxiliary forces; the Third Legion Gallica remained in its Jerusalem camp.

Zenub stirred and sat up. "How long have we been sleeping?" I looked at her naked body, admiring her long legs and full breasts. She was of mixed blood and as tall as me. Her mother was from Nubia, south of Egypt, where people are long limbed and ebony black. She had inherited the best of both black and white races; her hair was particularly delightful, falling in wavy, black tresses over her shoulders almost inviting you to stroke it.

"What are you smiling at?" she asked, knowing full well

the reason.

"There is plenty of time yet. I think I'm ready for more."

"You were certainly in a hurry today, Lucius, not your usual style. Are you sure you won't miss your evening roll call?"

"I am not on parade today. I have to preside over a court martial."

"What happened?"

"It's sad because it concerns a young legionary who showed promise. He's only twenty and fell in love with a Jewish girl who lives with her family just outside Jerusalem. When her parents found out they moved home and settled somewhere in Galilee. Our young soldier then let his heart rule his head and deserted to follow her. Fortunately, he was recaptured before the Zealots could get to him; a single Roman wandering alone through Galilee cannot expect to live long."

"I thought the Zealots abandoned violence after the rebellion?"

"Officially yes, but a few still carry on as before."

"What will happen to your young soldier?"

"He will be found guilty of course, but as we are under peacetime regulations, I will be able to show mercy. Had we been at war there could only have been one sentence."

"Death."

"Yes, but as we are at peace I will be able to consider mitigating circumstances. He will have to be dishonourably discharged as a minimum, but I will permit him to take his accrued pension with him. It won't be much; he only has three years' service."

"I am pleased you will not be harsh Lucius, but apart from your natural gentleness is there a particular reason?"

I knew the cats' code required any conversation in the bedchamber to be regarded as confidential, but I still chose my words carefully. "A few years ago, a good and trusted friend of mine fell in love with a beautiful Galilean girl and she with him. It could not last because he was one of three of us being held hostage by the Zealots and likely to be murdered. Mary was betrothed to Joseph, one of the Zealot leaders, but as she nursed Caius, who was near death from battle wounds, they fell deeply in love. Because of that two things happened; she and her close friend helped all three of us to escape, but then later she discovered she was pregnant. Surprisingly, the Zealot leader accepted the child as his own, partly to avoid scandal but mainly because he loved Mary too."

"That does not sound very Zealot-like to me," interrupted Zenub.

"True. Later, I got to know Joseph quite well. We were as close to being friends as a Zealot and a Roman could ever be. If they were all like him the land of the Jews would be a happier place."

"So, what happened to Caius?"

"He now lives his life knowing he has a son he will never see and a woman he will always love but can never have. It turned a brave young soldier with everything to live for into a sad and wise man before his twentieth birthday, so I have seen what young love can do. It's wonderful and I owe my life to it, but it can also be destructive. Does that answer your question?"

"Intriguing," mused Zenub. "This Caius, is he by any chance that tall, handsome Caius with golden hair who comes here to visit Esther?"

"Yes, but he wouldn't appreciate me telling you this."

"It will not become gossip, I promise. And Mary, she sounds like an interesting woman."

"Beautiful and highly intelligent, just like you."

Zenub smiled, "She would make a good cat then?"

"You can't have two queens in a cattery, and this one has you."

"You're being very complimentary today Lucius. I may be obliged to offer you a discount."

"No need, you're worth every sesterce. I think Mary would be a good businesswoman too if her husband allowed her to help in his business, but Jewish men do not usually encourage their women into male domains."

"Nor do Roman men."

"Perhaps, but they are less strict about it than their Jewish counterparts. I am told there are many businesses run by women in Rome, but I have never seen the great city so I cannot be sure."

"In Alexandria where I grew up, it's common to see women actively engaged in the world of commerce."

This was the first time Zenub had mentioned her childhood to me; I was interested to learn more. "I know it's not good manners to ask a cat about her previous life, but I had no idea you were from Alexandria." Zenub got out of bed, walked to her wardrobe and put on a white gown. The sunlight shone through the thin material so I could clearly see the outline of her elegant body. She flicked her long hair over the collar of her gown; it reached almost to her waist. For a while she was silent looking through the un-shuttered window into the city.

"Have I offended you?" I asked.

"Of course not, Lucius. You made me think of my mother, that's all."

"What is she like?"

"She was a cat too. Her Roman name is Julia."

"So, you are a daughter of the legion."

"Yes."

"I am a son of the legion."

"Yes, you told me."

"So, we both have the same father, the Third Gallica."

"Actually I know who my father was, though I have never met him. My mother was unwell for most of the month in which I was conceived. The only man who visited her during that time was a tribune, Titus Scaevola. My mother chose to tell him about me and he was pleased. He gave her a generous donation which she used to pay a scribe to teach me to read and write and speak two languages."

"Which are?"

"Greek and Aramaic. My mother tongue is Latin."

"What happened to Julia and Titus?"

"My mother still lives in Alexandria. I visit her once a year if I can. Titus became a senator in Rome, but I do not know if he still lives."

I got up, stood beside Zenub and put my arm round her narrow waist. "I never met my mother. I am told she died of fever while I was still a baby. All I know is her name, Antonia. The skill of languages is a great gift; your mother has done well for you. I am pleased you still see her. Can I ask you something?"

Zenub kissed me on the nose, "I think I can guess."

"No you can't."

She looked surprised. "Well?"

"Would you teach me Aramaic? I would come to you when you are unavailable for business but would still pay as for a normal visit."

She stepped back, looked at me and smiled broadly, "You're right Lucius, I would never have guessed that. But why?"

"When I retire from the legion I shall probably buy a farm near the coast, Caesarea, Sidon, Tyre, somewhere like that.

Syria and the land of the Jews are all I know, and the most common language is Aramaic, so it makes sense to be able to speak it. Also, apart from gambling, there is nothing much else for a soldier stationed in the east to do. The emperor has decided that his empire should expand no further eastwards, and all our dreams of conquering Parthia should be abandoned because it would cost too much. It is said that Emperor Augustus is a merchant at heart and sees everything in terms of financial returns."

"Then we are fortunate to have an emperor with such common sense instead of a glory seeker, but he is getting old is he not, so what of his successor?"

"His stepson, Tiberius, will follow him and he is from much the same mould. He has already won glory in Germania so he has nothing to prove. He will continue Augustus' peace and prosperity policy which is good for the empire, but not so good for its soldiers."

"Why not?" asked a perplexed Zenub.

"Our history shows us that when there is no enemy to fight, our army starts to turn on itself. Civil war is the worst of all types of war and I thank the gods Augustus put an end to it."

"But surely we will always need our army to protect us against the less fortunate peoples who live outside our borders?"

"True, but in the meantime will you teach me Aramaic?"

"Yes, but I warn you," she added with an impish grin, "I shall be a very strict teacher."

I looked at the water clock again. There was still plenty of time, so we went back to bed.

***

II

In a pointless attempt to show how different he was to his father, Herod, Archelaus replaced Joazar the high priest shortly after he took power, but none of Joazar's successors proved as co-operative as he had been and refused to overlook Archelaus' debauched lifestyle and the expenditure that went with it. Eventually the ethnarch bowed to the inevitable and recalled Joazar a few years later which meant he could return to his old ways undisturbed.

None of that was of any interest to us. From a Roman perspective, one high priest was much the same as any other, but the return of Joazar meant that Archelaus was, once more, free to spend as recklessly as he wished with no consideration for the consequences. This did indeed ultimately affect us, because as the ethnarch got deeper into debt, he increased taxes and made the capital mistake of allowing the pay of his Galatian guards to fall into arrears. He ended up paying dearly for this error of judgement in the rebellion that was about to break out, but ironically, the immediate cause of the rebellion was not caused by the ethnarch but by one of the few poor decisions made by our ageing emperor, as I shall shortly relate.

I continued to visit Zenub regularly and by the time Joazar was re-instated I could, thanks to her expert tuition, speak Aramaic well enough to converse adequately in day to day matters although I could neither read nor write the script. But my relaxed and peaceful life was soon to suffer a set-back.

On a bright, early spring morning in the thirty fourth year of Augustus' reign I arrived at the Antonia fortress for one of my normal, non-teaching visits to Zenub. As soon as I entered I could sense something was wrong. The queen of the house, a retired cat whom I knew well, stopped me at reception.

"Lucius, there's been trouble here. Yesterday evening Zenub was beaten up by a client. She's in a bad way."

My blood ran cold with shock. "Has a physician seen her?"

"Yes, but only this morning. No-one realised what had happened so Zenub lay unconscious and bleeding all night. By the time she was found she was close to death."

I did not wait to hear more and ran up the stairs three at a time to find Zenub lying on her bed with Esther, Caius' favourite, sitting beside her changing a bloody bandage on her forehead. Esther, a girl from Samaria with large, round eyes said, "Last night's beating would have killed most women but Zenub is strong. I think she'll recover but she needs plenty of rest. This sort of thing might happen in back street brothels, but never amongst us until now."

I looked at Zenub's bruised and battered face. The attack had been prolonged and vicious, but she was sleeping now and breathing strongly. I moved to touch her but Esther stopped me. "Do not wake her Lucius, sleep is the best cure now."

"Who did this?"

"A centurion from your cohort. His name is Marcus. You know him?"

"Yes." I said nothing more for a while and we sat in silence, lost in our own thoughts. I realised how fond I had become of Zenub and how lucky I was she had survived. She would not remain a cat for ever and my term of duty in the legion had six years to go. I wondered if I could put our

55

relationship on a more permanent footing. Then my mind turned to Marcus Sempronius.

"Esther, you said this sort of thing never happens amongst the cats?"

"It's true that some men give us a slap now and again, especially those who think it's our fault they can't maintain an erection, but I have never seen anything like this." I pictured the arrogant Marcus beating my Zenub with closed fists. Anger, a cold implacable anger, welled up inside me; I had never hated anyone until that moment. "Marcus cannot be allowed to get away with this. Tell Zenub I will deal with him."

"What will you do Lucius?"

"Give him a taste of his own medicine."

"Does he outrank you?"

"Why do you ask?"

"What is the penalty for striking a senior officer?"

"Death. Since Titus Cotta retired to his house in Sepphoris, Marcus has been our senior centurion. He commands the first century, I command the third so yes, he does outrank me."

A muffled voice from below us said, "Then don't do it." Zenub had overheard everything. One eye was half open; she tried to smile and I was pleased to see her perfect teeth were still in place.

I stroked her hair, "I shall be careful. He will not know who attacked him but he'll know why he's been punished. He may guess it was me but there will be no evidence. It is a matter of honour as well as revenge for you. Why did he do this?"

"He wanted to sodomise me which is something we do not have to permit. When I refused he became violent. I fought back and there will be scratch marks to prove it, but that only made him worse."

"Well, you rest now and I will come and see you as often as I can while you recover."

Esther asked, "Won't that draw suspicion on to you when Marcus receives his punishment?"

"Everyone already knows Zenub is special to me so it would seem strange if I did not come to her. Anyway, I'll make sure nothing can connect me with Marcus' fate. Only you and Zenub will know."

Once I had thought about things some more, I realised I would need an accomplice and there was only one man I could trust absolutely. Rufio was trustworthy but a drink or two might loosen his tongue. I could be sure of Caius so, after the evening roll call, I went to his office in the fifth century's barracks, explained what had happened and asked if he would help me.

"I would have been disappointed if you had asked anyone else," was his reply. "What is your plan?"

"Marcus is a creature of habit. He always visits the cats after the evening parade, which at this time of year means it will be dark when he returns. He'll leave the city by the south gate and use the causeway to get back to the camp. We'll surprise him at our end of the causeway."

"But the camp guards will hear us."

"Not if we're skilful. Esther will get word to us when his next visit is arranged. He must not recognise us. Although there'll be no sympathy for him, Piso, as our tribune, will be obliged to follow disciplinary procedure if there is enough evidence to demand it. Could you lie to Piso on oath?"

"No."

"Neither could I, so we must make sure Marcus cannot bring charges for he will certainly guess who his attackers are."

We did not have long to wait; Esther's message came just four days later. After the evening roll call Caius and I went to the centurions' mess and made a point of talking to as many comrades as possible. I left first saying I had to return to my quarters as I still had next day's duty roster to prepare. Caius left a little later. I spoke to some of my men telling them I did not want to be disturbed, and then locked myself in my office. As far as they were concerned I was there all night.

It was already twilight when I slipped out of my window, closed the shutters behind me and met Caius behind the latrine block. We wore Jewish clothing; ankle length, brown robes covered by a short, hooded tunic with the hood pulled well forward. Apart from Caius' height, we looked no different to any other Jewish vagabond lurking in a dark alley for an easy victim. We unbolted the night soil gate, which was never guarded because the Jews were horrified at the idea of coming into contact with human excrement and ran the fifty paces to the cover of the ditch which ringed Jerusalem's outer wall. The moon was three quarters full in the cloudless, cold sky and cast enough light for us to avoid mistaking the identity of our victim.

Now, out of sight of the camp guards, we headed towards the causeway and waited in the ditch at the place where the causeway joined the road leading to the north gate of our camp. As we settled down to wait, I recalled that this was where the fiercest fighting took place during the great rebellion and where we lost Severus Pollio and the entire first century. Twice we heard the city gates swing open, only to see off duty legionaries pass by as they returned to camp. It became very cold. Our Jewish clothes were little protection and I started to shiver.

Caius said, "Either Marcus is really indulging himself

tonight or we've been misinformed." I was about to answer when the city gates creaked open again. We peered over the lip of the ditch. In the moonlight we saw a single figure walking unsteadily towards us. When it was halfway across the causeway we could just hear it humming a bawdy marching tune.

"That's Marcus," I whispered. "Have you got the hood ready?"

"Yes."

"Let him pass and we'll take him from behind."

Our victim was within a few paces of us. My muscles tensed ready to pounce but we had to wait yet longer as Marcus stopped, belched loudly and urinated into the ditch just missing Caius' shoulder. It seemed to go on for ever, he must have had the bladder of a camel, but at last he finished and tottered past us. We sprang forward. Before the inebriated Marcus could turn, I struck him with a clenched fist just behind the ear, a blow that always induces immediate unconsciousness. He fell instantly in an untidy heap. Caius put a cloth bag over his head and tied it round Marcus' neck with a cord which had a toggle at one end in the form of a black cat. The cat would be enough for Marcus to deduce why he had been punished, without being adequate evidence to justify a formal investigation – so I hoped.

Staying within the city's perimeter ditch, we kept out of sight of the camp and moved towards the Kidron valley with Marcus slumped over Caius' mighty shoulder. Just before we reached the Kidron, we climbed out of the ditch and headed south towards the old quarry where the city's night soil was dumped. Here Caius dropped Marcus unceremoniously onto the rocky ground beside the lake of human ordure and looked at me. "We could get rid of him permanently."

"That would mean killing one of our own. I don't think I could live with that and I'm sure you couldn't. I'll cut some breathing holes into the hood and we'll just roll him into the edge of the shit without drowning him in it, much as I would like to."

And so, with Marcus just beginning to stir as we abandoned him in the city sewage, we entered the camp again by the same way we came and quietly slid the bolt back into place.

When I arrived for morning parade there was a commotion because the cohort's senior centurion had already been reported missing by his century, so when the parade was over Piso, our commanding officer, ordered me and the other four centurions to his office.

"Has any of you any idea what's happened to Marcus?"

Marcus Aius centurion of the fourth century, who along with Septimus Nasica centurion of the sixth had joined us after the great rebellion, said, "He went to visit the cats after yesterday's evening parade sir. Maybe he ran into trouble in the city."

"If that's so it's bad news for all of us," replied Piso. "That sort of thing ended after the rebellion. We've enjoyed good relations with the Jews since then. It could be the start of a return to the old ways." Then turning to Gnaeus Servilius, centurion of the second century, he said, "Gnaeus, organise a search party. Check if Marcus ever reached the felicifera in the Antonia fortress. If he did, scour the area between the fortress and the city's south gate first."

"And if he didn't sir?"

"Come straight back here and we'll begin a systematic search of the entire city."

But before Gnaeus could leave, we heard laughter coming from the direction of the parade ground. Then suddenly the door to Piso's office was flung open by a bedraggled, stinking wretch. Piso, who had been seated at his desk stood up, his face flushed with anger, "Marcus Sempronius! How dare you come to my office in such a state! Clean yourself up and return only when you're fit for duty."

"But—"

"No but's. Go now!"

As the humiliated centurion disappeared, Gnaeus said cheerily, "Well at least he's still alive."

"But covered in shit!" laughed Marcus Aius, who had become the comedian amongst us.

Piso, our tribune and always a stickler for personal cleanliness, brought the meeting to an abrupt end. "Return to your duties and carry on as usual until I find out what's happened and why. At least we're not facing another uprising."

Just before the noon meal, I was summoned to Piso's office again. This time we were alone. I stood to attention in front of his desk.

"At ease Lucius." Piso looked out of his window which opened on to the parade ground and sighed, "Marcus Sempronius has launched an official complaint against you. It involves striking a senior officer which is a capital offence." I stared blankly at the wall behind the seated tribune. "Have you nothing to say Lucius?"

"Nothing except the man's a fool. If he's been struck then it wasn't by me."

"He has evidence."

"He can't have."

Piso threw the black cat toggle onto the desk. "Marcus says you left that behind."

"It's not mine. Is that all the evidence he has?"

"Yes, and I agree it's not much. He says you were given this by a cat whom he reprimanded for disobedience." I wanted to tell Piso what Marcus', so called, reprimand had been but that would have invited deeper questioning so I confined myself to a minimal response.

"Sir, you can buy trinkets like that anywhere in the market place."

"True. What if I asked you under oath?"

This was what I feared. For the first time I looked directly at Piso. It was clear he knew more than he was saying. News of Zenub's near fatal beating had reached the camp by other means than me because she was popular amongst the senior officers, and it was well known she was my favourite.

"Sir, if this toggle is the only evidence against me, then I hope you will do me the honour of not putting me on oath and instead treat this complaint with the contempt it deserves."

Piso seemed relieved. I could see he knew full well I was guilty, but he also knew I would not lie to him on oath. He quickly made his decision. "Very well, putting a man on oath requires witnesses and I will not subject my best centurion to that on such flimsy evidence. It would set a bad precedent. Unless Marcus can come up with stronger grounds to substantiate his accusation, this matter is closed. Dismissed."

"Thank you, sir." I turned to leave but before I reached the door Piso added, "Lucius, Marcus believes it was you, evidence or not. Whatever else he may be, he does not lack determination. He will do his utmost to get revenge even if it takes years. Be careful."

I should have paid more heed to Piso's warning.

***

III

Another three years passed. We were now in the thirty sixth year of the reign of Augustus Caesar who was in his sixty seventh year. The emperor had always managed the affairs of the empire with consummate skill but, perhaps caused by his increasing age, he now made the first of two disastrous decisions which blighted his later years.

Publius Sulpicius Quirinius was now Governor of Syria which still included the land of the Jews within its boundaries. He was less avaricious than Varus had been but still managed to line his pockets well enough to retire in luxury at the end of his term in office. But he was a good soldier and could sense trouble when it was approaching. In a well-meaning attempt to reduce the tax burden on the peoples conquered during his reign, and there were many, Augustus issued a decree that every man together with his property and assets in these new provinces should be registered for direct taxation. This would cut out the corrupt tax gatherers and their fat commissions and so keep the revenues coming into the imperial treasury but at a lower cost. But most of the peoples in the new provinces were still semi-barbarous and saw this as an infringement on their honour and a first step into slavery. Consequently, rebellion broke out.

The Jews were neither recently conquered nor barbarous but, presumably for administrative efficiency, they too were included in the new taxation arrangements and thus the fig leaf of independent government by their own rulers was blown away leaving the naked reality of Rome's power clear for all to see. This was just what the numerous fanatics roaming throughout Judea and Galilee were hoping for, so Quirinius put his legions on stand-by.

Meanwhile Zenub made a full recovery and my thoughts began to turn towards retirement for I had completed sixteen of my twenty year term. Around the spring equinox the first sign of trouble appeared. We had just finished the noon meal and I was preparing to visit Zenub when I was summoned to Piso's office. As I entered, our tribune was gazing at the parade ground through his un-shuttered window. "Sit down Lucius," he said. "It seems our easy lives are about to be upset once more. Our legate, Marcus Tullius, has received notification from Quirinius that the Jews are to be included in the register for taxes. It will not go down well."

"Can the governor not write to the emperor explaining what will happen?"

"Quirinius is from the old school; he obeys orders without question. The Jewish rulers have already been ordered to implement the decree. Antipas, Tetrarch of Galilee, is worried. He has asked Marcus Tullius for help to nip any trouble in the bud. Galilee already has more than its fair share of fanatics."

"Is not Marcus due for retirement?"

"Overdue but another legate has not yet been appointed."

"What of the other Jewish rulers? Do they not share Antipas' fears?"

"Philip has no need to worry for there are few Jews in his domain and Archelaus doesn't care what happens outside his own palace just as long as he can live his debauched life in peace."

"What will we do for Antipas sir?"

"Tullius is sending the Numidian auxiliaries to Galilee and wants a century from my cohort to meet them there. It will be your century, Lucius." Piso saw the look of disappointment on my face and added, "I can't send the first century, Marcus has the tact of a frustrated buffalo, and Gnaeus of the second is ill with water fever so you are next in line I'm afraid."

"My orders?"

"To report to Antipas and give him as much visible support as possible to discourage unrest."

"That's rather vague sir."

"Which is another reason I'm sending you. We have no idea what form or how much trouble to expect, so you'll have to judge things as they happen for yourself. Also, the Numidians are brave soldiers but have an unfortunate habit of plundering friend and foe alike. Stay close to their commander, Juba. You may have to remind him whose side he's on. Prepare your century to leave tomorrow."

"Yes sir. May I make an observation please?"

"Of course."

"It concerns the replacement for Marcus Tullius. Is there any chance you will be given the command of the legion? Everyone in your cohort believes you would be an ideal legate and many in the other cohorts think so too."

Piso smiled and shook his head. "Thank you for that Lucius, but these decisions are made in Rome. My family are not part of the imperial establishment. The Piso's are seen as being too republican, too critical of rule by a single man because it smacks of kingship in all but name. We must expect a political appointment. Let us hope that whoever it is has at least some military experience."

By the time I had drawn the stores and completed the arrangements for my century's departure it was mid-afternoon and I arrived at the Antonia fortress almost at the end of my allotted time with Zenub. "I'm sorry I'm late. I was called to the tribune's office. My century leaves for Galilee tomorrow."

"Is the mission dangerous?"

"No."

Zenub smiled and poured me a goblet of wine. "Relax Lucius and drink this." She was wearing a long, tight fitting, red robe which enhanced her enticing curves. This had the usual effect on me but then, glancing at the water clock, I saw with horror it was empty. My time was up!

"Your face is a perfect picture," laughed Zenub. "Come and sit beside me."

"But—" She quietened me by putting her forefinger to my lips and guided me to the bed. I drew breath to speak again but once more she forestalled me.

"Lucius, do not worry; we have plenty of time."

"How so? The clock is empty. Your next client must be waiting."

"There is no next client."

"I don't understand."

She stroked my face and sighed. "Lucius, I have become fond of you, more than a cat should for a client. For the last few years I have seen no-one else on the days of your visits."

"You've kept yourself for me?"

"In the only way a cat can."

A flush of affection pulsed through me. "I am truly flattered and delighted to hear that because I too have become fond of you. I haven't visited another cat for a long time."

"I know."

We were silent for a while, then I said, "We've been meeting for about ten years. How old are you if you don't mind me asking?"

"Twenty-seven."

"I'm thirty-three. I finish my term in four years. How much longer will you go on for?"

Zenub replied, "I haven't really thought about retirement yet. I suppose I don't need to work because I've invested my money carefully. I own a house in Alexandria, which my mother lives in, and another in Caesarea which is rented through an agent. I think I would like to buy a third to be sure of a comfortable life when I finally retire."

"What will you do then?"

"Go to Alexandria and live with my mother."

"Would you consider living with me when I leave the legion?"

"Don't trifle with me Lucius."

"I'm not, I mean it. I am offering marriage."

"Offering marriage doesn't sound very romantic."

"Then will you marry me? Please! It will have to wait until I finish my term, but we could agree to it now." Zenub did not respond. She looked at the floor in silence. I saw a tear run down her cheek. "Zenub, have I upset you?" She shook her head and held my hand. I knew I should say no more, but I could not help myself. "You would not have to leave your mother, she could live with us." That produced a muffled giggle which broke the stress of the moment.

"You don't know my mother."

"I am sure I could cope. Now you're trifling with me."

She wiped her eyes and looked at me. "Lucius, this is

unexpected. I don't know what to say."

"How about 'yes'?"

She kissed my hand and whispered, "Yes."

"Well, that's settled then."

"Not quite. I know you mean what you are saying Lucius but you are extremely eligible and I would not want you to regret your decision. Ask me again one year before your term ends. If you still feel the same, the marriage contract can be prepared."

I was deflated by her caution. "Zenub, you may change your mind too."

"That will not happen." The words were spoken with the certainty of an oath.

"Then commit now. I am not after your houses or your mother. I have accumulated wealth of my own over the years and there will be my end of term payment which is generous for an experienced centurion."

"You do not have to persuade me. I am committed, but things may not be the same in the next few years. Men can change, even men like you. Please bear with me on this. If it helps, and as an expression of how I feel, you are now my lover not a client. I will no longer take payment for your visits."

"Very well, but it will help tighten our bond if you accept the payments I would have made and invest the money in our joint names for the future."

She kissed me on the lips and whispered in my ear, "Agreed. Enough talk, let's make love."

Without the pressure of time, I stayed with Zenub for the rest of the day. Just before I left an afterthought occurred to me which I should have considered sooner. "Zenub, what happens if you get pregnant?"

"By you or a client?"

"A client. Would you still want me?"

"It could happen I suppose but I've been lucky so far. Cats know the times of the month when they are most likely to conceive, so we avoid business on those days. It's not perfect and some girls get caught out or choose to take risks. Would that make a difference to us?"

"Not as far as I'm concerned. We both have our work to do. Will we have children?"

"Of course, lots of them."

"I like the idea of that. I must leave now for the evening parade. Stay well and I'll see you as soon as I get back from Galilee."

I placed my payment on the table beside her and said, "Invest our money wisely!"

***

IV

I did not hurry the march to Galilee and took a leisurely few days to reach Antipas' palace complex. I use the term 'palace' with a certain amount of latitude because it was temporary accommodation outside Sepphoris. Antipas had taken over a large village about a mile north of the city, ejected the inhabitants and converted the buildings into a grand interim base from where he could personally oversee the reconstruction of Sepphoris. A circular ditch and earth wall had been dug around the village buildings, which were converted into accommodation for his five hundred Galatian guards, palace officials, servants and slaves. A new, large stone building had been erected in what was previously the marketplace, for the tetrarch's own household.

My century and I arrived early on the fourth day of our journey and marched through the south gate where my men were allocated comfortable quarters near the palace. I reported to the office of the Galatian commander who, to my great pleasure, was Eumenes, previously second in command to Attalus in Jerusalem. We had become friends during the great rebellion but had not seen each other since then because he had chosen to serve Antipas in Galilee when Herod's kingdom was broken up rather than Archelaus in Jerusalem.

"Well, you Galatians certainly know how to make yourselves comfortable," I said as I looked at Eumenes' office from the comfort of a padded chair and munched on the bread and buffalo cheese left over from his breakfast.

"All the Herods enjoy their personal comforts and expect us to do likewise. Antipas is no different from the rest."

"Clearly you benefit from it Eumenes; you haven't aged at all since we last met whereas my hair is already beginning to go grey." In truth, the handsome young man I remembered had put on some weight since I last saw him, no doubt from too much good living, but then so had I. "Why did you choose to serve Antipas instead of Archelaus?" I asked.

"I prefer Galilee to Judea. I am not really a city dweller by nature. I found Jerusalem oppressive and the people untrustworthy. The Galileans are simple, uncomplicated folk who speak the truth and while Antipas leaves something to be desired as our master, he is a great improvement on Archelaus."

"I have not met either of them."

"Then you have not missed much Lucius, but Antipas is much more competent than his brother. Of all the family he is most like his father in character and appearance, but then you must remember that as a young man Herod proved himself to be a good general and conquered a kingdom before he was forty. He only became debauched in later life. Antipas is aware of this and yearns to emulate his father's achievements."

"Where is he now?"

"Gone hunting. He won't be back until dark. I expect he'll summon you tomorrow morning."

"Has there been any reaction yet to the taxation decree?"

Eumenes shook his head. "Difficult to say, but everything seems eerily quiet. We expected a riot or a demonstration at least. Some of my men are on patrol up north. That's where the trouble will start if there's going to be any."

"Do you doubt there'll be trouble?"

"Not really. The only question is how bad it will be."

"Any sign of the Numidians?"

"Not yet but they're expected at any moment. They'll be a welcome addition to our strength."

I finished my breakfast, went to my century to give orders for the day and left Rufio in command. Then I returned to Eumenes and spent the rest of the day with him looking at the construction work taking place in Sepphoris. The scale of it was vast and I could not help wondering how Antipas was able to squeeze enough taxation from his rural people to pay for it all in addition to his dues to Rome. With or without the taxation decree, Galilee was a tinder box waiting to be ignited.

In the evening we returned to the Galatian quarters but, just as we were about to enjoy the last meal of the day together, a sentry arrived and reported to Eumenes. "Horsemen approaching from the northwest sir. It's too dark to identify them yet; they're about a mile and a half away."

"Very well, I'll come. Lucius?"

"I'll come too," I answered.

We walked over to the west gate, climbed up the ramp to the top of the earth wall and peered into the twilight. At first, all we could see was the black outline of the Galilean hills contrasting against the charcoal grey of the night sky; the moon had not yet risen. My eyes slowly adapted to the dark but Eumenes saw them first. He pointed to the west. "Over there in the shallow valley about a mile away." I stared into the gloom and saw an irregular line of white specks picked out by the starlight. They were approaching rapidly. It did not take long for the specks to develop into horsemen but I shall never forget the remarkable appearance of the Numidians on that chilly, spring night. They wore long white cloaks with the hoods pulled forward to protect them against the cold. Their robes flowed behind them as they cantered towards us but in the darkness their black faces were invisible inside their hoods and their unshod ponies made almost no sound, seeming to glide just above the ground rather than on it. To me they looked like wraiths from the underworld coming to wreak havoc amongst the living.

"Frightening aren't they," whispered Eumenes. "Let's go out to meet them." We emerged from the west gate just as the leading wraith reached the earth rampart closely followed by his riders. Sliding easily from his horse, a tall figure in thigh length boots strode towards us. I still could see nothing inside the hood and briefly wondered if this indeed might really be a wraith, but the figure stopped in front of us and threw back his hood to reveal one of the most memorable faces I have ever seen. The black skin seemed to be stretched directly over the skull with no muscle or tissue in between. The whites of the eyes were yellow but when this creature smiled a greeting at us, the teeth were even whiter than his robes. His face bore the scars of many conflicts; especially noticeable was an old wound which stretched from his right eyebrow down to his neck. I later discovered this was an old spear wound which had pierced his throat turning his voice into something between a growl and a hoarse whisper.

"I am Juba," he hissed in execrable Latin. "Who commands here?"

"I am Eumenes, commander of the tetrarch's Galatian guard," answered my companion who was almost as comfortable speaking Latin as his native Greek.

"And you?" demanded Juba, turning his large round eyes

on me.

"Lucius Veranius, centurion of the third century, fifth cohort, third legion Gallica."

"Ah, I have heard of you. The fifth cohort is Piso's is it not?"

"Yes."

Then addressing Eumenes again Juba said, "We left Caesarea this morning and have ridden all day. Where can we make camp?"

"An area has been cleared for you outside the north gate. There is fresh water, a paddock for your horses and dried wood for your campfires. I will have food brought out to you immediately."

"Any wine?"

"As much as you can drink."

"That is much! You have thought of everything Eumenes. Take us to our camp."

And thus I met Juba, who turned out to be every bit as formidable as he appeared.

All remained quiet throughout April and May but in early June, when the command for every man to register at his nearest town took effect, trouble flared up. It was the day after the first Sabbath in the month. About mid-afternoon, I received a summons to attend on Antipas immediately, which did not auger well because the tetrarch was usually polite in his dealings with me. This time I was received in one of his private chambers instead of the audience hall. Eumenes was already there as was another man who was sweating, unwashed and looked as if he had just run many miles. Antipas was agitated; he did not even ask us to sit down, which he always did because he was extremely conscious of his short stature. As usual, he was immaculately attired in a long purple robe, multitudes of amulets and rings, and his beard was neatly trimmed, but his eyes darted to and fro and his brow was furrowed under his golden crown. He was winding and unwinding his hair ringlets around his forefinger which I had seen him do only once before when he had just escaped an assassin's knife.

I asked, "What has happened Your Majesty?" He was not a king but he liked the title and it did no harm to humour him.

Addressing both Eumenes and me, Antipas said, "I believe you both speak Aramaic?" We nodded; the normal court language was Greek. "Then I would like you to hear for yourselves what this man has to say. He is my agent based in Dan." Then changing from Greek into Aramaic he ordered, "David, tell these men what you have just told me, then you may rest."

"Yes, Your Majesty," answered David, who was a slim, fit looking man of about thirty. "I have come straight from the foothills of Mount Hermon, so my news is two days old. Judas the Galilean has captured Dan. His men have looted the city and committed acts of rape and murder against their own people. From one of the buildings looking out onto the marketplace, I saw Judas ordering summary executions of the city elders and any others who would not accept him as the Messiah. The man is clearly mad, but his followers obey him absolutely. He has named Sepphoris as his next target and our tetrarch as his next sacrificial victim."

"How many men does he have?" Asked Eumenes.

"Impossible to say. They are in no particular order but the hills around Dan are alive with them."

Eumenes pressed him. "Try and give an estimate. Are we

talking hundreds, thousands?"

David thought for a moment. "Many, many thousands but they move slowly. I think we have at least three days before they get here."

"Three days! Is that all!" Gasped Antipas who had by now turned quite pale. "What are we going to do?"

"Find out more," I replied. "If Your Majesty and Eumenes agree, I shall ride north with the Numidians and assess the quantity and quality of the men this Judas has. We can assume some in Dan will join him out of fear if nothing else, but they will probably run away at the first sign of real fighting. We may also be able to delay them while Eumenes musters Your Majesty's forces and prepares the defence of Sepphoris."

"Agreed," said Eumenes. Antipas just nodded distractedly.

And so, I went to war again, not trudging the dusty roads like a legionary, but flying like the wind with the best light cavalry in the world.

CHAPTER THREE

It was the thirteenth day of Adar (February) in the ninth year of Herod Antipas' rule in Galilee. Mary walked into Joseph's office and said starkly, "Joseph, I am with child again."

Joseph rolled up the scroll of the latest business accounts, which Judas had given him earlier that morning, got to his feet and kissed his beautiful wife. "When?"

"In six months' time."

"This is wonderful news Mary. Let us pray for our first daughter, then we shall name her after you." He put his arms round her and added, "Then our family will be complete. Five children, if you count Jesus, is a good number."

Mary pulled back from his embrace, the warmth of the moment gone. "I know I was at fault but you did agree to accept Jesus as yours. You did not have to, but I am heartily grateful you did."

"It was because I loved you as I still do now, and have I not treated Jesus as my own?"

"You have, but you are harder on him than the others."

"That's because he is not only the eldest but also the Messiah."

"But he isn't really, is he? He's half Roman!"

Joseph pointed to the chair where Ehud or Judas often sat. "Mary, sit with me and let us discuss this now. Perhaps we should have spoken much sooner, my office is hardly the ideal location, but now we have started let us continue."

Mary sat down, unsure of what was coming next, and said,

"Husband, I am ready."

He immediately sensed the defensive tone in her voice and chose his words carefully; his wife did not take criticism well. "I know your feelings about the Zealots and the dangers that will face Jesus when he gets older."

"Because they think he's the Messiah. Well, we can easily put that right and tell bar Abbas the truth."

"But then the title would fall upon James and we would still have the same problem. Belief in the Messiah is the only thing that can unite our people. Without it we will never throw off the Roman yoke."

"The Roman yoke, as you call it, does not seem so bad to me. We hardly ever see the Romans, we can worship as we like and our borders are protected from our enemies. Herod Antipas rules in Galilee with a light touch except for those who oppose him and moving his palace to Sepphoris will bring business opportunities to all the builders in the area. It is only that wastrel fool Archelaus in Jerusalem that's the problem. He bleeds the Judeans white and lines his own pockets to finance his debauched life while telling his people it's all the fault of Roman taxes. Your Zealot friends would do well to send an embassy to Augustus Caesar asking for Archelaus to be replaced."

"By whom?"

"Gebel, our senior donkey would do a better job, but surely there must be someone in Judea more suitable."

"Whoever it is would need to unite us quarrelsome Jews."

"The Romans have already done that! They are the people we love to hate, yet they leave us alone."

"I suppose the obvious choice would be Antipas," mused Joseph, "But the Herodian family is unpopular in Judea."

"So, must it be war? How many mothers' sons must die before you get what you want, and if you do, what will stop us from tearing each other apart again? And what of Jesus? Must he die too?"

Joseph did not respond for a few moments. Mary had come up with an idea that had not even been considered by the Zealot leadership. She had more common sense than any of them. "Mary, I shall take your advice to the Zealot council. We will try to obtain the support of the Pharisees and the Sadducees, but if all three sects are represented within the embassy you spoke of, that will increase its impact in Rome."

"What about the Essenes?"

"I don't think so. They're basically unwashed lunatics."

"Well that rules them out then," laughed Mary, who had little sympathy for the primitive way of life the Essenes chose to inflict upon themselves.

Joseph smiled, delighted to hear his wife's tinkling laughter again. "Mary, you put us all to shame. We are too slow to debate, too quick to argue and far too quick to reach for the sword instead of searching for compromise."

"But will your council accept a proposal put forward by a mere woman?"

"Probably not, though you are far from being a 'mere woman' so, with your permission I shan't tell them, at least until the embassy has left our shores."

"Granted."

Now that the conversation had warmed up a little, Joseph felt the time had come to ask the question he had been afraid to ask throughout their ten years of marriage. "Do you still think of him?"

Mary had been waiting for this moment for years and had

her reply well prepared. "I will not lie to you Joseph. Are you sure you wish me to answer?"

"Yes," he replied dully, fearful of what was to come.

"I do not think of Caius often, but sometimes when I see him in Jesus, I do. Apart from those moments, I think only of you, the man I love. I consider myself to be the most fortunate woman in Galilee to have Joseph bar Jacob as my husband."

Joseph felt his eyes moistening when he heard Mary's bold and honest response which far exceeded anything he dared hope for. "I am the fortunate one to have a wife who is as intelligent as she is beautiful. In truth I tried hard to hate Caius, but he was a difficult man to hate. Nor shall I ever forget that it was Caius and his centurion Lucius Veranius, who rescued us on that terrible night when Herod murdered all those babies in Bethlehem."

"Lucius was another Roman who was difficult to hate. I know Ruth thought so. She became fond of him but nothing came of it."

Joseph nodded in agreement. "You are right about Lucius. During our desperate escape to Egypt with that cohort of crude Germans, Lucius and I stayed up late one night talking by a campfire when neither of us could sleep. We came as close to becoming friends as is possible between a Jew and a Roman. I bear no ill will towards him and wish him well wherever he may be."

"And what of Ruth? I was always grateful you did not throw her out on to the streets of Nazareth but from what I hear, the marriage you arranged for her with Ehud has not worked out well."

"I know Ehud has shortcomings but he is a hard and loyal worker. Ruth is the one person I cannot forgive because she was your chaperon. She lived in my house with you but failed in her duty when she could easily have stopped the relationship blossoming between you and Caius. Protecting and guiding you was her purpose in being here."

"I am not an easy person to guide."

"I know that Mary, but do not ask me to forgive her."

"I shall not, but she will pay the price for something she could not have stopped as easily as you say, for the rest of her life. I have seen her only twice since she was married, each time by accident in the marketplace. On both occasions her face was bruised from the regular beatings Ehud gives her; no doubt there is worse elsewhere on her body."

Joseph sighed, "I do not wish for that but I will not interfere between a man and his wife; it would only make matters worse."

"I understand that husband, but Ehud is deep. Do not rely too heavily upon his loyalty."

***

II

It was now the tenth year of Antipas' rule in Galilee, which equated to the thirty sixth year of Emperor Augustus Caesar's rule over the Roman empire. Mary was right about the contracts generated by the building of the palace and ancillary works at Sepphoris. Antipas spent lavishly on his new capital and although Joseph initially failed to win any of the contracts for the preliminary works, his company's reputation was good enough for it to be pre-selected for the tender list for the main palace construction project. This was the most prestigious contract of the entire Antipas relocation development so the tetrarch's construction manager decided that, depending on how close the bids were, there could also be a building competition to assess the quality and speed of the highest bidders, which would help to determine the ultimate winner.

Jesus was now ten years old so Joseph decided to take him on the five-mile journey to Sepphoris where he could begin the apprenticeship that would give him the skills he would need to take over the business should his future as the Messiah not come to pass. All Jewish men were expected to have a skill and Jesus was no exception. It was early Iyar (April) and snow still dressed some of the Galilean hill tops as numerous hopeful building companies converged on Sepphoris to take advantage of the opportunities that were now on offer. Joseph needed his best managers with him, so Ehud and Judas also accompanied him. They walked quickly with young Jesus keeping up well, so they reached Sepphoris before noon, but there was no time to relax. Judas was given the critical task of analysing the contract documents while Ehud was sent to the area south of the city, where the competitors were assembling, to discover their identity and assess their prowess. Here he found out that there were only two other companies selected to tender for the main palace work, the Amos Construction Company a local Sepphoris business and the bar Micah brothers who, like Joseph, were also from Nazareth and had an uncanny habit of always beating Joseph for the contracts that really mattered.

Armed with this important information, Joseph and his team returned to his office in Nazareth and worked late into the evening to complete their bid. This was necessary because the following day was the Sabbath when no work was permitted, yet the deadline for the bids to be returned was noon on the day after the Sabbath.

"Well, we have now prepared our bid price and the time within which we are committed to completing the contract," said Joseph as he pushed back his chair and rolled up the scroll on his desk which would be submitted to Antipas' contracts manager. "All that remains now is for us to enjoy a well earned supper and for you, Ehud, to select our best construction team."

"Do you think there really will be a construction competition to decide the winner?"

"Almost certainly Ehud. The bidding for the palace work will be very tight and I'm convinced that Antipas' contracts manager will want to assess for himself the quality and speed of our work compared to the other two bidders."

At Judas' insistence, Jesus was present throughout the meeting and, even though it was well past his bedtime, the boy seemed as alert as he had been in the early morning and was not in the least overawed by the adult company he was in.

Judas put away his calculations and frowned. "The tender document was put together by someone who knew what he was doing. There is very little room for unforeseen extras or things that might happen that are entirely out of our control. There is also a stiff penalty if we miss the completion date but no bonus if we finish early."

"So, the price we bid is the price we must live with come what may," said Ehud.

"Precisely," agreed Judas, "So whatever we add to our bid cost to allow for risk will be critical. We should be asking ourselves how much we really need this contract, and therefore what margin we should accept, bearing in mind the unexpected."

"Winter is over," replied Joseph, "So the weather risk is minimal but, as I see it, the greater risk comes from the reliability of our suppliers. How do we stand there Ehud?"

"Fortunately, the mudbricks, which are the main variable, will be supplied by the client so the risk, if any, will be the same for all the contractors. Therefore, we need take no account of that so provided we have done our research thoroughly, the risk factor is minimal for this contract."

"Are you saying we should allow nothing for risk?" asked Judas.

"Yes, if we want to stand a chance of winning."

"Then it all comes down to what margin we are prepared to accept for what is likely to be the biggest contract in the history of our business."

"Exactly, Judas," said Joseph. "If we win this one our reputation will soar and we will be able to add the badge of honour *'Provider of the Tetrarch's palace'* to all our future bids.

It will not be just another contract but an investment for the future, so I propose a profit margin of just one fiftieth of our costs."

Judas objected, "But that is no profit at all because there are bound to be some unexpected extra costs; there always are."

"Typical accountant's view," scoffed Ehud. "There are bound to be some unforeseen savings too."

That was exactly what Joseph wanted to hear. "So, we are agreed then. Ehud, have your best work team prepared for the construction trial, we can't afford any mistakes or delays. Judas, please re-check your figures once more and have the bid ready for me to take it personally to the client's office. You shall accompany me, and you too Jesus."

None of the adults had noticed how closely Jesus was following the debate, after all he was only ten, but his intelligent eyes had been observing intently and, although not all the words had been fully understood, the thoughts and meaning behind them were crystal clear to him. He asked the simplest, but most perceptive question of all. "Father, is it possible the other businesses have received information we do not have? We may be bidding at a disadvantage."

Joseph frowned. "What do you mean Jesus?"

"Ehud has told us that the supply of mudbricks will be the same for everyone, but what of wood for the doorframes and lintels, iron for the nails and door hinges or anything else that could slow us down? If we are let down by just one supplier, we could end up paying time penalties that would more than wipe out our profit margin."

Judas remained silent but smiled with pleasure at his young student's observation and the measured way he explained it, but Ehud was dismissive. "Child, you are too young to understand these things. You are here to listen and learn, not to speak."

"Be that as it may," interjected Joseph springing to Jesus' defence, "It is a point well made and should be included in the risk assessment of the bid."

"Yes sir," replied Ehud sullenly.

"We will be advised of the winning bid during the afternoon of the same day the bids are submitted," continued Joseph. "Ehud, have your team ready to come to Sepphoris as soon as Judas returns here with the result. If we lose, Jesus and I will come home too and you can stand your men down, but if we win or are selected to take part in the construction trial, we shall lodge in the city and await your arrival. With God's help we will win."

"Amen to that," said Judas.

"And with any other help we can get," added Jesus, but the adults just smiled at the ramblings of a precocious child.

It was four hours after noon when the representatives of the three bidding companies for the palace complex work were called to the office of Antipas' contracts manager, a thin, grey totally unmemorable civil servant who read aloud from a large scroll. After the standard complimentary comments about the quality of the bids, he reached the part everyone was waiting for. "And so, in third place is Amos Construction of Sepphoris, in second is Joseph bar Jacob of Nazareth, and the winner is…" There was no need to listen to the rest.

Joseph had been beaten by the bar Micah brothers yet again. Judas closed his eyes, Joseph leaned forward and put his head in his hands. Only Jesus remained impassive.

But all was not lost. The contracts manager had more to say. "However, all three bids were so close that it has been decided a construction trial should take place. Depending on the performances of each company, the result may change so I exhort you all to have your best teams ready to commence work at noon tomorrow."

"There is still hope Father," said Jesus as they walked slowly back to their lodgings.

"A little but not much, my boy. The construction trial is to build part of the palace stable block. Each company will be given an identical stable to build. These are simple, standard structures which will not give us the chance to show our superiority in workmanship. That means the only way we can hope to overtake the bar Micah team is to build faster than them. Even then, we don't know how much faster will be enough to beat them. Ehud's team will do its best, but we must brace ourselves for a disappointment."

Jesus pondered for a moment. "Where does the competition take place?"

"Quite near our lodgings. All three of the stable block foundations have been pegged out ready for tomorrow."

"Do we know which one is ours?"

"Yes, there is a large notice with our name on it. The other two are identified in the same way."

"Can we see them before we go to our lodgings?"

"Of course, my boy. I'm gratified by the interest you're taking in all this. You are already shaping up to be a good builder."

"Thank you, Father."

Some hours after Joseph and Jesus retired for the night, Joseph was woken as Jesus quietly re-entered their room in the lodging house. "Where have you been?" he whispered.

"I am sorry Father, but I was caught short and had to relieve myself. I'm sorry if I disturbed you. I think it may have been something to do with this evening's meal."

"Well, the meat was certainly heavily spiced. That could easily affect a young stomach. How are you feeling now?"

"Much better Father. I think I'll sleep peacefully for the rest of the night."

Next morning there was an almost carnival atmosphere in the open plain west of Sepphoris where the stable blocks were to be built. Word had spread about the construction trial and a crowd had gathered to watch. It was estimated that the work would be completed on the third day of the competition, so an assortment of tents and temporary shelters had appeared where the contesting teams could sleep overnight. Work would only be permitted during daylight hours and a team of judges were on site to make sure there was no cheating. Joseph and Ehud oversaw the last-minute preparations of their team while Judas explained to Jesus what was happening and why. At noon, one of the judges raised the flag which was the signal to begin. Working conditions were not ideal because of a cold wind and steady drizzle, but that did not cool the ardour of the contestants.

At the end of the first day it seemed, judging by the number of courses of bricks that had been laid, that the Amos and Joseph teams were in the lead with the bar Micah brothers a little behind. "So far so good," said Judas as he walked round the competitors' sites with Joseph during the evening, "But something seems to be worrying the bar Micah team. There was a lot of head scratching going on this afternoon."

"I can see why," replied Joseph. "Look at their brickwork. There are some large gaps on the corners and the walls don't seem to be properly aligned."

"Perhaps they're feeling the pressure."

"Maybe, but although they are our fiercest rivals and there is no love lost between us, I would never say their work is shoddy. Anyway, let's see what tomorrow brings."

By the end of the second day, hopes were rising in Joseph's team. They had pulled ahead of the Amos team and had already fitted the stable roof framework while the Amos workers were still completing their last course of bricks. But the bar Micah team was lagging further and further behind and had completed barely half of the brickwork for their stable.

An hour and a half before noon on the third day, Ehud's workers hammered the last iron nail into the main hinge of the stable door to complete their task. Three and a half hours later the Amos team finished, but the bar Micah team had still not completed when the judges ended work for the day. After a tense wait of nearly an hour, Antipas' contracts manager announced that not only was Joseph of Nazareth the winner of the construction trial, but the margin of victory was so great that he was also the overall winner of the palace building contract. The winning contract would be signed the next day. Amos was second but, to add insult to injury, the bar Micah workers were not permitted to finish their task because they were disqualified for poor workmanship. In fact, their work was so bad, their stable block would have to be demolished and rebuilt by a competent builder.

Celebrations in the Joseph team went on well into the night though Ehud seemed a little subdued, but although there were some sore heads in the morning, nothing could spoil the sweet taste of victory when the winning contract was presented to

Joseph. But the victory was not yet certain. The bar Micah brothers claimed the test was flawed because the pegs on their plot which provided the baseline for the brickwork had been inaccurately placed. This was a direct criticism of the client's contracts manager and was therefore received coolly, but the marker pegs were now gone so the accusation could not be proven. After a superficial inquiry by the judges, the bar Micah's complaint was rejected for lack of evidence, but this set Joseph thinking so he called Judas and Ehud to the lodgings where he and Jesus were staying.

Judas arrived an hour after noon, but there was no sign of Ehud. "Welcome Judas," said Joseph. "There will be just you and I at this meeting because Ehud has returned to Nazareth to deal with an urgent, private matter."

"Will Jesus be joining us?"

"Not yet, because he is the reason for this meeting. You and I must speak alone first."

"Very well," replied a concerned Judas. "He did seem unusually quiet at the award presentation. Is he unwell?"

"Far from it I am pleased to say, but I am troubled by the bar Micah brothers' complaint."

"Sour grapes I would say."

"Possibly Judas, but nonetheless convenient for us. It is true that the bar Micah business is our bitter rival but their workmanship has always been top quality just like ours. It seems strange does it not, that at the very moment both our skills needed to be seen at their best, their workmanship failed them, not just by a small amount, but so disastrously that they were disqualified. I believe their objection may well be justified."

"Oh, come now Joseph. You have just won a great victory, yet you question it. Could it be that you expected to lose because the bar Micah brothers always beat us when it really matters?"

"Maybe, but it is more the manner of their defeat. It rings false to me."

"And you think young Jesus may have had something to do with it? But he was with us all the time."

Joseph shook his head. "Not all the time. Call him in. He's waiting outside."

When Jesus entered, Judas took a fresh look at the boy he had been tutoring for the last six years. He was unusually tall for his age. His limbs were long and sturdy and his hair was reddish brown, almost the colour of freshly wrought copper, which was unusual amongst the Jews, but commonly seen further north amongst the tribes of Syria and Galatia, some of whom, long ago, came south to become mercenaries in the armies of David and Solomon. But most striking were his large eyes which were the golden green colour of hazel leaves in the autumn. Judas had seen nothing like them in Judea or Galilee and felt it entirely appropriate that the Messiah should have a feature which distinguished him from all his fellow countrymen, the people he would eventually lead to freedom.

Joseph said, "Sit down my son. I have some important questions to ask you."

"Have I displeased you, Father?"

"I do not know yet but we shall soon find out. Now Jesus, what is the most important thing when answering questions from your father or mother?"

"To tell the truth."

"Good boy, that is correct. Do you remember four nights ago, when you woke me up after you came back from relieving yourself?"

"Yes Father."

"Did you do anything else that night?" Jesus frowned and

stared hard at his feet but remained silent.

"Answer, my son," demanded Joseph. "Did you do anything else?"

"Yes Father. I went out to the construction trial site."

"And?"

"I moved some of the pegs on the bar Micah plot, but only a little so that the change would not be noticed."

"How much?"

"Half a hand width."

"Enough to misalign the foundations?"

"Yes Father."

"So, we only won by cheating."

"You did not cheat Father, you did not know."

"What you did was wrong. I cannot allow us to benefit from cheating. Do you understand!"

"Yes Father, but the bar Micah company always beats us yet you are the best builder in Nazareth. They must be cheating too!"

"Two wrongs do not make a right, do they?"

"They do not Father, but -"

"No more buts. Judas, what do you say?"

Unlike Joseph's stentorian tone, Judas spoke gently and smiled at the unhappy boy. "There is no doubt that what Jesus did was wrong, but at least his motives were good. He gained nothing out of it for himself and moved those pegs out of love and loyalty to you. Also, moving the pegs just enough to cause a problem without being noticed to start with was very clever."

"Judas, your answer surprises me."

"Joseph, I can only speak as I find. Love and loyalty are the greatest virtues. If Jesus were my son I would be bursting with pride. Sometimes we must be pragmatic. The bar Micah brothers have had the beating of us on all important bids for years. I could never understand why. I have no proof of cheating, but Jesus has voiced my own long-held suspicions."

"But that does not entitle us to win by cheating too."

"True, but if you tell the judges what has happened, what will become of Jesus' future as the Messiah? There will be a stain on his character which could undermine his leadership and play into the hands of the enemies a Messiah is bound to make. No-one is perfect. Did not King David himself commit a far greater sin when he stole Uriah the Hittite's wife? But God forgave him, and I am sure Jesus will learn from this and grow up to be a better man for it."

Joseph shrugged, "You are persuasive Judas, but I am not sure."

"Jesus is the Messiah, the anointed one. He is the future King of the Jews. There is no need to do anything today. Sleep on it, and if you still feel the same tomorrow, do what you must."

"That is sound advice Judas," said Joseph. Then turning to Jesus, he added, "Whatever I decide, my love for you will remain as strong as ever."

"Thank you, Father. I am very sorry to have put you through this. Will you tell Mother?"

"Of course, but her opinion will be the same as Judas', of that I am certain."

The next morning, Joseph followed Judas' advice and was justified soon after.

***

III

Six days earlier, on the evening the successful bid had been prepared in Joseph's office, a tired Ehud returned to his fine house in Nazareth's upper town, threw the final bid document onto the table in the reception room, and called loudly for Ruth.

"Wife! I need some wine. You may sit with me while I drink it." Eight years of marriage to her brutish husband had only been bearable because of Ruth's ability to hide her true self behind a mask of obedience and submission. Any sign of spirit or defiance invariably resulted in a beating from Ehud who was a powerfully built man. She had long ago learned to move with the blows rather than resist them, which minimised the injuries she received. Her husband's temper was not improved by the fact she had born him no children, which was hardly surprising because of the constant stress she lived under. Although she hated him, she hated his fawning, interfering mother more who constantly reminded her son of his wife's inadequacies and how he deserved someone better.

But tonight, Ehud seemed to want to talk, which was usually a good sign, so she decided to humour him. She brought a half full goblet of wine, a full goblet often brought on violence, and sat down opposite him. "Did you manage to finish the work on the Sepphoris bid, Dear?"

Ehud took a long pull at his wine, wiped his lips on the back of his hand, and held up a small scroll. "Yes, we've just completed it despite some moaning by that fool Judas. He thinks he knows all about business, but he knows nothing. He's just an overpaid scribe who never gets his hands dirty."

"Just as well then that Joseph has you to guide him. Was the bid completed the way you wanted it?"

"Yes, despite the fact that Joseph insisted on having his precocious son present."

"What are your chances?"

Ehud drained his goblet. "Fair to middling, I suppose. The bar Micah brothers are bidding too, so they're the ones to beat. We'll know the result the day after tomorrow."

"Another goblet of wine dear?" Asked Ruth, hoping that would make him go to sleep straight away when they went to bed.

"No, I've got another job to do which won't take long. Maybe I'll have another when I get back, but I'll pour it myself. Don't wait up for me."

"As you wish Dear."

But Ruth had no intention of going to bed yet. Going out at night after a bid had been prepared was becoming something of a routine, and each time Ehud returned he would be uncharacteristically cheerful. Tonight, Ruth decided she would follow him. As soon as she heard the front door close, she slipped on a dark cloak, covered her hair with a hood and went out into the night. Ehud was easy to follow because he was carrying a lamp, but Ruth did not need one because the night sky was clear and full of stars and an almost full moon lit up Nazareth in a bright, silver light which cast plenty of shadows if she needed them.

Surprisingly, Ehud did not head towards the town centre but walked up the hill where most of the wealthier townsfolk lived. Here the houses were spaced further apart and the shadows were fewer, so when a small, feral dog barked at Ruth she had nowhere to hide. She stood stock still. Ehud, who was about forty paces ahead of her, stopped and turned to face the commotion behind him. The night was cold, but Ruth could feel a bead of nervous sweat trickle down her brow as her husband scanned the area from where he had heard the bark. Slowly, he began to retrace his steps. She felt like running but fear kept her rooted to the ground. She dared not move but as he came closer she felt certain he would discover her. Suddenly the dog trotted off towards a midden heap to scavenge. Ehud saw it and, satisfied there was nothing to worry about, turned round and resumed his journey.

Ruth let out a huge, but quiet, sigh of relief. After half a minute or so she began to follow her husband again, but at a greater distance than before, until Ehud had almost reached the northern boundary of the town. She was mystified because there was no-one in this part of Nazareth that her husband had dealings with, as far as she knew. At last, he stopped outside a large, three storeyed building surrounded by a neat, well laid out garden, but this house was the office of the bar Micah brothers! She waited under a shadow cast by a large cedar tree and watched with growing dismay as she saw Ehud walk across the garden and knock at the door of the bar Micah establishment. Seconds later the door opened and he entered without challenge or question. She had seen enough and waited no longer. She now realised that her husband was a traitor to the business that had employed him for the last fifteen years and ran home wondering what she should do next.

When Ruth awoke on the Sabbath morning, Ehud was in a jovial mood; clearly whatever had happened at the bar Micah residence had gone well for him. He even spoke of extending the house and beginning the roof garden she had always wanted. This set off another train of thought in her mind. In the past she had always assumed Ehud received financial support from his parents which allowed him to afford a lifestyle that far exceeded the salary of a construction manager, but now she understood where the money was coming from. She decided to write to Mary for she could not speak to her directly because she was not permitted to leave the house alone; either Ehud or his mother would always accompany her, so she would have to trust Hiram, the house slave, to deliver the letter. This would be a risk because it was not possible to tell what went on in a slave's mind. In any event, she would have to wait until Ehud was working away from home so she could safely gain access to his office where he stored his writing materials. But the opportunity came sooner than she expected.

On the morning after the result of the Sepphoris palace bid was announced, Ehud departed with his building team to take part in the construction trial. With him out of the way, Ruth was able to write her letter to Mary.

Fifteenth day of Iyar, tenth year of Tetrarch Antipas.

My Dearest Mary,

I deeply regret not being able to meet you in the years since my marriage, but this is because my husband treats me like a prisoner. I am not permitted to leave the house unless he, or his doting mother escorts me. Consequently, the hopes I had of meeting you and exchanging news in the marketplace have not been fulfilled.

But now I must risk writing to you using our house slave

Hiram as the carrier of this letter. I hope it reaches you safely. I have recently discovered that my husband Ehud, your husband's business manager, has been having secret meetings with the bar Micah brothers. These meetings only take place when bids for important contracts have been prepared which they and your husband are competing for. I have no absolute proof, but I believe that Ehud is passing on details of Joseph's bids to his fiercest rivals. This would explain Joseph's consistent failure to beat the bar Micah firm for important contracts. I do not know what you can do about this, but poor Judas should at least be told the reason for his otherwise inexplicable failure to manage Joseph's business successfully. He was being cheated by the very man who took his place as Joseph's deputy.

I pray that somehow we will be able to meet soon, otherwise I see no point in continuing with this miserable existence. I am trapped in a life where I am being treated worse than a slave. I can see only one way out of this hell on earth and, even though it is against God's law, the real Hell can be no worse than what I am going through.

My love to you and Jesus. May God smile upon you both as he has failed to do upon me.

Ruth.

She rolled up the parchment and used her husband's clay cylinder to seal it. Then she went to the shed in the courtyard where Hiram lived and knocked on the door.

The house slave from Samaria, a small, shrivelled man now well into his fifties, was startled when he opened the door to find the lady of the house standing there. "Mistress Ruth! Please excuse me but I am unprepared for your visit. If you would please wait, I will tidy my dwelling before you enter."

"That will not be necessary Hiram, I shall not stay long. I have here a letter I wish you to deliver for me. It's for Mary, Joseph bar Jacob's wife. It is very important that it reaches her safely but, as you must already know, I am not permitted to leave this house alone."

Hiram paused. He seemed to want to say something, but checked himself and simply replied, "I will see to it at once my lady."

"If for any reason Mary is not there when you call, you may leave the letter with Joseph or Judas, but no-one else."

"I understand my lady. I will leave in a moment."

"Thank you, Hiram. God go with you."

The old slave watched Ruth return to the main house with pity in his eyes. She always treated him well but he was well aware of how much she suffered in Ehud's household. Sadly, as a slave, he could not permit his feelings to show; it would be far too dangerous.

Hiram departed just before noon but, by one of those bitter twists of fate which can foil even the best laid plans, Golda, Ehud's corpulent mother who was unaware her son had gone to Sepphoris, was coming to visit him. She saw Hiram just as he was leaving and stopped him. "Where are you going?"

"I am delivering a message for Mistress Ruth."

"I said where are you going, not what are you doing!"

"To the house of Joseph bar Jacob."

"What is that you are carrying?"

"It is the message."

"Give it to me."

"My instruction from the lady of the house is to deliver it directly to the recipient."

Golda's eyes narrowed. "I am the mother of the master of this house. He will be displeased if you defy me. Well you know that! Now do as I say."

Hiram had no choice and handed her the letter, but when Golda saw it was sealed she thought twice about opening it. After Hiram explained that her son had left for Sepphoris with his building team, she decided to take the letter home to her husband; waiting a little longer until he returned home from the synagogue, where he worked as a scribe, would make no difference because, like most Jewish women, she could neither read nor write.

"You did the right thing Golda," said Aaron, as he fingered the sealed letter after they had eaten their evening meal, "And you also did right to leave the letter unopened."

Golda beamed at the praise she received from her beloved husband. "Then what should we do?"

Aaron was not blind to the treatment his son inflicted upon his wife, but that was all part of marrying below himself. "We should not interfere between man and wife, but nor should Ruth be writing letters without her husband's knowledge. We'll send a reliable house slave to Sepphoris with the unopened letter and let Ehud make of it what he wants. He is a clever boy and will know what to do but, if he needs advice, he will ask us as he always does."

"That Ruth was always wilful."

"That's true Golda, but we must not be blind to the fact that Ehud is not the most patient of men."

"Ruth would drive any normal man beyond endurance! I wonder he has not divorced her; she's obviously barren."

"There is still plenty of time. It is said that children born to mature women are often highly intelligent."

Golda sighed, "Well that's something I suppose. I would so love to be a grandmother before I'm too old to care."

When Ehud read Ruth's letter, he boiled over with rage. Deceitful, disloyal and wilful; she had all the faults that angered him most. If he had been at home he would have given her a thrashing she would never forget, but by the time he cooled down a little he realised that being five miles away was fortuitous. He could plan what to do next without letting his ire cloud his judgement. He would have to be careful because Ruth had information that could destroy his reputation, but as he weighed up the possibilities facing him, a seed of an idea developed in his mind which, if carefully nurtured, might resolve all his difficulties at a single stroke. It involved risk, but only a small one, compared to the disaster confronting him if he did nothing.

Ruth viewed Ehud's return home with terror because Hiram, at great risk to himself, had told her about his encounter with Golda. If she'd had somewhere to go she would have fled, but her family had lost interest in her years ago, so her only choice was to live on the streets like a beggar or remain at home and face what was coming. Ehud had sent word ahead that he would come home on the day after the contract was signed. He expected to arrive in the evening and would require a meal. The message, delivered verbally by one of his workers, was so ordinary that Ruth concluded he could not yet have seen the letter.

The dreadful day arrived. Ruth waited, cold with fear, but she had secreted a carving knife inside her gown. If Ehud intended murder, she would not go down without a fight. The sun was just setting creating a warm, red glow on the underside of the clouds that blanketed most of the evening sky when she heard Hiram open the front door to his master. She stood beside the large, dining table in the reception room, trying unsuccessfully to stop herself from shaking.

There was an inaudible conversation between the two men, then silence as the slave returned to his quarters.

The door to the reception room swung open. Ruth felt her legs beginning to quake and gripped the back of a chair to stop herself from falling; she had never felt such abject terror. Ehud stood in the doorway; he was smiling! "Hello, my Dear. Will you not embrace your husband on his return?" Ruth could not move; she could not even speak. "Very well," said Ehud in a friendly, conversational tone, "Then I shall embrace you." He strode towards her, arms outstretched. She fumbled in her gown for the knife but could not find the handle amongst the folds in her clothing before he reached her. She closed her eyes waiting for the first blow. It did not come. Instead, he put his arms round her and kissed her. She opened her eyes again in astonishment.

Ehud stepped back and looked at her. "There is no need to fear me. Yes, I have read the letter but I will not harm you. Hiram is bringing some wine, and we shall talk. Then we shall eat together and I shall retire early because I've had a busy day. Now please sit with me."

Ruth sat down and Hiram brought wine and two goblets. By the time the slave left the room, her fear had been replaced by confusion. Ehud raised his goblet, "To my beautiful wife," and drank. Then he waited for her to do the same.

Ruth took a small sip in case her wine was poisoned and said, "But you have read the letter, yet you are not angry?"

"I admit I was at first, but then I began to wonder how it could be that a wife hates her husband so much. While you were wrong about my motive for visiting the bar Micah brothers, the simple fact that you truly believed me to be capable of such treachery was appalling. That gave me cause to take a long, hard look at myself, with as much impartiality as is possible when doing such a difficult thing. I did not like what I saw; an angry, self-centred, violent individual who works hard but shares none of his concerns with the wife he truly loves. I have been unfair and unkind to you. I apologise for that, and from now on I am resolved to do better."

Ruth could hardly believe what she was hearing, but although hugely relieved she was not taking the beating she had expected, eight years of misery could not be erased by mere words. "Husband, I am greatly heartened by what you have just said, but will you tell me how the change in you will affect my life? Will I truly become the lady of this house instead of your mother?"

"Certainly! And no more drunken beatings. When the contract in Sepphoris is completed, you will be free to come and go as you please and organise all matters concerning the welfare of our home."

This was more than Ruth could have hoped for, but the delay in awarding her the status she craved until the Sepphoris contract was finished seemed odd. "Husband, being established as the lady of this house will give me great joy, but how long will it be before the contract you speak of is ended?"

Ehud was silent for a moment. She wondered if she had angered him again, but then he smiled once more. "The contract period is nine months, but upon reflection, that is far too long to make you wait. Therefore, I will bring forward the change in your status to when the contract begins, which will be in two or three weeks. How does that sound?"

"Wonderful!" She stood up and put her arms round him with genuine warmth for the first time in their marriage. "I thank God for this change in you. Now we have a new future to look forward to."

But as she embraced her husband, she could not see the look of triumph in his dark, unfathomable eyes.

***

IV

On the sixteenth day of Sivan (June), Joseph, Ehud and their team of skilled workmen began the Sepphoris palace contract. The weather was sunny yet cool which was ideal for working. Everyone was in high spirits but none more so than Ruth who was now free to go wherever she wished. Ehud kept his word and even his mother stayed away. Ruth decided her first trip would be to the marketplace where she hoped she might meet Mary, but, on this occasion, she was not there. Surprisingly Jonathan, the younger of the two bar Micah brothers, was. He seemed to recognise Ruth though that hardly seemed possible for she had been locked away for eight years. As best as she could remember, he might have been a guest on her wedding day. Still, he was a tall, handsome fellow so she did not mind too much when he spoke to her.

"I have not seen you before, but I think we might have met?"

"Were you a guest on the day I married Ehud?"

"Ah, that would be it, but that was some time ago I think."

"Eight years."

"As much as that!"

And so, the inconsequential chatter continued until Ruth began to feel uncomfortable because a married woman should not be seen engaging in conversation with an unaccompanied man when her husband was absent. She politely brought the meeting to a close, purchased a few items from a food stall, and went home.

She thought no more about it until the next day when she returned to the market looking for Mary, but Jonathan was there again. He seemed to be waiting for her. This time the conversation became more difficult when Jonathan asked after Ehud in a way that invited Ruth to be critical of her husband. Fortunately, she saw Mary arrive which enabled her to conclude the conversation without causing offence.

Mary was delighted to see her best friend again after such a long time and the two women chatted happily for more than an hour. Perhaps it was the new sense of freedom she was experiencing or, more probably, the unexpected change in Ehud's treatment of her that made her refrain from telling Mary about his dishonest dealings with the bar Micah brothers, but whatever the cause might be, Ruth found herself feeling a sense of loyalty to her husband for the first time in eight years. The change in him had caused a change in her. After all, she might have misinterpreted the reason for Ehud's nocturnal visit to the bar Micah household. Even now, she sometimes wondered if she was dreaming and that she would wake up to the bad times again.

Then suddenly something happened which no-one in Nazareth anticipated.

***

V

Augustus Caesar's decree that all men in the kingdom once ruled by Herod should present themselves for taxation sparked another rebellion. The conflict began in Judea but soon spread to Galilee. Bar Abbas responded quickly and summoned his council to the Zealot headquarters in Jerusalem. The council included Judas who left Nazareth on the twenty third day of Sivan (June) to attend the meeting.

Four days later the council assembled, though bar Abbas' attendance was kept secret until the last moment because he was still a fugitive from the last rebellion ten years ago. Sitting either side of the long council table in the upper floor of the Zealot bureau were Ariel, the grey haired, official leader of the sect, Asher, the young military commander who was also a fugitive from the earlier rebellion, Isaac, the leader of the sinister Shadows, Judas, the financial controller and, of course, Eli bar Abbas himself. For the sake of the safety of Asher and bar Abbas, the meeting was held at night.

Bar Abbas opened the meeting. "My friends, you will know by now that rebellion has broken out in Judea. This is led by Alexander, a giant of a man, who claims to be Herod's grandson. He has no real credentials to his name except 'sheep stealer' but, significantly, he has gained support from some elements of the official Judean army, so he has disciplined, well-armed troops with him which makes him a real threat to Archelaus."

"Where is he?" Asked Asher.

"On the other side of the Jordan, half a day's march from Jericho."

"Less than two days from Jerusalem then?"

"Yes, Asher, but now the Romans have a legion stationed in the city. Alexander will be beaten."

Isaac asked, "Should we not consider helping Alexander?"

"No," answered bar Abbas, "For two reasons. First, Alexander also claims he is the Messiah, which we know is false, and second, the true Messiah will not be ready to lead his people in person for at least another eight years. We have already learned a bloody lesson from fighting too soon."

Judas asked, "How does Alexander pay his troops? Where does he get the money?"

Bar Abbas smiled, "As usual Judas Sicariot, you go straight to the heart of the matter. Alexander is a peasant. He has not thought such important details through. I hear his only method of payment is promises for the future and any plunder his troops can find which, of course, will be extracted from our own people. Consequently, he must gain a quick victory else his army will desert him."

Ariel commented, "Our people are easily discouraged by delay or failure, but they will move mountains for the true Messiah."

"Thank you, Ariel," acknowledged bar Abbas, "And the reason I called this meeting concerns the true Messiah. Rumours have reached us that our old enemy, Judas the Galilean, is on the move again. It's said his first target is Dan, but after that he will head for Sepphoris where he has many sympathisers. Sepphoris is only five miles northwest of Nazareth. If Sepphoris falls to the Galilean, the true Messiah will be in danger so Judas, it will be your responsibility to ensure Jesus and his family leave Nazareth immediately and, with Reuben's protection, come to Jerusalem until the danger has passed. The safety of the true Messiah must be our first and only priority."

"It shall be so Eli," replied Judas. "Do you want me to accompany them?"

"No, you must remain in Nazareth and send word when you believe it is safe for Jesus to return but also, and almost as important, you must discover the location of Judas the Galilean because we have a score to settle with him. That is why Isaac and some of his Shadows will accompany you back to Nazareth. They will afford you protection during the turbulent times ahead while avenging poor Daniel's death."

Judas replied, "I understand Eli and should you need money your treasury is full."

***

VI

News of Judas the Galilean's rebellion was in Nazareth before Judas returned. Herod Antipas had panicked and already left Sepphoris making sure to suspend all construction projects before he departed. This disappointment for Joseph was made worse when Judas informed him he must immediately leave Nazareth with his family and make for the sanctuary of Jerusalem. So, on the fifth day of Tamuz (July), Joseph with Mary, now eight months pregnant and his children left Nazareth for Jerusalem. This brought back ironic memories of a similar journey to Bethlehem ten years earlier, when Mary was heavily pregnant with Jesus, but it was also the opportunity Ehud had been waiting for.

Joseph was the highly respected chairman of the Nazareth Council of Elders. He was also the only obstacle left to thwart Ehud's plan to do away with Ruth because Joseph's deputy, Jonah bar Joash, was a reactionary traditionalist who believed that the laws of Moses should be strictly enforced with no room for discretion or modernist interpretation. Now, if Ehud acted quickly, it would be Jonah who would lead the elders in judgement of the ordeal he had planned for his wife.

The morning after Joseph and his family left Nazareth, Ruth was at home preparing for her daily trip to the market. Suddenly there was a loud banging at the front door, so Hiram went to see what the problem was because Ehud had left the house earlier that morning. The house slave was brushed aside and two large synagogue servants burst into the reception room where Ruth was packing her bag before going to the market.

"Ruth, wife of Ehud bar Aaron!" said the senior of the two.

"Yes, but who are you? How dare you force your way into my husband's house! He shall hear of this."

"He already knows. You must come with us to the synagogue where you will be held on a charge of breaking the law of Moses."

"Nonsense! On whose authority are you here?"

"That of Jonah bar Joash, chairman of the Council of Elders."

"Joseph bar Jacob is the chairman. Everyone knows that."

"But he is not here, so in his stead you are summoned by Jonah."

"I refuse to go!"

The second servant pushed past Ruth and stood behind her, then his senior said, "This is official business. We will force you if we must."

Ruth realised she had no choice but said defiantly, "Very well, but my husband will deal with you for this violation."

"I think not. He is the one who brings the charges against you."

As she was escorted out of the house, Ruth called to the terrified Hiram, "Find my husband and tell him what has happened. There must be some mistake!"

Ruth spent the rest of the morning languishing in a small antechamber of the synagogue, confused and frightened by this sudden change in her life. She struggled to believe that her newly reformed husband was the cause, yet deep down she knew that he was certainly capable of such a thing. Hopefully there had been some sort of misunderstanding which would soon be resolved, for she knew she had done nothing wrong.

Two hours after noon, her chamber door was unlocked by the senior synagogue servant. He beckoned her to follow him. "Come with me. The Council of Elders is ready to examine you now."

"Where is my husband?"

"He awaits you with the council." Ruth was taken to the main chamber of the synagogue, which she knew well because here the families of the faithful met every Sabbath for prayers and readings from the Torah. Now it was empty except for the servants, five elderly men who sat along the wall that faced Jerusalem and standing to one side her husband. Ehud refused to look at her as she was presented to the council for interrogation by the senior servant.

Jonah, a grey haired grim faced man with a beak like nose and small, cold eyes sat in the middle of the five. His voice was as hostile as his face. "Ruth, wife of Ehud bar Aaron, you are accused of adultery which is against the law of Moses. If you are found guilty the penalty is death by stoning. What is your answer?"

Ruth hardly heard the charge. Her mind was racing as she began to comprehend that Ehud's kindness over the past few weeks had been a ruse. He had planned this all along. She had to face a mortal charge alone and friendless. Some women would have crumpled at this realisation, but not Ruth. Her initial shock and desperation were quickly subsumed in anger at Ehud, but also rage for allowing herself to be taken in by this callous, hateful man who wanted to be rid of her. "The accusation is false! Who brings it!" She demanded.

"Your own husband," replied Jonah.

"And by what right do you accuse me Jonah bar Joash! I

demand to be tried by Joseph bar Jacob, the true chairman of the council of Elders."

"You may demand what you like but it will make no difference. Joseph fled from Nazareth with his family yesterday. He has abandoned Nazareth, so I am chairman now."

"Fled? Joseph is not the sort of man who is easily frightened. Fled from what?"

"Judas the Galilean. His army captured Sepphoris yesterday. Now you must stay silent while the full charge is read out to you by your accuser."

Ehud unrolled a scroll and began to read. "Ruth, my wife who I have loved and cherished for eight years -"

"Eight years! Not even eight weeks!"

"Quiet woman!" Snarled Jonah. "If you interrupt again, I shall have you gagged! Ehud, you may continue."

For the first time during the mockery of a trial, Ehud looked Ruth in the eyes, gloating as his plan progressed perfectly. "I accuse you of adultery with Jonathan bar Micah. You have been seen by many witnesses talking intimately together in the marketplace. When questioned yesterday, Jonathan admitted committing adultery with you after you seduced him. He is Joseph's bitterest rival in business. How could you do such a thing! What have you to say?"

"All lies! Where is your evidence!"

Ehud turned to Jonah. "Bring in Jonathan bar Micah."

Jonathan's evidence was a complete fabrication, but it was convincing. Above all, he was able to describe the birthmark on Ruth's back and other personal details that only a husband or a lover would know. As the evidence unfolded, Ruth realised she was lost. Ehud had obviously provided the details Jonathan needed to make his statements sound convincing, and if she agreed to be physically examined by a panel of respected matriarchs, the result would only confirm the veracity of Jonathan's evidence. She tried to defend herself by saying the accusation was a conspiracy to hide the illegal relationship between Ehud and the bar Micah brothers, but her defence sounded hollow even to her own ears.

Jonathan humbly begged the council's forgiveness for his part in the crime and pleaded the extenuating circumstances of a young, virile man being tempted by a wily seductress. His plea was accepted though he was required to pay a small fine. Ruth was taken back to her prison while the council considered its judgement, but she had only a few minutes to wait before she was called back to hear the council's sentence.

Jonah delivered the verdict. "Ruth, wife of Ehud bar Aaron, you have shown no sorrow, no remorse for your sin. Instead all we have heard is defiance and disrespect. Consequently, any inclination this council may have felt for mercy has been extinguished by your own attitude. You will be given the rest of this day to consider your fate and make your peace with God if you are able to. Then, tomorrow at noon, you will be taken to the quarry outside the northern wall of our town where you will be tied to a stake and stoned by the good folk of Nazareth until you are dead. Thus will the law of Moses be carried out. Have you anything to say?"

"Yes. May you and your four stupid councillors rot in Hell where you belong!"

"Take her away!" Then addressing Ruth's accuser, Jonah said sympathetically, "Ehud, son of Aaron, this has been a difficult time for you but you have done your duty most honourably."

The morning of the twenty third day of Tamuz (July) saw a

beautiful, cloudless sky. Judas bade farewell to the Shadows who had accompanied him from Jerusalem and watched them head menacingly towards Sepphoris where Judas the Galilean was reported to be. As he was returning to his house, he noticed an unusually large number of townsfolk walking towards Nazareth's north gate, so he stopped a middle-aged man, who was accompanied by his wife and children, and asked, "What's happening? Where is everyone going?"

"To the quarry. Have you not heard? There is to be an execution at noon, the first for many years."

"Who?"

"Ruth, wife of Ehud bar Aaron. She is to be stoned for adultery."

Judas knew Ruth well. Ten years earlier, when she had been part of Joseph's household, they had shared in the dramatic escape from Bethlehem just days after Jesus was born. "But who chaired the trial?" He asked. "Joseph bar Jacob is not here."

"Jonah bar Joash," came the reply.

Judas ran to the synagogue where he found Jonah dressed in his formal regalia for the execution. "Jonah, what is the meaning of this? You have sanctioned an execution but you know that this should only be done by the true chairman of the council, Joseph bar Jacob."

Jonah shrugged. "But he is not here. He has fled before the approach of Judas the Galilean, but life, death and judgement must go on with or without our craven chairman."

Judas could not give the real reason for Joseph's departure without revealing the existence of the true Messiah, so he used the power of the law instead.

"Jonah, you make a big assumption as to why Joseph left

Nazareth, but be that as it may, you well know that the passing of a capital sentence needs to be sanctioned by the Roman authorities before an execution can take place."

"Really!" Scoffed Jonah. "I see no Roman authority here, but I do see the imminent approach of Judas the Galilean. We are only implementing the laws of Moses. It is well known that the Galilean disapproves of the way they have been diluted in recent times. I have no doubt he will applaud our actions this day. Rome's power is broken now."

"Jonah, if you think a Galilean peasant and a few ruffian supporters can break the power of Rome, then you are a bigger fool than I thought you were. When this Judas is beaten, as he assuredly will be, you will face retribution for killing this woman without due process of law."

But Jonah would not be diverted from his chosen course; his sense of self-importance would not allow it. Indeed, he was revelling in the stir he had created in the absence of the cowardly Joseph. Judas would have to think of something else, so he asked, "When is the execution due to take place?"

"Noon." That left him just under four hours to do something. Sepphoris was two hours' walk away. Roman soldiers were reported to be just west of the city, so he put on his most sturdy sandals and half walked, half trotted towards the city. He was determined to rescue Ruth for he had never liked or trusted Ehud and even if she was guilty of adultery, who could blame her?

Half an hour before noon, Ruth was taken from her prison and dragged to the north gate of the town by the two synagogue servants. Now that the moment of execution faced her, terror once more gripped her brave heart. As she stumbled down the rocky track to the quarry, she was shocked at the size of the crowd assembled there. It seemed like every resident in Nazareth had come to take part in the morbid ritual of execution by stoning. She was tied to a wooden stake with thick leather straps around her ankles, arms and neck to make her an easy, static target for the stone throwers. Just before the execution began, she was subjected to a torrent of abuse by Jonah, who was relishing every moment of his newfound power, but Ruth heard barely a word of it. The full horror of what was about to happen began to numb her wits. Death by stoning was said to be slow and painful. She prayed she would be stunned by an early blow to the head before the pain became too great.

Jonah's monotonous drone ended. He stepped away and within seconds sharp lumps of pale, grey rock began to strike home. The first hit her ankle; she cried out in pain. The crowd cheered. Next, she was struck on the shoulder, then by a glancing blow to her head. Just before she lost consciousness, she turned her head to the left to avoid another rock. It must have been wishful thinking, but as she finally closed her eyes she imagined she saw two Roman soldiers standing at the edge of the quarry.

CHAPTER FOUR

The Numidians travel fast so it did not take long to find Judas the Galilean's army. On the morning of the second day out of Sepphoris we approached the valley of the River Jordan from the west, just north of the Sea of Galilee. I was riding at the head of the column with Juba who started to look round as if we were lost.

"Is anything wrong?" I asked.

Juba frowned. "I have passed this way before. We should be able to see Mount Hermon from here, yet there is nothing."

"Heat haze?" I suggested.

"Too early in the day. I shall call a brief halt and go forward with a scouting party to investigate. Come if you wish."

We went down towards the Jordan leaving the rest of the Numidians on the high ground behind the lip of the valley out of sight of enemy eyes. A group of just five horsemen was unlikely to cause concern within the rebel ranks, so we did not try to hide ourselves from view. The ground was parched, there had been no rain for weeks and the reason we could not see Mount Hermon soon became apparent. A huge dust cloud created by thousands of marching feet had risen high into the sky obscuring everything behind it. There was no wind to disperse it so we knew the leading contingents of the rebel army would soon be in sight.

About noon we saw the outriders, twenty-two of them, just as we were passing the ruins of an old city on our left. The

Jordan valley is wide and flat here, so they saw us as soon as we saw them, but they made no attempt to chase us away.

"They seem very confident," I said to Juba. "You'd think they would want to find out who we are."

"True," agreed the Numidian, "But we must be cautious, so let us halt now and watch the rebels from here."

"Then we might as well wait out of sight in those ruins yonder. We don't want to encourage them to investigate us."

That turned out to be an inspired suggestion on my part because one of Juba's men found a deep well still full of sweet water within the ruins which, as I later found out, were those of Hazor, a city of the Jewish people which flourished for a while after King Solomon's empire split in two following his death. Consequently, we were able to replenish our water sacks and observe the approach of Judas the Galilean's army in comfort.

During the afternoon we realised that the Galilean had divided his army into two parts either side of the River Jordan. I was sitting with Juba in the shade of a large pillar that had once held up some sort of roof when suddenly, he turned to me and grinned. "Lucius, I think we may have an opportunity. How many men do you suppose are in the rebel army?"

"Difficult to say from here, but I would estimate between seven and eight thousand though we have no idea how many are real soldiers and how many are enthusiastic volunteers who will run at the first sight of blood."

"But how many are on our side of the Jordan?"

"A quarter or less. Most are on the east bank."

"Mmmm," pondered Juba. "What sort of obstacle is the river?"

I was now beginning to understand what the wily Numidian had in mind. "The meltwaters from the winter snow on Mount Hermon have finished, but the river will still be deep enough to slow down a crossing by an army. Cavalry horses should be able to swim it, but the current will still be too fast for all but the strongest swimmers to cross. The rebels will need to build a bridge or use boats."

"Hah!" It sounded more like a jackal's bark than a human laugh. "And there is no bridge between here and the Sea of Galilee. We shall attack early tomorrow morning, just before dawn."

"With what purpose?" I asked.

"To kill as many of those fools as possible and to frighten the faint hearted. Then we'll find out how many real soldiers they have. Most of the others will desert." He spat into the sandy soil. "I shall enjoy this. My men will get here after dark this evening and still have time to rest before the attack. Would you like to use one of our lances Lucius? Your short Roman swords are no use for cavalry fighting."

"No thank you Juba. I would probably be more danger to myself than the enemy, waving one of those long spears around with no skill or training, but I brought a long Galatian broadsword which Eumenes lent me. It's packed alongside my saddle cloth."

"Good, good. Now I shall send a messenger to bring up my men. Let us eat while we wait."

The moon was less than half full but the sky was clear and the stars bright. We could pick our way across the open plain towards the rebel camp without difficulty. The Numidian horses were unshod, so we were able to approach the rebel campfires unheard. Judging the moment to perfection, Juba dug his heels into his horse's flanks and croaked out a guttural sound which must have meant 'charge' in Numidian, for his horsemen surged forward as one and swept me up with them. The rebel sentries, unaware of our presence, must have been asleep. They were awake now, but it was too late; Juba's men were already amongst them using their lances to deadly effect. I drew my Galatian longsword but had no need to use it. By the camp firelight I could see the white clad Numidians at work, pig sticking half asleep, bewildered shapes on the ground with their fearsome weapons. There was no organised resistance yet, just blind panic as terrified men bolted in the direction of the river hoping to find some kind of escape there from these demonic wraiths of the night.

But there were at least two thousand rebels on our side of the Jordan. Juba's force amounted to just three hundred and eighty. After fifteen minutes or so, Juba's men were scattered. Some, including Juba, pursued their victims to the Jordan where the rebels faced the choice of swimming across the river or certain death at lance point, but most of the Numidians remained in the camp indulging their only military weakness; plundering. This should not have mattered too much if all the rebels on the west bank were untrained levies.

Quite suddenly we began to feel pressure coming from the north. The Numidians slung their plunder across their horses' backs and, without orders, turned tail and headed towards the ruins from where we had launched the attack. None spoke Latin, so I shouted orders in Greek and then Aramaic. I was either not understood or ignored, but the result was a waste of breath and only seconds later I too fled as a body of disciplined, armoured infantry broke into the camp, eager to avenge the shambles which had just taken place.

We waited in the ruins for the seventy men who had been cut

off from us when we abandoned the rebel camp, but only thirty-three returned, in small groups having done their duty unlike the rest of us. Fortunately, one of the survivors was Juba.

"I tried to stop the plundering but no-one could understand me," I said.

Exhausted though he was, Juba beamed a smile and patted his saddlebags which responded with a metallic clink. "It would have made no difference. Plundering is in our blood. It is our payment for a great victory."

I was not at all sure that it really was such a great victory, but I let the comment pass unchallenged. "Then what now Juba?"

The wily, old warrior pointed to the east. "The sky is grey. It will soon be dawn. We must be gone by then."

A day and a half later we reached Sepphoris, thirty-eight men fewer than when we set out. Although Antipas had abandoned his new capital and fled to the security of Caesarea Maritima, Eumenes was still there with four hundred of Antipas' Galatian guards. Eumenes was the senior officer present, so Juba and I reported to his office. I let Juba do most of the talking because, as a cohort leader, he was senior to me. We were both exhausted and needed rest, but when our Galatian commander placed two goblets of wine in front of us, Juba made a miraculous recovery. To be fair, his report only embellished the facts a little and Eumenes accepted the Numidians' failure to follow up their victory for the sake of plunder as something to be expected. This would not have been tolerated within the Roman legions.

"It seems to me that we need to buy time," said Eumenes as he began to sum up our position. "Antipas has sent a message to Quirinius in Antioch asking for two legions to be sent to help us."

"Will two be enough?" asked Juba.

"Based on your report the answer is yes, but the legions will not reach us until well into next month, so we must stop Judas the Galilean at Sepphoris otherwise his rebellion could spread to all of southern Galilee and maybe Samaria too. The trouble is we don't have enough men. My Galatians and your century Lucius, add up to four hundred and seventy, and with your Numidians Juba, we have another three hundred and thirty if they can be persuaded to fight as infantry behind city walls."

"They will do as I order," replied Juba menacingly.

"But it may not come to that," added Eumenes. "Your men are much greater value to us as cavalry so, until Sepphoris is almost surrounded, I would prefer them to shadow the rebels, report back on their movements and numbers and make a general nuisance of themselves whenever they can without taking silly risks."

"That is what they do best," acknowledged Juba.

"But what of the citizens of Sepphoris?" I asked. "Can we trust them? During the last rebellion they opened their gates to Judas the Galilean."

"And were punished for it," answered Eumenes darkly. "I have informers amongst them who receive regular payments from me, so if treachery is being planned we shall have advance knowledge of it. If we are obliged to abandon the city, we can reform further south and use harassing tactics to slow the rebels until help arrives. But for now, we shall prepare Sepphoris for a siege. Did you see any evidence of a siege train within the rebel army?"

"No," answered Juba, "But that does not mean there isn't one. The dust cloud limited our view."

"Very well. When your men and horses are rested, start your observation of the enemy. The storerooms here are full, so take what you need but leave us some wine!"

Juba's horsemen proved not only to be superb scouts but also masters of the art of skirmishing which slowed the rebel advance to a crawl. By the time the Galilean's army appeared before the walls of Sepphoris, it was already early June. Eumenes was delighted because a messenger had come from Quirinius telling us that the tenth legion, nicknamed The Larks, would reach Caesarea Maritima by the end of the month. Ideally, we would have preferred The Larks to have marched directly to us but Antipas' message had asked them to go to Caesarea first to protect his precious skin. Even so, that was only a small diversion and we knew they would be with us some time in July.

But on the thirteenth day of July, I received an urgent summons to report to Eumenes' office. Juba was out on patrol, so the meeting involved just the two of us.

"Lucius, I have received reliable information from one of my agents that the Sepphoris city elders have decided to throw open the city gates to Judas the Galilean."

"But why would they want to do that?"

"It's quite simple really. The elders fear him more than they do us. Word has reached them of what Judas did in Dan. That city defied him. After it was captured and plundered, the city elders were marched out to the marketplace and publicly beheaded. That was followed by the massacre of everyone who refused to acknowledge Judas as the Jewish Messiah. Before I advise you of my decision, I would like to know what action you recommend."

"You already mentioned abandoning the city if we could not trust the citizens," I answered, "Well now is the time to do it. We number less than four hundred, but there are more than six thousand rebels out there, some of whom are professional soldiers as Juba found out to his cost. With the citizens against us too we'll be lambs led to the slaughter. Whatever Juba says, his men will add little value in street fighting, but they'll have a huge impact in the open countryside where their cavalry skills can be used to their full potential."

Eumenes nodded. "I share your opinion Lucius, but if we leave Sepphoris, what would you do next?"

"Set up a loose, flexible cordon of your men and mine a couple of miles south of here covering Nazareth. Keep Juba's horsemen in reserve to counter any attempt by the rebels to break through. Meanwhile send an urgent message to the legate of the tenth to get here as soon as he can."

"Thank you, Lucius. Your thoughts match mine absolutely. I feared you might prefer a glorious last stand in true Roman style."

"Not at all Eumenes," I smiled. "I love glory, but I love life more and so do my men."

***

II

The reason my century was the only Roman contingent facing Judas the Galilean was because of trouble in the south. Rebellion had also broken out in Antipas' trans-Jordan territory, Perea, which was opposite Jericho and dangerously close to Jerusalem. While I was heading north with Juba's men to appraise the Galilean's army, the new legate of the Third Gallica, Quintus Metellus Albinus, called his most experienced tribune to a meeting which would determine the Roman response.

Quintus came from a respected family of ancient lineage. The Metelli were originally from plebeian stock, but through business acumen and astute marriages they clawed their way up to the summit of Roman politics a hundred years ago. They managed to survive the civil wars that saw the end of the republic and were still firmly entrenched in the senatorial class in Rome. Quintus was in his mid-thirties, which was young for a legionary commander but he was ambitious, eager to learn, and well aware of his inexperience compared to his ten-seasoned cohort commanders. Above all, the tribune of the fifth cohort, Licinius Piso, was the most respected throughout the legion. He could pose a threat to the authority of the legate, especially as their families were bitter rivals in the Roman senate.

When it was clear that the republic would fall, the Metelli changed sides and supported Octavian, who eventually became our emperor, Augustus Caesar, but the Pisos never really gave up their republican principles. This was why our Piso was passed over for legionary command. Using the political instincts ingrained into him since childhood, Quintus decided he would watch the tribune of his fifth cohort closely and at the same time gain the benefit of his experience.

Piso, whose cohort was based in Bethlehem, six miles from Jerusalem, arrived at the legate's office on the twentieth day of June. "Please sit," said Quintus, who chose to remain standing because he was much shorter than Piso. The tribune sat down on a light, campaign chair and glanced round the legate's office. Busts and statues of some of the distinguished Metelli of old were liberally spread around the room on stands and cloth covered tables reminding anyone who entered that they were in the presence of a man imbued with all the qualities of a great family. Piso was not impressed.

"You will already know," began Quintus, "That rebellion has broken out on two fronts. Messages have been sent to Quirinius, our governor in Antioch, but we have not yet asked for help and will not until we know more. It would be good if we could deal with this on our own."

"Let us hope so," replied Piso.

"Our families are rivals in Rome but that will not affect our relationship here, will it?"

"I will do my duty sir."

"Good, I thought as much. You have been based in the east for many years while I have only been here for a month and a half, so I will need your advice. All Jews look the same to me hidden behind their heavy beards. How can we tell friend from foe?"

"Romans are generally hated here, so it is best to assume

all Jews are enemies unless there is good reason to believe otherwise. The ruling class, which is small in number, can be trusted because they gain from the stability we bring and the taxes they extort for themselves while conveniently blaming us for the poverty most Jews have to endure. Similarly, the merchants and traders gain from our presence but would not dare to thank us openly for it."

"Then how is it that the ruling class has allowed these rebellions to take place?"

"The rebellions are actually against the ruling class rather than us but inevitably we, as the imperial power, get drawn in."

"Then what are the Jewish armies doing?"

"We don't know yet, but we must find out. In the rebellion after Herod's death ten years ago, some of the Jewish regulars joined the rebels."

"But they're only Jews."

"Do not underestimate them sir. When properly armed and trained, the Jews make formidable soldiers."

"What of the Galatians?"

"I fought alongside them in the last rebellion. They are excellent soldiers too."

"But they're just mercenaries and I hear they are refusing to fight."

"That's because Archelaus has not paid them for more than a year! I doubt Roman soldiers would put up with that, and to say the Galatians refuse to fight is not strictly true. They refuse to leave the citadel in Jerusalem, but they will fight if attacked."

Although he had asked for advice, Quintus was becoming irritated by his tribune continually correcting him, so he decided to assert his authority. "Well, I have already determined our course of action. We shall concentrate all our cohorts at

Jerusalem which should prevent rebellion spreading to the capital. We'll bring in the auxiliaries too, except for a few cavalry squadrons which will cross the Jordan to find out how large the rebel army actually is. Then, depending on that information, we shall either attack or wait for reinforcements from Quirinius."

Piso knew full well that he had annoyed his commander, but whilst that did not worry him at all, he tried to be more conciliatory for the sake of ensuring the correct campaign decisions were made.

"I applaud your decision to send forward scouts sir. Our best scouts, the Numidians, were sent north before you arrived when reports started coming in from Antipas about trouble being fomented by Judas the Galilean, but in their absence, I recommend you use a squadron of Friedrich von Vechten's Germans who are also experienced scouts."

"Your recommendation is accepted," replied a slightly mollified Quintus.

"Concentrating the legion at Jerusalem also makes good sense but I do have a view about waiting here until the scouts report back."

The legate frowned, "Well, go on then."

"Sir, waiting would be the right thing to do if we were opposed to a regular army like the Parthians for instance, but we are not. Rebellions have a habit of feeding on success, real or perceived. The longer no action is taken by us or the Galatians to quell the revolt, the more successful it will seem to the Jews. This will swell the numbers joining the rebels; their army could easily double in size within a month. The quality will not be up to much, but the temptation facing the officers in the regular Jewish armies of Judea and Galilee to join the rebellion may become irresistible to many of them as the prospects of success improve."

"Then what do you suggest Tribune?" asked Quintus laying great emphasis on the word *you*.

"Leave a cohort in Jerusalem and march the rest of the legion and auxiliaries to the Jordan without delay. It will be an aggressive move that will disconcert the faint hearted amongst the rebels as the prospect of real fighting confronts them. We can be at the Jordan in two days which means we'll get von Vechten's report earlier and, if you deem conditions are suitable, we can attack immediately."

"Thank you, Tribune. I shall consider what you have said. You may return to your men now. Dismissed."

When Piso stood up to leave, he realised he was almost a head taller than Quintus. The two men's eyes met; there was no love lost there.

The legate followed Piso's advice to the letter. After he had calmed down and thought rationally about it, he realised that a quick victory without the help of the Governor of Syria would enhance his reputation considerably. If the enemy forces were too large to attack, he could always retreat or, perhaps, fight a holding action on the west bank of the Jordan, but he would certainly have to do something about Piso. The 'wonderful' tribune of the fifth cohort had been unable to mask the contempt he felt for his commander. Such disrespect could spread.

During the last week of June the Third Gallica marched out of Jerusalem. Two days later the legion made contact with von Vechten's Germans between Jericho and the Jordan. Von Vechten reported to Quintus that the rebels numbered around eight and a half thousand but, worryingly, a quarter of them were Jewish regulars who had deserted Archelaus. They were still a day's march east of the Jordan so if the Romans were to cross now, they would be unopposed. Our men numbered four thousand legionaries plus the two auxiliary cohorts of Germans and Syrian mounted archers, making a total of almost five thousand. Quintus was unnerved by the size of the rebel army, particularly the number of regulars, but he could not show weakness by summoning a war council, so he called Piso to his tent.

"Von Vechten says the rebels number over nine thousand, possibly ten thousand, at least a third of whom are regulars. What is your advice?"

Quintus did not know that von Vechten and Piso were friends and had already spoken, so the legate's exaggeration of the rebel strength did not fool his tribune. "Where is the German now sir?"

"I sent him back to the Jordan in case we decide to cross."

"That was a good move sir. We should ford the river as soon as possible and engage the enemy before their numbers increase further."

"And fight with a river at our back! That is against all military practice. What if we have to retreat?"

"At this time of year the river is not an obstacle this far south because it's so shallow, but if we give the rebels time to reach it, an opposed crossing will be costly."

"We could wait on the west bank and let the Jews try an opposed crossing instead."

"As I said before sir, their numbers grow by the day. They could divide their army in two and use one half to oppose us at the Jordan while the other half crosses further downstream.

Then they would cut off our road back to Jerusalem and take us in the rear. We must cross the river immediately!"

Piso could see the fear and indecision in his commander's face, so he appealed to his vanity. "If you go forward now and attack, you will forever gain the respect of your men whatever happens, but if you hesitate..." He did not need to say more.

"Very well Tribune, I shall give the order that you desire."
"And that you too desire sir, I am sure. I will prepare my men."

The rebels were slow to move, so it was two days later when the armies confronted each other three miles east of the River Jordan. The land here was a flat, featureless semi-desert which had seen no rain since winter and even then not much. The stream beds were dry and the only source of water came from wells. No army could survive here long in such conditions; a battle would have to be fought soon or not at all.

The Jewish army had grown in the four days since von Vechten had counted them and, ironically, was close to the exaggerated estimate Quintus had given Piso at their meeting. But they were weak in the cavalry arm which left us with a distinct advantage. Quintus arranged our army in the standard formation of infantry in the centre with cavalry on both wings. Our line was extended and thin, overlapping the Jews on both sides. Alexander, the rebel leader and false messiah, had arranged his army in a densely packed formation which to the eye of an untrained observer, would easily break through the Roman lines, but we had never forgotten the painful lesson Hannibal inflicted upon us at Cannae, three hundred years ago. If the Jews attacked, we knew our line would bend but not break then, just as Hannibal did to us at Cannae, our cavalry would sweep in from both flanks, compress the enemy, and the slaughter would begin.

But then, to everyone's surprise, the Jews sent forward an embassy under a flag of truce and waited four hundred paces in front of our third cohort whose tribune, Aulus Scapula, went out to meet them. Conveniently, our legate had stationed himself and his staff just behind the third cohort, so he was able to summon quickly all his other tribunes to hear for themselves Aulus' report.

"In order to save unnecessary bloodshed, the rebels are proposing to settle matters with a trial of champions, a single combat," said the grey-haired, battle-scarred veteran of fourteen campaigns.

Quintus, invigorated by the sight of his legion in battle formation, now had one of those sudden changes of mood that are often seen in inexperienced officers. The cautious commander of two days ago was eager to attack. "I take it gentlemen, that you agree we should refuse this offer?"

"Not necessarily sir." It was that irritating Piso again who responded. "We have nothing to lose by this but a lot to gain."

"Which is?" replied Quintus with an air of lofty boredom.

"If our champion loses, it will anger our men and they will fight even better to avenge him, but if the rebel champion loses, the Jews will become disheartened for they will believe their god has turned his back on them. They only have one god whereas we have many, so if one of our gods lets us down we can always call upon the help of others."

"But if our champion loses, we lose the campaign. That is the whole point of a trial of champions," objected Quintus.

There were a few, barely suppressed smirks from the seasoned cohort tribunes as Piso answered, "No-one in this tent ever heard of a trial of champions ever deciding anything except in fairy stories. As soon as the trial is over, whatever the result, battle will commence; you can be assured of that."

Quintus nervously looked to the other tribunes for support but, finding none, sighed, "And who will be our champion?"

Piso replied, "Tell the Jews we accept their challenge and that we require one hour to select and prepare our champion. I am sure we'll have no difficulty finding one."

The clamour of those wanting to volunteer to be the Roman champion suddenly went silent when the Jewish champion strode forward to join his embassy between the two armies; it was the rebel leader, Alexander himself. He was a giant of a man standing seven feet tall and dressed in the best Greek style armour which reflected the sun in burnished bronze. The greaves protecting his shins were longer than an average man's arm, he carried a huge battle axe as if it were a dried-out twig and most imposing of all, his crested helmet with its black, horsehair plume added yet another foot to his immense height.

The enthusiasm in Piso's cohort to challenge the Jew disappeared as in all the other cohorts but for one man; Caius Pantera centurion of the fifth century. Caius was a big man too, well over six feet tall, but compared to Alexander he seemed puny.

"Caius, you don't need to do this," whispered Piso as the centurion stood his ground while all the other volunteers hurried back to the anonymity of the ranks.

"Someone must fight him, or we'll be shamed."

"But why you?" said Piso, who did not want to lose a first-class centurion. "Let one of the other cohorts find someone."

"Very well sir, I will stand down as you wish but only if another volunteer comes forward."

After ten minutes no-one else had volunteered so Caius was selected as the only choice. Gnaeus Servilius, centurion of the second century in Piso's cohort and a friend of Caius' joined his tribune who was helping Caius to prepare. "Sir, I remember a man of similar proportions to this Jew who lived in the same village as me back in Sicily. He was immensely strong, but his size was born out of some illness he contracted in his mother's womb. Although formidable in appearance, he was slow and cumbersome. I have been watching the Jew and he moves in the same slow, plodding manner. The Sicilian had weak joints, especially the knees and ankles, and when we were working in the fields as youngsters together, he tired quickly; no stamina."

"What happened to him?" asked Caius.

"He died before he was thirty. He fell and broke his ankle, complications set in and his blood became poisoned. If your opponent has the same illness, which I believe he has, you may win by tiring him out then attacking his legs."

"Thank you Gnaeus, I shall bear that in mind."

"What weapons will you use?"

"A standard legionary shield but I'll abandon the gladius and use a longsword if I can find one."

"Use my spatha," said Piso. "It's a well-balanced cavalry longsword which I used at the Battle of Mukhmas."

"Thank you, sir. I'll make sure I wipe the blood from it before I return it to you."

As they watched Caius march out to meet Alexander, Gnaeus said, "Well at least he's confident."

"Indeed," agreed Piso, "and he's fit and very brave too."

It was a little past noon when single combat commenced. There would be no quarter given, for this was to be a fight to the death. Slowly, the two champions, who were both right handers, began circling to their right, each looking for an opening to strike. Both armies looked on nervously, willing their man a quick victory, and it was not long before Alexander decided to force the issue. Suddenly he lunged at Caius swinging his huge axe in a vertical stroke designed to split his opponent in two from head to groin, but the alert Caius saw it coming in good time and neatly side stepped to his right, allowing the axe head to plunge into the sandy earth to roars of approbation from the Romans and groans of disappointment from the Jews.

But Alexander quickly recovered and swung at Caius again, this time with a horizontal stroke which was more difficult to avoid. The Roman tried to step inside the arc of the axe head but was not fast enough. Fortunately, he just had time to adjust his shield so the axe struck at an angle rather than full on, turning it into a glancing blow, but the power in the strike was still huge and sent Caius staggering to his right almost toppling him over. Now it was the turn of the Romans to groan as their champion seemed badly shaken and hopelessly outmatched.

Piso turned to Gnaeus who was still standing beside him. "There seems nothing wrong with the Jew's joints to me. Maybe he's not got the condition your Sicilian had."

"But he moves ponderously. If only Caius can avoid another hit like that for a few more minutes, his chances will greatly improve."

Worryingly, after five more minutes, Alexander seemed to have no discernible problem with his stamina and Caius had taken two more glancing blows without making a single attacking move himself. The men in Piso's cohort began to fidget nervously and started to shout yells of encouragement which sounded hollow against the silence of the rest of the Roman army.

The other cohorts began to despair because the shame of their champion being killed without delivering a single aggressive stroke would reflect on all of them.

An angry Quintus strode across to Piso. "This is humiliating! I should never have listened to your advice!"

"It's not over yet sir," replied Piso calmly. "Caius is both brave and resourceful; do not give up on him so soon."

The one-sided contest continued for nearly ten more minutes with Alexander swinging and missing most of the time but scoring two more ferocious glancing strikes which must have numbed Caius' left arm from wrist to shoulder. At last, the Jewish champion began to slow down. Swinging a heavy axe and missing puts a massive strain on the sinews no matter how strong you are, but just as the Romans began to sense their champion might have a chance after all, Alexander landed a direct hit which tore Caius' shield from his arm and left him prostrate on the sandy soil at the feet of his opponent. The Jewish champion bellowed a victory roar, which was answered in kind by the rebel army, as he dropped his own shield so that he could deliver the death blow two handed. He stepped forward and stood over Caius who sat up seemingly stunned and bewildered, but as he raised his mighty axe, Caius grabbed a handful of sand and threw it in his face, momentarily blinding him. The Roman still had the spatha in his right hand and in the three seconds his unexpected move had given him, he scrambled forward on his knees and delivered a ferocious slash which cut the ligaments behind Alexander's left knee. The giant howled in pain and fell backwards, dropping his huge axe so he could use his hands to break his fall. It was a fatal mistake. Caius sprang to his feet and followed up his advantage over the half blinded, unarmed Jewish champion with a powerful thrust of his longsword into his throat. A mighty cheer erupted from the men of the Third Gallica, who had been expecting imminent defeat as the huge body writhed and twitched before finally lying still.

It took Caius three mighty hacks to sever the head from the body but at last, battered but victorious, he removed the helmet and raised the head in triumph for his comrades to see. The noise became almost deafening as the legionaries began to beat their shields in unison with the pommels of their swords.

"Order the advance!" shouted Piso to his legate. "The men are desperate to charge and the Jews won't stand now!"

"But shouldn't we—"

"No buts! Just do it!"

Quintus gave the signal and the trumpeters sounded three long blasts on their war horns. The men cheered even louder and the whole legion surged forward marching in time to the rhythmic beat of sword pommels on shields. It must have been terrifying for the Jewish levies who ran well before contact was made. The regulars gave a good account of themselves and took heavy losses but, outnumbered and disheartened, they finally broke before following the levies in flight. The pursuit was left to the German and Syrian cavalry while the legionaries fell to plundering the Jewish camp. The battle was over.

It was a complete victory. Roman losses numbered around forty, but more than three hundred and fifty Jewish corpses littered the battle ground when the fighting ended. We never found out what their true losses were, though the cavalry pursuit probably accounted for another three hundred. But in any event, the battle ended the rebellion in the south.

In the evening Quintus, flushed with his first victory as a legate, called Caius to his tent along with some of the officers who had distinguished themselves in the fighting. Piso was not invited. Caius, who was a modest man, found the fulsome praise he faced embarrassing, and when some of the officers began insulting the severed, bloody head of Alexander which had been skewered on a spear outside the legate's tent, he requested permission to leave citing a severe head pain caused by his dual with the giant. Quintus, partly inebriated, put his arm round Caius' large shoulder and insisted he should accept fifty silver denarii from his personal purse as a reward for his achievement. This eased the pain a little, because the legate had put his arm round the shoulder injured by Alexander's last blow, the one that tore the shield from Caius' arm and sent him sprawling across the ground. Fifty denarii was a large sum of money so Caius willingly accepted, gave his thanks and retired to his tent to nurse his bruises and enjoy a well-earned sleep after his successful and profitable day.

There was no time to rest because the rebellion of Judas the Galilean was still in full flow in the north. Secure, after his victory Quintus could afford to be generous so he sent four cohorts, including Piso's, to assist Antipas in Galilee. Although Piso was his most experienced tribune, Quintus, who decided to remain in Jerusalem, put Aulus Scapula in command. The insult was obvious, as it was intended to be, but Piso was too professional to be offended by such a smallminded act. Scapula, who was a solid, level-headed commander, was only too pleased to have Piso alongside him; there was no rivalry between the two.

Latest reports said the rebels were only a day's march from Antipas' new capital, Sepphoris, but Scapula's cohorts were three days away so there was no time to lose if the city was to be saved. They did not know we had already abandoned Sepphoris.

***

III

Judas was almost in sight of Sepphoris when he stumbled into a Galatian patrol. The Galatians were unconcerned about the stoning of an obscure Jewish woman in Nazareth, so Judas asked for directions to the camp of the Roman commander. As luck would have it, my century was stationed on top of a small knoll only half a mile away where I was with my senior file leader the toothless veteran Galerius. We were observing the movements of some rebels just outside the city and wondering why they were making no attempt yet to break through our thinly stretched out cordon.

The Galatians approached me accompanied by a dishevelled looking Jew. The officer addressed me. "Centurion, this Jew has come to ask us to stop an execution about to take place in Nazareth. I've told him we have more important things to do than interfere in local domestic matters, but he would not be put off and asked to see the Roman commander. As you were nearby, I thought it could do no harm to bring him to you."

"You did the right thing Agoras," I replied. "Return to your post and I will deal with this."

Agoras saluted and departed with his men. Then I turned to the Jew who seemed to be staring rather than looking at me. "Well, what's this all about?" I asked in Aramaic.

"An execution by stoning will take place in Nazareth at noon, but it has not been authorised by the Roman authority. As I am sure you already know, we Jews may practice our laws freely and without interference from you with the exception of capital crimes which must be reviewed and approved by the Roman commander of the occupying forces before the death penalty can be carried out."

"But that's our legate and he's a hundred miles away!"

"Then it must be you in his stead."

"But I know nothing of your law. Just get on with what you must do."

"But the victim is Ruth. You already know her Lucius Veranius, even if you don't remember me."

I was dumbstruck. How could this man know who I was? Then slowly my memory began to create pictures in my mind. I recalled the silent, sinister, dark eyed Jew who accompanied Joseph and his family on that terrible night ten years ago when Caius and I reached Bethlehem just before the arrival of the Galatians who had orders to kill all the male babies in the city in the hope of keeping Herod safe from the Jewish Messiah.

The Jew smiled, "Speak to me in Greek or Latin if you prefer. Yes Lucius, I am Judas, the one in Joseph's party who you never really knew."

"You are a Zealot!"

"Yes, but much has happened since then. The Zealots are not part of this rebellion, we are at peace with you, but we have no time to stand here talking. If you want to save Ruth come with me now or we'll be too late! I'll explain everything as we go."

I had no choice. I left Galerius, who was much too old to hurry, in charge of the century and took Rufio and his file of eight with me. We left immediately but by the time we reached Nazareth it was already noon. Judas had told me the details of the injustice about to take place but if the execution had started on time, we were probably already too late. He guided us to the quarry outside the town where we beheld a young woman strapped to a wooden stake being battered by a crowd of people hurling stones at her. For a terrible moment I thought she was already dead but then I saw her move as a large rock glanced off the side of her face.

"Rufio! To me!" I shouted, then quietly to Judas, "Stand back and do not let yourself be seen. I will do the rest."

Then facing the crowd, I bellowed in Aramaic, "Halt! Stop this at once or you will pay with your lives!" Rufio, bless him, drew himself up to his full height, which was considerable, and flashed his sword. The stoning stopped immediately. A grey-haired man, one of the elders, tried to stand in our way but I pushed him to one side and we placed ourselves between Ruth and the crowd, daring them to hurl a stone at two Roman officers. Yet even with the impressive Rufio standing beside me, one fool chanced his arm and threw a rock at us which bounced harmlessly off Rufio's shield, but when my file leader started to walk towards him, the stone thrower's courage failed and he ran off into the crowd.

Satisfied that the stoning had ended, I sheathed my sword, dropped my shield and turned to Ruth, who was still breathing but unconscious, and cut her free from the stake with my dagger. Blood streamed from cuts to her forehead and neck. Her long, black hair was sticky with matted blood but, as far as I could judge, she would recover. "Rufio, call your file here. We must get this woman's injuries treated."

As Rufio left to fetch his men Judas, who had ignored my request to stay out of sight, appeared behind me. "Bring her to my house; it's not far away. Then I'll fetch Deborah from Joseph's house; she'll know what to do."

"Is that the same Deborah who was with us when we fled from Bethlehem all those years ago?"

"Yes."

I remembered a stout, strong willed matriarch who organised all the necessaries for Jesus' birth in adverse conditions with the skill of a veteran nurse. "She'll be ideal," I replied, "But we'd better leave here quickly; there are only ten of us and the crowd's mood may change."

Judas' house had a fine garden which easily accommodated Rufio and his men. I followed Judas up the stairs to the sleeping area where I gently placed Ruth on a bed. Judas brought fresh water and some linen for bandages, then departed for Joseph's household where Deborah lived. I glanced round the bedroom. There was no evidence of a woman's touch, no perfume or ointments to adorn the face, no flowers and, above all, no mirror.

"Lucius!"

I looked down at the bed where two beautiful brown eyes and a warm but bruised mouth smiled at me. "Lucius, you came for me!"

I stroked her face and wiped some of the blood from her forehead. "Yes, I came for you but had it not been for Judas I would never have known about your misfortune. He is your real saviour."

"But it was you who saved me."

"Plus, Rufio and eight tough Roman soldiers. Judas told me what happened to you, but you are safe now, I promise."

She squeezed my hand. "I always hoped you would come for me one day, but I never believed it would really happen."

"Left it a bit late didn't I!"

"God has smiled upon me at last."

"From what Judas told me, you have more than earned your reward for years of pain and misery."

Ruth suddenly seemed to gather her wits and whispered, "Judas does not know the truth. He believes Jesus is the Messiah descended from the line of David, not a Roman soldier."

"Caius is a centurion now and a fine one too," I said, "But the secret is safe with him and me. No-one else knows except you, Mary and Joseph."

Memories came flooding back again; how Caius, Rufio and I had faced certain death as hostages of the Zealots after the Battle of Mount Carmel, how we were liberated by Mary and Ruth thanks to Caius' passionate affair with Mary which was to result in Jesus. Ruth was punished by Joseph for her part in facilitating Mary's love for Caius, but he was basically a kind man and could never have anticipated how badly she would be treated by Ehud, the man he decided she would marry or be thrown out onto the streets.

"What is it, Lucius? You have fallen silent. Is something wrong?"

"Nothing is wrong Ruth," I answered. "I was just recalling some of the events we went through together and how you helped to save my life and my two comrades from the vengeance of the Zealots and also how sad I was when the time came for us to part."

"Well, you managed to hide your feelings well enough. I thought you did not care."

"Of course I did, but I did not get the chance to show it. We were never alone together."

With some effort and help from me, she sat up on the bed and held out her arms. "I know I don't look my best at this moment, but you may show it now if you wish."

I did not hesitate though I should have for Zenub's sake, but as I looked at that wounded but still beautiful woman I could not resist. Nor could I kiss her because of her cut and bruised lips, so we just held each other in a tight embrace, hoping the moment would never end.

Eventually, a noise downstairs ended our moment, but not before Ruth whispered in my ear, "Never leave me."

"I am a soldier and must obey orders, but my term of duty does not have long to go. I shall make sure you're safe until then." That seemed to satisfy her but I knew what I was saying would mean a terrible choice and that there would be a day of reckoning to come. But just then, Zenub seemed a long way away and Ruth was in desperate need of comfort and security.

She smiled again, "You have learned Aramaic since we last met. How did that happen?"

"Soldiers without a war to fight become bored. Learning your language helped to pass the time."

Before she could enquire further, Deborah bustled in. "My poor child, what have they done to you!"

"The execution was interrupted, and I was saved by Lucius."

"And Judas," I added.

Deborah glared at me. "Men! Arrogant, useless creatures who make laws for others they do not themselves obey! Still, there are some exceptions I suppose. Lucius, you've put on weight since I last saw you."

"Thank you, Deborah, it's good to see you've lost none of your fire."

"I'll have to remove some of Ruth's clothing to treat her wounds so make yourself scarce and wait in the garden with your men."

I found Rufio and Judas engaged in animated chatter at the foot of the stairs. Rufio beamed, "Lucius, a messenger has just passed through Nazareth from Jerusalem. We've won in the south. Complete victory! Four cohorts are on their way to help us. They should be here in two days' time."

"Then we must get back to Eumenes at once in case Judas the Galilean decides to attack us before help arrives. Prepare your men to leave."

"What about Ruth?" asked Judas.

"I'll find out what she wants to do," I answered as I began climbing the stairs again, momentarily forgetting why I had been sent away. I walked into the upstairs room where Deborah had already begun cleaning Ruth's wounds. Ruth was naked to the waist. Deborah turned on me furiously. "Get out of here at once!"

"I'm sorry," I said turning my back on them both, but not before noticing Ruth smile. "We must leave at once. News has just come in from the south making our return to the army urgent."

A few seconds passed, then a mollified Deborah said, "Very well, you may turn round now."

"Are you feeling a bit better?" I asked.

Ruth nodded. "Yes, thank you, but must you really leave so soon?"

"I'm afraid so. We may be attacked in the next few hours so I must return to be with my men, but help is on its way so the rebellion will end soon. I'll come back as soon as I can. Do you have anywhere you can stay in the meantime?"

Ruth shook her head but Deborah intervened. "Of course, she has. Ruth will come back to Joseph's house with me until she is fully recovered."

"And after that?" I asked.

"She has been mistreated and abandoned by her husband, but there is still the marital home."

"I thought Jewish women could not own property."

"It is unusual but possible under certain circumstances. I am sure Joseph will see to it."

"Then I can leave knowing all will be well until my return."

"Yes, and make sure you do."

"I will."

"And soon," added Ruth.

"I will, though I don't expect to be away long."

I could not have been more wrong.

When we reached the Galatian camp I was greeted by Eumenes with more good news. "Lucius, the legate of the Tenth Fretensis, Antonius Primus, has changed course and instead of marching on Caesarea, he is coming direct to Sepphoris. He should get here on the same day as the Third Gallica."

"Hurrah for Antonius Primus and the Larks! Now the rebels will be squeezed from the north and south."

"Indeed," agreed Eumenes, "And this time we'll make sure there is no escape for Judas the Galilean."

But the Galilean's scouts kept him well informed and the following night he abandoned his army. With just a few close companions, he left Sepphoris and headed north for the safety of his sanctuary within the folds of Mount Hermon, but unfortunately for him he ran straight into one of Juba's night patrols which brought him back to our camp to await his fate. Next day word reached the city of what he had done and his supporters melted away leaving the unfortunate citizens to face the wrath of Rome which knew no mercy for rebellion.

In the end Judas the Galilean did not need to fear our retribution because the Shadows got to him first while he was still in our camp under Galatian custody. Early in the morning when the Third Gallica was due to arrive, four shame faced Galatians, who had fallen asleep when they were supposed to be guarding the Galilean, reported sheepishly that he was still in custody but his head was missing. Eumenes was angry, but not overly so, and the guards were fined a week's pay for dereliction of duty. They never realised how lucky they were. Had they been awake the Shadows would have slit their throats.

The citizens of Sepphoris were not so fortunate. For the second time in ten years their city was sacked by Roman soldiers and many of them died in the frenzy of looting that took place. As for me, my hopes of a quick return to Ruth were dashed when our legate decided to rid himself of Piso's annoying presence by sending him and his cohort north to pacify the region around Mount Hermon and Dan.

But the most tangible result of the rebellion was the removal of Archelaus. The embassy to Augustus Caesar had left Jerusalem before the rebellion broke out, but the purpose of the visit of the deputation of worthy Pharisees, Sadducees and Zealots was made easier when news of the rebellion reached Rome. The emperor accepted that Archelaus had failed in his duty and agreed to send a prefect to govern Judea, Idumea and Samaria.

The prefect, a magistrate of middle rank in Rome called Coponius, arrived later in the year and in deference to the sensitivities of the Jews, set up his office in the non-Jewish city of Caesarea Maritima which was near enough to Jerusalem if trouble broke out but far enough away to please the Judean establishment. Coponius and his early successors served terms of three years each. Naturally they lined their pockets but the extravagance of Archelaus was ended and the hard-pressed people of Judea entered into a period of increasing prosperity which lasted a generation.

CHAPTER FIVE

Only two days after I left Nazareth with Rufio's file, Judas received an unexpected visit. Deborah had already moved Ruth to Joseph's house so he was alone. The sun had just set, the sky was a rich crimson colour, and the bustle in the town had subsided as the townsfolk sat down for their evening meal. Judas was placing some silver denarii brought by a fund raiser into the Zealot treasury hidden beneath the floor of his house, when he was startled by a sharp rap at his door.

"Wait a moment!" He shouted, as he hurriedly put back the wooden boards that hid years of accumulated Zealot wealth and covered them with mats. Who on earth can that be at this time of day, he wondered as he unlocked and opened the door. He was confronted by four black cloaked figures which were hooded and masked so that only their eyes were visible. To the average Nazarene they would have looked like spectres from Hell, but Judas knew exactly who they were.

"Come in," he said warmly. "Have you travelled far?"

"Only from Sepphoris," answered Isaac, the leader of the Shadows, as he threw back his hood and entered. "We completed our mission last night, laid low for most of today and left the city two hours ago."

"Did you have trouble with Roman patrols?"

"Not Roman ones; you could hear them coming from a mile away."

"Though we almost bumped into one of their auxiliary

units," added Reuben, "Black skinned men dressed in white robes and riding ponies that seemed to glide just above the ground."

"The Numidians," acknowledged Judas. "I have heard they are excellent scouts."

"Well, they certainly look formidable," agreed Isaac, "And we wouldn't have wanted to meet them with the trophy Reuben has in his bag."

"Which is?" asked Judas.

Reuben opened the leather bag slung over his shoulder and pulled out the head of Judas the Galilean. "Ten years ago, when I heard of Daniel's murder by this man, I vowed I would avenge him. We grew up together in the same village and were more like brothers than friends. I made sure the Galilean remembered him before I slit his throat. He squealed like a stuck pig. By God! That revenge was sweet."

Judas, who had witnessed Daniel's murder, sighed, "At last the monster has paid for his crimes. I only wish that it was I that carried out the execution."

Reuben returned the head to its bag. "If it is any consolation Judas, I told the Galilean I was going to kill him for you too."

"It is. What will the Shadows do now?"

Isaac answered, "We will leave Nazareth before dawn tomorrow and go to Jerusalem where bar Abbas shall see the Galilean's head for himself before we burn it. The rebellion has collapsed, so it is now safe for Joseph and his family to return to Nazareth. Then you may resume tutoring the true Messiah and prepare him for his mission."

"I hope we are more successful than Judas the Galilean."

"We will be," replied Isaac. "We are gaining support day by

day amongst the ordinary Jewish people, not the bloated sycophants of the Romans who call themselves our leaders, and I know bar Abbas hopes to persuade the Essenes to join us despite their aversion to bloodshed and violence."

"That would be a major step forward," agreed Judas, "But getting the Essenes to abandon their oath against violence is ambitious. But if we could find a way to harness their single-minded dedication to our cause in some other form, our power would be considerably enhanced."

"You may well find yourself part of that process, my friend," said Isaac, "But now we Shadows will sleep for we must leave early tomorrow."

When the Shadows reached Jerusalem with their news, Mary, against medical advice, insisted on returning home for the birth of her fifth child even though she was almost at the end of her term. Reuben accompanied her, Joseph, Jesus and the rest of the family on the return journey, for bar Abbas had ordained that the young Messiah should always be under the protection of the Shadows. They reached Nazareth four days later with Mary still well and in good heart, but her spirits lifted even more when she saw Ruth had returned. Joseph immediately accepted Ruth back into the household when he heard the truth about Ehud and told her she could stay as long as she liked, so when Mary finally went into labour she was attended by Deborah and Ruth, just as she had been when her first child was born in Ezra's outhouse near Bethlehem ten years before. The child, a girl, was named Mary after her beautiful mother.

At the beginning of the first week of Elul (August), Judas was called to Joseph's office after his morning tuition with Jesus. Joseph greeted him warmly and pointed to the chair opposite his desk that had once been Judas' before Ehud displaced him. "Please sit Judas."

Judas did as he was bid and asked after Mary and the new baby.

"Both are well," beamed Joseph proudly. "Young Mary has powerful lungs too and wakens the entire household when she wants milk."

"I am happy for you."

"Thank you, Judas, and your happiness is my concern too. That is why I have called you here today. It's many years since you sat in that very chair to begin your mission to tutor Jesus. Soon, you also became an important asset to my business but never had the chance to prove yourself because of Ehud's criminal disloyalty. I deeply regret my bad judgement when I promoted Ehud above you, yet you still remained loyal to me. I cannot thank you enough for that."

"Joseph, he deceived us all. You should not blame yourself."

"Well, now you shall have the chance to re-establish yourself in my business. Even as we speak, Sepphoris is being sacked for opening its gates to Judas the Galilean. It is tragic that the citizens should suffer for the bad judgement of their elders, but it will mean great opportunities for all construction businesses in the area in the coming years. So, as of today, you are re-instated as my business manager and we shall work together to make the business a success."

"This time we will flourish, I'm sure of it, but what of the bar Micah brothers?"

Joseph frowned. "Our elders also failed us while I was away. There will have to be an inquiry into the whole sordid affair, which will include Ehud's part in the corruption."

"And his attempt to have Ruth stoned to death for something she did not do?"

"Certainly. That was a case of false witness and attempted murder if ever there was one, but Ehud has fled his retribution so the inquiry will proceed in his absence. The behaviour of Jonah bar Joash will also be examined, so the chairman of the inquiry must be carefully selected."

"Surely that will be you, Joseph. You are the chairman of the Council of Elders."

"No, I must stand down for this because, as one of the victims of Ehud's treachery, I am an interested party."

"But you still have influence."

"That is true, and I shall use it to ensure a steady, honest chairman is selected who is beyond reproach. You can count on that!"

The inquiry took two full days. It would have been longer but the chairman was Joachim the Zealot, Mary's father. The old warrior made sure that the witnesses stuck to the facts; flights of fancy and personal opinions were not permitted. Consequently, on the morning of the third day he was able to announce his findings to a packed audience. No-one could remember the synagogue being so full in living memory. Joachim, who was in his sixty-third year and seemed to be carved out of gnarled, old wood spoke calmly and without emotion.

"I shall start at the top, that is the Council of Elders, which cravenly allowed itself to be browbeaten by its self-appointed, substitute chairman Jonah bar Joash. He was on a mission to satisfy his own self-importance. The evidence against Ruth, the woman accused of adultery, was unsupported by anyone outside the husband and the so-called adulterer, Jonathan bar Micah who has since withdrawn his evidence. Consequently, the sentence of death by stoning according to the laws of Moses was wrong. Therefore, the Council of Elders is hereby dissolved and new elections will take place as soon as possible, but Jonah bar Joash is permanently excluded from standing for election."

This was greeted by a murmur of assent within the synagogue; many were delighted to witness proud Jonah's downfall. "Now, I come to the complicity of the bar Micah brothers," continued Joachim, "The younger of whom, Jonathan, has shown remorse by withdrawing the evidence which was a powerful factor in Ruth's conviction for adultery. Compensation will be agreed by a special committee for a sum of money to be paid by the bar Micah brothers to Joseph bar Jacob for years of cheating when bidding for contracts, which is in breach of the Seventh Commandment. The compensation sum will no doubt be considerable. In addition, the bar Micah brothers will not be permitted to trade in construction and related businesses for two years. Now we come to even more serious crimes. Jonathan bar Micah has already admitted to bearing false witness, which breaches the Eighth Commandment, but this almost led to a breach of the Fifth Commandment, thou shall not kill. Murder was only prevented by the quick action of Judas bar Menahem, who is congratulated by this inquiry. Jonathan's punishment is mitigated a little by his open acknowledgement of his sin, but nonetheless he has a debt to pay. He will be banished from Nazareth for two years and may not return before then on pain of death."

Jonathan, who was present, stood up and walked slowly out of the synagogue. His tears flowed freely. He made a pathetic sight for his only real flaw was weakness because he was too easily influenced by others.

Joachim's voice hardened as Jonathan left. "Finally, we come to Ehud bar Aaron, the root cause of this sorry series of events who has sought refuge in flight. He has been found guilty in his absence of crimes against the Fifth, Seventh and Eighth Commandments which demand the ultimate penalty. We shall do our utmost to track him down and bring him to justice but in the meantime Ruth, his wife, is entitled to satisfaction for the ordeal she has suffered. This inquiry has not investigated the relationship between Ruth and her husband. The dealings between a man and his wife are private matters, but it is clear cruelty and vindictiveness played a large part, and the crime of attempted murder is certainly within our scrutiny. This poor woman had to endure the terror of execution by stoning. She really believed she was going to die, and indeed she received injuries before she was rescued thanks to Judas bar Menahem. Her husband has abandoned her through fear and shame so she has no means of support. Consequently, this inquiry has determined that the ownership of the marital home together with all its contents, including Hiram the slave, should be transferred to her to use as she sees fit."

This brought spontaneous applause from the women's side of the synagogue and also from some of the men too. Mary stood up and clapped while her husband smiled with satisfaction at the balanced judgement Joachim gave that day.

But if those present thought they had heard the last of Ehud bar Aaron, they were mistaken.

***

II

A month passed. Sepphoris was in ruins. Herod Antipas returned to view the remains of his future capital and gave orders for reconstruction to commence at once. Jesus, now approaching his eleventh birthday, had just finished his morning tutorial on the Greek language and was enjoying the garden while Judas prepared some bread and cheese for their noon meal before he returned to his father's house. Although autumn had come early, it was still warm enough to eat outside, but today was unusual because of the silence. Judas would normally expect to hear his garrulous charge chatting to the birds or singing one of the many folk songs he had learned from his mother; but not today. He did not give it too much thought and finished the preparation of lemon juice diluted with water which would accompany their meal, but when he walked into the garden he almost dropped the tray he was carrying with the food and drink on it.

Jesus was sitting cross-legged on the ground. His eyes, wide open and unblinking, were staring at something in the sky behind Judas' shoulder. Judas turned round and looked, but he could see nothing except blue sky and a few white fine weather clouds. He placed the tray on one of the garden tables and started to walk towards Jesus fearing he was having some kind of fit or seizure, but before he could touch him Jesus raised his arm with the palm of his hand facing his tutor in the gesture to stop. The boy did not speak or look at him but simply continued to stare at something in the sky. Judas had never seen anything like this before. He had no idea what he should do, but Jesus was obviously aware of his presence and seemed to be in no pain, so he decided to do nothing and wait.

It was a full quarter of an hour before Jesus moved. Suddenly he blinked, looked at Judas and began to shake. Judas knelt beside him and asked, "Are you unwell? Shall I fetch your mother or Deborah perhaps?"

"I am not unwell," replied Jesus quietly, "At least I don't think so. Have I been away long?"

"Away? You've been here all the time."

"Then I must have been dreaming. Why am I trembling?"

"I do not know. Tell me what happened."

"I'm thirsty." Judas picked up one of the goblets of lemon juice from the tray and handed it to Jesus. It was consumed in seconds. Jesus wiped his lips on his sleeve and started to speak. "I remember waiting in this garden while you were preparing something for us to eat, but then I think I must have fallen asleep because I had some strange but wonderful dreams. First, I became aware of light all around me, warm friendly light that brought with it comfort and safety. I looked down and saw that the light seemed to be coming from within me, though I did not understand how that could be. Then I seemed to leave the ground and float into the sky. Higher and higher I went until I could see all the world below me." He paused. "May I have another drink?"

"Of course," said Judas and handed him the goblet he had kept for himself. "What did you see?"

"Wonderful things! Many beautiful cities with people working in them just like ants do when they build their nests, but there were also cities that were deserted, destroyed, but I could not tell how or why. I wanted to help but did not know how to. There seemed to be great love in me. I wanted to bring joy and happiness to everyone and make them feel how I was feeling but something held me back. I do not know what it was, but what I do know is that there is a great task ahead for me."

"That should not be a surprise. You are the Messiah, the King of the Jews anointed by God himself."

"But my dream was for all people, not just the Jews."

That comment gave Judas pause for thought and for the first time he realised that the Messiah might not be what bar Abbas and the Zealots were expecting. This child, who was not yet eleven years old, was speaking not just of the future Kingdom of Israel, but the whole world. Then, with a flash of insight, Judas understood what had happened. "Jesus, listen carefully to me. You have just been granted a revelation. This is something given only to a very few people and certainly not to me, but such a thing was once described to me by someone who had experienced one."

"Who was that?"

"A wise man called Abbas, the father of Eli bar Abbas. We were locked up in Herod's prison together for a while. I was released but he was murdered. Abbas' revelation brought him trouble and comfort at the same time which helped him to endure the suffering he was undergoing. The same will happen to you. I believe you have experienced the first of many revelations. I do not know when or where they will take you but they are messages direct from God and you must be guided by them. You are privileged but also cursed because your life will no longer be your own. Such is the fate of all great leaders."

Sure enough, the second revelation occurred in the following year but not before disquieting news came from the north. On the second day of Iyar (April) a messenger arrived from Dan carrying a letter addressed to Judas bar Menahem. It was early afternoon and Judas was in his garden pruning an olive tree when the messenger knocked at his door.

"I have been asked to wait until you have read the first letter sir," said the young man who spoke with a pronounced northern accent.

"Have you eaten today?" asked Judas.

"Not yet sir."

"Then come in and I will provide you with some refreshment while I read the letter."

Judas broke the seal on the scroll and saw that the outer letter and the inner were both written in the same hand. The inner letter was sealed separately and addressed to Ruth. The outer letter was addressed to Judas.

Tenth day of April, thirty seventh year of the Emperor Augustus Caesar.

Hail Judas bar Menahem,

I trust this letter finds you in good heart. Although I can speak Greek and Aramaic, I can read and write in neither but I know you are fluent in Latin which is why these two letters are written in my own tongue. I cannot remember thanking you for your vital role in rescuing Ruth, and for this I apologise. Please accept my sincere thanks now, for Ruth is someone who is special to me. I do not know how to contact her and, as you well know, we left in haste so may I presume upon you to ensure she receives the letter enclosed within this one. You will need to read and translate it for her for which I also thank you. You will understand why I have written to Ruth when you read the letter to her. You may trust the messenger who brings this letter. Please give him two denarii. I will pay you back when I next see you.

May your God keep you well.

Lucius Veranius, Centurion third century, fifth cohort, Third Legion Gallica.

Judas asked the messenger, "Where will you go when you leave here?"
"I shall return to Dan."
"One of these letters needs a reply. You may stay here until tomorrow if you are willing to wait."
"Thank you, sir. I shall enjoy walking in your garden. I have a small one at home which gives me great pleasure."
Judas hurried to Joseph's house where Ruth was now living. The marital home she had been awarded by the inquiry had been rented to a grain merchant because it would have been unwise for a young woman of means to live alone. The rent would enable her to make a contribution to the running costs of Joseph's household. Judas found her in the kitchen garden collecting herbs for the evening meal. Together they sat on a bench amid the delightful scent of thyme as Judas broke the seal on Ruth's letter and began to read slowly, translating as he went.

Ninth day of April, thirty seventh year of the Emperor Augustus Caesar.

Hail Ruth,

We only had a few moments alone together on that terrible day of your execution. In that short time, we gave our hearts to each other knowing we should have done that more than ten years ago; a whole decade! I am sorry to say that an unpleasant rumour is circulating which, if true, means we will again see nothing of each other for a long while. Simply put, the Third Legion Gallica is going to lend its fifth cohort, my cohort, to the under-strength Eighteenth Legion for a campaign in Germania which is at the opposite end of the empire from Galilee. The Germans are tough warriors so the fighting will be hard but I will be careful and make sure I return to you and pay Judas the two denarii I owe him!

Even if my cohort does not return, my term of duty has less than three years to run. I know you will have many suitors but I hope you can find it in your heart to wait for me. I joined the legion when I was just seventeen so I will only be thirty-seven when I retire. A centurion's pension is generous, and I have prize money too.

If you have doubts, seek advice from Judas. He doesn't smile much (sorry J), but he is good hearted, sensible and brave. He is also the reason we met again for which I will be eternally grateful. I shall try to take some leave so I can see you before we march to Germania, but it may not be possible.

May your God watch over you until I can.

Lucius Veranius, Centurion.

When Judas looked up from the letter, Ruth was smiling and her eyes were sparkling with happiness. "You love this man?"

"Yes! Yes! He is all I could hope for."

"So, you will wait for him?"

"Yes, of course!"

"He is not of your blood or your God. Most Roman soldiers worship Mithras."

"He can worship who or what he likes. It will make no difference to me."

"I can see that. How fortunate he is to be loved like that."

Ruth quickly understood how her own elation contrasted with the lonely life Judas led. She gently took the letter from him, rolled it up and placed it inside her sleeve. "Lucius is not the only one who is eternally grateful to you. You brought us together again even though we must wait for a while to become one. I will pray you find the same happiness as you have given us."

"Thank you, Ruth, but for such a gift as that one must be lovable. I am not such a person. What you now have is reserved for a select few. If you wish to reply to this letter, the messenger is waiting. I shall write down your words in Latin so Lucius will understand them."

***

III

The second revelation took place in the winter of the same year. This time Judas did not see it because Jesus was alone in bed when it happened. It was the middle of the night. Jesus suddenly woke up, or was awoken, he was not quite sure which. He stared hard into the darkness but could see and hear nothing. Then the same warm light that emanated from his body appeared again and grew in strength until he could see the details in his chamber as if it was full daylight. Just like the first time, he experienced that same sense of well-being and comfort as he floated upwards, but now the view he saw from the sky was very different. Instead of busy cities teeming with people he saw parched, waterless empty desert. Then, out of the corner of his eye, he spied movement coming from a hole in the ground. He could not tell what sort of animal this was as it struggled with the roots and rocks blocking its path, but at last it pulled free of the obstacles holding it back, stood up and stretched itself to its full height. It was a human being! He called out and offered to help but instead of coming to meet him, the human figure disappeared back into its hole. Then more humans appeared, some from holes in the ground, others from caves in the pale rocks that lined the edge of the desert. The humans were Jews though dressed in the simple, white raiment of the desert with no bright colours or adornment of any kind. Then, Jesus looked to his right where the desert ended and beheld a large, blue sea but there were no vessels upon it, nor any settlements beside it, not even a fisherman's hut.

When he awoke from his dream, Jesus was shaking and very thirsty again. He was also troubled. Who are these strange people who live in holes and caves? When he spoke of the dream to Judas at his tuition the next morning, his tutor understood immediately. "Your second revelation, for that is what it was, took you to a place in the desert south of here between the hills of Judea and the Great Salt Sea. The people you saw were Essenes who are an unusual and interesting Jewish sect. Now is the time I must tell you about them because they will certainly have a great impact upon your life."

"They seemed to be peasants."

"They most certainly are not. They have chosen to live a plain, uncomplicated existence which, they believe, is pleasing to God and brings them close to the way of life of the Israelites of Moses' time."

"How will that affect me?"

"Because the Essenes, though small in number, have great influence amongst our people. They lead the life many of us feel we should follow but are too weak willed to do so. The abstemious ways of the Essenes build moral strength and personal fortitude, but the rest of us prefer not to give up life's little pleasures. They also reject violence in all its forms, so when the time comes to rise up against the Romans, they will not fight."

Jesus paused for a moment, then said, "I think dedication to peace is worthy of praise."

"Of course, it is but if we are ever to regain our freedom we will have to fight for it. The Romans will not just walk away because we ask them to. Look what happened to Judas the Galilean. Look what happened to his followers in Sepphoris!"

"Were they really his followers or did he force them to be? Could we not speak to the Romans and make them part of our mission?"

"Jesus, you do not know the Romans. They treat rebellion mercilessly."

"I am not talking of rebellion, but persuasion. If you are so convinced that fighting is the only way, could you not persuade the Essenes to join us?"

"Bar Abbas thinks they might abandon their devotion to peace for the cause of our independence, but I am not so sure, though the Essenes would make formidable warriors if they ever did change their minds. Maybe the time has come for you to be revealed to their leader. I am sure he can be trusted with such an important secret as the identity of the true Messiah, and even if he refuses to fight there may be other ways he can help when you begin your mission as the Messiah."

"Does that mean we will visit him in his desert cave?" asked Jesus eagerly.

"Perhaps, though he does not live in a cave. I will speak to your father and bar Abbas. If they both approve, you and I shall visit his home in Qumran together."

Permission was granted, reluctantly by Joseph because Mary had little sympathy with Essene values but eagerly by bar Abbas who was desperate to recruit the Essenes to the Zealot cause. So early in the spring Judas, Jesus and, of course, Reuben, their Shadow guardian, set off for the Essene settlement of Qumran at the north western end of the Great Salt Sea. For the first time in his short life Jesus encountered true desert conditions; blistering heat, relentless blue sky and an unforgiving, burning sun. Fortunately, the distance from the Judean hills to the Essene settlement was less than a day's walk but the three travellers were still obliged to halt for a while in the shade of a small wadi until the full midday heat had passed.

"How can people live in heat like this?" asked Jesus.

Reuben answered, "I have been here before. There is plenty of cool, sweet water just below the ground which is fed by springs from the hills of Judea. The Essenes only have to dig down a few yards to find a plentiful supply of water, enough for them to enjoy their ritual of bathing every day."

Jesus frowned, "But surely that cannot be good for the body?"

"I don't know," smiled Reuben, "But the Essenes seem to thrive on it. It is said the average Essene lives longer and more healthily than the rest of us."

"And it is part of their law," added Judas, "Which is enforced by their leader, the Teacher of Righteousness, to whom all are pledged to obey without question."

"Does this teacher have a name?" asked Jesus.

"Indeed," answered Judas. "The current Teacher of Righteousness, who is elected by his people, is called Judah."

Reuben shaded his eyes and squinted upwards. "The sun is lower in the sky now. It is time to finish our journey."

Qumran was not a series of caves and holes in the ground, but a small village of stone houses set upon a terrace overlooking the flood plain of the Great Salt Sea. The travellers were given the warm welcome which was customary from the Essenes, because they received few visitors, and were taken to a small building which enclosed a well and a stone bath filled with water from the well. Here they were required to bathe before being presented to Judah. Then they were escorted through the village to a house, a little larger than the rest, where the Teacher of Righteousness lived. Inside, they were presented to a remarkable individual who seemed to Judas as old as the hills. Seated on a simple wooden chair, he was as still as a statue, almost as if he had been carved out of ancient rock. His beard was thin with age and pure white, matching his classic Essene raiment. He wore no head covering allowing his long, white hair to fall to his shoulders. Bushy eyebrows almost covered the small, dark eyes either side of his beak-like nose, and when at last he moved, he pointed to three chairs with a scaly, claw of a hand; the resemblance to a wise old eagle was striking.

"Please sit, I am too old to stand up and greet you properly." He spoke lucidly in the rich, mellow voice of a man of fifty but Judas guessed he must be almost twice that age. "Please identify yourselves." Judas looked awkwardly at the two Essenes who had accompanied the travellers from the bath house. Judah seemed to understand what he was thinking and signalled them to withdraw. "Now you may speak freely and in confidence."

It was uncanny. Judas felt the words in his mind were being read before he spoke them. "How should we address you Teacher of Righteousness?"

The dark eyes seemed to twinkle. "Judah will suffice."

"I am Judas bar Menahem, sometimes called Sicariot," replied Judas. "I am a Zealot from Jericho but now resident in Nazareth. On my left is Reuben our protector who is also a Zealot and one of bar Abbas' secret order the Shadows. On my right is Jesus bar Joseph, the Messiah."

"I am glad you did not say 'the true Messiah'. We have had enough of those lately, but did not the Messiah perish during Herod's purge of male babies in Bethlehem?"

"He survived as you can see. We were warned of what was to come by two Roman soldiers and escaped with just minutes to spare."

"Why would Romans do that?"

"I asked Joseph the same question. He said it was a debt of honour."

"That could mean anything," sniffed the teacher sceptically.

"When I pressed him he did not wish to say more."

"Well, we can leave that for now. Jesus, stand up please."

Jesus obeyed and the dark, bird-like eyes examined him. "How old are you?"

"I am twelve years old Teacher of Righteousness."

"You are tall for your age."

"Yes."

"You do not look very Jewish."

Judas interrupted. "There is northern blood in his family."

Judah raised a bushy eyebrow, "Really? How sure are you of his ancestry?"

"Certain. Both mother and father can trace their bloodlines back to King David himself. Their records are amongst those that survived the destruction of Solomon's temple by the Babylonians."

"How convenient, and what do you expect from Jesus?"

"When he becomes an adult, he will raise his banner and lead the Jews to independence from Rome. Then he will re-establish the Kingdom of Israel. Only then will we regain our rightful place as God's Chosen Race."

"Well, I'll admit you don't lack ambition. What do you expect from the Essenes?"

"When the time comes, we Jews should be united as we once were under David and Solomon. The Zealots cannot do this alone. We cannot rely on the Pharisees and Sadducees for they have too much to lose; the Romans have bought their loyalty. But with your help we can win. You have many influential communities scattered throughout Judea and Galilee. We need you to join us."

"To fight?"

"If necessary."

Judah sighed and shook his head. "Then you do not understand the essence of what it means to be an Essene. We will never shed blood whatever the cause, but you may tell bar Abbas we will help in other ways. Bring Jesus back here when he is fourteen and, if he can withstand a thorough examination from me concerning his status as the Messiah, we will agree a means by which the Essenes can support your cause without shedding blood."

"But that's two years away!" exclaimed Judas. "You may be er, well…"

"Dead?" smiled Judah. "That will not be the case, be assured about that. My death has been foretold and, despite my age, it will not be for a while yet. We will meet again two years from now. There has been enough talk. Let us eat and drink together and speak of less weighty matters before you leave."

Judah clapped his hands and a tall girl of about fourteen entered. She was not perfect. Her eyes were set too wide apart, her nose was aquiline, her lips were full and her hair was dark brown rather than true Jewish black, but the combination of these imperfections was devastating. This was not the beauty of angelic delight, but unbridled charisma that drives men wild. Judas appreciated this but felt nothing, Reuben was a Shadow and masked his feelings most of the time, but neither of them noticed the radiant sparkle in young Jesus' eyes. He was smitten.

The girl's name was Mary Magdalene.

***

IV

Just after his thirteenth birthday, Jesus had his third revelation. He had continued to grow rapidly and was now as tall as Judas, but his mental maturity seemed to be developing even faster. But on a cold, wet Shevat (January) morning, Jesus arrived for his tutorial with Judas looking pale and nervous and for the first time, he had not completed the work given him the previous day for this morning's Greek language lesson.

"Are you unwell?" Asked a concerned Judas.

"No, just a little tired."

But when Judas took the unfinished clay tablet from him, he noticed Jesus was trembling. "Have you eaten this morning?" Jesus shook his head. "Then I will fetch you some bread and cheese. Breakfast is the most important meal of the day."

When he returned, Jesus had stopped shaking and some of the colour had returned to his cheeks. "You've had another revelation, haven't you?" Jesus nodded. "But you weren't going to tell me about it. Why was that?"

"You will not like it."

"That does not matter. It will help you if you tell me, but you are not obliged to. Eat first then see how you feel."

By the time Jesus had eaten and drunk a little milk, his normal, cheerful nature began to reassert itself, but he was still hesitant to talk about his revelation. "Do not be shy," urged Judas. "You are thirteen now. If your revelation involved a girl it is natural, especially at your age."

"I have already had dreams like that, but this was a revelation and altogether different. It was dark and full of hate. I saw terrible things."

"I cannot help unless you tell me about it."

Once he started to talk, Jesus held nothing back. "It happened just after I woke up this morning. I was sitting on the side of my bed and about to get up and wash, which is something I do every morning since our visit to the Essenes. Suddenly I felt a sharp pain in my stomach, the sort of pain you have when you know something bad is about to happen. Then my room seemed to darken. Once more I seemed to float upwards, but this time there was no pleasant sensation, no warmth or comfort, just a growing sense of desolation. I looked down and below me I saw our holy city, Jerusalem. It was in flames. Dead bodies lay everywhere, men, women and even children. Screams of agony pierced the night sky. Roman soldiers were rampaging through the city killing at will and laughing as they did so. I looked towards the temple. It was also on fire but here our soldiers were still fighting along with priests and anyone else who sought refuge inside the temple walls.

But as I watched, the Romans broke into the Court of the Priests, the last defence before the Holy of Holies. They flooded in like a torrent of black hate. I could bear it no longer, turned away and closed my eyes, but I could still hear the screams and clamour of destruction. Then suddenly there was silence. When I opened my eyes, I was standing in a scented garden.

Beautiful trees were in blossom, birds were singing songs of spring and flowers of all kinds were everywhere. This matched my idea of how Heaven must be. Before me was an avenue of acacia trees which were just beginning to display their sky-blue flowers. Two people were in the avenue walking arm in arm away from me. One was a Jewish woman with long black, uncovered hair which reached almost to her waist but her partner was a Roman attired in full armour. He was not wearing his helmet so I could see his short-cropped hair was the colour of ripe straw. Suddenly they turned and began to walk towards me. The woman was my mother though she seemed older than she is now. I did not recognise the Roman which is no surprise because I do not know any Romans. They stopped and looked at each other. He put his arm round her waist and I am sure they were about to embrace, but there the revelation ended.

After Jesus finished speaking, there was silence for a full minute as Judas pondered on his words. Finally, he asked, "What is your interpretation of this revelation?"

"Do not make war on Rome," answered Jesus emphatically. "We can achieve our aims through a peaceful way, the Essene way. War will be a disaster for our people."

"But Jesus, you are the Messiah, anointed by God as the King of Israel."

"Maybe so, but I also know that if we make war on the most powerful empire the world has ever seen, we will fail."

"But can you not see that with the Messiah to lead us we will be invincible!"

"Actually no I cannot see that, but I can see what the revelation showed me; death and destruction for Jerusalem."

Judas saw all his years of tutoring the Messiah crumbling before his eyes because of a single revelation. "So, what do you think we should do?" He asked desperately.

"That was made clear in the last part of the revelation. We should hold out the hand of friendship to the Romans. They are not a stupid people and would far rather have a compliant Jewish nation which is allowed to practice its own customs without interference, much as happens now, instead of an angry, rebellious people who will cost them men and money to keep subdued."

Judas recalled the meeting with Judah, the Essene leader, who questioned the veracity of Jesus' ancestry. Then he considered the last part of Jesus' revelation. Thirteen years ago, Judas had met Caius Pantera who, with Lucius Veranius, had saved the new-born Jesus and his family from Herod's massacre in Bethlehem. Jesus' description of the Roman in his revelation fitted Caius perfectly. A fleeting thought occurred to Judas but he quickly dismissed it as absurd and preposterous. But a little niggle at the back of his mind remained, for he had always wondered about the Messiah's height and the colour of his hair.

"Jesus," he said, "We will talk of this again soon, but I need time to think. Until then will you promise me you will speak to no-one about this revelation?"

"Certainly."

"Thank you. The things you have just said are, well, not what the Zealots expect to hear from their Messiah. We need time to determine how we should deliver your message most effectively." Judas was struggling to believe he was talking to a boy of only thirteen.

"I understand Judas. You have faith in me for which I am grateful, and I shall speak to you first as you ask. But somehow, I do not expect to have another revelation for a long time. My message is clear, to me at least, and now God expects to see some sign that I will act upon it before he grants me further insights into my mission."

Judas did not doubt this, but he could not have known that this was the last time Jesus would disclose a revelation in its entirety to him.

CHAPTER SIX

Our deployment to Dan was a much longer mission than anyone in the fifth cohort expected. Despite the demise of Judas the Galilean, there was still an undercurrent of rebellion amongst the local tribe which manifested itself in small scale irritations such as occasional stone throwing at our sentries on guard duty, defecating in our usually unoccupied observation posts at important road junctions and river crossings, and shouting insults at our patrols, all of which were pointless because apart from me, none of us understood Aramaic. It all combined to deliver a message that northern Galilee was not yet tamed. But such harmless provocations were considered by Metellus Albinus, our legate, serious enough to keep our cohort in Dan. None of us could understand this because we did not yet realise how much he hated Piso, our noble tribune.

Matters took a turn for the worse at the beginning of the third month of the thirty eighth year of the rule of Augustus Caesar when our six cohort centurions were summoned to a meeting at Piso's office after the evening parade. "At ease gentlemen," said our tribune as he gestured towards the six campaign chairs opposite his desk. "I am afraid I have news which most of you will not like, so prepare yourselves." There was a certain amount of nervous throat clearing as Piso continued, "Publius Quinctilius Varus, who most of you will remember was our Governor of Syria until a few years ago, has had his appointment as Governor of Germania Magna confirmed. He intends to lead a campaign against the remaining recalcitrant German tribes living between the rivers Rhine and Elbe to complete our conquest of Germania and secure everlasting glory for himself."

"Where's the profit in that?" asked Gnaeus Servilius, commander of our second century. "The Germans are just primitive, starving barbarians. They have no wealth worth plundering!"

"True," agreed Piso, "But they are natural warriors and will make a good source of recruits for the legions once they are tamed. Unfortunately, Varus has only five under-strength legions with which to accomplish his task and has therefore requested reinforcements from other provinces in the empire to bring his army up to full strength. I must tell you now that our legate has donated the fifth cohort to Varus for this imperial venture. We shall march for Germania in a month or two's time with a view to taking part in a campaign scheduled for next year, which will extend the boundaries of our empire from the Rhine to the Elbe."

This was devastating news. Postings in the eastern part of the empire such as ours were considered soft and luxurious compared to those in the west. The Rhine and Danube frontiers were said to be harsh, where only hard fighting and freezing winters could be expected. For some of us the move would be particularly difficult for though legionary rules forbade marriage, this did not prevent long lasting relationships developing with local women which were marriage in all but name. Indeed Gnaeus, who had served with me for many years, had two young children by a Judean woman and managed to spend more nights with her than in our camp until our transfer to Dan.

"Sir, how long will this transfer last?" asked Septimus Nasicus, who looked far too young to be the centurion of the sixth.

Piso shrugged. "If I knew I would tell you Septimus. Much will depend upon how Varus handles the Germans. They are a proud, independent-minded people much like the Jews. I remember fighting them during my early days on the Danube frontier under a good general called Domitius Ahenobarbus. Although we beat them, Ahenobarbus only brought them to heel by treating them with respect. If Varus does not do the same, we could be in for a long, hard stay in Germania."

"Why were we selected to go?" asked Marcus Sempronius of the first century.

"I do not know," answered Piso curtly. "Speculation will not help. We have a direct order and that's an end to it."

"How far away is Germania?" wondered Marcus Aius, centurion of the fourth.

Piso said, "I too have asked that question. It seems the best estimate is about two thousand miles from here to the western edge of Germania, which is where we are going, but there is more than one route to choose from. But the roads are good and at twenty miles a day it should take us about three months to get there. The march will toughen us up for what lies ahead."

Caius, who commanded the fifth, asked, "Are we the only ones being transferred to Germania?"

"No, we'll be accompanied by Friedrich von Vechten's Batavian cohort which will doubtless be a great asset when the campaign begins. The Batavii tribe are absolutely loyal to Rome."

Young Septimus raised an eyebrow, "Why should that be so, sir?"

"Because the Batavii and their allies, the Frisii, are blood enemies of the tribes further east. The German tribes seem to hate each other more than they do us."

"And it is not in the nature of Germans to be disloyal," added Caius. "My father, who came from the Suebi tribe, made it clear to me that disloyalty is one of the few weaknesses that can never be forgiven."

Marcus Sempronius, who disliked Caius almost as much as he hated me, was always ready to sneer. "Then are you a Roman or a German?"

"I am a Roman just like you. You well know that almost none of the men in the legions are true born Romans, the exception being the Praetorian Guard. Were either of your parents born in Rome?"

Marcus stuttered, "Well, as a matter of fact, I er –"

"He doesn't know," interrupted Marcus Aius, the joker amongst us. "Maybe he was a foundling!"

Caius said, "My father was German and my mother was Jewish, at least I know that much. I was born within the boundaries of the empire which makes me a Roman."

"Enough!" interjected Piso, who was enjoying the arrogant Sempronius' discomfiture, though he could not show it. "We are ordered to Germania and that's all that matters. I will be able to give you a departure date soon. It is likely to be in May, so that will give you plenty of time to send your goodbyes to those who care for you. Now return to your centuries and brief your men about what will shortly happen."

After the meeting ended, Caius and I met in the camp parade ground to talk about the implications of our transfer. "What are you going to do about Ruth?" asked Caius. "You still have enough time to marry her if you wish."

I had not seen Ruth since interrupting her execution, though I had written to her using Judas as the intermediary. She had returned an affectionate letter to me, but now the drama of her rescue was over, I began to see things in a more balanced way. "I am in a quandary," I replied to Caius' question. "I love Ruth, but I love Zenub too."

"The cat in Jerusalem who was beaten up by Sempronius?"

"Yes, I have offered marriage to both of them when my term in the legion expires, which is now less than two years away."

"Zenub has accepted?"

"They both have."

"Then you must choose one and disappoint the other. How could you let yourself get into such a mess?"

"I don't know. It just happened. I feel wretched."

"Of course you do, but it's a situation of your own making. You must choose, but you can leave it until you return from Germania. Who knows what will happen there? At least you are fortunate enough to have a choice. I can never have the woman I love."

"Never is a long time Caius. At least you know Mary and Jesus are well and you are still young."

Caius was silent for a while as we strolled slowly across the parade ground. He was five years younger than me but seemed older and wiser. "Which one will you marry?" He said suddenly.

"I really don't know. I love both of them."

"Then if I were in your position, I would consider which of the two needed me most and which could best manage without me."

"On that basis I would choose Ruth. Zenub is experienced

and quite wealthy."

"Well, whatever you decide, you must tell the loser face to face and not by letter."

"I know that."

"Then look on the bright side. I have a bad feeling about the Germania campaign. We may never come back and then you won't have to decide at all!"

"Oh, what a bundle of joy you can be Caius Pantera! Why are you so pessimistic about Germania?"

"There is no logical reason. I just feel it in my bones. Varus is not the right man to take on the Germans. He underestimated the Jews. I have a feeling he will do exactly the same in Germania."

***

II

On the sixteenth day of May we broke camp and began the long march to Germania. Everyone knows how big and powerful the Roman empire is, at least they think they do, but it is not until you have marched from one side of the empire to the other that you can truly appreciate its vastness and diversity. Twenty miles a day was not an ambitious target because of the excellent, paved imperial roads that link all the provinces to Rome and each other. We followed the coast road north through Syria, crossed the Taurus mountains into Cappadocia, and marched through Galatia and Bithynia until we took our first long rest in a busy town called Byzantium just after we had been ferried across the narrow straight separating Europe from Asia. The rest was welcome, especially for Caius, who had begun to limp because of a return of the soreness in his leg caused by the wound he had received many years ago in our first battle together on Mount Carmel.

In Byzantium Piso was faced with a choice. We could have either headed west on good roads towards the Adriatic Sea and followed the Dalmatian coast northwards, which would mean crossing the Alps to reach Germania, or use a much shorter route across recently conquered territory, where good quality roads had yet to be constructed, and follow the valley of the River Danube upstream which would have taken us directly to the southern marches of Germania.

We ended our stay in Byzantium on the eleventh day of

July. It was a hot day so we prepared to set off just before dawn but there was an unexpected delay when a group of angry tavern owners approached Piso complaining that they had not been paid by some of our soldiers for food and drink supplied the night before. Two of these men were Roman citizens so their complaints had to be taken seriously. Our tribune stood us down for an hour while a hastily arranged inquiry took place. I decided to walk to the fishing port to enjoy watching the sun rise on the Asian side of the straight. It was not often that a centurion got leisure time alone, so I sat down on a disused mooring bollard and watched the eastern sky turn from dark grey to deep blue. The fishermen were still slumbering, there was no-one about. It was bliss.

But my moment of quiet euphoria did not last long. "Lucius!" called a voice just behind me.

I looked round, irritated by the interruption. "Who is it?" I demanded, trying to sound less annoyed than I felt.

"Lucius, may I speak with you?" Although I could barely make out the figure in the pre-dawn gloom, I recognised the voice of young Septimus Nasica, centurion of our sixth century. He sounded worried.

"Of course, you may Septimus," I replied, pointing to another bollard near mine. "I am about to enjoy the sight of dawn in Byzantium. Come and watch it with me." Septimus sat on his bollard but remained silent.

"Well, what is it?" I asked. "Are you going to keep me in suspense much longer?"

He sighed, "Lucius, I am troubled."

"About what?"

"I am unsure how to lead my men when we go into battle in Germania. They are mostly experienced veterans but, apart from some stone throwing by rioters in Jerusalem, I have never seen action."

"A stone can kill you as easily as a sword point, but if you have not been in action how is it that you are a centurion? Distinguished war service is a pre-requisite for promotion to centurion status."

"That is true which only makes things worse. The Nasicas are a senatorial patrician family but, as you will gather from my name, I am a seventh child. I have four elder brothers whose careers had to be settled before mine. We are not a rich family so by the time my turn came, all that my father could afford to arrange for me was a centurion's position in a remote eastern outpost. Even that was a favour because in the senate my family is closely allied to that of our legate, Metellus Albinus."

"Who knows little enough of war himself so I am told, or he would not have offered a centurion's post to a greenhorn. He's a greenhorn himself which is why he got rid of the experienced Piso and the fifth cohort so quickly."

"I hear the Germans are formidable warriors," continued Septimus, "And although I know all about organisation, drills and training, I am not fit to lead good men into battle. How can they respect a centurion like me? I don't even know if I have the courage to fight let alone lead in battle."

"Septimus, you are right to question yourself but that is an encouraging sign. Personally, I do not believe you will lack courage when the time comes to face the Germans. It is true they are fine warriors and have occasionally beaten a Roman army but usually we win. They have great strength and vigour but we have discipline and stamina. Provided their first charge is held, we always outlast them."

Septimus nodded an acknowledgement but remained silent. By now the light was improving as the rim of the sun's golden disc appeared over the eastern horizon casting a rich crimson colour on the scudding clouds above us. I took the opportunity to take a closer look at my young companion who looked more like a priest than a soldier. He was slim and fine boned with very white skin, the sort that does not take kindly to excessive sunlight and burns rather than browns. His reddish hair suggested an origin from northern Italia but I already knew that his family came from Veletri, just ten miles south of Rome. His only distinguishing feature was his green eyes, a colour that often accompanies red hair. He looked very young.

I broke the silence. "How old are you, Septimus?"

"Nineteen."

"Young for a centurion. How long do you intend to stay with the army?"

"The full legionary term."

"Twenty years!"

"Yes."

"But most senatorial appointments to the army last less than two years. The army is just one of the stepping-stones on the route to the senate."

"I know, but I have always wanted to be a soldier. I feel that is where my future lies."

"Just like our own dear tribune. I shall make sure your men get to hear about this. They will respect you for it."

"There is nothing I want more than to earn their respect, but I am inexperienced and fear making a mistake in battle either through ignorance or terror."

"You are not alone in that. We all have to go through our first test. I remember seeing Piso in his first battle. It was thirteen years ago at Mount Carmel and was more of a heavy skirmish than a true battle. I saw the fear in his eyes as Zealot sling stones flew past his ears, but he had the moral fibre to overcome his fear and commanded well, as I am sure you will.

My advice to you is to bring some of your senior file commanders into your confidence. Ask their advice and gain the benefit of their experience."

"But won't they despise me for doing that?"

"Certainly not! They will respect you for it. What arouses their contempt is the arrogant officer who tries to hide his ignorance with bluster."

"Do you remember your first action Lucius?"

"I shall never forget it. It was seventeen years ago and, co-incidentally, against two German tribes, the Marsii and the Cherusci. Our commander was Drusus, younger brother of Tiberius who will be our emperor when Augustus finally dies. The Germans surprised us and caught us on the march forcing us to fight with our backs to a river. It was win or die. Along with some other eastern recruits, I had been transferred to Germania for a season to be toughened-up but we were fortunate with our centurion who steadied us when the Germans attacked. He was a veteran of thirty campaigns and was on his second term with the legions. 'Stand firm and remember your training then all will be well,' he said quietly as the German charge approached. 'You are better than they are so let them know it!' I remember I stopped shaking when I heard his calm voice and gripped my pilum ready to hurl it when the word of command came. Those heavy spears disrupted the impetus of the charge. The Germans tumbled over their fallen comrades and when the clash finally came they had slowed to little more than a walk. Our line bent but held. The noise was mind-numbing. I couldn't think because of the yells and screams coming from all around me, but above the tumult I could still hear our centurion's booming voice, 'Stand firm! Stand firm! Remember your training!' The Germans were brave and ferocious, but our shield wall held while our sword thrusts began their deadly work. From being terrified, I remember confidence flooding through my body as I realised the Germans were as frightened as we had been. Soon we began to push them back, slowly at first but then faster and faster until they broke and ran. The whole event could not have lasted more than five minutes, and although I was exhausted in that short time, I shall never forget the feeling of elation that followed. I had fought my first battle and won!"

"So, you no longer fear battle Lucius?"

"I fear losing and bad generals, but Drusus was a good general and led from the front that day as he always did. It was a great loss to Rome when he died young."

Just then the recall sounded. "Seems like Piso has satisfied those tavern keepers. We'd better go back now," I said.

"Thank you, Lucius. I feel much better now, and I'll try to model myself on that centurion who commanded during your first action."

"That's what I have tried to do. Coolness in battle is what the men respect the most."

We walked back to our camp in silence. I wondered why Septimus had approached me instead of Gnaeus, who had a more easy-going nature than me, or Caius, who was nearer his age. In truth I was flattered and pleased to be able to help the young centurion who, as it turned out, was to find an early opportunity to prove himself. As for me, I felt a fatherly affection for Septimus and decided to watch over him as best I could. I realised I was now ready for parenthood. My thoughts turned to marriage and the choice I would one day have to make between the two women I loved.

***

III

We marched up the valley of the River Danube which now marked part of the northern boundary of our empire. Evidence of recent fighting was everywhere. Burnt out villages, cowed, nervous people and vicious feral dogs are my abiding memories of that long march, but as we trudged steadily upstream we at last reached more prosperous provinces that had been annexed long enough for the people to enjoy the benefits of Roman peace.

Towards the end of August we entered the upper reaches of the River Rhine and reached a town, whose name I do not remember, on the German side of the river about fifty miles upstream from Moguntiacum. Although technically outside the boundary of our empire, there was plenty of cross-river traffic and a Roman quarter had developed within the town which housed our merchants and traders. By now we were exhausted. Our military sandals were worn out and so was the reserve pair we always carried with us. Caius was limping again and we all needed a rest but Piso knew that Vetera, our destination, was still hundreds of miles away so he went to the Roman quarter and, out of his own pocket, rented fourteen flat bottomed barges and crew which were large enough to carry the entire cohort plus horses and equipment. Unlike the Danube, which flowed against our line of march, the Rhine flowed with us so, sending Friedrich's Batavian horsemen ahead, Piso gave the rest of us a day's rest while the barges were being arranged and loaded. We all blessed out tribune for his generosity and understanding.

Just two days later we reached Moguntiacum, the headquarters of the army of the Upper Rhine which consisted of two legions plus auxiliary cohorts commanded by Nonius Asprenas, a general with a senatorial family background but who had achieved his status in the army on merit. Piso briefly disembarked to pay his respects and collect any news relevant to us, then we continued downstream towards Vetera. The difference between the left and right banks of the Rhine was striking. On the left, the Roman side, the landscape was predominantly comprised of well-tended farmed fields with a few early attempts at viticulture, presumably using vines imported from Gaul or Italia. The German bank was a stark contrast. Dark forests made up of huge trees stretched as far as the eye could see. I noticed Caius, who was on the same barge as me that day, also staring at the great German forests.

"How's your leg?" I asked as I walked up beside him.

"It aches, but thanks to Piso I can rest it until we reach Vetera. It'll be all right by then."

"I saw you looking at those great forests. They make me nervous."

"Me too Lucius. I seem to feel thousands of malevolent eyes glaring at me from within those dark, brooding masses of green."

"Ideal for surprises and ambushes; not our sort of warfare."

"Indeed not. Although my father was German, I sense no deep desire within me to visit my ancestral land. I feel far more affinity with my mother's homeland, Judea, where you can at least see the sun and the sky every day. You could walk for months in the forests of Germania without seeing either."

"But presumably the leaves drop off the trees every autumn like any other forest," I replied cheerily, "And there must be some clearings for the towns and villages."

Caius shrugged, "Maybe so, but I still don't like the idea of fighting in a forest."

We stood and watched the German riverbank pass by in silence for a while, then in order to break the gloom I said, "I spoke to Piso earlier this morning. Asprenas told him that Varus is taking just three legions into Germania next year."

"Is that all?"

"And an auxiliary cavalry cohort for each legion. No serious fighting is expected. According to Asprenas, Varus says that all Germania east of the Rhine as far as the River Weser is already subdued. Our task will be to complete the pacification as far as the Elbe though I'm not sure what that means exactly. I suppose there must still be some troublemakers who refuse to accept the benefits of being within our empire."

Caius frowned. "I overheard The Germans talking when they were loading our barges, they didn't sound pacified or subdued. I'd describe them as sullen and ready to fight given any excuse. I hope Varus knows what he is doing."

"Well, he was a success as Governor of Syria."

"Lucius, he was just lucky. Had it not been for Piso's leadership when the Zealots revolted, Varus would have been obliged to recapture Jerusalem by storm and he would have very likely failed."

"True, but he would say that it was his excellent choice of placing Piso in command of our soldiers in Jerusalem that assured victory for Rome which, in effect, gives the credit for the success to the Governor of Syria."

"I suppose so."

"But when you think about it," I continued, "Taking three legions into Germania makes no sense at all. If Germania really is pacified then one legion plus an auxiliary cohort is plenty. Three legions look like an invading army. But if the Germans intend to fight, three understrength legions are wholly inadequate. Even when you add our cohort to the total, I doubt there will be even thirteen thousand legionaries plus three thousand auxiliaries in the army. Drusus and Tiberius each had three or four times that number when they began their conquest of Germania."

"And still they only gained a partial victory. It seems that Varus does not believe what he is telling his own officers."

"Or," I added, "He is afraid to ask the emperor for more men. We all know that Augustus only approves conquests that will improve his balance sheet."

Caius sighed, "Well I expect you're right. Anyway, Varus has all winter to reconsider his strategy. The fighting season will be all but over by the time we reach Vetera."

Our journey down the Rhine was slow and relaxing. We arrived at Vetera, fully rested, by the beginning of September. The army headquarters was based in a camp constructed by Drusus twenty years before. It was big enough to accommodate two legions though only one, the Eighteenth, occupied it now. Even now the camp, which was made of wood, still had a temporary look about it as if it was a jumping off point for further invasions rather than a permanent, imperial boundary. It stood on a prominent hill overlooking the Rhine just downstream of its confluence with the much smaller Lippe.

While we helped to unload the barges, Piso reported to the governor's residence in the middle of the camp which had previously been the legate's headquarters. He was not kept waiting because Varus was pleased to see him. "Welcome Licinius! It's been a few years since we last met."

"Thirteen, sir," replied Piso as he glanced around the most richly furnished legate's office he had ever seen. Gone were the hard wooden chairs and simple fittings of a legate's headquarters. Instead, the tribune was directed towards an ornately carved chair padded with green linen cushions adjacent to a small companion table upon which was placed a silver goblet full of wine even though it was still well before noon.

Piso, who had abstemious tastes, took a polite sip from the goblet and looked at Varus. The Governor of Germania was now in his mid-fifties but he had not aged well. Since their last meeting he had grown fat, wrinkled and lost most of his hair; what was left of it was entirely grey. On a brighter note Brasidas, the governor's Greek secretary and note taker was present. He had hardly changed at all apart from a slight thickening around the waist and the appearance of lines under his dark, alert eyes.

"You already know Brasidas," said Varus. "He will record our conversation."

There was a silence; clearly Piso was expected to speak first. "I hear you have achieved great things in Rome sir, a second consulship no less."

"Yes, marrying into the emperor's family does have its advantages."

"And now you have secured the most important governorship in the empire!"

"Well, it will be when we have completed our work Licinius. I confess I am surprised that Albinus has sent me the best cohort in his legion. I well remember your excellent defence of Jerusalem against heavy odds during my last year as Governor of Syria. You and your fifth cohort fought like lions! All the other legates sent me the dregs of their legions when the call went out to bolster the armies of the Rhine."

"I think the legate of the Third Gallica knew exactly what he was doing sir," replied Piso in a neutral voice.

"Be that as it may, I have a vacancy for the post of legate of the Eighteenth legion. I would like you to take it." The offer was unexpected and beyond Piso's wildest dreams. He was briefly lost for words. "Well?" said Varus.

"It would be a great honour sir. I never thought to achieve such a position because my family is always out of favour in the senate."

"Only because of your loud mouthed, republican cousin Calpurnius," agreed Varus, "But I am pleased to say that a governor in an area of potential conflict has full authority to appoint his own legates. Your promotion will have to be confirmed by the emperor in due course, but that will only be a formality."

"Thank you, sir. I will not disappoint you."

"I know that. Now when your cohort has disembarked, split the six centuries into three groups of two. These will then be added to each of the three legions, including the Eighteenth, which I shall take into Germania Magna next year."

Piso's brief moment of delight was suddenly shattered. The dismemberment of the cohort that had been his home ever since he joined the army had never crossed his mind. He cleared his throat. "Sir, cannot the fifth cohort be kept together? You said yourself that it has distinguished itself in battle."

Varus frowned. He hated to be thwarted. "Licinius, we all must make sacrifices for the sake of advancement. I must bolster all my legions. If I did not disband a cohort newly arrived from the east and instead took apart an existing cohort from within the Eighteenth legion having already promoted you above other tribunes' heads, how do you think that would appear?"

"Favouritism, sir."

"Exactly! So, you will understand the problem that faces me. Morale is all important."

"I do understand sir but I am afraid I cannot help. I must stay with my men."

"And walk away from a legate's appointment?"

"If needs be sir."

Varus signalled Brasidas to stop recording. The warmth drained from his voice. "Tribune, I urge you to think again. I applaud your loyalty to your men but you must think of the greater good."

"Sir, I do not see how the greater good can benefit from the break-up of one of the best cohorts in the army."

Varus shook his head with an air of resignation. "I see your mind is made up. Very well, I will accede to your request though it will create ill feeling within the Eighteenth. The fifth cohort of the Eighteenth will be the one that is broken up so you will be able to retain your cohort number, but the price will be your legate's appointment."

"I accept with gratitude sir."

"Very well," sighed the governor. "You may go."

After Piso shut the door to the governor's office behind him, Varus turned to Brasidas. "What do you think of that?"

"I am but a slave sir —"

"Don't give me that rubbish. Answer!"

"Piso is a man of honour. He saved my life in Jerusalem when most would not have bothered for a mere slave. If I were a free man, I would join his cohort immediately."

"Well, you're not and you'll damn well stay here with me!"

Piso said nothing about this to us. I did not find out about his sacrifice until a year later.

***

IV

Winters in Germany are cold and wet. It snowed in January, spring was late in coming, so the campaign that was supposed to start at the beginning of the thirty ninth year of the rule of the emperor Augustus was delayed for a full month. The constituent parts of 'The Army of Germania Magna' as the governor grandly named it began to consolidate around Vetera at the end of March. The Seventeenth legion arrived from its base sixty miles upstream from us on the last day of the month. The Nineteenth legion was waiting for us at Aliso, which was an advance legionary base built by Drusus forty miles up the Lippe valley just before he died.

Aliso guarded the best route into Germania Magna but it also served to remind the fractious local tribe, the Sugambri, that the might of Rome was not far away.

Of the three auxiliary cavalry cohorts designated to accompany the legions into Germania Magna, Friedrich's Batavians had spent the winter with us while a Gallic cohort joined us on the day after the Seventeenth legion arrived. Last to join the army was the Cheruscan cohort. I remember that day well. It was shortly after noon on a clear spring day. Caius, Friedrich and I had just finished our midday meal and walked down to the river to watch our engineers replace some of the worn-out barges and boats that supported the bridge over the Rhine, the only permanent crossing of the river this far north.

Caius looked up and pointed to the far bank which had been cleared of trees for two miles before the forest closed in again. "Look! Horsemen approaching from the east." The engineers quickly suspended work, armoured up and joined the sentinels on the far bank while someone sounded the alarm horn. Before the horsemen had covered half the open ground between the forest and the river, the cohort on guard duty for the day had assembled on our side of the river while the engineers stood ready to cut the ropes on the far bank and haul the bridge into the middle of the river if necessary, should the newcomers prove to be hostile.

We waited in silence. The horsemen stopped half a mile from us, then three riders approached the river. One of them shouted in guttural Latin, "Make vay for de cohort of Arminius, Prince of de Cherusci!"

"Hermann is prince now," said Friedrich. "Someone must have died."

"Or been murdered," added Caius.

"Yah! Yah!" laughed Friedrich. "Dat is Cheruscan vay!"

The sentinels were unsure what to do until a young tribune galloped up from the governor's office and shouted, "Stand back and allow the Cheruscan cohort to cross the river! They are our comrades now, remember! I shall escort Arminius to the governor."

The Cheruscans began to cross the bridge of boats at a steady trot. I have to admit, they looked superb. There were about four hundred of them all told, wearing the helmets and chainmail armour of Roman legionary cavalry. In fact the untutored eye would quickly have accepted them as true Roman cavalry but, upon closer inspection, their hair was long and they carried spears instead of long swords. An astute observer would also have noticed that their horses were bigger than ours, which they needed to be in order to support the weight of the large, armoured men who rode them. Arminius, whom Caius and I had met before, came in last instead of first like a shepherd herding his flock. Friedrich, who at one time was Arminius' commander, raised his arm in acknowledgement but his erstwhile subordinate ignored him even though he could not have failed to recognise the rotund, red-haired Batavian.

"Hermann has not changed," said Friedrich sadly. "Alvays sehr proud; too gut for Batavians. I vorry much about him."

"But his cohort looks good," replied Caius.

"Yah, but who dey fight for? Are dey mit uns or Germania?"

"But are not the Cherusci our allies now?"

"So dey say Caius, but ich nicht weiss vat dey really are."

I said, "Well if he's our enemy, he's taking a big risk."

"Not so big Lucius because Varus tink sun shines out of his, how you say?"

"Arse?" suggested Caius.

"Yah! Yah! Sun shine out of Arminius arse! Varus tink Arminius good camarade, but I vorry much about dis. Cherusci can never be trusted."

During the next few months we were to find out the truth.

The army began its eastward march on the twentieth day of April and, after two days, we arrived at Aliso, the Nineteenth legion's base. Varus seemed to be in no hurry because we were told that we would remain at Aliso for at least ten days. The reason for this was that the Governor of Germania Magna, as Varus now called himself, wished to consult with his senior officers on matters of strategy, while at the same time filling his supply wagons with food and provisions taken from the Aliso hinterland, which did nothing to endear us to the local Sugambri tribe. In fact, most of these supplies were loaded onto the boats which were to accompany us up the Lippe and would remain close by us as long as we stayed near the river.

For us, the boats were an important emotional link to Rome, providing comfort for us as we strayed further and further from our imperial boundary.

On the seventh day of May, Varus called the legates of the three legions, the leaders of the auxiliary cohorts and the most senior tribunes, including Piso, to a strategy meeting to be held at the army headquarters in the centre of the Aliso fort. Caius accompanied Friedrich on account of the Batavian's poor understanding of Latin. It is Caius I have to thank for the account of the extraordinary decisions that were taken at that critical meeting, a meeting that decided the fate of the Germania Magna campaign.

It was a cool, blustery day with a wet wind blowing rain in from the west. The Aliso fort, which was located on the side of a hill overlooking the Lippe, was alive with activity because orders had been received from headquarters that the eastward march would resume the following morning. Outside the entrance to the headquarters building, Caius and Friedrich arrived to find the senior officers of the legions huddled inside their red cloaks, sheltering as best they could from the chilly rain as they waited for Varus to let them in. They had been told by a body servant that the meeting would be delayed a little because the governor had not slept well, so when the doors were finally opened more than an hour late, tempers were already frayed.

Varus had not lost his politician's sense of theatre and had arranged for four long tables to be formed into a square in the audience chamber so everyone would be able to observe the proceedings clearly. The table facing the river was occupied by Varus and Brasidas, his long-time secretary and servant. On their left on the same table, and to everyone's surprise, sat Arminius the Cheruscan prince; the German had obviously been summoned before the rest of those gathering there. The tables on the governor's left and right were occupied by the legates and senior tribunes while opposite him, with their backs to the river, sat the two remaining auxiliary cohort commanders and Caius. Caius could already feel Friedrich bristling with indignation when he saw the privileged position awarded to Arminius.

Without reference or apology for the late start, Varus opened the meeting. "Gentlemen, you are here to listen to my plan for the conduct of the coming campaign and, after you have heard it, I shall welcome any questions or comments you may have." The way this was said suggested he expected very few comments, if any. He was greeted with silence so he continued, "Our task is delicate. We have a number of subjugated German tribes to deal with, in particular the Bructeri, Angrivarii, Usipatii and the most recent addition to the empire the Sugambri, in whose land we now reside. These tribes were all defeated by Drusus and Tiberius but subjugated and pacified are not the same thing. Our campaign is intended to pacify the tribes I have just mentioned and thus extend the limit of imperial Rome to the River Weser. In fact, with the support of our Cheruscan allies," Varus nodded towards Arminius, "That boundary can quickly be extended to the River Elbe."

The newly promoted legate of the Eighteenth legion,

Lucius Eggius, who had taken the appointment Piso should have had, asked, "Governor, why are we doing this? There is no wealth in Germania, no towns of any consequence, just forests, rivers, wild men and more forests. What benefit to the empire can this campaign bring?"

Varus frowned, irritated that his oration should have been challenged so soon. "Lucius, you are new to your role so I will make allowance for your inexperience, but legates are not expected to question a governor's overall strategy. You are here to ensure that my strategy is accomplished by the best means possible. That is all, but I will still answer your question." There were nods of approval from the more sycophantic present, but those who were long term professional soldiers were pleased that Eggius, who was a soldier's soldier, asked the question we all wanted answered.

"It is true," continued Varus, "That there is little commercial wealth in Germania Magna at this time, but it must be clear to you that Germania Minor, that is Germania west of the Rhine and within our empire, is flourishing. That proves that given the right conditions and sustained peace which only our empire can bring, the Germans can create wealth through trade and commerce just like any other people and, as you know, wealth can be taxed. In addition, the Germans can bring another asset to the empire which many other people cannot; that is a huge resource of accomplished warriors who will provide an excellent recruiting ground for our legions. Even as I speak, one of our legions at Moguntiacum is composed primarily of Germans from the west bank of the Rhine. The First legion Germania does not bear that name for nothing and the German legionaries, who are also Roman citizens, have proven themselves to be fine soldiers. So just imagine how much stronger our empire will become with more legions drawn from the pacified tribes between the Rhine and the Weser."

This answer seemed to satisfy Eggius, but just as Varus was about to resume his lecture, Piso asked another question. "Governor, if we march to the Weser our lines of communication with Vetera will be seriously stretched. We could end up becoming isolated in enemy territory with only a small army. Are you comfortable with this?"

Varus was unable to keep the anger from showing on his red, fleshy face but he was a politician and knew how to exercise self-control when needed. He remained silent for almost half a minute as he gathered his thoughts and when he replied his answer was withering. "Piso, I am surprised you felt the need to ask such a question as that. Do you think I have not considered these matters in depth? Remember I was already a governor of a Roman province when you were still a child! You will therefore be pleased to know that the Lippe is navigable for supply vessels almost as far as its source. Tiberius, our future emperor, built a legionary base at this place which I am assured," he nodded towards Arminius, "is still in fair condition and can be restored to full military readiness with minimum effort. So, in the unlikely event that we should need to defend ourselves, we have a base by the Lippe which can be supplied direct from Vetera by river. Therefore, if we ever have to retreat under pressure, we have direct access to the Rhine by boat and barge without the need to use the land route. As you can see all eventualities are covered. I trust that answers your question?"

Before Piso could respond, Eggius spoke again. "Governor, it seems to me that your strategy depends heavily on the good will of the Cherusci. But if your faith in them turns out to be misplaced, we could still find ourselves isolated in hostile terrain facing an enemy hugely superior to us in numbers."

Varus could no longer mask his irritation. "Lucius, you should not doubt my strategy or the Cherusci. I have known Arminius for many years. Nineteen years ago he came to Rome as a child hostage from a beaten enemy. Since then he has learned our ways, speaks our language better than his own and has been appointed to the equestrian order which is just one rank below the senatorial class. This is a status few of you here have. If the German tribes, despite our best efforts decide to fight, then the Cherusci, the most powerful of them all, will be with us." Then turning to the Cheruscan prince Varus asked, "Arminius, would you like to say a few words?"

The German nodded and stood up, towering above us all from his full height of six and a half feet. He had filled out with muscle since Caius last saw him and looked the very epitome of the great god Apollo. He spoke quietly in a restrained, controlled manner and in perfect Latin. "Thank you Governor for affording me this privilege. All I have to say is this. Yes, I am now more Roman than Cheruscan but I have maintained contact with my people. They understand the great advantage it will be for them to join the Roman empire of their own free will, not just as allies or confederates like the Batavii," he threw a dismissive glance in Friedrich's direction, "But as a people fully integrated into your empire ready to fight and die for you! I hear you speak with fear of the tribes between the Rhine and the Weser, but you have the Cherusci with you. I can assure you that if the tribes create trouble, you will have no less than eight thousand fully armed Cheruscan warriors at your side, the equivalent of two legions. We shall fight and conquer together!"

Arminius could speak well. From his quiet start, he had gradually raised the pitch of his voice so that the last sentence sounded like a rallying cry. Most of those listening responded with spontaneous applause. Varus was delighted and no-one noticed the few words Arminius whispered to him as the applause died down.

Now, in a much better frame of mind, Varus smiled, "Gentlemen, I think Prince Arminius has answered any lingering doubts you may have, so before I close this meeting, I have one more precautionary measure to announce. You will not know but the Batavii are blood enemies of the Bructerii and the Angrivarii, two of the tribes we must pacify this year. Therefore, the Batavian cohort will remain here at Aliso with two cohorts of the Nineteenth legion under the command of Lucius Caedicius, the camp prefect, to ensure our line of retreat, should it be threatened, will be secure."

Friedrich, who was coming to a boil as he sat listening to Caius' translation, could contain himself no longer. He jumped to his feet and shouted, "Nein! Nein! Dis must not be! Vat for you do dis!"

The governor's good humour of a moment before evaporated. His brow furrowed as Friedrich followed his outburst with a torrent of angry, guttural German. "Who speaks for this man!" demanded Varus.

Caius got to his feet. "I do sir."

"And you are?"

"Caius Pantera sir, centurion of the fifth century, fifth cohort of the eighteenth legion."

Varus paused briefly as he dredged the depths of his long memory. "Have we met before?"

"Yes sir, fourteen years ago in Antioch just before you joined our cohort to put down a rebellion in Galilee."

"Ah yes, I remember now. You have a German father, so your mother tongue is German." The words were spoken almost as an accusation.

"No, sir. My mother is Jewish and my mother tongue is Hebrew. My father is German, of the Suebi tribe, but I am most comfortable in Latin because I am Roman like you."

"My memory is clearing Caius Pantera. I see you have been promoted. You have done well."

"Thank you sir and, if you will permit, I shall translate von Vechten's words for you."

Varus sighed, "If you must, but be brief. There is still much to be done before tomorrow morning's march commences."

After a quick consultation with Friedrich, Caius said, "von Vechten's words are these. 'We Batavians have many times proven our loyalty to Rome on the battlefield, but you have now decided to leave us at Aliso while you march into danger because of your misplaced trust in a Chersucan prince. I know Arminius. He was an officer in my cohort some years ago. He has no love for Rome. He speaks fine words, but that is all they are, just words! You rely too heavily on him. If he betrays Rome, you and your army will be destroyed. Can you not see that! You must take the Batavian cohort with you'."

The governor looked at Arminius who simply shook his head sadly as if Friedrich was a raving madman. "Very well gentlemen, that concludes our discussion on strategy. The rest of this meeting will determine tomorrow's order of march, logistics and so on. Those who will remain at Aliso may return to your duties now. That includes you von Vechten."

Piso was required to stay at the meeting, so Caius and Friedrich came to my quarters to vent their frustration. After sinking a large goblet of wine, Friedrich wiped his mouth on his cuff and banged his mighty fist on the barrack room table. "Dis vill end badly, ich weiss. Hermann sets trap for Varus and Varus walks into it like fly to spider."

"What will you do?" I asked.

"Vat can I do! I must obey orders. I sprech mit camp commander Caedicius. He gut man. I ask to send long distance patrol up Lippe valley to help survivors."

"Then you're sure there'll be a disaster?"

"As sure as I sit here und sprech mit you Lucius."

"Varus was always arrogant but never a fool," muttered Caius.

"Then his yearning to complete the conquest of Germania Magna must have blinded his judgement," I replied. "We must speak to Piso as soon as the meeting finishes. At least we can be prepared so we are not taken by surprise."

"Yah, but remember Hermann is clever. He vill not show true self too soon. Attack vill not come till after harvest. By den Varus vill tink he has won und all is gut."

The march from Aliso to Varus' summer camp on the Weser began on the eighth day of May, and after four days, we arrived at the abandoned camp built by Tiberius alongside the Lippe four years earlier, which was where practical river navigation ended. All the earthwork defences were still in place just as Arminius said they would be, so we pitched our tents inside the earthworks and unloaded our supplies from the boats that had accompanied us this far. Two days later the wagons and pack animals had been loaded, so we began the last part of the journey that would take us overland to the legionary camp, on the Weser, which Drusus had built after his crushing defeat of the Cherusci nineteen years ago.

Between us and Drusus' camp was a range of hills which slowed our progress, but our pace would have been reduced anyway because of the thousand or so camp followers which Varus had allowed to accompany us. There were merchants, traders and money lenders and of course, the ladies of leisure who were attached to all legions in peace time. Varus clearly anticipated we were on the verge of securing a final peace, but many of us were not convinced and wondered what fate would befall these non-combatants if Friedrich's fears were proved right.

Arminius had told Varus that Drusus' camp was still intact and, once again, he turned out to be correct. Just like the camp we had left on the Lippe the defences were still in place and fully functional. Varus' faith in Arminius seemed to be justified.

But all was not as it seemed.

CHAPTER SEVEN

Ananas bar Seth felt well pleased with himself. From his eyrie in the temple of Jerusalem perched far above ordinary people, he looked out at a city at peace with itself for the first time in many years. Archelaus, Ethnarch of Judea, Samaria and Idumea and Herod's incompetent eldest surviving son, had been replaced by the Roman prefect, Coponius. The prefect's instructions from Rome were to govern the Jews with a light touch as long as taxes were paid on time and in full to the imperial treasury. Ananas had made sure he was in the best position to replace Joazar, the previous high priest, who was so closely allied to Archelaus that his downfall was assured when the ethnarch was dethroned by Emperor Augustus.

All that had happened three years ago. Now, after three years of peace, the resourceful Jewish people were creating wealth through trade and commerce and there was more than enough taxation to satisfy Rome and maintain the prosperity of the temple of Jerusalem too. Better still, Coponius had agreed to keep Roman troops away from Jerusalem and set up his office on the coast in the pagan city of Caesarea Maritima, which was two days' march west of the Judean capital so that the ordinary Jew felt he was being governed by the temple from where Jewish law was created and observed.

A knock on the cedar wood doors of the high priest's office awoke Ananas from his musings.

"Who is it!" He called grumpily.

"Caiphas, your chief secretary," came the muffled reply from the other side of the doors. He was also Ananas' son-in-law.

"You'd better come in then."

Caiaphas entered with his usual irritating, supercilious smile. "We have a visitor, Ehud bar Aaron by name. I think you should see him."

"Should I? Why so? There's a time and a place for listening to common-place supplicants."

"I agree, but this supplicant is certainly not common-place, and he bears information you should hear. It concerns the Messiah."

"Absolute nonsense! Send him away. Herod murdered the Messiah in Bethlehem years ago along with all the other male babies."

Caiaphas shook his head, "So we thought."

"Are you saying he is not dead?"

"All I am saying is that you should hear what this Ehud has to say and then judge for yourself."

Caiaphas returned accompanied by a stocky man of middle age and weather-beaten appearance due to many years of working in the open on construction sites. He was obviously nervous about being presented to the high priest of all Jews who was now sitting behind his desk looking very severe. In order to put the supplicant at ease, Caiaphas opened the interview. "May I present Ehud bar Aaron, who was for many years the manager of the construction company in Nazareth owned by the chairman of the Council of Elders, Joseph bar Jacob. Ehud contends that Joseph is also the father of the Messiah who, until now, we believed was dead."

"Well?" demanded Ananas. "I am a busy man so say what

you must say and be quick about it."

Ehud, who was not asked to sit down, stammered, "During the many years I worked for Joseph, I learned much about his family."

"Did he tell you he is the father of the Messiah?" asked the high priest coldly.

"No, but he became so accustomed to my presence that I seemed to become part of the furniture. Things were said in front of me that should not have been said in my hearing, especially when the Zealots came to the office."

Ananas raised an eyebrow. "Is Joseph a Zealot then?"

"He says not but his son, Jesus, is both mentored and protected by two Zealots, Reuben and Judas bar Menahem, sometimes called Sicariot."

"Master," interrupted Caiaphas, "Ehud is right about Judas. He qualified from his studies at the temple in the same year as me. Now he is an influential member of the Zealot leadership."

At last, Ananas became interested and dropped his arrogant manner. "Continue Ehud bar Aaron. Would you like some refreshment?"

"Just a goblet of water sir."

The water was quickly brought and then downed in a few gulps by Ehud.

"Now tell me about the Messiah," said the high priest soothingly. "If your information has value, you will be rewarded."

"He is now thirteen years old and learning his father's trade. He's precocious and bright and should do well in business."

"Yes, but what makes you say he is the Messiah?"

Caiaphas intervened again. "His ancestry is indisputable.

We have the records here, which go back as far as King David. They are among the few documents that escaped the Babylonian destruction."

"And," added Ehud, now rapidly gaining confidence as he sensed the high priest's growing interest, "He survived Herod's massacre in Bethlehem because Joseph and his family were given early warning by two Roman soldiers."

Ananas frowned. "But why would they do that?"

"I don't know sir, but Judas was there to witness it."

"Ehud, why have I not heard of this before?"

"It is a secret known only to the Zealot leadership."

"And how do you know?"

"It was mentioned between Judas and Joseph within my hearing when I was working in the room next to Joseph's office."

"Are you a Zealot?"

"No, sir."

"That is good, but I am still unclear why you are reporting this now instead of when you first heard it."

"Retribution sir. Joseph was my employer. I worked faithfully for him for many years, but now that his son will soon come of age, my services have been terminated to make space for him."

"Revenge is a good, clean motive," mused the high priest. "Do you have work now?"

"No, sir. Joseph slandered my reputation to justify dismissing me. I cannot get work now."

"I understand. Caiaphas, see if we can find work for Ehud in one of our temple properties and, before he leaves, give him a small reward from the treasury."

"Yes Master."

"Ehud, have you anything else to tell me?"

"I have told you all I know sir."

"Very well. You may go home now. Caiaphas, return to me when Ehud has left the temple and be generous with his reward. We may need his help again, so make sure you know where we can find him."

"Thank you, sir, thank you," mumbled a grateful Ehud as Caiaphas ushered him out of the high priest's presence.

"And tell no-one about this meeting!" called Ananas just before the great cedar wood doors slammed shut.

A few minutes later, Caiaphas returned.

"How much did you give that worm?" asked Ananas.

"Twenty silver shekels Master. Was that too much?"

"Do you believe what he told us?"

"Yes, I do."

"So do I, so twenty shekels was cheap for information like that. Even so, I would still like Ehud's information verified as far as possible, especially the reason why he left Joseph which I do not find convincing, so you'll be able to do that when you go to Nazareth."

"Me?"

"Yes, you Caiaphas. This mission is far too important to send a menial. You are my son-in-law, my family, and one of the few people I can really trust. But now we must discuss what is to be done with the Messiah."

"To be done with him? The Messiah is the rightful king of the Jews, David's successor, the one we have been awaiting for generations and the one who will liberate us from Roman tyranny and return us to our rightful place amongst the great nations of the world."

Ananas shrugged. "A pretty speech but I see no Romans or

tyranny here."

"They are in Caesarea Maritima as you already know."

"My point exactly Caiaphas! Now go to my window, look out at Jerusalem and tell me what you see."

Caiaphas, somewhat perplexed, did as he was told. Ananas gave him a few moments then said, "Well?"

"I can see the marketplace. It is full of people buying and selling, traders are talking to each other and there is much laughter. The streets around the temple are crowded with people going about their business. The temple courtyards are also busy with the faithful bringing their animals for sacrifice."

"And outside the city?"

"The fields are being worked, the vines will be ripe in a few weeks. All is as it should be."

"Are the people happy?"

Caiaphas paused for thought. "I believe most of them are."

"See any Romans?"

"No."

"Caiaphas, what you have just described to me is peace and prosperity. True, we had peace in Herod's time and prosperity for a few, but his building projects and foreign wars demanded burdensome taxation which crushed everyone else. What do you think will happen when the Messiah raises his standard to lead us to a new, independent Israel?"

"There will be war with Rome."

"Correct! And do you think we will win?"

"Certainly, if God is with us."

"That's a big 'if'. God has not always been with us has he?"

"Well, er—"

"What about the sack of Jerusalem by the Babylonians

followed by exile for seventy years?"

"God was punishing us for our sins."

"Have we been sinless since then? How do you know God will not punish us again?"

"I do not know."

"Caiaphas, what I am saying is do we really want or need a Messsiah? We already have peace and prosperity. Our prefect, Coponius, has cooped up his Romans in Caesarea Maritima so, for all intents and purposes, we already govern ourselves. The Romans oversee us with the lightest possible touch. You are right that the Messiah will lead us into war, though not just with a regional power like the Babylonians were, but with the most powerful empire the world has ever seen whose resources are vastly greater than ours. Blood will flow, blood from many thousands of good Jews, and for what? To throw off a yoke we barely notice? Is that what you want?"

"Then what should we do with the Messiah?"

"Now you come to the nub of it. What, indeed, shall we do with him?"

"Master, the point is academic because we cannot do anything unless he is in our custody."

The high priest smiled. "In our 'care' I think you mean. We must be sure to create the right impression if we want the support of the people."

"But the Zealots seem to have a hold on him."

"Yes Caiaphas, that is a problem so we must act covertly and quickly which is why it must be you that leads this mission."

"I shall need Ehud with me to make sure there is no mistake regarding the Messiah's identity."

"True, and he will need protection from the enemies he has

undoubtedly created in Nazareth, so disguise him as one of your palace bodyguards."

Caiaphas frowned. "Of course, you realise that Nazareth is in Herod Antipas' territory. Should we not speak to him first?"

"Certainly not! If this were just a temporal matter you would be correct, but the arrival of the Messiah is above all that. It is a religious matter that affects all Jews wherever they may be, so the writ of the high priest must override a mere tetrarch."

"And when we find the Messiah, what then?"

"Bring him here."

"There may be opposition, especially if the Zealots are involved."

"Which is why your visit must be kept secret. Your arrival in Nazareth will come as a surprise, so twenty burly temple guards should be able to handle any difficulties you may encounter."

"What will we do with the Messiah after we have brought him here?"

"I am not sure, but I may change my mind and decide this is a temporal matter after all. You know what that will mean?"

"You'll hand him over to the Romans!"

"Yes Caiaphas, you get to the point quickly. I am glad I chose you to be my successor. The Messiah will claim to be the rightful King of the Jews; he must do because it is his duty as the Messiah, but that will contravene the settlement ordained by the emperor, Augustus. Now you know how the Romans hate rebellion."

"They will put him on trial for sedition and execute him."

"Correct, and we shall be blameless having done our duty to Rome and avoided the shedding of Jewish blood."

"Except the Messiah's."

"One death to save thousands. What is wrong with that?"

As he returned to his quarters later that day, even Caiaphas was surprised at how easy it had been to fall in line with the high priest's view of the Messiah. Better still, although there had been hints and suggestions before, this was the first time that Ananas had said in clear, unmistakable terms that Joseph Caiaphas would succeed his father-in-law as high priest.

***

II

The grape harvest was in and the atmosphere in Galilee was jovial as Caiaphas and his retinue approached Nazareth from the south. They had spent the previous night at nearby Shunam and so arrived at Joseph's town by the middle of the morning where they were directed to the dwelling of the chairman of the Council of Elders. This was located near the top of the hill around which Nazareth was built.

Joseph was working in his office when a servant knocked at the door and announced grandly the arrival of the chief secretary to the high priest of Jerusalem. Joseph immediately sensed danger but could not refuse entry to such an important visitor. He took the precaution of sending for Mary and requiring the chief secretary to leave his entourage outside the house and come to his office alone. When Caiaphas arrived, Joseph and his beautiful wife were ready to receive him. Caiaphas had already decided that guile rather than threats would be the most likely way to crown his mission with success, so he used charm which was one of the many weapons in his personal armoury.

"Joseph bar Jacob, you honour me by inviting me into your wonderful house. I am Joseph Caiaphas."

Joseph, who recognised guile when he saw it, replied, "And you honour us too, Joseph Caiaphas, by visiting us. May I present my wife Mary."

Caiaphas, who could not help being impressed by her

beauty, said, "Joseph, you are indeed blessed by God with a wonderful family."

"Thank you. How may we be of service to you?"

Having completed the pleasantries, Caiaphas immediately came to the point. "Joseph, I will not dissemble. Word has reached the temple that you and your beautiful wife are the parents of the one person whom the entire Jewish people have been waiting for, the Messiah."

Joseph felt Mary stiffen beside him. He asked, "How have you received such information?"

Despite his best efforts to be charming, Caiaphas could not stop his voice from hardening. "Is it true?"

Joseph, who was at least Caiaphas' equal when it came to charm, said, "Forgive me, I am forgetting my manners. Please sit while I arrange some refreshment for you and your companions. Mary will stay with you while I speak with the kitchen supervisor." Before Caiaphas could respond, Joseph left the office but not before giving Mary a reassuring squeeze on the arm as he passed her. She knew her husband well enough to realise he was taking action and she prepared to engage the chief secretary to the high priest in charming small talk until her husband returned.

Joseph knew he had only seconds to put Jesus beyond Caiaphas' clutches and ran down the stairs to the main house where he found Deborah, the manager of domestic arrangements, and Ruth talking to each other. "Deborah, we have an emergency. Take refreshment, anything you can think of, to the man talking to my wife in the office. Hurry, he is dangerous! Invite his companions in for something too. They can have anything but do your best to give us a few extra minutes."

"But what—"

"No time for talk Deborah, just get on with it!"

As the portly Deborah waddled off to the kitchen, Joseph turned to Ruth. "Ruth, the man in the office with Mary is Joseph Caiaphas who is chief secretary to the high priest in Jerusalem. He knows about Jesus and is asking questions about the Messiah."

"We have been betrayed!"

"It seems so. Now listen carefully. Caiaphas has come here with poorly disguised temple guards in his entourage. He is determined to find Jesus."

"And do what?"

"God knows, but it will not be good. Now go at once to Reuben and tell him what has happened. Then ask him to go immediately to Sepphoris where Jesus and Judas are working on the foundations for the extension to Herod's palace. Tell him to take forty silver and ten gold shekels with him from the Zealot treasury and give them to Judas. Then he must accompany Judas and Jesus and leave Sepphoris without delay and go to the Essene establishment at Qumran where they will be beyond the prying eyes of the high priest. They must not, I repeat not, return to Nazareth. It is no longer safe here. I will delay Caiaphas as long as I can and then go to Sepphoris with him but, by the time we get there, Reuben, Judas and Jesus must be long gone. Is all that clear?"

"Yes."

"Then go now and God be with you. I'll see you this evening when I get back from Sepphoris."

Before five minutes had elapsed, Joseph returned to his office where he found Caiaphas and Mary in seemingly relaxed conversation. "The refreshment is on its way and we are also providing something for your companions," said Joseph as he sat down again beside Mary. "Now where were we?"

"I was asking you if it is true that your son is the Messiah," replied Caiaphas, scarcely masking his irritation at the delay.

"So, we have been informed."

"Ah, then I would like to see him."

"He is working on a building project with Judas."

"Judas? The one sometimes called Sicariot?"

"Yes."

Any lingering doubts Caiaphas might have harboured about Ehud's information were now quashed. He was in no doubt that he was talking to the parents of the true Messiah. He quietly marvelled that this had come to pass in his lifetime. "I must see him," he said starkly.

"Why?" asked Joseph. "He has not yet reached manhood. He is but thirteen years of age so why should I expose him to someone who might have been part of the murderous plot to kill him when he was just born?"

"I was not part of that. It was Herod's order which was carried out by his Galatian guards. No Jew would have implemented an order like that."

"As the Messiah's mother," interjected Mary, "I believe I have the right to question you before allowing you access to my son. You come here with no warning, no invitation and a small army accompanying you demanding this and that. We have no proof you are who you say you are, therefore you must satisfy us before we allow our son to enter the same room as you. It is our duty as parents and guardians of the Messiah. You could be an agent of Rome for all we know."

Caiaphas glanced at Joseph, who nodded his approval of Mary's statement and said, "Can you not see that what my wife says is reasonable? There has already been one attempt on our son's life. Would you not expect us to be cautious?"

Now Caiaphas realised he had pushed too hard. He became his charming self again. "You are right. I should have considered the important matter of identification more carefully before coming here, but I believe I have an answer that will satisfy both of you. Joseph, you said that Jesus is accompanied by the one called Judas Sicariot?"

"Yes."

"You trust him?"

"Totally."

"Good, then if he identifies me will that satisfy you?"

"Certainly."

"Then are you prepared to accompany me to wherever it is that Judas and the Messiah are working together?"

Joseph paused sensing a trap, but Mary answered for him. "If you are prepared to go with my husband and take just two of your bodyguards with you and leave the rest of your little army here, then my husband will take you to the Messiah."

"That is acceptable," replied Caiaphas, who now realised that Joseph would not agree to anything without the approval of his forceful wife. "Can we leave now?" he asked.

"In about an hour," said Joseph. "We will be away for almost a full day, so I must ensure arrangements are in place for the smooth running of the household in my absence."

"And you have not yet taken your refreshment," added Mary.

Caiaphas nodded his acceptance though he was quite certain that any so-called arrangements could easily be organised by Mary without help from her husband. But searching for the Messiah with Joseph's co-operation instead of his opposition was worth an hour's delay.

Meanwhile Ruth had run to the house shared by Reuben and Judas but to her horror, Reuben was not at home. They had no house servant, so she quickly wrote a message using the small roll of parchment and charcoal stick she always carried with her and slipped it under the door. It said:

Reuben,

Jesus is in danger. The high priest knows of him and has sent searchers to Nazareth. I shall now go and warn Jesus and Judas. You, go immediately to Mary at Joseph's house for instructions. Hurry, there is little time.

God be with you,

Ruth.

She desperately hoped Reuben would return soon but she could do no more in Nazareth and set out alone on the five-mile journey to Sepphoris.

But Ruth was not alone. A pair of hungry, lascivious eyes had seen her as she left Joseph's house and, without a second thought about deserting his new master, Ehud slipped away and followed the woman he still regarded as his wife. He watched her as she got no response at the Zealot house, and when he saw her leave Nazareth and head towards Sepphoris, he was easily able to piece together what was happening. Instead of reporting what he had seen to Caiaphas, Ehud followed Ruth for a short while at a respectful distance to ensure he was not recognised. This was not difficult because she was walking fast and he doubted he would catch her anyway so, knowing she was likely to return alone after warning Judas and Jesus, he found a comfortable lair sheltered from the wind in a recently harvested vineyard close to the Sepphoris road and waited. He had plenty of time to decide what he was going to do to his disobedient, wilful wife.

It was more than an hour after Ruth left her message before Reuben returned home. Over the years he had built up his own circle of friends in Nazareth and enjoyed chatting in the marketplace while he purchased provisions for the day. The terror of King Herod's anger at the birth of the Messiah seemed a long time ago, his savagery in Bethlehem murdering all the male babies, a distant memory. But Reuben's relaxed existence was destroyed when he read Ruth's message. He had become complacent! Years of peace had given him a false sense of security that no danger threatened the Messiah at least until the time came when he would make his mission known to all Jews, which was still many years away. Now he was mortified. He had become reasonably comfortable allowing Jesus out of his sight as long as he was accompanied by Judas or one of Joseph's family, but he had not foreseen a visit from the high priest's lackeys. He ran to Joseph's house ashamed and angry with himself for failing in his prime duty; the safety of the Messiah. His humiliation was made worse when he discovered that Joseph had already left the house with Caiaphas, but fortunately Mary was still there to advise him.

"When did they leave?" he asked breathlessly, having just run up the hill from the lower town.

Mary, in control as always, replied, "Sit down Reuben and calm yourself. Everything is under control – I think. What did Ruth's note say?"

"Here it is," answered Reuben as he handed it to her.

After she read it, Mary realised that her eldest son's life was now balanced on a knife edge. "Reuben, you are about an hour behind Joseph and Caiaphas. If Ruth left Nazareth immediately after she left you this note, then she will be arriving at Sepphoris about now.

Therefore, there is nothing you can achieve by following them. Just before he left here my husband told me that Judas and Jesus must flee to the Essenes at Qumran without coming back to Nazareth first. Only there will my son be safe from the malicious intent of the high priest; therefore you must pack everything that will be needed for a long stay with the Essenes which will certainly be months or possibly years. You must go there direct from here. Judas and Jesus will avoid Nazareth so you must go to Qumran and meet them there. You may take one of our donkeys to carry your luggage and take some money from the Zealot treasury to pay for your up-keep amongst the Essenes."

"You know about the treasury?"

"Of course I do Reuben. A good husband and wife have no secrets between them."

"Are you sure I should not go to Sepphoris?"

"Certain! God willing, Judas and Jesus will already have gone. If not they will be arrested or dead by the time you arrive. Go straight to Qumran and prepare old Judah for their arrival."

Reuben left and, as the door closed behind him, Mary knew she had done all she could. Now all that was left was to wait and pray.

Ruth found Judas and Jesus in Sepphoris at about the same time as Reuben was packing the luggage for the indeterminate stay with the Essenes. Judas immediately understood the gravity of the danger approaching them and, after thanking Ruth for her help, left Sepphoris with Jesus for Qumran by the easterly road which followed the Jordan valley and avoided Nazareth.

After a short rest, Ruth started out on the return journey to Nazareth, walking more slowly this time and guessing she was likely to meet Joseph and Caiaphas as they headed north in search of a bird that had already flown. Sure enough, when she was a little less than half-way on her southward journey she saw four men about half a mile away hurrying towards her. She could not be sure who they were until they were almost within hailing distance, but then she recognised the oldest of the four as Joseph, so one of the others must be Caiaphas. Ruth decided not to hail or even acknowledge the approaching group unless she was hailed herself. None of the other three knew her so if Joseph remained silent, so would she.

The road was narrow so she stood to one side, as a respectful Jewish woman should, to let the men pass. Joseph looked her directly in the eyes as they passed by and she gave him the faintest nod. He smiled, knowing that Judas and Jesus had been warned, and prepared himself to face an angry chief secretary to the high priest when he discovered his prey had slipped through his fingers. Caiaphas could say what he liked but Joseph did not care because he would be amongst his own workmen who would ensure their paymaster was not harmed.

Now Ruth continued her journey in good spirits knowing that Mary would be pleased. It was about three hours after noon when, at last, she saw Nazareth on top of its hill no more than a mile away looking warm and welcoming in the afternoon sun light. She was tired and no longer alert. She thought the danger was gone so she failed to notice the movement in the harvested vineyard which lay nestled against a righthand bend in the road ahead. Suddenly, a familiar and unwelcome figure burst out of the vineyard and stopped ten paces in front of her blocking further progress. She quickly looked round to see if there was anyone else in sight, but she was alone.

"Bad luck my dear! There's no-one else here, just you and me."

"What do you want Ehud?"

He laughed, a wicked triumphant laugh that chilled her spine. "What do I want! What do I want, by God! I've waited a long time for this moment, and I shall enjoy it to the fullest!"

Ruth took a step back. "What are you going to do?"

"Take my revenge of course, what else?"

"You cannot. I have Roman protection now."

Ehud shaded his eyes with his hand in an exaggerated gesture of search. "Well, well, I see no Romans here. What a shame! Your last day on this earth will end with me. How appropriate! First, I shall enjoy my rights as your husband and then," he paused and touched the hilt of the dagger in his belt, "I shall slit your throat if a feel merciful or kill you slowly if I do not."

She turned to run but she had already walked the best part of ten miles that day so her legs could not provide the speed she would normally have expected. Ehud caught her in seconds, pulled off her shawl and dragged her by her long, black hair into the vineyard.

Years of marital violence had taught Ruth to ride the blows rather than resist them so, between slaps and punches, she was still able to think. She knew she must fight back or die but Ehud's determination to rape her before murdering her gave Ruth a slim chance of survival. She remembered him touching the hilt of his dagger as he taunted her.

After the next slap, she fell to the ground and rolled on her back pretending to be semi-conscious. The slapping stopped as Ehud knelt over her and began tearing at her clothing. He forced her legs apart with his knees. She could smell the stench of his foul breath as he positioned himself to violate her without troubling to pin her arms down. His rough beard scratched her face. The disgusting animal noises he made, a sort of growling gobble which she had heard so often during their married life, told her that his attention was now fully engaged. She knew she would have only one chance, there could be no fumbling, no mistakes. Fear gave her the strength she needed.

She put her arms round his waist as if welcoming him. She remembered the dagger in his belt was on his left side so she could use her right hand. She touched the hilt with her fingertips then gripped it firmly, withdrew the blade from its sheath and stabbed him hard in his side. The growling stopped. It was probably not a lethal strike, but it went in deep, just below the rib cage. Ehud reared up, grabbed her throat in both hands and began to squeeze. Now panic set in. She stabbed him again but the grip on her throat only tightened. She could no longer breathe but if she lost consciousness she would certainly die. The sky seemed to darken, the end was near. Again, she stabbed him and again and at last his death grip loosened. She gasped for air, the sky brightened again and she wriggled free from the heavy weight above her.

Now blind fury driven by panic and the pent-up anger caused by years of humiliation pushed Ruth into a murderous frenzy. Ehud was still breathing as he slumped forward onto the ground where she had just been lying. She stabbed him wildly in his shoulders, neck and back; anywhere she could strike. She tried to turn him over so she could stab his face and cut his throat and do as much damage as she could to the man she hated, but he was too heavy, so she plunged the knife into his back again and rested to regain her strength. Ehud's body began to twitch and for a terrible moment she wondered if he still had enough life left in him to attack her again. She stabbed him twice more and then his body went still. He let out a long sigh and she heard the death rattle.

She was free of Ehud bar Aaron at last.

***

III

Ruth slowly staggered to her feet, exhausted by her life and death struggle. She looked down at Ehud and then at herself and realised she was covered in his blood. She dropped the dagger and staggered back to the road. No-one was in sight in either direction so, bruised and aching, she made her way back to Nazareth as fast as her weary legs would permit. She managed to cover most of the blood stains with the shawl Ehud had ripped off her before he dragged her into the vineyard, so she was able to reach Joseph's house unchallenged and went straight to Mary who was writing a letter in her day room.

By now Ruth was in the last stages of exhaustion and fell to the floor beside Mary's chair dropping the shawl and revealing her blood-stained clothing. Mary was horrified, thinking at first that the blood was Ruth's. "What happened! Wait here, I'll fetch a healer."

"For God's sake no!" implored Ruth.

"But you're wounded."

"The blood is Ehud's not mine. I have just murdered him!"

Mary gently helped Ruth into her chair and asked, "Are you injured?"

"Battered, bruised but otherwise unhurt but I am very tired. I must sleep."

Knowing full well the penalty for murder, Mary replied, "Soon but not yet. You must tell me exactly what happened. Only then shall I know what to do."

Ruth's account was barely coherent because of her exhaustion, but at the end Mary had heard enough to realise that urgent action was needed. "Listen to me carefully Ruth. What you did was self-defence, not murder, but we cannot rely on the Council of Elders coming to the same conclusion because Joseph cannot take part in any judgement. He will have to stand down as an interested party."

"What then?"

"We must deal with this ourselves. I know you're tired out but I must ask you for one last effort so that I can make sure there is no miscarriage of justice. Ehud's body will soon be found and you will come under suspicion. You must take me to the place where he died, then you may rest. I will do whatever is necessary."

"I need sleep first."

"You cannot! Joseph and Caiaphas are returning from Sepphoris even as we speak. I must dispose of the evidence before they get here. You must come with me now!"

"Very well."

"But first put on some clean clothes and hide what you are wearing until I can burn them."

While Ruth changed her clothes, Mary went to the kitchen and removed a meat cleaver and a large vegetable sack. Then, with Mary cajoling and almost dragging Ruth with her, they set off on the Sepphoris road together. To make matters worse, a cold, penetrating rain set in from the north and Ruth began to shiver and stumble like a drunkard. By the time they reached the vineyard, Mary herself felt her strength starting to ebb but her determination drove her on.

As soon as Ruth showed her the body Mary said, "Now you may rest for a short while. Go back to the road and warn me if anyone is approaching. On no account allow yourself to fall asleep. Do you understand?"

Ruth nodded and stumbled the few paces back to the road.

Biting her lip, Mary took the meat cleaver from the vegetable sack and began hacking at Ehud's neck. Now was not the time for weakness but she felt her stomach heave as she continued her grisly work. It was vital she separate the head from the body in order to prevent identification of the corpse. The neck was thick and meaty but at least the body was cold now, so she could carry out her task without becoming splattered with blood. The meat cleaver was overdue for sharpening and it seemed to take an age to cut through the neck but at last, she managed to sever the last sinew and placed the head, which was surprisingly heavy, into the sack. She remembered to remove Ehud's outer garment, which identified him as a temple servant, and placed it into the bag too, but she failed to see Ehud's dagger lying where Ruth had dropped it because Ruth suddenly re-appeared before she could complete a final search of the area around Ehud's body.

"Mary, come quickly. Four men are approaching from the Sepphoris direction. I think it may be Joseph's group."

"How far away?"

"About a quarter of a mile."

"What! Is that all! You fell asleep didn't you?"

"Sorry."

"Then hurry. At least this road is on a bend. We must be out of sight before they get here."

Fear released unexpected reserves of strength in both women and, before Joseph and an angry Caiaphas rounded the bend, they had disappeared beneath the crest of a small hill. Soon they reached the quarry where Ruth had almost been executed three years before.

"Mary panted, "Can you get home from here alone?"

"Why?"

Mary held up the sack. "I must dispose of this."

"Where?"

"In the town cess pit yonder. No-one will search there."

"Yes, I can manage from here."

"Good. Then go now and go straight to bed and, if anyone questions you, just say you're ill."

"What about Joseph?"

"I'll get back before him and be washed and scrubbed as if I've been at home all day. Now go!"

Mary needed all her strength to cast the heavy bag into the stinking ordure of the cess pit. She allowed herself a few precious seconds to watch it sink out of sight then fled back towards Nazareth. As she entered the day room she had left an hour earlier, she just had time to reflect upon the appropriate ending of the horrible Ehud before vomiting into an empty fruit bowl.

But Ehud still had a sting in his tail even from beyond the grave or, in his case, the cess pit.

***

IV

When Judas and Jesus reached Qumran three days later, Reuben was waiting for them. He had already briefed Judah, the Teacher of Righteousness, about the plight of the young Messiah and his mentor; consequently, accommodation had been prepared for both of them.

As before, Judas, Jesus and Reuben met Judah as representatives of the Zealot sect in the house where they had first met but this time it was Judah who spoke first. "You are early. Did we not agree to meet again when Jesus is fourteen years old?"

While Judas was considering his response, Jesus answered for him. "That is true Teacher of Righteousness, but circumstances have changed as you already know, and I shall be fourteen years old in less than three months." Judah turned his old head from the adults and faced Jesus, but before he could speak Jesus added, "And you're not getting any younger."

The dark, hawk-like eyes on either side of the beaked nose twinkled as the thin lips broke into a disarming smile. "You are bold for your age young man."

"It is probably ignorance Teacher of Righteousness. I did not mean to be impertinent, just direct."

"There is nothing wrong with what you said. In fact boldness spawned from bravery should be encouraged. Have you learned much since we last met?"

"Yes. Judas my guardian has taught me languages, politics

and religion and I have also had my revelations."

"How many?"

"Four, Teacher of Righteousness." That answer surprised Judas because Jesus had said nothing to him about the fourth revelation.

"Would you like to speak to me about them?"

"Yes, but it will take a long time."

"Then I shall make time for you tomorrow." Turning back to Judas and Reuben, Judah said, "I have not heard much but I have heard enough to know that the Messiah is with us. He shall have the protection of the Essenes for as long as he needs it and he will also have the companionship of his cousin, John, son of his aunt, Elizabeth. John already dwells here."

At that moment not even Judah could have foreseen the unwelcome rivalry that would develop between the two young men.

Early next morning, Reuben requested a meeting with Judas alone. "Let us sit outside and enjoy the view over the Great Salt Sea while we talk," he said. Judas did not like the sound of this. 'Enjoying views' was not usually part of Reuben's down to earth manner. He seemed to be trying to put Judas at ease but something unpleasant was obviously going to come up. Reuben remained silent for a while as they sat side by side on a flat rock just outside Qumran in the early morning sunlight. Judas thought, it's going to be a pleasant day but not for me.

"You no doubt realise," began Reuben, "That had it not been for the quick wits and bravery of Ruth, both you and Jesus would now be in the custody of the high priest."

"Yes, I do realise that but, thanks to Ruth, all is well now."

"For you and Jesus yes, but not for me. I failed in my duty

as your Shadow, and I see now that I have lost my edge."

"Nonsense Reuben! You are as sharp as ever."

"Thank you, Judas, but you are wrong. I have been your Shadow since Jesus was a baby. I have enjoyed the comfort of living in Nazareth and being one of the select few who have befriended the Messiah, but it is time for me to hand over my responsibilities to a younger man. I should never have allowed either of you to go alone to Sepphoris yet, during the past few years, I have permitted such things to happen without a second thought because I believed we were safe in Nazareth."

"Reuben, you are too hard on yourself. You must not go. We need you."

Reuben continued as if Judas had not spoken. "At least I know you will both be safe here with the Essenes while I go to Jerusalem to report to Isaac, my commander. He will no doubt consult with bar Abbas in Bethlehem before selecting my replacement, so you will not hear anything for a week or so."

"As soon as that?"

"Remember that while we are here the entire treasury of the Zealot sect lies unguarded under the floor of our house! We must get a Shadow there as soon as possible, don't you agree?"

"Of course I do."

"I shall make two recommendations to Isaac in view of my failure three days ago. The first will be that any Shadow guarding you and Jesus should be replaced after two years. I became too comfortable in Nazareth and the result was we almost lost the Messiah. The second will be that we must move the Zealot treasury somewhere safer. The high priest now knows that Jesus' home is in Nazareth so we can be sure that the town will be carefully watched. Strangers come and go every day. The treasury should be moved to a less conspicuous place."

"And soon," agreed Judas. "Our revenue is increasing almost by the day with the security of peace. I was already wondering how we would store it because there is almost no space left under our front room floor!"

"Finally," said Reuben, "It is time I had a family. I am almost thirty-one years old and my mother has found a nice girl for me at home in Hebron. I shall ask Isaac if I can be allocated duties more fitting for a married man although I shall always be available if the Messiah needs me."

Judas could see there was no point in trying to persuade Reuben to change his mind. He had obviously thought deeply about this even before Caiaphas' attempt to arrest Jesus, so he simply said, "Reuben, then now is the moment I must thank you from the bottom of my heart for your fourteen years of dedicated service to the Messiah and myself. I wish you good fortune in your future life and many fine children."

The exile amongst the Essenes was to last far longer than either Judas or Jesus expected, and the eventual reason for their return to Nazareth was even more unexpected. But before the end of the year something happened in the distant west which was to have far reaching consequences for the Roman empire as dark rumours concerning the fate of an entire Roman army began to emerge from the misty forests of Germania.

CHAPTER EIGHT

Varus, Governor of Germania Magna, frittered away the entire summer at his camp beside the River Weser dispensing justice, as he saw it, and collecting taxes from the local German tribes in exchange for the benefits of Roman peace. Sadly, the Germans saw it differently. To them Roman law was complex and cumbersome. The traditional German way of settling differences was either by a decree from the tribal chief or trial by combat, which was quick and final though admittedly quite often unjust. As for taxation, the Germans saw this as downright robbery by the occupying power. They had nothing like this in their own society. Varus made a big mistake by imposing taxation far too soon, as I was about to discover.

It was the middle of a hot August when I was summoned to Piso's tent near the north gate of our camp by the bank of the Weser. He seemed ill at ease. "Lucius, our tax gatherers are coming under increasing risk of physical assault as they go about their duties. They need our protection."

"No tax gatherers are popular," I replied, "But legionary support seems a bit excessive."

"I would normally agree with you, but the tax gatherers are not Roman administrators doing a peace-time job."

"Who are they then?"

"Gallic auxiliaries. Don't ask me why Varus is using them to carry out such a sensitive task, but I suspect he has not taken the trouble to find out more about them. In fact they are from the Nervi tribe who are part of the Gallic confederation called the Belgae. The great Julius Caesar recorded that they were the toughest opponents he ever faced in Gaul."

"I am none the wiser sir."

"Then you have clearly not read Caesar's account of his Gallic wars. The Nervi live close to the border with Germania Magna a little further downstream on the Rhine from Vetera. There is a long history of raids and counter raids between the Belgae and the nearby German tribes which includes our own brave allies the Batavi. Consequently, there is no love lost between the Germans and our Gallic allies who are using the opportunity Varus has given them to settle old scores under the guise of taxation. Our governor could hardly have made a worse choice even if he tried. The Gallic cohort needs to be restrained otherwise Varus' illusion that the German tribes west of the Weser are pacified will dissolve into flames."

"Now I understand sir. We must ensure that our Gallic allies behave properly."

"Exactly so, which is why your mission requires delicate handling and careful management."

"Thank you, sir. When do we leave?"

"Tomorrow morning. The Gallic commander, Allix, outranks you but I shall make sure he understands why you are with him and what the consequences will be if he contravenes your wishes."

"I understand sir. I shall go and prepare my century now."

"One more thing Lucius. You will be away for at least seven days so you need to know that the rest of my cohort will have been transferred to the River Lippe camp by the time you return."

"The camp where we parted company with our river-borne

supply transport?"

"Yes, so do not return here but come back on a more westerly route direct to the Lippe. We have been ordered to take our turn there guarding the army's line of retreat should it ever be needed."

"Is there a road we can use or must we cut across country?"

"It seems that Tiberius built a road during his last campaign in this area thirteen years ago. It should still be there, if a little overgrown, but Allix knows where it is, so he'll be able to guide you."

Ironically, if I had not asked about that road, I would not now be alive to write this story.

We departed just after dawn the next morning. Of course, I already had a passing acquaintance with Allix but I did not really know him. We met by the west gate of the Weser camp. The three squadrons, which were half of his four hundred strong cohort, were drawn up outside the camp ready for the march. To me, they looked very much like the Germans and their fine, large horses could easily have been Batavian, but as people they could not have been more different. In contrast to the dour Germans, the Nervi Gauls were cheerful, friendly fellows who lived life to the fullest. They seemed to have no cares in the world and were proud of being part of the Roman empire. Their commander handed his horse's reins to his deputy and strode towards me. He was short and stout, rather like Friedrich, but his hair was remarkable not so much for its fullness and length, but for its colour which was a bright, burnished copper that seemed to shine in the early morning sunlight.

We shook hands and he said in surprisingly cultured Latin, "I am Allix."

"Just Allix?"

He laughed. "You would not be able to pronounce my first name."

"I am Lucius Veranius. I look forward to working with you."

"And giving those German bastards a good kick up the arse!"

"I don't believe that is part of my orders Allix."

He laughed again. "Then we shall use our initiative. Where would you like my squadrons?"

"Two squadrons in front of my century and the third behind if you please. Do you know where we are going?"

"There is an Angrivarian settlement two days' march northwest of here. It's large by German standards so we'll collect our taxes there."

"What form will these taxes take? The Germans have no coinage."

"At the moment I've no idea, but we'll find out when we get there. If we mount up now, we should be able to cover about twenty miles a day if your foot sloggers are up to it."

"Excellent! Then let's get started."

And so, we set off with my seventy legionaries accompanied by three times their number of chattering Gauls, but I had deep misgivings about how difficult it was going to be controlling these cheerful fellows when it came to extracting taxes from their arch enemies.

We saw nothing of the Angrivarii on the march, save for a few herds of goats managed by skulking children which, I suppose, was hardly surprising as they were sure to know what our intentions were. The Germans always seemed to be well informed about what we were about to do. On the second day of the march we entered a dense forest of huge, broad trunked trees that cast so much shadow it was almost like marching at night. My men were nervous of marching in woodland where it was impossible to see more than a few yards either side of the track, but the Gauls seemed untroubled so we continued at a good pace because the summer had been dry and the ground was firm. Consequently, we reached the Angrivarian settlement about an hour before noon of the second day of the march which was obviously earlier than the Germans expected.

The scene that greeted us was a picture of domesticity. The settlement was just a clearing in the forest no more than eighty paces wide at its greatest extent. Women were cooking over open fires, collecting water from a small dew pond and tending groups of children playing near animal pens beside the forest edge. Most of the men were doing nothing as far as I could see except drinking that horrible brew of barley that they call beer, which is the only way to get drunk this far north where vines refuse to grow.

Our arrival clearly took them by surprise. One of the women shouted a warning as the first of the Gauls emerged from the forest. The other women quickly abandoned their domestic tasks and gathered the children, about forty of them, into a group at the far side of the clearing.

Most of the men were too drunk to stand, though a few managed to stagger to their feet aided by their womenfolk. It looked as though the Gauls would be able to take what they wanted, but they reckoned without the spirited nature of German women.

Allix, who like many of his people spoke German to some extent called out, "Who commands here?"

A tall, straight-backed woman of about forty years of age stepped forward and replied in their guttural language. Allix dismounted and they conversed for a few moments. The conversation ended when the woman stepped back and shouted, "Nein! Nein!" Then she called to all those in hearing distance and suddenly the peaceful scene of a few seconds before turned into mayhem. Those German men who could still stand fumbled for their weapons which lay strewn across the ground while the women grabbed whatever was nearest to hand, wooden poles, branding irons, fire pokers, anything that could be used as a weapon and began attacking the Gauls who were in the process of dismounting from their horses. I ordered my men to stand back as we beheld a scene unfold before us that was totally unforgettable.

Initially, Allix's men were caught off guard and quickly yielded ground as the all-female assault struck them. Helmets flew off, spear shafts snapped and shields clanged as the improvised weapons delivered vicious, powerful blows that could easily crack bones and break skulls. The drunken German men were worse than useless. Waving their axes and clubs at any shape their blurred eyes could see, they were more a danger to each other than us, but their women were managing well enough without them. My men began to laugh but the laughing soon stopped when a fallen Gaul had his brains smashed out by two ferocious German women.

Now I was obliged to intervene. "Our Gallic allies are under attack. We must help them! File leaders, keep your men close to you and do what you must to help the Gauls. Be in no doubt, those women will kill you if they can. You must not hold back. They are the enemy! Forward!" We trotted into the clearing in ten groups of seven, each file leader choosing his point of attack. The two squadrons of Gauls, which numbered about one hundred and fifty men, were beginning to recover and, despite most of my men ignoring my order not to hold back, military weapons and discipline quickly began to assert themselves. When two of my files got close to the children, the tall woman who had given the order to fight barked out another order. Immediately the women broke off the fight and ran to form a protective cordon around their children. Leaving a few Gauls to keep an eye on the useless German men, we approached the cordon and stopped about twenty paces away while Allix went forward and spoke to the tall woman again. This time she did not speak. Instead, she just nodded acceptance of whatever it was Allix said and signalled the women and children to sit down.

By now the third Gallic squadron, which had been our rear guard, arrived at the clearing. They remained mounted, ready to hunt down any German foolish enough to attempt to run away while Allix came over to me, stepping over the body of one of his two troopers who had been killed in the short but vicious fight. "Lucius, we must hurry. I am not sure how long I can restrain my men. They want to avenge their fallen comrades."

"That is only natural."

"I have told that she-wolf that we will take all their pigs, cattle, goats and horses in taxation and compensation for the deaths of my comrades, but we will allow their children to remain with them instead of taking them as slaves. She has agreed but we must get away from here before the men sober up and the rest, who are out harvesting, return. They are probably hurrying back even as we speak. Those screeching women must have been heard miles away."

I looked over Allix's shoulder. "It looks like your troopers are taking their revenge on the men already. They've speared most of them."

"Yes, but just like your men, they held back from the women who were the ones who killed my two troopers. Now they want to rape the women, all of them, then kill them but there isn't time."

"Just as well. This is supposed to be a peaceful tax gathering mission."

Allix shrugged. "And our governor says the Angrivarii are pacified. I'd hate to see how an unpacified German tribe behaves."

***

II

As Piso had predicted, Allix was familiar with this part of Germania Magna and had no difficulty locating the direct road south to the Lippe which Tiberius had built. The 'taxation' that the Gauls extracted from the Angrivarii slowed us down considerably; there are few beasts more obstinate than pigs who do not want to leave home. I was sure the Angrivarii would catch up with us but, strangely, they did not pursue. It was almost as if they were biding their time.

As soon as we reached the camp on the Lippe, Piso called me to his tent. The summons was urgent, so I did not have time to enjoy the bath I was looking forward to after six days on the march. It was late in the day but the sun was still warm and I gladly accepted the goblet of wine that Piso offered me as I sat down to give my report.

"Lucius, I will hear your report after I have given you my news," he said as he filled a goblet for himself. "Our army will leave the Weser camp on the seventh day of September."

"That seems early to go into winter quarters."

"I know, but we will be following a different route to Vetera and fighting a battle or two on the way. Arminius has informed our governor that Cheruscan territory has been raided by Bructeri and Angrivarii war parties. Varus wanted to deal with the matter through legal means, but Arminius persuaded him that a show of force is necessary if peaceful Germans like the Cherusci are going to retain their faith in the much vaunted Roman peace that Varus has been preaching about all summer. Their confidence has already been shaken by the simple fact that the Roman peace failed to prevent the attack on Cheruscan land in the first place. All German eyes are now on the Governor of Germania and the action he takes."

Somehow, I could not stop myself feeling that the change in our route back to the Rhine and the lack of pursuit by the Angrivarii were linked, but I could not explain why, so I simply asked, "What are the orders for your cohort sir?"

"To send whatever taxes you have secured by river back to Vetera, then march quickly back to the Weser leaving just one century here to guard this camp. I have decided that century will be our first century."

"Marcus Sempronius'?"

"Yes."

The thought of the arrogant Marcus having to load all those awkward pigs and cattle onto boats pleased me. "Then when do we leave for the Weser camp?"

"Tomorrow. Marcus Sempronius is ordered to remain here until the first day of October and, if he has received no further orders by then, to embark his century on boats if available, or failing that, march back to Aliso and report to Caedicius for further orders. Now I will hear your report."

The seventh day of September duly arrived and the entire army of Germania Magna assembled outside the Weser camp in review order ready for the march to commence. But the start was delayed by a few hours for two reasons. Firstly, Varus wished to convey a message to every man concerning where we were going and why. Secondly, this day coincided with the men's quarterly payday which always put the soldiers in fine spirits. In later years some critics claimed that Varus' army was too small for the task expected of it and, with the benefit of hindsight, they were right, but on that sunny, early autumn morning the sight of all three legions plus auxiliaries, thirteen thousand fighting men deployed across the open plain of the Weser valley made us feel invincible. Even though the legions were under strength at about four thousand men each, they still stretched six miles on the line of march. When added to the auxiliary cavalry cohorts, baggage train, pack animals and essential camp technicians such as wheelwrights, blacksmiths, carpenters, farriers, medics and so on, the army column was nearly ten miles long which meant that the head of the column was well over half-way to its next camp for the night before the rear guard had even left the morning camp.

Varus' message to the men was given to the cohort commanders who then rode back to their cohorts and relayed the message directly to their soldiers. In essence it was that the army was going to return to Vetera by a different but shorter route so that the two rebellious tribes, the Bructeri and the Angrivarii, could be chastised for breaking Roman peace by raiding the land of our allies, the Cherusci. Arminius, a prince of the Cherusci, was even now riding to gather his formidable tribesmen whom he would bring up to support us and help teach the Bructeri and the Angrivarii a lesson they would never forget. And to ensure our soldiers would warm to their task, Varus gave them permission to loot and destroy any settlements they came across.

When Piso finished relaying this message to the fifth cohort, he turned to his centurions who were standing beside him and added quietly, "So much for pacification. It would seem that this summer's campaign has been a complete waste of time."

The column set off about midmorning. Arminius left a Cheruscan squadron behind to lead the march while he went off to gather his army. We were in Cheruscan territory so his troopers knew the land well. They were followed by the Seventeenth legion, then Varus and his headquarters staff. After that came our legion, the Eighteenth, followed by the baggage train and the Nineteenth legion. Finally, Allix's Gallic cavalrymen formed the rearguard but there was another, unofficial group who followed the column a few miles behind the Gauls. Varus had ordered all non-essential camp followers, tradesmen, merchants, cats and the like, to leave the Weser and make their way to the Lippe camp where they could embark on supply ships and travel downstream to Vetera in safety. Most obeyed, but about fifty hardy souls who were well aware that the soldiers had just been paid, decided to follow the army and make some easy money. Sadly, this group included five cats.

We saw no sign of the enemy during the first day's march, so we covered the regulation daily target of sixteen miles by early evening and made camp without incident. But the next day everything changed. We resumed the march just after dawn in the same marching order as before and all went well until midmorning when the head of the column entered dense, heavy forest. Here the path narrowed, and the pace of the march soon slowed down. The width restriction caused the army to string out and by the time the rear guard entered the forest the length of the column had stretched to at least twelve miles.

The effect of the gloomy forest on our men was startling. Normally when on the march they would chatter, laugh at bawdy jokes and sing equally bawdy marching songs but now, marching in the shadows of huge, ancient trees which had watched the comings and goings of puny humans for many centuries, they all fell silent. All I could hear was the trudge of feet on the forest floor; which was soft and springy from the rotting detritus of hundreds of seasons of fallen leaves, and the occasional barked order from a centurion or file leader. Even when the men had cause to speak, it was with the hush of lowered voices, as if malignant spirits of the trees were hunting for them.

And all the while we wondered where the Germans were. To them the forest, which was oppressive to us, was friendly and protective. While they knew every path, almost every deer track, we were lost and far from home in a hostile land relying on the goodwill of Germans who only Varus trusted.

The attack hit us about noon. The first we knew of it was the sound of warning shouts and war cries coming from somewhere near the front of the army. The column soon ground to a halt. There was nothing we could do except wait. Orders from the front of the army would take hours to reach us, so we made ready to receive an attack and then sat down to eat our midday rations. It would have been madness to leave the path and struggle through the forest which was already crawling with German tribesmen.

After a while the sound of fighting began to subside but only to be replaced by another attack, this time at the rear of the column. We were just as powerless to help as we had been when the first attack struck, but it was a reasonable guess that we would be on the receiving end of the third attack. Sure enough, about an hour later we heard movement amongst the trees on our right. We formed two lines, shields locked together and prepared ourselves, while a third line faced about in the opposite direction in case the Germans launched a surprise assault from there. My mouth was dry with tension. This sort of warfare did not suit our style of fighting. I looked right and left at the men standing beside me. Their jaws were set and their bodies rigid as they stared into the green gloom, willing the attack to come soon. I was sure they would acquit themselves well this day.

The quiet of the forest was shattered by a booming German war cry. The trees seemed to erupt with wild, vengeful tribesmen. They charged in small, tight knit groups and thundered into our shield wall yelling and screaming. These were large men by our standards and the legionaries had to dig deep into their reserves of strength to withstand the shock. I remembered my centurion's calm voice when I first encountered a German attack and did my best to emulate him.

Our shield wall bent but did not break. We gave ground, but not much, and the furious assault quickly spent itself like waves on a rocky shore. This gave me a few precious seconds to appraise our enemy. They were indeed vigorous and frightening, but they were poorly equipped and unarmoured. Many carried wooden cudgels as their primary weapon and most of the others short, wide bladed stabbing spears. A few carried the short Roman gladius sword that had doubtless been taken from some of our men earlier in the day, but they were ineffective because the Germans did not know how to use them. In the legions we would sharpen the points of our swords and the blades for just a few inches above them. The rest of the blade was left blunt because the gladius was a thrusting weapon designed to kill or debilitate at the first blow. The tribesmen wielded them as slashing weapons, which was their instinct, but the blades above the point were no sharper than the day the blacksmith first made them, so while they might cause a fine bruise or two, they could not cut properly. The Germans certainly made plenty of noise as they hammered on our shields but very soon my men, who were mostly veterans, realised that beneath the frenzy they had little to fear if they kept their discipline.

I still do not know if we were fighting the Angrivarii or the Bructeri, all German tribesmen looked the same to me, but once the charge had been held and the deadly gladius began its work in Roman hands, the tribesmen broke and ran for the cover of the forest. I do not remember killing anyone but my sword blade was covered in blood, none of which was mine. My century cheered with relief and elation as the Germans fled, but the skirmish had cost us too as I could tell by the number of bodies on the ground which included my dear old file leader, Galerius, who lay on his back staring upwards with lifeless eyes and a spear in his guts.

"Stand fast and stay on the path!" I shouted as some of the bolder souls in my century started to pursue their foe. "File leaders to me with a casualty report!"

The first to come in was Rufio, the big Pannonian who had been with me for fifteen years. His helmet was dented. He laughed, "That was lively! But more bluster than substance. Two slightly wounded but still fit to fight. One dead."

"Thank you. Galerius fell today."

The smile left Rufio's face. He and Galerius were old friends. "I am saddened to hear that. Galerius would have been a difficult man to kill. Maybe one of those damned beardless warriors caught him by surprise."

"What do you mean? All Germans are unshaven."

"That's what I thought but there were some beardless ones today. We assumed they were boys, but we were wrong. You saw what happened at the Angrivarian settlement when we tried to extract taxes from them last month."

"Yes, but what of it?"

"Well, while some of my men were checking German corpses for plunder, they found two clean shaven Germans. On closer examination they turned out to be women!"

"So German women sometimes fight alongside their men?"

"It seems so, but we should not be surprised."

"True. Rufio, pass the word to the other file leaders. I'll do the same for the other centuries as soon as I can."

"Yes, sir."

Rufio turned to go but I stopped him. "And one more thing Rufio. We lost Galerius today, so take care of yourself. I cannot bear the thought of losing two old friends on the same day."

The big Pannonian smiled, "I'll be careful sir."

The march resumed. It was excruciatingly slow and made worse by an outbreak of heavy rain which was enough to turn the woodland path into a morass as thousands of feet, hooves and wheels trampled along it. But at least it seemed to deter the Germans from attacking us again that day and, as evening drew near, the head of the column at last broke out of the forest into open terrain once more. As soon as the army was clear of the trees, Varus ordered us to halt for the day and pitch camp. It was still pouring with rain but our spirits lifted now that we were rid of that interminable forest gloom for a while. Our cohort was one of the lucky ones which was ordered to erect our tents and dry out while others dug the ditch and rampart that would surround our square shaped camp. The Nineteenth legion was the least fortunate of all because to its men fell the task of guard duty in case the tribesmen attempted a surprise attack while the camp was being constructed.

The Germans, who must have been even colder and wetter than we were, remained quiet, and by the time Piso called his centurions to his tent to tell us about the council of war he had just attended we had eaten our evening rations and dried out nicely beside the campfires.

"Centurions," he said, "You will be pleased to know that our losses in the fighting today were quite light for the most part, and that tomorrow we shall remain here and rest before continuing the march."

Marcus Aius, commander of the fourth century and the joker amongst us replied, "Excellent! And let us pray to the gods that the Germans attack us here where we can at least see what we're doing!"

Piso smiled. "I doubt they'll be so stupid Marcus. They took a beating today even though it might not feel that way to us. Another reason for waiting here for a day is to give Arminius and his Cherusci time to catch up with us. With the addition of his nine thousand warriors, Varus is convinced we shall soon win a great victory."

Caius exchanged glances with me and said, "Doesn't it depend on whose side Arminius is really on? The squadron he left with us to be our guides disappeared during the fighting today."

"Captured or killed?" speculated Septimus Nasica.

"That could be one explanation," acknowledged Piso, "But there is another possibility which Caius has just hinted at."

"That doesn't bear thinking about," muttered Gnaeus Servilius. "If Arminius has betrayed us, we could be facing disaster."

"Even if he has," said Piso, "Three understrength legions should still be enough to deal with the Cherusci too as long as we stay out in the open and avoid that infernal forest. In any event, we will soon know. Early tomorrow morning, two scouting parties will be sent out. One will head west to try and locate the Bructeri and the Angrivarii, who have for the moment disappeared. The other will return the way we have just come, find Arminius and urge him to get his warriors here as soon as he can so that we can conclude this campaign as quickly as possible. I know some of you have misgivings about Arminius but, so far, he has shown total loyalty to Rome."

"So, there's no truth in the rumour that Segestes, Arminius' own father-in-law, has warned Varus not to trust Arminius?" asked Gnaeus.

"I cannot answer that, but it is true that the relationship between the two Germans is bad because Arminius married Segestes' daughter without his permission. It might be that this rumour is a means by which Segestes can pay Arminius back."

"The plain fact is," I said, "there is nothing we can do about Arminius and his intentions now, but we'll know by tomorrow night."

"Thank you, Lucius," responded Piso, "So, all of you return to your tents, get a good night's sleep and enjoy your rest day tomorrow. Obviously, not a word of this discussion to your men. They will need to be in good heart whatever happens."

The torrential rain continued throughout the following day, removing any remote hopes we had that the Germans might attack our camp. The scouts who had been sent forward returned in the early afternoon and reported no sign of the tribesmen ahead, but the route we were following plunged back into the forest again within two miles of our camp. This was disheartening news, but as the day wore on without any sign of the return of the scouting party sent to find Arminius, the terrible truth began to dawn even on Varus.

By nightfall there was a remarkable change in the Governor of Germania Magna. Gone was the aging, slothful leader looking for ultimate glory without bothering to put in the effort needed to achieve such fame. Now, those like me who had known him as a younger man saw the re-emergence of the intelligent and resourceful general who had been successful against the tough Alpine tribes and the warlike peoples of the Upper Danube, pacifying the desert nomads of North Africa and firmly crushing a major rebellion in Judea. He summoned his legates and senior cohort commanders and gave them clear, unambiguous orders for the following day. The army would resume its march westwards with the intention of subjugating the Angrivarii and the Bructeri and, if necessary, the Cherusci too. Having achieved that task, we would continue our march until we came into contact with proven German allies, the Batavi and the Frisii, and when we reached the Rhine we would embark on boats up the river to Vetera where we would go into winter quarters. It all sounded so simple.

Due to the dreadful ground conditions, all wheeled transport would be left behind because struggling to drive carts through thick mud would cut our daily mileage by half. Also, abandoning the vehicles would shorten the length of the column by at least a quarter and improve battlefield communication which was lacking during the fighting two days previously. Only essential equipment would be taken with us carried by pack animals and the soldiers themselves. The severely wounded who could not walk or ride would be carried on litters.

For this part of the march, the Eighteenth legion formed the rear guard with Allix's Gallic cohort behind us. Behind them, the hapless camp followers were beginning to realise that they had made a terrible mistake by disobeying Varus' order to go to the Lippe camp and embark for Vetera.

And so, we marched towards the climax of Varus' bid for everlasting fame, still hopeful that victory was within our grasp.

***

III

We set off early next morning full of apprehension about entering the forest again, but there was no choice because Varus was determined not to re-trace his steps; that would be admitting defeat. We, the rear guard, had been in the forest for less than half an hour when the attacks began again. This time they were much more intense. Instead of assaulting parts of our column in sequence, the whole length of the army was attacked at the same time. The Germans must have been heavily reinforced to enable them to do that; we could guess who by. Some of the newcomers were wearing Roman style helmets and mail shirts, the sort our Cheruscan auxiliaries wore. Arminius had openly declared himself at last.

My century was bringing up the rear of the Eighteenth legion with the Gauls close behind us when we fell victim to a particularly ferocious attack which seemed to be designed to separate us from the Gauls. Allix's men were walking and leading their horses, which was the surest way of getting their fine mounts safely through the sodden ground already churned up by the rest of the army. Consequently, they were obliged to fight with one hand only, or let their horses loose. The Germans sensed victory and fought with much more vigour than previously. It was impossible to send messages for help up the column; the path was blocked by the fighting. We were on our own. It was do or die.

We managed to beat off the first attack but the Germans

would soon be back, so during the lull I called Rufio and Allix to me. "Rufio, what of your file?"

"Down to five fit for duty including me sir."

"And Nubi?"

"He's still fit, and well and itching for more." Nubi was a dark-skinned soldier from Nubia, south of our Egyptian province. He was also large, fast and athletic, just the sort of fellow for the task I had in mind. "Tell Nubi to force his way through the column and run to cohort headquarters. Then he must tell Piso that my century has suffered heavy losses and will not be able to withstand another attack without help. We will stand our ground here for as long as we can."

As Rufio ran back to his file, I turned to Allix. "Your brave men are no use as cavalry in this forest. You must fight as foot soldiers. Let your horses go if necessary."

"I cannot give my men an order like that," he answered, "Because I know they will not obey it. Our horses mean everything to us. We can certainly fight dismounted but one in five of my men will need to come out of the line to tether five horses each and a squadron of fifty will be required to guard them. That leaves a few less than two hundred to fight on foot alongside you."

"Then that will have to be sufficient. Order it now!"

Fortunately the tribesmen gave us a full half hour before they came back and by then Allix had prepared his cohort. My men were ready too but there was no sign of help coming from headquarters. There was also a yawning gap of about two hundred paces between my left hand file and the next in line in the column, so there was every chance that the next attack would cut us off from the rest of the army. My century was now down to just forty-one men fit for combat, as a German war howl announced the next assault. They emerged from the forest at a steady, determined trot. When fighting in woodland, it was always impossible to tell how many men you faced but there seemed to be many hundreds of them. Together, my century and the dismounted Gauls numbered just two hundred and thirty. Instinctively the legionaries huddled closer together, shutting off any gaps in our ranks. The Gauls did the same and we braced ourselves for what was to come.

When the leading Germans were just twenty paces from our line, I bawled out the order to hurl the last of our pila at the wave of screaming humanity intent on our destruction. As always, the pila did their deadly work and slowed the assault, but we were already exhausted and the weight of the attack forced us back off the path and almost into the forest behind us. On our right the Gauls were pushed back too but they remained in contact with us and the line held, but on our left where our flank was unprotected, the Germans were already enveloping us and would soon be able to take us from behind. As the pressure grew our line began to break up from the left. It looked like the end. I had no more orders to give. All that we could do was to fight and stay alive for as long as possible.

Then suddenly the pressure eased. We were at the mercy of the tribesmen, who were well led and fighting with skill, but they began to back away as if we had suddenly doubled our numbers. The war howls stopped, the tumult went quiet, then almost as one they turned and ran. I looked towards our endangered left flank and saw about eighty paces away Nubi leading Roman legionaries, coming to our aid at a fast trot. It was our second century commanded by Gnaeus Servilius. I blessed him, Nubi, Piso and anyone else I could think of as I staggered to greet them like a drunken man, exhausted but elated.

Gnaeus glanced at the bodies scattered around the battleground. "Looks like you've been busy here Lucius."

"Never have I been happier to see you Gnaeus!"

"You can thank Piso and this large, black legionary beside me for that."

I looked at the Nubian. "Thank you Nubi. Your conduct today will be recorded in the cohort log. Now return to your file and rest. You deserve it."

Nubi just smiled and left. He knew that all distinguished battlefield conduct was rewarded in Piso's cohort.

"Lucius, are you wounded?" asked Gnaeus.

"I don't think so, apart from some shallow cuts on my sword arm, but I've lost many men today, far too many."

"I'm afraid that's true for the whole army. We've taken a battering. The casualty reports were just starting to come in when I left cohort headquarters to help you."

"Has the fighting finished then?"

"It seems that way. Yours was the last action. The Germans have had enough for today."

"And all the gods know, so have I! I must check on Allix and the Gauls. They covered our right flank and fought manfully too."

"Then I'll come with you while my men help to tend to your wounded. My century escaped lightly this day compared to some."

It was now about midday and the march resumed. There were no more attacks and, as a result, we covered at least five more miles before the head of the column broke out of the forest and entered open terrain once more. Now, our scouts could see more clearly the options open to us. To our left, the west where we had just left the forest, was a range of hills covered by woodland which looked distinctly uninviting to us. On our right was a vast area of open marshland which would give us a good early view of an enemy approach but might also swallow us up in bog and quicksand. But to the northwest, between these two alternatives, there seemed to be a pass which should lead us direct to our truest allies, the Batavi. Between us and the pass was a spur of unforested high ground jutting out from the hills on our left which would have excellent views all round. It made an ideal location for our next camp and Varus directed the army towards it.

While we were constructing the camp, Varus ordered all of our cavalry, which numbered about nine hundred riders, to leave the army, ride hard for the pass and try to reach the Batavi with orders for them to come to our aid. There was still no sign of the enemy, so they departed immediately. We watched them go with mixed feelings. True, it would be good to have our Batavian friends fighting alongside us, but how long must we wait for them? Meanwhile, we would be marching blindfolded in hostile territory with no vanguard or rear guard. Nevertheless, the cavalry made a fine sight as they cantered into the open plain under the command of Numonius Vala, our legionary cavalry tribune who I hardly knew but whose reputation was that of a dashing, fearless leader.

I turned my attention back to the squads digging the ditch which would protect the east side of the camp but only a minute or so later, I heard groans of despair coming from those who were still watching Vala's men. I scrambled out of the ditch and my heart sank as I saw a body of horsemen, many thousands strong, appear over a ridge in the east riding hard to head off

Vala's troopers from reaching the pass. Although their horses were fresh, our men were already tired, and it soon became clear that their escape route would be blocked before they could reach it. Worse still, the leading enemy squadrons were wearing the armour and accoutrements of Roman auxiliary cavalry. They could only be Arminius' Cheruscan cohort.

Allix's Gauls were the first to see the position was hopeless and drew rein. After a brief pause during which Allix must have given his orders, they scattered into small groups and galloped southwards in the direction of our camp on the Lippe where Sempronius and our first century were blithely unaware of the disaster unfolding fifty miles north of them. Allix was pursued by at least three times his number of Cheruscans, but that still left more than enough Germans to overwhelm and annihilate Vala and the remainder of his horsemen.

The effect on our morale was devastating. Until now we had always assumed our leaders were in control and that, after some hard fighting, we would ultimately win through as Romans always did. But now a blanket of black gloom settled upon us as we finished our work in silence and returned to our tents to await news.

It took a while, but when news eventually came it did nothing to lift our depression. At nightfall, we centurions were summoned to Piso's tent. Surprisingly Brasidas, Varus' personal secretary, was present but thankfully all the fifth cohort centurions were present too. Piso, pale and grim faced, did not ask us to sit down or offer us the customary goblet of wine. Instead, he said quietly and without emotion, "Varus, Governor of Germania Magna, is dead." That simple statement hit us like a thunderbolt; some of us had seen him less than half an hour before talking to his commanders outside his tent. "I will tell you exactly what has happened and why Brasidas is here with us," continued our tribune. "The destruction of our cavalry, which you all witnessed, means that we are now alone with no hope of help. We must therefore save ourselves with our own resources and fight it out with the Germans man to man. The army lost many good men today including the legates of the Seventeenth and Nineteenth legions. The Nineteenth was so badly mauled that what remains of it will be re-allocated to the Seventeenth and Eighteenth which will bring them back up to around four thousand men each, perhaps a little less. Command of the Seventeenth has been given to Caeonius, the senior tribune. Eggius, our legate, now replaces Varus as general in command of the whole army. He also retains control of the Eighteenth."

"I didn't realise Varus had been badly wounded," said Gnaeus quietly.

"He wasn't, at least not physically," replied Piso. "He blamed himself for our present difficulties caused by his blind faith in Arminius."

"Well, he was warned often enough," muttered Marcus Aius, now no longer the joker.

Piso shrugged, "Well be that as it may, Varus decided to end his command and save his family in the only way he could. So, having written his last will, he freed Brasidas from slavery and, with his help, fell on his sword. Even as I speak his body is being cremated but with difficulty because all the wood around here is green and just smoulders instead of burning. Before he died, he gave permission for the cohort commanders to reorganise their cohorts into more practical units which reflect the level of casualties we have suffered. Consequently, my cohort will now be reformed into just two units. The first will comprise the second, fourth and sixth centuries under Gnaeus' command. The third and fifth centuries will merge to form the second unit under Lucius' command. Before dawn tomorrow, we will march northwest and head for the pass that the cavalry failed to reach today."

I asked, "Sir, what about the wounded? There are many of them."

Piso paused and took a deep breath. "I know that Lucius but our orders are to leave behind all those who cannot walk. Any medics who volunteer may stay with them."

"But the Germans will kill them all!"

"Very probably Lucius, but our men are already exhausted. They cannot carry the wounded and we have no vehicles to put them in."

"The Germans will torture them before they kill them," said Gnaeus sombrely.

"Any who choose death now will be killed quickly with little pain by their comrades. I do not like this any more than you do, but the only alternative is to stay here and let death come to all of us."

"Some of our Gauls may reach the Aliso camp," said Septimus Nasica. "Help might come if we dig in and stay here."

"That is possible," agreed Piso, "But not before winter sets in. We will run out of food well before next spring but the Germans will still be waiting. By then we will be emaciated from starvation. If we fight now we will still be strong. The decision to leave the wounded was not taken lightly but it's the only way to avoid a military disaster."

"How far is it to the land of the Batavi?" asked Caius.

"About three days' march according to the Gauls who know this area," answered Piso, "and less than half the distance back to the Rhine if we try returning by the way we came."

There were no more questions, so our tribune brought the meeting to a close. "Now my friends, I know I can call you that after all our years together, I do not know any better than you about what will happen tomorrow. The Germans will certainly try to stop us before we reach the pass because a victory over Rome will consolidate Arminius' desire to lead not only the Cherusci, but all the tribes west of the River Elbe. I am, of course, confident of a Roman victory but the fighting will be hard and if I should fall I want you to know it has been an honour to serve our empire with you." I felt my eyes beginning to water for that sounded like a farewell speech. I could not want or imagine any other commander but Piso. "Finally," he said, "Try to get a good night's sleep because we have an early start tomorrow. Brasidas has asked to remain with my cohort so I will allocate him to you Lucius. Try and find him something useful to do."

"I shall sir."

We were ready to march an hour before dawn. This time the Eighteenth legion was leading with the Seventeenth close behind. The Germans were alert and, despite our best efforts to move quietly, we could hear them following us on our left, no doubt waiting for dawn before they attacked. Soon, it was light enough to see movement in the shadows. We were still in open terrain, which was a relief, and as the light improved, it became evident that the Germans, who were about half a mile away, were marching parallel with us instead of closing in. The sun's golden orb appeared at last on our right and revealed a near cloudless morning. We relished the warmth after so many days of cloud and rain.

I spoke to Caius who was marching alongside me. "Strange

they're holding back. I would have thought they would want to finish us as soon as possible."

"It seems that Arminius has given them discipline Lucius. You can be sure there'll be a good reason."

There was. The ground on our left began to rise a little and, as we crossed a small stream which flowed from the forest into the marshland on our right Caius, whose eyes were better than mine, pointed to the northwest, the direction of the pass we were hoping to use. "The Germans are making sure we follow the route they want us to take. We're being herded like sheep to be slaughtered."

"We're not sheep, and how can you know what the Germans are thinking?"

"About two miles ahead there are some sort of earthworks lining the top of the rising ground on our left. They'll try to stop us there, I'm sure of it."

About half an hour later, our scouts returned and went straight to Eggius with their report. A few moments later the column was halted and we were given orders to deploy for battle. The Seventeenth legion had fallen back a little way and were now at least a mile behind us so, for the moment, we were alone. By now it was clear even to my middle-aged eyes that the earthworks Caius had pointed out were ramparts topped with thick, wicker fencing and occupied by a large number of tribesmen. When added to those marching parallel with us it was obvious that the Eighteenth was heavily outnumbered, but Eggius decided to attack anyway because he already knew the reason why the Seventeenth was lagging behind; its rear-guard was under heavy pressure from Cheruscan cavalry.

Three cohorts deployed to form our front line; we were placed on the right. Behind us were three more in close support ready to exploit any breakthrough we might achieve, and two were held in reserve. There should have been two more but we had lost so many men we were down to just eight understrength cohorts instead of ten. But just before we attacked, a remarkable event occurred which heartened us all.

We had closed to within two hundred paces of the German rampart and halted awaiting the command to charge. As always before any action, my mouth was dry with tension. Caius stood beside me, calm as ever, when suddenly a huge German clambered over the wicker fence, trotted fifty or so paces towards us, stopped and began shouting at us.

"What's he saying?" I asked.

"He wants to fight our best warrior," answered Caius. "He's saying that Germans are better than Romans and he will prove it."

There were many legionaries in the Eighteenth who had learned enough of the German tongue during years of patrolling both sides of the Rhine for the message to be clearly understood. Unsurprisingly, no-one relished the prospect of confronting this giant of a man. All eyes in our cohort turned towards Caius who had overcome an equally big man in single combat when he killed Alexander, the so-called Jewish Messiah just before the battle at the River Jordan.

"I'd better go and get Piso's permission to accept the challenge," he said.

"You're already too late," I replied. "Look!" To my horror, young Septimus Nasica, centurion of our sixth century, had left our cohort and was trotting towards the giant German to meet the challenge. An audible groan went up from our men for there could only be one outcome to this uneven contest. My thoughts immediately went back to that conversation I had with Septimus in Byzantium beside the Bosphorus. Had I said something to the young centurion which had driven him to this suicidal act?

Caius sighed, "He must be mad."

"No," I replied, "Just very brave."

As Septimus approached, the German could not believe his eyes. He began to laugh, a deep booming sound which easily reached our ears. Then he grounded his spear and drew a massive wooden club from his belt which seemed almost as big as Septimus. Our brave, little centurion was now within forty paces of his opponent. I noticed he was carrying a pilum, a standard legionary throwing spear, which was singularly unsuitable for close quarter fighting. The German turned his back on him and shouted something to his comrades which drew peals of laughter.

"What did he say Caius?"

"Words to the effect 'Fetch my grandmother. If this is the best the Romans have got, then she can deal with him'!"

Overconfidence can be just as deadly in battle as terror. Septimus was indeed small, but he had powerful shoulders and a good throwing arm. Thinking he was out of range of the approaching Roman, the German champion did not hurry to turn round and face the impudent shrimp, knowing full well that Romans never threw their pila until the enemy was within twenty paces. But Septimus stopped thirty-five paces away, braced his legs and hurled his pilum with all his strength.

His aim was true. Like most of his comrades, the German was clad in a padded leather jerkin which provided no protection against the barbed point of the pilum. It penetrated his body just to the left of the backbone and when he swung round in shock, we could see the pilum's head sticking through his chest just below the heart. The Germans fell silent but a rousing cheer went up from our ranks as Septimus trotted back to our lines as if he had just left a family picnic. The German champion sank to his knees, coughed up blood and fell forwards. He died quietly with his face in the mud where it belonged.

I could not control my delight and ran to Septimus. He stopped and smiled broadly as I put my arm round his shoulders and shouted to his century, "Behold Septimus Nasica, conqueror of the German champion. Follow him to glory today!" All those within hearing distance cheered, and beneath the uproar I whispered into his ear, "Well done! You have nothing to prove now. Your men will follow you to Hades and back if you ask them to!"

Septimus smiled again, shook my hand and returned to his century. That was the last time I saw him.

***

IV

Lucius Eggius knew the moment was right and ordered three long blasts on the horn to be sounded; the signal to charge. We surged forward, determined to break the arrogant foe that stood between us and safety. My command, the remains of the third and fifth centuries, amounted to ninety-five men deployed in three lines of just over thirty men in each. Caius and I took our places in the centre of the front rank where we could set the pace at a steady walk; any faster would break up the shield wall we relied upon to stop the enemy infiltrating into our ranks. Piso took his place with Gnaeus' men on our right. To our left were two more cohorts of the Eighteenth.

We advanced steadily towards the enemy rampart without loss because the Germans had no missile weapons, but when we came within twenty paces, we were assailed by a barrage of hand thrown objects, mainly rocks and stones but also lumps of wood, charcoal and anything else that was small enough to throw. Apart from rattling our shields, they were ineffective and just seconds later we closed on the screeching tribesmen and began exchanging blows across the wicker fence that topped the rampart.

Although it looks fragile, wicker is an awkward obstacle because it is flexible and difficult to cut. As I have said before, the gladius is a thrusting weapon and therefore useless for cutting a way through a wicker fence, so we were obliged to try and climb over the top of it which gave the defenders a huge advantage. They easily began to pick us off with their hand spears and soon we lost order and degenerated into a disorganised, frustrated mob struggling to find a way to dislodge the Germans.

We became discouraged until Piso shouted the order, "Second, fourth and sixth centuries testudo! Third and fifth push on!" Gnaius' men quickly formed the well-practised testudo formation which mimicked the defensive armour of a tortoise and was often used when assaulting a fortified position. The men in the inner ranks raised their shields flat above their heads and locked the edges together to form a sort of raised pavement. The men in the outer ranks locked their shields together to form a continuous wall to protect their comrades in the middle and together they slowly edged towards the enemy defences. Caius and I ran to the rear of the testudo, beckoning our men to follow, climbed up onto the pavement of shields and ran to the front edge of the testudo from where we launched ourselves over the top of the wicker wall, hoping our men would follow. Fortunately, they did. Caius cleared the wicker easily but I fell a little short and tripped over the inner edge of the wall hitting the ground hard. I was briefly dazed and needed a few moments to gather my wits when a large tribesman loomed above me. He held a woodman's axe and raised his arm. I tried to move my shield to deflect the imminent blow but realised, as my senses began to return, that I was lying on it. I was helpless but Rufio, who had leaped across the wall just behind me and retained his balance, thrust his sword into the tribesman's armpit just before the German delivered what would have been a fatal strike.

I staggered unsteadily to my feet but had no time to thank Rufio because more Germans pushed forward desperate to drive us out of the toehold we had gained in their defences. But our brave legionaries were already swarming into the enclave we had created and managed to stop the tribesmen in their tracks. Gradually we were able to force them back and link up with another enclave cut out by Caius and his men. We seemed to be winning. Victory was close.

But the two cohorts on our left were being held by the Germans and the cohorts behind us were slow in coming forward. The fighting started to slacken as both sides began to tire. Life and death hand to hand fighting is exhausting and can only be maintained for a few minutes at a time. Only those who have gone through it will appreciate this and will understand how unplanned pauses happen as if by agreement so that each side can regain its strength to renew the combat. It was during this brief rest that I discovered that our success was transient.

Caius tapped me on the shoulder. "Lucius, look at the forest edge behind the Germans about five hundred paces away."

I did as he bid. For a moment my vision was blurred. I may still have been feeling the effect of my fall at the wicker wall, because the tree line seemed to be moving. Then I realised it was not the trees but hordes of tribesmen issuing from the depths of the forest. There seemed to be thousands of them. If they caught us exposed in the middle of an attack, we would be slaughtered.

Fortunately, Piso had also seen what was happening. His was the only cohort that had broken through the German defences but he could not risk us being cut off from the rest of the army so, reluctantly, he gave the order to abandon our hard won enclave. Now, the more experienced amongst us knew this battle was lost. The consequences were unthinkable but for the moment we were too busy preparing a defensive line ready to fend off a German attack to worry about what was likely to happen next.

Once again, the enemy showed unexpected discipline and paused to re-order their ranks before following up our failure to capture their rampart. Eggius rode up to Piso, who was standing near me, so I was able to hear the exchange.

"Licinius, your cohort is now the rear guard. We're going to make for last night's camp."

"Yes sir. When do we leave?"

"As soon as you're ready. The rest of the Eighteenth is already on the move to help the Seventeenth which is under heavy pressure from the Cherusci."

"Then don't wait for us sir. We'll soon catch up with you."

As always, Piso was as good as his word and we quickly caught up with the rest of the legion, but our noble tribune was troubled and sent for me. He took me out of earshot of anyone else and said, "Lucius, listen to me carefully and keep your questions until you have heard all I have to say to you." I nodded and he continued, "This battle is heading for disaster. We are about to be beaten by an enemy commanded by Arminius who is familiar with Roman tactics and discipline. I hope I am wrong, but the time has come to make sure that if disaster happens it does not spread further than necessary. Therefore, prepare your men to leave the column, and make your way back to the camp on the Lippe." He took the signet ring from the little finger on his right hand and gave it to me. "Time is short, and I have no writing materials at hand to give you official orders, but this ring has my name inscribed on it and will at once be recognisable to senior officers in the army. When you reach the Lippe camp show Marcus Sempronius my ring and tell him to obey the orders I am about to give you.

There can be no arguments; it is of paramount importance that Caedicius at Aliso is forewarned of what has happened here. He is a good man and will send a message to Asprenas in Moguntiacum. If things end up as I expect, the whole of Germania Magna will rise up in rebellion so we must make sure all the Rhine crossings are reinforced to prevent a German invasion of Gaul. Is all that clear?"

"Yes sir, but what if Sempronius refuses to obey your order? You know how he hates me."

"Then you will have to take his authority from him. Send Caius to me after we have finished so you have a witness to what my orders are."

"I will sir."

"Good. Now look to the southwest and you will see a line of trees, mostly willows, which mark a small stream flowing from the wooded hills into the marsh east of us."

"I see it sir. I remember crossing it this morning."

"When we cross that stream I want you to leave the column and take your men back to the forest. Stay low and follow the stream bed so you are not seen by the enemy. Find the path we used earlier today and hurry back to the camp on the Lippe. Collect Sempronius and his century and march down the Lippe valley as fast as you can until you reach Aliso where you will report to Caedicius. Is all that clear?"

"Yes sir, but why have you chosen me when you have Gnaeus here?"

"Because you led the tax gathering expedition into the same area we have just come through, so you have the best chance of finding your way out of this mess."

"I understand sir, but I sincerely hope you are wrong about impending disaster."

"So do I. Now send Caius to me and go and prepare your file leaders. I will give you written orders if I have time."

Those orders never came because the Germans following us attacked a few minutes before my departure. To my great sorrow, I never saw my noble commander again.

We soon reached the stream that Piso had mentioned. It was only four hundred paces away. I directed my men to follow it upstream having explained to Caius what our mission was.

Always practical, Caius asked, "Have you been given written orders? This could look like desertion in the face of the enemy."

"There was no time, but we both know what Piso's orders are. He gave me his signet ring to prove good faith to anyone who might question his orders."

"Sempronius probably will. You know how he hates us both."

"A disaster of the magnitude Piso predicts should dwarf such squabbles but I shall be ready for him if he causes trouble."

"And I'll stand by you, come what may."

"Thank you, Caius, I never doubted that."

I never thought I would be glad to re-enter that gloomy, forbidding forest, but fighting a lost battle would have been worse. I waited until all my men were under cover then took a last look at the tragic scene unfolding behind us. The Seventeenth legion had almost joined up with the Eighteenth but not as a single, disciplined unit. Instead of marching in orderly columns the legionaries were trotting in small groups, probably the remains of centuries or even cohorts. Interspersed amongst them were other groups, some mounted but most on foot. At first, I took these to be auxiliaries, but then I realised they were attacking our men at will. The legionaries were putting up almost no resistance. All they seemed to care about was escaping from their German tormentors and reaching the protection of the Eighteenth. For the first and thankfully, the last time in my life I witnessed the break-up of a legion. With tears of pity and shame in my eyes, I turned away and followed my men into the forest.

CHAPTER NINE

Despite our best efforts, our departure from the Eighteenth legion had been observed by the Germans. As we plodded through the forest, searching for a track that would take us southwards, we became aware of noises amongst the trees behind us which, we were soon to discover, were the harbingers of the pursuit closing in on us. For the rest of that terrible day, we struggled through dense undergrowth, and I began to wonder if we would ever find our way out of what seemed like some huge arboreal tomb, but just before daylight finally faded, we stumbled across the forest path that the army had used in the morning. The Germans following us were quiet, so it was a reasonable risk to stop and make camp for the night. We were exhausted but sentinels were needed more than ever so I agreed with Caius to take the first watch and he would take the second.

The Germans must have been exhausted too because we were not disturbed during the night and resumed our march unhindered just before dawn. There were no sounds of pursuit, the Germans must have slept longer than us, so we relaxed a little and followed the path until we came across the remains of the battle that took place on the day Varus fell on his sword. The detritus of conflict lay everywhere, dead mules, broken weapons and bodies, mostly German, scattered in disorderly heaps across the forest floor. The sight was even worse when we came across the dead of our own cohort, men we recognised but whose features were already disfigured by forest scavengers.

"Should we not bury our dead?" said Caius who was marching beside me as usual.

"At this moment that is my greatest wish, but we dare not risk the living for the dead."

"But we don't even know how many tribesmen are following us. We still number over a hundred but for all we know we could be running away from half our number or even less!"

Although that was unlikely, Caius made a valid point. We should at least try to find out how many Germans were behind us, so when we entered a small clearing caused by some ponds and marshland, I stayed behind with Rufio after we had all filled our water canteens and hid behind some thorny bushes to count the number of tribesmen following us while Caius led our little column further down the path and waited a safe distance away.

The first of the Germans arrived less than two hours later. Like us, they drank from the ponds and then waited for their comrades. There were many of them. They flooded into the clearing all suffering from thirst, drank deeply and waited while yet more arrived. We counted six hundred and forty-seven before their forward scouts started to take an interest in our side of the clearing. It was time to leave.

"Six hundred and forty-seven is not a huge number," panted Rufio as we trotted down the forest path. "We could easily ambush them and send them running back to Arminius with their tails between their legs."

"Perhaps Rufio, but they had not all appeared before we were obliged to leave our observation post. If Arminius has organised them on Roman lines, as seems to be the case, then six hundred and forty seven is well over a typical cohort of four hundred or so. Therefore, it is reasonable to suppose that there are at least two cohorts chasing us, perhaps even more, which is too much for us to take on even by ambush. We cannot risk a battle against such odds. Our orders are to reach Aliso as soon as we can."

Rufio shrugged and said nothing for a while, but then he suddenly blurted out, "By the gods! I would dearly like to avenge our comrades, especially Galerius."

"I am sure that opportunity will come, and one more thing. I never thanked you for stopping that tribesman from dashing out my brains when we crossed the wicker wall."

"That's all right, sir. You'd have done the same for me."

We must have covered more than twenty miles that day, and when at last we rested for the night it was in the settlement where Allix and I had faced the formidable German woman who objected to our tax raising mission. Now, the settlement was deserted but at least this confirmed we were heading in the right direction to reach the Lippe camp. We set off the next day in good spirits and confident that the pursuit was not gaining on us, but just after the path broke out of the forest for a while, we came across the remains of some of the camp followers who had disobeyed Varus' order not to follow the army. To get this far south, they must have turned back after our last battle in the forest, but now we knew that hostile tribesmen were ahead of us as well as behind us. All the dead were men, so if there had been some cats with them, at least they had been spared for the services they could render to their captors, and where there was life there was hope. But now my greatest fear was that instead of finding Sempronius and his century at the Lippe camp, we might encounter Germans instead.

It took another two days to reach the Lippe. During daylight hours, the lightly armed Germans began to gain on us, but we countered this by starting earlier in the morning than them; they seemed to need more sleep than us. When we finally broke out of the forest on the morning of the fifth day after leaving Piso's cohort, we could see the Lippe camp just half a mile away. All seemed well but we approached cautiously until we saw two Roman soldiers leave the camp by a side gate carrying buckets to collect water from the river. We cheered and yelled with relief as we realised that our sanctuary had not been captured by the Germans. The men of the first century were equally pleased to see us because of an unsettling change in the behaviour of the local tribe, the Marsii, who had a long history of opposing Rome.

Caius and I immediately went to Sempronius' tent to relay Piso's orders. We found him eating hazel nuts and drinking wine even though it was still two hours before noon. He did not offer us a seat or bother to stand up himself. "I wondered what all that shouting was about." His speech was a little slurred. "It sounded like a riot."

"Nothing like that," I replied, "Just the arrival of the remains of the third and fifth centuries."

"Remains?"

"Yes, there has been a battle, a disastrous one. Our army was destroyed."

Now we had Sempronius' full attention. He frowned and pondered for a moment as he struggled to gather his wits. "That might explain why all our local tribesmen and traders suddenly disappeared yesterday morning. We've seen nothing of them since. What of Varus?"

"Dead."

"And Piso?"

"Alive when we left but certainly dead now. Caius and I bring you his last orders."

"Then give them to me."

"They are verbal. We were in the middle of a battle. There was no time to write orders."

Sempronius summoned one of the two guards who were on duty outside his tent. "Send Vannius to me at once." Vannius was a middle-aged file leader who had re-enlisted for a second term. He was a German by birth and, like Caius, stemmed from the Suebi tribe which had been subdued by the great Julius Caesar and was now a fertile source of quality recruits for the legions. While we waited, I spoke again to Sempronius this time with more urgency. "Marcus, there is no time for delay. There are upwards of a thousand Germans pursuing us. They'll be here in less than three hours!"

Sempronius remained unmoved. "That may or may not be the case but, if I am to receive verbal orders from the two men who hate me most in the cohort, then I shall need a witness."

I placed Piso's red stone ring on the table beside his wine goblet. "When our tribune saw the battle was lost he gave me his signet ring to show that I speak with his authority."

"You could just as easily have stolen it from his body as you deserted the battlefield."

Now Caius intervened. "Don't you understand? There's a major disaster unfolding around us yet all you can do is squabble about protocol and accuse us of desertion!"

Sempronius drew breath to respond in like manner but

Vannius arrived so he thought better of it. "Vannius, you recognise the centurions of the third and fifth centuries?"

Vannius, a weather-beaten, brown haired man with sky blue eyes answered, "Yes sir."

"I want you to witness the verbal orders they say they received from our tribune before leaving the army in the middle of a battle."

Vannius just nodded, as if this sort of thing happened all the time, and stood beside Sempronius who, at last, troubled himself to stand up. "Proceed with your report Centurion Veranius."

I relayed Piso's words as accurately as I could remember and ended by explaining why it was so important that Caedicius should be alerted at Aliso, but I could see that my report was falling on stony ground.

"I see, so let me sum this up," said Sempronius pompously. "I have here written orders from out tribune instructing me to remain in this camp until the beginning of October, which I fully intend to do. Now you arrive here using Piso's signet ring to change those orders verbally and tell me to run away from the enemy just as you have done. Well let me tell you now, I will not run away and nor will you. If the Germans are following you as you say, we shall meet them head on here and stand and fight them. There'll be no running away like cowards." I could feel Caius bristling beside me and put a restraining hand on his large arm. "And now," continued Sempronius, "You will take your orders from me as the senior officer here. How many men have you?"

"One hundred and four fit for duty and seven walking wounded." I answered.

"Then go with Vannius who will show you the sector of the

camp you will defend if the Germans ever get here. Dismissed."

"Not so fast Marcus. What about our wounded? Do you have any boats here or do you expect them to die uselessly like you will?"

Sempronius paused for a moment. He did not wish to appear callous in front of his senior file leader. "We have one boat. You may take it if you can find a pilot."

"We have a river man who used to row a ferry back and forth across the Danube," said Caius.

"Very well, Vannius will take him and your wounded to it after he has finished showing Veranius where his duty lies. Now you may go."

Caius was not ready to leave, and I almost had to manhandle him out of the tent, but not before I had picked up Piso's ring, the only hard evidence I had of my authority.

"Lucius, you cannot let him get away with this. What of Piso's instruction to you to take command?"

"I have not forgotten that and I'll deal with it in my own way. Now return to our men and get them re-provisioned as quickly as you can. We shall resume our march within the hour."

Vannius heard all this but said nothing. I said, "Take me to the sector your centurion wants us to defend."

The file leader looked at me strangely and gestured towards the riverside of the camp. "Over there, sir."

When we were halfway to the sector and well out of earshot of anyone else, I ordered Vannius to halt. "Now listen to me file leader. You heard everything in that tent and will no doubt have already formed your own opinion, but I must tell you that whatever you think, my men and I will obey Piso's orders. What I did not say earlier is that our tribune ordered me to take command of all the soldiers here if Sempronius refuses to obey these orders. I do not want to see any more Roman blood shed, least of all on the sword points of other Romans, but we must alert Caedicius at Aliso so he can take measures to prevent a German invasion of Gaul. I will not order you to disobey your centurion, but you will be doing a service to Rome as well as your comrades if you help us get to Aliso instead of waiting here for certain death. Speak to your fellow file leaders. Please come with us. If you choose to come, I will say I ordered you to, so if things go badly you will not be to blame. If you decide to stay then we shall leave anyway even if you choose to oppose us. Do you understand?" Once again Vannius nodded but remained silent. "Very well file leader. We will depart within the hour so make your decision quickly."

I returned to Caius and asked, "Who is this Danubian river man who can pilot Sempronius' boat?"

"Berea is one of my file leaders and very reliable. I have no idea if he can really pilot the boat or not, but when I spoke to him, he said he thought he could. The only other choice is to stay here and await the tender mercy of the Germans. I hope he's a quick learner. I have told him to request an urgent meeting with Caedicius when he gets to Aliso so that he can pass on the orders Piso gave us."

"Excellent! So even if we are caught by the Germans, the Rhine garrisons will be prepared for a German attack. That's a huge weight off my mind."

"And mine," agreed Caius, "But I would prefer not to be caught by the Germans!"

"I rather think that will depend on what the first century file leaders decide to do."

We need not have worried. By the time the third and fifth

centuries were ready to leave, the first century had already joined us in full marching order.

Vannius approached me. "Centurion, the first century now places itself under your command."

"You are all agreed on this?"

"Almost all of us sir." For the first time since we met, the dour file leader smiled giving his leathery, weathered face a remarkably pleasant aspect. "All except our centurion. All the other file leaders are happy to follow you sir."

"Thank you Vannius. As promised, I now formally order you to join us. What made you come to this decision?"

"It was not difficult, sir. To us file leaders, a tribune outranks a centurion so Piso's orders are the ones that must be obeyed."

"But they are only verbal orders."

"Yes sir, but we in the first century are all aware of your reputation and Centurion Caius'. Neither of you would lie because you are both men of honour."

"How did your own centurion take this decision?"

"Not well to begin with. He wanted to arrest me but when I explained he would have to do that himself because all the other file leaders in his century agreed with me, he changed his mind."

"Again, I thank you and your comrades Vannius. I do not know what your centurion will do, but he must remain in command of your century unless he openly disobeys me. Do what you can to enable him to maintain his self-respect."

"I understand sir, but remember, if things get difficult we are now committed to you."

"I will not forget, and I shall watch closely to make sure you do not suffer for what you have done."

Shortly afterwards we abandoned the camp on the Lippe and began the westward march to Aliso. The third and fifth centuries led with the first following. Sempronius took his place at the head of his century as if nothing had happened and I began to hope he had seen the sense of what we were doing.

***

II

The next few days were hard but at least the rain held off. We knew the Germans were gaining ground on us because sometimes we caught sight of them just a mile or two behind us at the far end of one of the long bends in the Lippe. On occasions such as these I would try and assess their numbers, but I was never able to see the rear of their column, so all I could deduce was that there were at least fifteen hundred of them. On the third day out of the Lippe camp, I was beginning to accept that they would catch up with us before we reached Aliso. We pushed on as hard as we could with the river on our left and the great German forest on our right, but shortly after we passed a deserted marching camp built by Drusus many years ago, it became clear that we would have to stand and fight our enemy who were now only half a mile away. This was all the more frustrating because we were only a long day's march away from Aliso and safety.

It was early afternoon when we reached a tributary stream that flowed from the north and merged with the Lippe. I had barely noticed it on the outward journey in the spring, but the heavy rain we had experienced during the forest march with Varus had swollen it into a torrent thirty yards wide. Now, the only way across it was by way of a sturdy, wooden bridge half a mile upstream from its confluence with the Lippe.

I called Sempronius to me. "Marcus, how close are the Germans to us?"

"Their forward scouts have already made contact with our rear guard."

"My men are travelling light. Before we reached your camp, we were obliged to get rid of all unnecessary equipment to stay ahead of the Germans. What of your century?"

"The first is fully equipped," he replied pompously.

"Including entrenching tools and the like?"

"Naturally."

"Excellent!" I exclaimed, hoping to get a positive reaction to what I was about to propose. "The flooding stream in front of us might just be what we need to save our skins. We will cross by the bridge upstream. It is strongly built, but if you cross and order your men to break up the bridge behind us, we may gain just enough time to reach Aliso before the Germans catch up with us."

"But we don't have the equipment to pull up the piles the bridge sits on," objected Sempronius.

"Don't even try to. Just break up the bridge decking and let the beams float downstream into the Lippe. Even if you only cut out a twenty-pace gap, that will hold up the Germans for at least an hour. Aliso is only a day's march from here. That hour could prove vital."

Sempronius was no fool, and even though he did not want me to be successful, he wanted to save his own skin even more. "Very well," he agreed. "I shall order it at once."

I stayed with him and watched the work begin while Caius led the third and fifth centuries towards Aliso. I tried to engage Sempronius in conversation but he remained monosyllabic, though his men did well and managed to remove almost all of the bridge decking before the Germans arrived. The Germans howled with frustration. I would have given a year's pay to have a troop of Syrian archers with me, but we had no missile weapons, and before we left we had to content ourselves with some vulgar Roman gestures which were doubtless lost on the barbarians.

As we turned to go, I was surprised to see that Brasidas was still with us. Usually, he marched with Caius with whom he had formed a strong bond caused by the perilous journey they undertook together during the great Zealot rebellion following King Herod's death. They had volunteered to take a message to the Governor of Syria based in Antioch, who happened to be Varus at the time, warning him that the Roman garrison in Jerusalem was under siege and was sure to fall without urgent help. But getting that message to Antioch meant creeping through the Zealot lines at night with the prospect of certain death if they were caught.

I left Sempronius and walked over to him. "Hello Brasidas. Why aren't you with Caius?"

"I've been keeping a journal of this campaign. Most days there was nothing much to write about until Varus started his final march, but since we left Piso there's been plenty to say. The breaking of this bridge will make good reading."

"Have you recorded Piso's orders concerning the command here?"

"Yes, Caius told me and also how Sempronius reacted."

I laughed, "Well, you'd better not let Sempronius know what you're doing. Who will read this journal?"

"I am thinking of making it into a book."

"You won't get many readers. Rome does not like to dwell on its defeats."

"True, but when the wounds have healed, there will be lessons to be learned."

At the time, I had no idea how important that journal would be to me.

The relief of knowing we would reach Aliso safely created a light-hearted atmosphere amongst us. Even Sempronius smiled when I complimented him on the diligence of his men, but we were celebrating too soon. By mid-afternoon, I estimated we were no more than three miles from Aliso but as we rounded another righthand bend in the Lippe, the forest was replaced by a large, open area of cultivated land stretching miles away to our right. Normally we would have been pleased to see this, but our view was blighted by an army of German warriors about eight hundred strong blocking any further progress. They were drawn up in no particular order astride the path we were following. Aliso might now just as well have been the other side of the world.

"Sugambri?" asked Caius.

"Probably," I replied. "They must have heard about Varus and thrown in their lot with Arminius. This is their land. They look a bit different to the Germans we encountered before. Their hair is cut short and they seem to be better equipped, more swords and axes and fewer home-made wooden clubs."

"There are a lot of them."

"About four times our number but fewer than those following us. We must attack or be squeezed between two superior armies."

Caius looked at the Lippe. "Well thankfully, the river covers our left flank, so we only have the right to protect."

"Unless those behind us get here sooner than we expect. We'll attack at once. Caius, you may lead the attack or cover our right flank. Which do you choose?"

"To lead the attack."

"Very well, take the third and fifth with you and form up in two lines. I will stay with Sempronius and the first and cover the right and rear. Go forward immediately."

"I will Lucius and may Mithras protect you."

"And you too and look after little Brasidas."

"I will."

Within a few minutes we had formed up and began to march towards the Sugambri. There was no need for speeches or exhortations; every man knew we had to break the enemy before our pursuers caught up with us. As always, the Germans looked large and fearsome and made a great deal of noise, but we had already proven that we would beat them in open terrain as long as the odds against us were not too great. They waited for us in a dense mass that easily overlapped our two lines, which were only sixty paces wide. When we were about thirty paces away from them, some tribesmen could no longer contain themselves and charged at us. Others, somewhat confused, followed hesitantly while most stayed where they were. It was a ragged, ineffective charge. There was no sign of the discipline Arminius had instilled into his men and, best of all, there was no cavalry.

We halted, locked shields, and took the impact of the charge quite easily but, as those behind the front runners began to push forwards, the pressure on our front rank started to build. As is natural when a frontal attack is held, the Germans began to feel for an exposed flank to turn. Soon the first century found itself in danger of being enveloped. I had placed myself a little behind Sempronius' men, with a tactical reserve of thirty legionaries, so we went forward and extended the line to prevent the Germans from getting behind us. But more tribesmen arrived and lengthened the German line to our right.

This forced us to swing backwards until we were almost at right angles to Caius' line. If we retired any further, the Germans would be free to attack Caius' line from behind.

I did not know what orders to give next. The battle was drifting away from us. Suddenly, an unmistakably German war horn sounded from behind the Sugambrian warriors.

Vannius, who was fighting beside me gasped, "Centurion, it seems we're done for. It sounds like the Sugambri are bringing up their cavalry." But the Sugambri also hesitated, seemingly surprised by the arrival of their own horsemen. The horn sounded again, then again. Faintly, above the noise of battle, I could just hear a voice I recognised bellowing, "Wir kommen! Lucius, wir kommen! Die Batavii kommen!"

The Sugumbrian pressure slackened. I could not see what was happening, but I could feel the thunder of cavalry hooves in the ground under my feet. Again, I heard, "Lucius, wir kommen!" Then suddenly, our opponents turned and scattered before our eyes as the Batavian cohort galloped into their ranks crushing men and spreading confusion all round them. The battle was over; we were saved.

While the Sugambri fled before the Batavian horsemen, we centurions counted our losses which were eleven dead and seventeen wounded of whom three were likely to die, but I now knew that more than one hundred and fifty Roman legionaries would reach safety. I walked over to Brasidas who was helping to bandage the wounded. "Are you all right?"

"Yes," he replied, "but a little shaken. I've not been this close to combat before."

"Something more for your book then?"

"Indeed yes, but not until tomorrow. I don't think my hands will stop shaking before then."

"Thanks for your help with the wounded."

Just then Friedrich rode up, dismounted and handed his reins to one of his troopers. He embraced me with the fiercest bear hug I've ever experienced and, breathing onions all over me, asked, "Lucius, you are not hurt?"

"No, just a few cuts and bruises. By holy Jupiter! I never was more pleased to see you!"

"Yah, me too. I vorry ve may be too late. Your man Berea kommt in boat mit vounded. He zay vat happen to Varus. Caedicius send me here plenty quick. Ve have spare horses. Dey carry your vounded to Aliso. Ve hurry now. Sugumbri and Cherusci kommen back here soon. Caedicius march for Vetera tomorrow. Goodbye Aliso."

We reached Aliso just as the sun was setting. I immediately went to Caedicius' quarters to report and told him everything that had happened since we left Varus. I left out the confrontation with Sempronius, which turned out to be a mistake. After a few questions concerning German weapons and tactics, Caedicius said, "Thank you Lucius. You have done well to get your men here. We had already heard rumours of a disaster from our German allies but could not believe them until your man Berea arrived. Now you have confirmed them. We shall leave for Vetera tomorrow morning and begin reinforcing all the Rhine defences in our sector. I have already sent preliminary warnings to Asprenas in Moguntiacum; now I shall confirm them. As for you, take yourself a well-earned bath and get a good night's sleep because we shall start early tomorrow."

"Thank you, sir, I shall happily obey that order."

Later that evening I was preparing to go to bed after a hot bath in the centurions' barracks when there was a knock at my door. Before I could respond, a centurion I did not know entered followed by four legionaries. He unrolled a piece of parchment and said, "Centurion Lucius Veranius, you are under arrest. You must come with us."

I struggled to believe what I was hearing and demanded, "What hole in Hades have you climbed out of! Go away!"

The centurion nodded to two of his men who roughly manhandled me to my feet. "You are under arrest," he repeated.

"What is the charge?"

"Sedition, disobeying orders from a senior officer and cowardice in the face of the enemy!"

***

III

The bloody nose the Sugambri had suffered at the hands of Friedrich's Batavians enabled Caedicius to complete his withdrawal to Vetera without too much interference from the Germans. It only took two days but all this time I remained in close confinement marching under guard with the baggage train. I was not allowed to speak to anyone. When we reached Vetera I was escorted to the isolated detention block in the legionary camp where, as best as I could tell, I was the only prisoner. I cannot say I was treated badly as far as food and basic comforts were concerned, but I had plenty of time to think because, apart from dour prison guards, I languished there alone and isolated for two and a half months!

By the time I received my first visitor, who was Caedicius, I had become bitter and very angry. When he entered my cell I stood up more in anger than out of respect. He saw the look on my face and held up his left arm in the sign of peace. "Lucius, say nothing until you have heard me out, then as your superior officer, you have my leave to speak freely to me without fear of punishment or reprisal." I nodded and sat down again while Caedicius remained standing. He was a short, sturdily built man of fifty years or so. His close-cropped grey hair and battle-scarred face reflected an experienced veteran who was now approaching the end of his second term with the legions.

I pointed to the solitary chair opposite mine, the only furniture in my cell apart from my bunk, and he sat down gathering his thoughts for what he was about to say. "Lucius, I am sorry you've been stuck here for two months—"

"Two and a half!" I interrupted.

His grey eyebrows furrowed. I knew I had gone too far. "Sorry, I shall not interrupt you again."

"For two and a half months," he sighed. "I had intended to speak to you on the third day of your confinement, but Asprenas reached Vetera that same day and took over command. His was the order that you should remain in solitary confinement until further notice."

He paused so I asked, "Then what are you doing here now?"

"On the pretext that I must ensure our prisoner remains in good enough health for the trial he must undergo. Lucius, you and I are of the same mettle. We come from humble stock, but we have risen through the ranks to our present positions and understand the feelings of our fellow legionaries. Asprenas is different. He comes from a respected senatorial family. Did you know that Varus was his uncle?"

"No."

"Well, he was, but although he's very conscious of his elevated status, he has already proven himself a good general and did the right thing by moving his two legions here as soon as he heard the news of his uncle's disaster."

"Did Arminius counterattack then?"

"No, I suspect the Germans lost almost as many men as we did in that final battle. They certainly showed no appetite to attempt a Rhine crossing, but during the last two months," he paused and smiled, "The last two and a half months, I have used my humble background to test the feelings of the men and I think I now understand the true position. You were indeed instructed by Piso to leave Varus' beaten army and since which you have followed his orders to the letter. Your men adore you and so do Sempronius' which explains their decision to support you against their own centurion. But unlike you and me, Sempronius comes from a high-ranking family which will stand him in good stead for when you have to face each other in a court of law. Do you still possess Piso's ring?"

"Yes." I handed the precious object over to him. He looked at it, turned it over in his fingers and saw Piso's name inscribed upon it. Then he handed it back to me. "Lucius, guard this well. You may soon be on trial for your life and the odds will be stacked against you, but this ring could be the one object that stands between you and execution."

By now my hostility towards the old campaigner had disappeared. I realised I had an ally in Caedicius but I doubted his support would carry a great deal of weight in the trial I was about to face. "Well what happens now? How soon will I have to undergo this trial that awaits me?"

"Not for a while yet because the emperor himself has shown an interest in your case. He has taken the Varus disaster badly because he feels it reflects on him; Varus was a member of his family if only by marriage. Consequently, your examination and trial will take place in Rome."

"Rome!"

"Yes, which will give Sempronius a big advantage over you. He will be a thousand miles away from those whose lives you saved by overriding his faulty decision to remain at the camp on the Lippe. Instead, he'll have the benefit of his high-status family around him who will no doubt be able to afford the best lawyer available in Rome. You, on the other hand, are permitted just two companions to accompany you to our capital.

You will have an armed escort to prevent you trying to escape because you will face the death penalty if you lose."

"What if Sempronius loses?"

"At worst he will be discharged from the army."

"Then I owe it to my men to make sure he loses. What's happened to them?"

"They've been redistributed amongst other cohorts."

"But that should not have happened. Piso's cohort was only loaned to Varus. Whatever is left of it should be returned to the Third Gallica in Judea."

"I am not sure if the Third's legate wants your cohort back, but in any event you must fight your own battle first. If you win, then you may come back for your men. Now who do you want to go with you to Rome?"

"Centurion Caius Pantera and…" I paused for thought. I almost said 'File leader Ostorius Rufio' who any man would want by his side in a fight, but this was not to be an ordinary fight. Brains would be more valuable than brawn. "Brasidas," I replied, "Varus' private secretary."

Caedicius raised an eyebrow. "But he's only a slave. His testimony will be of no value to you."

"He's a freedman. One of Varus' last acts before killing himself was to release Brasidas from slavery. I know there is written evidence of that."

"Very well," agreed Caedicius, "it shall be so. Use the rest of today to make ready to leave because you will depart early tomorrow for Rome."

Rome, the capital of our great empire is also the largest city in the world containing over a million inhabitants, but I do not suppose that anyone has actually counted them all. By the time I reached the city with my two chosen companions and a troop of thirty legionary cavalry commanded by a young decurion called Albus, it was the beginning of the new year and very cold. At first, I did not even realise we had reached the outer fringes of the great city. There was no wall or any other defining boundary. All that happened as we travelled further south was that the space between small, grubby villages gradually became less and less until the countryside disappeared and we were enclosed by a myriad of small buildings as far as the eye could see. These were mostly the dwellings of the urban poor. We were obliged to pick our way through a maze of narrow streets and passageways seemingly making no forward progress at all until we reached a small square with a gap in one side which revealed a view of the great buildings of the imperial city capping a series of low hills ahead of us.

We stopped and looked in wonder. "Impressive aren't they Lucius," said Caius.

"Yes, but we're still miles away from them and we've still got to find our way through this infernal jumble of backstreets."

"I think I can help you there," said our young decurion who was riding just behind us. "I was born and bred in this city. I know the best roads to use. Rest assured, we will be at the Basilica Julia, which is our destination, before dark."

"I should hope so," grumbled a saddle sore Brasidas. "I wouldn't want to be lost in these unsavoury back streets after dark."

Albus laughed, "Have no fear! The main streets can be just as unsavoury as the back streets when the lights go out!"

Caius whispered to me, "We could always escape from our escort within this maze. We'll never be found amongst these alleys and dead ends."

"True, but that means I would have to remain a fugitive for the rest of my life or live outside the empire. Neither is appealing."

"Nor is death from an unfair trial."

"I must clear my name. I owe it to you and others to do so. Let's just follow our decurion to the Basilica Julia and see what fate has in store for me."

Sure enough, Albus guided us safely to the forum where the Basilica Julia was located. Like most of the buildings in the forum, it was large and imposing. Built of white limestone, it faced the Curia, where the senate carried out its duties, and sat neatly between the temple of Castor and Pollux and the temple of Saturn. The basilica was oblong in shape and three storeys high. The ground floor was surrounded by a spectacular colonnade and contained a single, large audience chamber where legal proceedings, such as my trial, were carried out. The upper floors were composed of offices and lodgings for visitors and, to my surprise, we were taken upstairs together with Albus and six of the escort and given rooms to use while the rest of the escort found lodgings and stables elsewhere in the city.

Caius, Brasidas and I shared one room while Albus and his troopers shared another three. Our surroundings were plush, our escort was inattentive. Now if ever was the time to escape. I thought again about what Caius had said. The prospect of freedom, however restricted, began to seem preferable to a coward's death, which seemed the most likely outcome if I did nothing, but ultimately the prospect of dishonour was the greater evil so I gritted my teeth and decided to confront what was to come.

I slept surprisingly well that night and felt refreshed and

invigorated to face the new day. As we prepared our uniforms to look the best we could after a winter journey of a thousand miles, Caius said, "It seems strange that we are being treated as guests rather than the companions of a man charged with capital offences."

Brasidas, who had more legal knowledge than either of us, replied, "Lucius has not yet been charged with anything. He's been accused by a senior officer of serious crimes but so far we have seen no formal charge sheet."

"But I'm here under guard!"

"As I said," continued Brasidas, "You have not yet been formally charged. Also, you have no legal representation so I don't see how a trial can be imminent. Be prepared for a surprise or two."

We were escorted downstairs to the audience chamber which was already filling up with senators and other important people. I have faced fear, and occasionally terror, in battle but the next two days were something different, something I never experienced before or since: unmitigated, debilitating stress. It was a true ordeal. Any silly mistake or slip of the tongue could mean the end for me. The Basilica Julia was where most of the high-profile legal cases were heard involving people far more important than me. The surroundings were unnerving to a humble centurion. I was led with my two companions into the middle of the audience chamber which had lines of wooden benches on one side for those who wished to attend trials as spectators, a raised dais in the centre where the presiding officials sat and, opposite that, two sets of wooden benches separated by an open area occupied by a file of tall, imposing soldiers dressed in uniforms of burnished gold armour and purple cloaks.

"Who are they?" gasped Caius in admiration.

I had no idea but Brasidas, who had visited Rome many times with Varus, answered, "They're Praetorian Guards, the emperor's select bodyguard and the cream of our army, so it is said. The guards are here to ensure that opposing lawyers and their clients cannot come to blows with each other if emotions run too high." I had Albus' troopers at my side, but they looked small and scruffy beside the praetorians.

There were already at least forty senators and men of the equestrian order, the second most important order in the Roman social and political hierarchy, occupying the spectator benches but, as yet, there was no sign of my accuser. We were obliged to wait for almost an hour before the presiding officials arrived who were a consul and two praetors. During this wait my nerves became taught and my confidence waned. I knew Sempronius came from a good family and would be at ease in this formidable place which to me seemed awe inspiring. How could a simple child of a legion hope to compete in such exalted company?

The three presiding officials took their places on the dais opposite me. After a few words to each other and some shuffling of scrolls, the man in the centre of the three spoke first. He was slim, middle aged and weather-beaten. He seemed to have military experience if his clear, precise manner was anything to go by.

"My name is Publius Cornelius Dolabella. I am the senior consul for this year." Then he introduced the two praetors, the next highest officials in Roman politics after the consuls, but I do not remember their names. One of the praetors read out the accusations, which were much the same as those read out to me when I was arrested.

Then Dolabella spoke again. "Centurion Lucius Veranius, you have heard the accusations. How do you plead?"

"Not guilty to all of them."

"Very well. I must now make clear that this is not a trial but an inquiry to establish whether or not you have a case to answer. If you do, you shall remain here to await a trial for your life. If you do not, you will return to your legion with your record unblemished and the pay that has been withheld from you while you've been under arrest will be reimbursed to you in full." How I wished that all this was over, and I could return to my comrades with my reputation intact! Dolabella drew breath to speak again but checked himself and looked hard at something or someone behind me. Then he stood up as did the praetors and everyone else in the basilica. I looked round and saw an elderly man dressed entirely in purple, using a staff as an aid and walking slowly towards the spectator benches. The consul announced grandly, "Hail Caesar!" This was repeated by everyone in the basilica.

Augustus Caesar was now in his seventy-third year, but although weakened and shrivelled with age, he still carried the aura of power remarkably well. I watched him settle down on one of the spectator benches amongst the senators and thought he looked more like a kindly old grandfather rather than the man who had won the seemingly endless civil wars and ruled ruthlessly but successfully for forty years over the most powerful empire the world had ever seen.

Such was the impression Augustus had on me, I hardly noticed his companion who walked a respectful few paces behind and sat beside him amongst the senators. In his mid-twenties, he was tall, strongly built and had a military bearing. He was also handsome, in a rugged sort of way, and seemed to look upon Augustus with genuine warmth.

I whispered to Caius, "Who do you think that tall fellow is with Augustus?"

A voice from behind us whispered back, "That is Nero Claudius Drusus, son of the deceased General Drusus and nephew and adopted son of Tiberius, our future emperor." I looked round and saw a small, fox faced man of about forty-five behind me. "Gnaeus Calpurnius Piso at your service," he said. "Your tribune is, or rather was, my second cousin. I hope we get the chance to speak when this inquiry is over."

"I think that will depend upon whether I win or not, but I will be happy to speak if I get the chance."

"Good, good," replied the fox faced man, but just then the emperor gestured for us all to sit, which we dutifully did.

Once we were all settled, Dolabella outlined the terms of the inquiry. "We have called this inquiry rather than going straight to a trial because it may touch upon matters pertaining to a much greater inquiry that will take place later this year examining the cause and circumstances of the loss of Varus and his three legions." He looked at me. "Do you understand?"

"Yes," I answered. It was only when I heard Sempronius say 'yes' at the same time as me that I realised my accuser had arrived. He was sitting a few yards to my left and a little behind me. I could not see him clearly because of the intervening Praetorian Guards.

"You must both clearly understand," continued the consul "That from this moment you will follow the procedure I am about to explain to you. First, you will not at any time speak to each other while this inquiry is proceeding. There will be no arguing here. When you are permitted to speak you will always stand and address your comments to me, no-one else. I will decide when you speak and what questions you may answer. If you have a question or are uncertain on any matter, you will raise your arm and keep it raised until I acknowledge you."

"Yes sir, we both replied together."

"What did I just say!"

I frowned and looked blank but Sempronius stood up and said, "Yes sir." I got to my feet belatedly remembering the instruction about only speaking when standing and repeated another 'Yes sir', angry that I had made a fool of myself before we had even started.

As the accuser, Sempronius was instructed to speak first. He gave a reasonably accurate account of what had happened at the Lippe camp with only minor embellishments to the confrontation we had before I took command of his century. Nothing was said about the events following our departure from the Lippe camp, which was understandable since there was nothing to criticise me about, unless Sempronius was prepared to lie outright. Realising there were many witnesses still available who knew the truth, he sat down and said no more, satisfied that the evidence he had provided was sufficient to justify a trial.

After taking a few moments to complete his notes, Dolabella turned to me. "Well, you have heard the accusation. What is your reply?"

Remembering to stand up first, I answered, "Sir, apart from some minor details about what happened, my accuser's account is substantially correct but with the major exception of his interpretation of my motives. Yes, we were indeed running from an enemy greatly superior in numbers, but my orders from my tribune were to escape the disaster unfolding around us, save as many men as I could and get through to Aliso where I could report to the commander who would then advise Asprenas at Moguntiacum of the gravity of the situation. That way the Rhine crossings could be strengthened or even destroyed if necessary to forestall a German counterattack on Gaul."

"This is all hearsay," interrupted Dolabella. "You have no written orders to support your statement."

"That is true sir, but the Germans were attacking in overwhelming numbers. We were hard pressed, there was no time to write orders, so my tribune gave me his signet ring to use as a means of underwriting the truth of my orders. It has his name inscribed on it."

"Let me see it," said the consul. I handed it to him. He turned it over a few times and read the name inscribed on the inner side of the ring. "Well, it looks genuine but we have the head of the family here who can verify it. Gnaeus Calpurnius Piso, come forward!"

The same fox faced senator who was seated behind us stood up and went to the dais. He examined the ring, turned to face the assembly and pronounced, "This is the family ring worn by my second cousin Licinius, commander of the fifth cohort of Legion Eighteen of Varus' army. Let there be no doubt about that." He returned to his place giving me a friendly nod as he passed by.

"Then all that remains in doubt is how you came by it," continued Dolabella looking at me. "Were there any witnesses to the hand-over of the ring?"

"I do not know sir," I answered. "Witnesses were the last thing on my mind at the time."

The consul now addressed Sempronius, so I sat down as procedure required. "What do you say to that?"

"Sir, there were no witnesses so Veranius can say what he

likes. He could just as easily have removed the ring from Piso's finger after he had been killed. His cowardly actions afterwards suggest to me that is a far more likely explanation."

Turning back to me, Dolabella said, "I think now is the time we should hear your account in full starting from the moment Varus killed himself. Take your time, spare no detail and be prepared to answer questions as you proceed."

My account took the rest of the day. There were many questions: 'Why were you chosen to leave the battlefield?' 'How did you know the number of Germans following you?' 'Why did the first century accept you as its commander so readily?' And many more. By the time Dolabella ordered an adjournment until the following morning, I had been fighting for my life for many hours; one slip could have been fatal. My mind was drained like a wrung-out sponge. In the evening I ate little and went to bed early.

"Lucius, wake up!" It seemed as if I had only just closed my eyes, but I had slept for almost twelve hours. Caius was waking me with a none too gentle shake. "Brasidas has disappeared! He's missing!"

I tried to gather my wits. "Missing? Where's he gone?"

"I don't know. If I did I would go and look for him."

I sat up and rubbed my eyes. "Of course you would but Brasidas is smarter than either of us. He knows what he's doing. Just leave him be and let us return to the trial that is not a trial but only an inquiry."

When we reassembled, Gnaeus Piso sat behind us again but there was no sign of Nero Claudius Drusus who I shall henceforth refer to by the title 'Germanicus' which he was later awarded for his hard-fought victories in Germania Magna. The emperor was present but this time he was accompanied by another impressive looking young man who was attired in the purple uniform of the Praetorian Guard. This man was as tall as Germanicus but less easy on the eye because of his coarser features. His dark brown eyes flickered this way and that as if he was memorising all those present in the basilica.

I whispered to Caius, "Who do you think that is sitting beside the emperor today?"

"I've no idea. I've not seen him before."

Once again we were enlightened by the same voice as before, belonging to the head of the Piso family. "That is Aelius Sejanus, son of the Praetorian prefect, Seius Strabo. Be wary of him for though he's young, he's ambitious. Where is the third member of your party today?"

I answered, "I don't know sir. We haven't seen him since yesterday evening."

"Perhaps he's given up on a lost cause," said Gnaeus Piso, "But tell me, what do you intend to do with my cousin's ring when this ridiculous inquiry is finished?"

"You are the head of the Piso family so I will give it to you. I am sure that's what your cousin would have wanted."

"Thank you, Centurion Veranius. I wish you well with your struggle here, but I am told that your opponent has influence in high places which you do not."

"The impartiality of Roman justice is renowned throughout the empire."

Piso frowned. "Perhaps, we'll soon know. Here come your inquisitors."

Dolabella and his two praetors entered the audience chamber and sat down at the table on the dais in front of us. The consul opened the proceedings with a long summary of the evidence given the previous day but when he began his conclusion, my hopes of success began to fade. I glanced at Sempronius whose eyes met mine. He gave me a sickly, confident smile and shook his head as if he was sorry for my imminent defeat.

"And so, we come to the judgement regarding whether or not Centurion Veranius has a case to answer," continued Dolabella, rolling up his scroll and speaking without the aid of notes. "We have before us a multitude of opinions but very few facts, and it is by facts alone that this inquiry will determine the fate of Veranius. The most important, undisputed fact we have is that a junior officer, Centurion Veranius, not only disobeyed the written orders of his superior officer, but by means yet to be determined, subverted Centurion Sempronius' authority and took command of his century on the basis of a ring which may or may not have been given to him by the cohort commander, Licinius Piso. Therefore, I—"

"Stop! Stop!" All eyes turned towards the main entrance of the basilica where Germanicus had appeared waving two scrolls above his head. He was followed by the small, slender figure of Brasidas. Germanicus strode to the centre of the chamber and repeated "Stop!" The red leather casings of the scrolls were familiar. I nudged Caius. "Look! He's carrying Brasidas' journal!"

Germanicus stopped in front of Dolabella and placed the scrolls in front of him. "Sir, I place before you as evidence a journal written by Varus' personal secretary, Brasidas, which describes in detail day by day all the events that took place from the moment Centurion Veranius left the main army with the remains of two centuries until he reached Aliso."

"But Varus' secretary is a slave is he not?" objected Dolabella. "A slave's evidence carries no legal weight."

"He is not and was not when he wrote this journal. Varus gave him his freedom before he fell on his sword. I have here the document signed and sealed by Varus himself. I propose you adjourn this inquiry to give you and your praetors time to read this journal which not only mentions Piso giving Centurion Veranius the ring, but also unwittingly describes a textbook example of a fighting withdrawal led by Veranius. Thanks to this centurion, Rome is one hundred and fifty brave legionaries better off than would have been the case if Centurion Sempronius remained in command. Just read the journal. It is the ultimate in contemporary evidence. Brasidas had no reason to favour either centurion; he simply recorded what he observed. It makes powerful reading!"

The case against me collapsed there and then. Thanks to Brasidas and Germanicus I was saved and Gnaeus Piso got his cousin's ring.

***

IV

The Basilica Julia emptied quickly after my acquittal. Caius and I remained seated still trying to come to terms with this sudden change in fortune while Brasidas went over to Germanicus to retrieve his journal. When he returned, Germanicus came with him.

We both stood up. I said, "Thank you sir for what you did today. Things were going badly until you and Brasidas intervened."

Germanicus smiled, a warm, generous smile. "I am happy to have helped to see justice done, but the real thanks should go to Brasidas. Without his help you would be facing a trial with little prospect of success, but you are a free man now Lucius Veranius so what are you going to do?"

"I have not yet had time to think much about the immediate future, but I suppose I shall return to Vetera."

"How old are you?"
"Thirty-six sir."
"How much longer have you to serve with the eagles?"
"I have just started my last year."
"But you have no legion to return to. No doubt you have lost many friends and comrades, but you still have two with you. If you were given your discharge now but with all the payments due to you as if you had served your full term, what would you do then?"

"Go back to Galilee where there is a wonderful woman I

love and who loves me. At this moment she probably thinks I perished with the rest of Varus' army, but I would return and marry her as soon as possible. Then I would buy some land and try my hand at farming."

"You have obviously thought about this."

"I had two and a half months of solitary confinement to think about things."

"I am sorry for that, but I could make all that possible now. There would be one condition however."

I could hardly believe my ears. The prospect of returning to Germania for revenge had no attraction for me at all. "Sir, there is nothing I could wish for more than a return to Galilee on the terms you have just offered, but what is the condition?"

"We will soon invade Germania Magna again. Our defeat must be avenged and Arminius brought to justice or killed. If we do nothing, others in the empire might be encouraged to emulate the Germans. As you well know, the fighting will be hard and more than one campaign will be needed to bring the Germans to heel once and for all. The emperor has already asked me to lead the invasion which I will happily do. I may well need experienced men like you, so the condition is that I may call upon you at any time in the next five years to re-join the eagles under my command. You would join as a member of my staff, not just as an ordinary centurion."

The thought of being able to go back to Ruth on a full centurion's retirement benefit was too attractive to resist, but at thirty-six years of age I had learned to question things that seemed too good to be true. "Sir, why is your condition limited to five years?"

"Because if I have not conquered Germania Magna within five years I shall have failed. I cannot expect the empire to finance a campaign with men and money for longer than that."

That seemed fair enough, so I replied, "I accept your condition sir, but what of my two friends here?"

"I have already considered that. With regard to your tall friend who Brasidas tells me is the Caius Pantera in his journal, I am assured by Aelius Sejanus son of the Praetorian prefect, that he would be welcomed into the ranks of the Praetorian Guard. They are paid double the rate of the legions and their contract of service is four years less at only sixteen years. Strabo, the prefect, is always on the look-out for men like Caius who are both physically imposing and experienced in battle. Caius, how many years have you left to serve?"

"Four sir."

"Then you would have to re-enlist, but if you retain your centurion's rank in the guard would you be interested?"

"Indeed, I would sir. It would be an honour to serve with the Praetorians and, like Lucius, I have no legion to return to."

Germanicus smiled, "Then consider it done. Your four remaining years with the eagles will be cancelled, so you will have just sixteen years to serve with the Praetorians. That only leaves the true hero of the hour, you Brasidas. Sadly, I have nothing to offer a scholar like you within the legions. I believe your talents would be more appreciated outside the army. I could look for a post for you within the senate administration if you wish?"

Brasidas appeared crestfallen, the outsider of the three friends, but I owed him a huge debt and could not see him abandoned. "Sir," I said, "I would willingly take Brasidas with me as my business manager. If he accepts, I would be free to do the physical work farming requires without worrying about the business side of things which has been the downfall of many a retired veteran. I have enough saved to purchase a small holding with a home for a manager who would share in the profits generated from the farm."

"I accept," said Brasidas almost before I had finished speaking.

Germanicus laughed, "Excellent! It seems the future for all three of you has now been agreed. I will arrange for the paperwork to be drawn up tomorrow morning. That just leaves one unanswered question which I put to you Lucius. While you are struggling behind the plough or harvesting grapes and olives or whatever you farmers do, there is an appointment which has recently become available at Herod Antipas' palace in Galilee. Do you know of him?"

"Certainly sir, I served at his court for a few months while my century was on loan to him during the last Jewish rebellion four years ago."

"Really! You speak Greek or perhaps Aramaic?"

"Both sir, though I cannot read or write Aramaic."

"That does not matter. Herod has asked for a Roman liaison officer to be made available at his palace in Sepphoris, but we've had some difficulty finding a suitable person who can speak to him in his own language. It will not be a fulltime post but you would be affiliated with the army even though you would still be classified as a retired veteran. That means you would receive part time pay, in addition to your pension, but you would need to make your home close enough to Sepphoris to be on hand when Herod needs you."

Nazareth is only five miles from Sepphoris. The idea of staying linked to the army in some way was attractive. "Sir, I gratefully accept. I cannot thank you enough for what you are doing for me and my friends."

"It is nothing. Now I must go and put the arrangements in place. Caius, be prepared for a noon meeting tomorrow with me and the Praetorian prefect. I wish all three of you well for the future. Remain here at your lodgings until one of my staff members brings you the necessary papers tomorrow morning."

With that, Germanicus shook each of us by the hand and departed. We stood there for a short while silently trying to comprehend what had just happened. Eventually Caius broke the silence. "I wonder if that man realises what a huge difference he has made to the lives of three humble citizens in just a few minutes."

"Probably not," replied Brasidas, "Because it was so easy for him to do."

"Well, if he is the nephew and adopted son of Tiberius," I said, "Who is already well past middle age, we have a wonderful emperor to look forward to. If there was ever a leader who could unite all the different peoples in our empire, Germanicus is the one."

"Except for the Jews of course," added Brasidas, "They can't even unite themselves."

"Which is just as well for us," remarked Caius sagely. "Lucius, what if Germanicus calls upon you to return to the eagles during the next five years?"

"Then I will have to, but he won't. A man of his importance will soon forget about me." But even as I uttered those confident words, I was not so sure.

By the middle of the morning next day, all our paperwork had arrived, and it was time to say our goodbyes. Albus and his cavalry troop had already left for Vetera and Brasidas was busy packing our luggage onto our horses. Caius and I stood side by side outside the Basilica Julia looking at the forum. We had been through a great deal together during the last fourteen years and had no idea when or if we would see each other again. The bond forged by men who have fought together is usually incredibly strong and ours was no exception.

"Caius, you will do well with the Praetorians," I said, unable to keep the sadness out of my voice. "You'll probably be a cohort tribune before long."

"Perhaps," he replied as if he had barely heard me. He was as sad as I was.

"When I reach Galilee, do you have a message for Mary?"

He said nothing for a while as we watched the sun appear from behind a cloud and cast a warm glow over all the superb buildings in the forum.

I waited in silence and eventually Caius sighed, "The truth is Lucius, I still adore her as much as I did when we first met. After all this time I have never seen a woman to match her, and I don't suppose I ever will. If she is contented with the life she has now, say nothing, but if not please give her my love. The trouble is I don't see how you can judge whether to speak of me to her or stay silent."

"Easy, I shall ask Ruth. She'll know."

"So, you have definitely chosen Ruth instead of Zenub?"

"Yes, but I shall return via Caesarea Maritima, where the Third Gallica was based when I last heard, and speak to Zenub first."

"Why?"

"It is the honourable thing to do of course. I can hardly end the matter by sending her a letter."

Caius shook his head in disapproval. "Listen old friend, you are not thinking straight. As we speak both Zenub and Ruth believe you are dead, lost with Varus and his legions. The news of the disaster is certain to have reached them by now. The fact that two or three centuries escaped will not be news. So, as Zenub thinks you are dead you should leave things as they are.

Why raise her hopes again, but only briefly, to tell her you have changed your mind? That would be cruel."

"But that does not seem honourable. What if she finds out?"

"Highly unlikely, though if she does she will learn the truth and work out for herself that you have changed your mind. But your proposal alters my 'highly unlikely' to 'absolute certainty,' so what's to be gained by it?"

"Nothing I suppose. Caius, I can't fault your logic, but it seems a cowardly way out."

"So, you would inflict double misery on Zenub to satisfy your sense of honour! Instead of losing you once as a hero she can remember with respect, she'll lose you twice and be rejected the second time."

"I can see you are right, but the idea will take some getting used to."

"Well get used to it quickly for Zenub's sake. She deserves it."

Just then, we heard Brasidas approaching with the horses loaded and ready for our departure. I embraced Caius, "Thank you for your advice which I shall follow. I will write to you and give you Mary's reaction to your message as well as news of Jesus. I will also give you details of where I live so we can continue to correspond. Please give me any news you can find out about Rufio."

"I shall Lucius."

"So, my friend, all that is left to say is take good care of yourself until we meet again."

Caius just nodded. The tears in his eyes spoke far more than words. Then Brasidas and I mounted up and began our long journey back to the east.

CHAPTER TEN

It was the fortieth year of the reign of Augustus Caesar. Spring came early in Galilee so Ruth and Mary were able to work in the small walled garden at the back of Joseph's house which was reserved for growing herbs of culinary and medical use. Earlier in the morning, Mary had purchased a lamb in the marketplace which would be prepared for the Passover feast that fell on the next day. She asked Ruth to help her select some fresh herbs to augment the flavour of the Passover lamb, not that she really needed help, but so they could be together enjoying each other's company. The moments when they could talk freely to each other without worrying about being overheard had become few and far between since Mary's father, Joachim died. As a consequence, Anna, her mother, had joined Joseph's household and tended to keep her daughter company as much as possible, which was understandable but also inhibiting from time to time.

"The rosemary is looking particularly good this year," said Mary as she cut a handful of the pungent herb and placed it in her basket.

"So is the sage," answered Ruth. "It augurs well for the Passover feast. What a pity Jesus won't be with us."

"And Judas too. I've changed my opinion about him. He's rather strange but there is an aura of sadness about him. He's good hearted and cares for Jesus."

"More than Joseph does."

"Well, that's understandable is it not?"

"But you have born Joseph four sons and a daughter. What more could a man want?"

"Three sons and a daughter," corrected Mary. "Joseph does not in his heart count Jesus as his."

"He has not forgiven you then?"

"Forgiven yes, forgotten no, but it does not alter the fact that I worry for my firstborn and loath all the Messiah nonsense that weighs so heavily on his young shoulders."

The two women worked together in silence for a while as they continued to cut herbs for the Passover meal until Ruth said, "You still miss him then?"

"Jesus?"

"Obviously, but I was referring to Caius."

"I have not heard from him for years."

"Well, he could hardly write to you without opening up old wounds with Joseph, could he?"

"I suppose not."

"And you certainly won't hear anything before this German war is over."

"I know. Ruth, I'm being selfish. Your man Lucius is involved with that war too, isn't he?"

"Yes, he's in the same cohort as Caius. I pray for both of them every morning and evening though I sometimes wonder if my prayers are ever heard."

"Jehovah is a man's god. Women's feelings do not matter to him."

"How could I forget it! We're reminded of that every time we visit the synagogue!"

Mary sighed, "But at least we have each other now. That is a great comfort to me."

Before Ruth could reply, a house slave entered the garden and addressed Mary. "My lady, the master wishes you and mistress Ruth to attend on him in his office."

"We'll be there soon," answered Mary.

The slave shifted uncomfortably. "I am sorry my lady, but the master's words were that you should go to him at once."

"Very well, go ahead and tell him we are coming."

When the slave had left, Ruth shrugged. "A man's god and a man's world."

Mary smiled, "But we know better don't we. Would you rather be a man?"

"No, but there are some times when I could be persuaded!"

The two women arrived at the office to be confronted by a solemn looking Joseph. "Ladies, please sit down. I have some bad news for you both." Mary and Ruth looked at each other with fear in their eyes and sat down opposite Joseph awaiting his next words with dread.

"I have just received a message from Jerusalem. The Roman army in Germania has been destroyed, wiped out. Apart from a few Gallic horsemen there were no survivors, none!"

Mary answered first. "This was Varus' army? The one with Lucius and…"

"Caius! Yes. It has been a complete disaster. The emperor is in mourning as is the rest of the empire."

"Except your Zealots," said Ruth. "They'll be delighted. I suppose we must expect another rebellion now. The Zealots won't want to be outdone by the Germans."

"Ruth, the Romans are an imperial nation but even empire builders must expect setbacks from time to time. This is not their first nor will it be their last."

"How many men have perished?" asked Mary.

"Three legions plus auxiliaries; about seventeen thousand in all."

"But what about prisoners and wounded?"

"The Germans do not take prisoners and kill all enemy wounded."

"So, there's no hope for a prisoner exchange?"

"None. There is no-one to exchange. I am truly sorry to tell you this. I did not wish it."

As the full horror dawned on her, Ruth felt her world crumble. All the hopes and dreams she had nurtured since we had last met were unceremoniously shattered. She was alone in this world once more. She tried to stand up, but her legs felt leaden. Mary put her hand on her shoulder. "Steady Ruth, let me help you." But for a full minute she could not move. She hoped this was just a bad dream and she would wake up soon, but she knew this was real; there was no escape.

Joseph helped Mary to get Ruth on her feet. "I am truly sorry Ruth. Is there anything I can do?"

She shook her head and whispered hoarsely, "I must go to my room."

"Then Mary and I will take you there."

When they reached the door to Ruth's room Mary asked, "Would you like me to sit with you for a while?"

"No, I just need to be alone now."

As they walked back to Joseph's office, Mary said, "Ruth was only living for the day Lucius came back. She used to tell me about all the things they would do together, discuss where they would live, how many children they would have, what crops they would grow and so on. She has nothing to live for now."

"That is sad. Life has been hard on Ruth, and we must watch her carefully in case she considers ending her place in this world early. And what of you Mary? You too have had bad news, yet you have said nothing."

Mary waited until Joseph had shut the office door behind them before responding. "Joseph, my husband, you and our children are my life now. It is true that I am saddened to hear of Caius' death, but he was a soldier and knew that death was always possible. He is part of my past, not the present."

An assurance like this, which was infrequent, was always gratifying to Joseph and he responded warmly, perhaps because the perceived threat, which never left him, was now gone. "Mary, I shall never forget that had it not been for Caius and Lucius risking their own lives to warn us in Bethlehem of Herod's murderous vengeance, you and I would have died protecting Jesus on that terrible day."

"All because your Zealot friends believe he is the Messiah which you and I know cannot be true."

"That secret was the price I had to pay to keep you. I could not bear to lose you and I would pay it again if I had to. Do you realise that with Caius and Lucius dead, you, I and Ruth are the only ones left on this earth who know the truth about the Messiah's ancestry?"

"Yes, but the terrible irony is that Jesus' life is threatened by a cause that is not his own. I have a feeling he will not turn out to be what his fanatical followers expect."

"Perhaps, and we can hardly be surprised if your prediction is realised. I believe Judas was becoming anxious about that very matter, but he only mentioned his concern indirectly. He never spoke directly to me about it before he fled with Jesus to Qumran."

"You must miss him helping you in the business. He seemed to have an aptitude for commercial work."

"He certainly has but James is coming on well, though he is not as advanced as Jesus was at the same age."

"Probably because he did not have Judas to teach him."

Joseph poured some wine into two goblets and handed one to Mary. "I know it is only just past noon, but I feel I need a drink after the news we have just received. Will you join me?"

Mary picked up the goblet, took a sip and put it down intending to go back to the garden, but Joseph put his hand on her shoulder and looked her directly in the eyes. "What happened to Ehud?"

The question came as a surprise, but she retained her composure. "If I tell you, your sense of justice might require me to be stoned to death. Do you want that?"

"Of course not! I am already party to the biggest deception in Jewish history so my sense of justice, as you call it, is certainly not strong enough to put my dear wife's life in danger."

"Very well, I will tell you, though you will not like what you are about to hear." Mary spared none of the gory details even as she saw Joseph's face turn ashen as the bloody events were revealed to him.

When she finished, he unlocked the drawer in his desk and said, "So, it was self-defence then?"

"Yes."

"Then why did you not come to me for help?"

A flash of anger pulsed through Mary at such a stupid, arrogant, male question, but she did not show it. "Two reasons," she answered. "Firstly, you were not there. You were with Jesus' arch enemy, Caiaphas, on your way back from Sepphoris.

Secondly, while I thank you for saying what you did about not allowing your sense of justice to put me in danger, I doubt you would have had the same concern for Ruth. I could hardly expect that could I?"

"She might have gone on trial, but she would have been acquitted because no crime was committed. It was self-defence."

"But, as an interested party, you would not have been able to give judgement and Ruth has already tasted Nazarene justice without your presence. And what about the removal of Ehud's head? I did that not Ruth. That makes me complicit in Ehud's death because I cleared up afterwards."

"You did a good job Mary, but you were not as thorough as you thought." Joseph took something wrapped in a cloth from his desk drawer, removed the cloth and placed a gleaming dagger in front of her. Mary's eyes widened. "Yes," he said, "It's Ehud's. He always carried it with him. The body was discovered on the morning after Caiaphas left us. I led some of the elders to the murder site to try and identify the body. We could not, so it was buried in an unmarked grave." He pointed to the dagger. "During the investigation I found this amongst the vines where I presume Ruth discarded it. I recognised it immediately and guessed that she might have been involved, so I hid it until I could return alone and collect it. It has been in my desk drawer ever since. I have spoken to no-one about this until now, so that makes me as complicit as you, does it not?"

"Certainly, but I always wondered what happened to that dagger. Ruth was too distraught to remember what she had done with it, and I did not have enough time to carry out a proper search of the area."

"Then what shall we do with it?"

"Cast it into the town cess pit where it can join its owner's head."

"I shall do exactly that Mary. So now you can trust your husband absolutely and at least we can comfort ourselves knowing that Ehud can do us no more harm."

Joseph could not have been more wrong about that. Meanwhile poor Ruth sobbed her heart out.

***

II

In the late afternoon sunlight, Caiaphas quietly watched Jerusalem's busy marketplace from the window of his office in the temple. He had just completed the arrangements for the Passover celebrations which would take place during the next few days. Ananas, the high priest, was away in Hebron where he was to attend a special ceremony for the patriarchs at the burial place of Abraham and his wife Sarah. While he casually observed the comings and goings in the marketplace below, Caiaphas considered the seminal events that had taken place during the last six months. It had been an unpleasant surprise to discover that the Messiah was still alive and very frustrating that he had managed to escape capture by a hair's breadth. Despite a thorough search of the most likely hiding places, the Messiah had evaded Caiaphas' agents and had probably gone to ground in one of the pagan cities such as Caesarea Maritima or Sepphoris. He may even be hiding right under the nose of the temple at Jerusalem but wherever he was, the Zealots had been strangely quiet about their success.

He was aroused from his musing by a palace servant who knocked at his door and entered without waiting to be invited to enter. "Sir, there is a visitor who requests an interview with the high priest."

"Does he have an appointment?"

"No sir, but he says the high priest and yourself met his son in the autumn of last year."

Suddenly Caiaphas' sensitive antennae twitched with excitement. This could be interesting. "Very well, bring him to me."

The servant returned accompanied by a small, innocuous man who would never see sixty again. He was the sort of person Caiaphas would normally instantly forget but for the first words the little man uttered. "Master, my name is Aaron of Nazareth. My son, Ehud, came to see you last autumn."

Always conscious of his own dignity, Caiaphas replied, "Do not call me 'Master'. I am not the high priest but his chief secretary. He confides in me so you may speak freely. I was present at the meeting with your son. You may refer to me as 'sir'."

"But the message I have is for the high priest alone."
"Then you will have to wait because he is in Hebron and will not be back in Jerusalem for another week at least. Is your message urgent?"

"I do not know sir."

"How can that be!" Snapped Caiaphas impatiently.

"Because the message is in the form of a sealed letter addressed to the high priest alone." Aaron took a scroll from the small bag he was carrying and placed it on the desk in front of Caiaphas. "You can see for yourself. It says, 'for the eyes of the high priest only.' It was written just after my son returned from his visit to the temple."

"I remember it well but tell me, why have you chosen this moment to bring the letter to the attention of the high priest? You could have done it months ago or months hence, so why now?"

"Sir, may I have some water? I have walked more than twenty miles today and, as you can see, I am not in the first flush of youth."

"Of course, you may," replied a mollified Caiaphas. Turning to the temple servant he said, "Bring this man some water and a chair then leave us." The chief secretary's instincts told him that this man might have important information though kindness rather than fear would probably extract the most out of him.

Once Aaron had drunk his fill and they were alone, Caiaphas used one of his most winning smiles. "Now Aaron, you have had a long journey and must be tired, so if what you have brought is of interest, I shall arrange accommodation for you here in the temple tonight."

"That would be a great honour sir."

"Yes, it would, so why have you chosen this moment to bring your son's letter to the temple?"

"Last year, after he returned from the temple, my son told me he was going to visit Nazareth with an escort of temple guards. He did not say why but he handed me this scroll saying he was about to navigate dangerous waters and though he hoped all would be well, there was a possibility that he might encounter trouble. Then he added that if I did not hear from him for three months, I should prepare myself because something may have happened to him, and if I had still heard nothing by Passover, he was probably dead. In that event I should hand this letter to the high priest because he would be very interested in its contents. My son is not perfect but he is a good boy and keeps in close contact with his mother and me. We have never gone this long without hearing from him, so we fear the worst. My wife Golda is distraught."

"Naturally, naturally," sympathised Caiaphas, "but at least I can tell you that your son accompanied me on my recent visit to

Nazareth. I'm surprised he did not contact you then."

"We no longer live there. Because of some unfortunate business matters in which Ehud was the victim of false accusations, we moved to Sepphoris where people are more friendly and Zealot influence is less strong."

"I understand completely," replied Caiaphas soothingly. "Your son left my retinue in Nazareth without permission, or so I thought at the time, but perhaps he had no choice in the matter. I sincerely hope your sorrow will not turn out to be justified, but it is wise to be realistic because it may well be that Ehud was forcibly taken from Nazareth. As you say, Zealot influence is strong there."

Aaron nodded, struggling to hold back his tears. "Then what should I do sir?"

Caiaphas knew he must not appear too eager otherwise he might frighten off this nervous little man, so he chose the path of disinterested reassurance. "Aaron, I will not presume to advise you. All I shall do is tell you what I would do in your position, if you wish me to."

"I do wish it sir, most definitely."

Pointing to the scroll on the desk, which he was desperately eager to acquire, the chief secretary said, "You clearly hold a letter of importance. Who knows what it contains, but I believe it is essential that the high priest sees it as soon as possible. It may well throw some light on the whereabouts of your son. As chief secretary to the high priest, I will place it under lock and key and send a message to Ananas asking him to return to Jerusalem immediately. I would not risk sending it to Hebron. The road is not secure at present because of the re-emergence of criminal, nomadic gangs which infest the area. My offer of accommodation here for you tonight is now confirmed so you can return to Sepphoris knowing your mission to the temple has been accomplished. I cannot promise good news concerning your son, I wish I could, but at least you may get some sort of closure to this terrible uncertainty for you and your wife by finding out what has happened to him."

Aaron looked at the scroll on the desk, he was clearly reluctant to part with it, and during the ensuing silence Caiaphas almost spoke again to urge him to do the right thing then checked himself, but only just. Finally, Aaron broke the silence. "Sir, I see the sense in what you say so I will leave this letter in your safekeeping because it's the only way I can be sure that whatever Ehud has said in it will be acted upon. Please take it and, if the high priest agrees, advise me of the contents at the address I shall give you."

He pushed the scroll towards Caiaphas who restrained himself from grabbing it and hiding it away. "Are you sure about this Aaron?"

"Yes sir."

"Then I will have a servant escort you to your quarters for tonight and bid you a safe journey tomorrow. Now if you will excuse me, I shall start writing the letter to Ananas which I am sure will bring him back here quickly."

As soon as Aaron had departed with the temple servant, Caiaphas at last picked up the scroll and stared at the seal. What he was about to do now could change his life or have no effect at all. The seal could not be broken and resealed, that was the whole point of a seal, but he had to know what was in that letter. He looked at his hands. They were shaking. He took out a small, bronze knife from the drawer in his desk and slid the point under the seal. He paused. The next move, if he had the courage to do it, might break him. But he had to know! He took a deep breath, paused once more then slit open the seal. Now there was no going back. He unrolled the scroll and began to read the text, which was written in the clear, neat hand of a construction surveyor.

Date: Thirteenth day of Heshvan (October).
To Ananas, the high priest or your successor, hail!
If you are reading this letter, I am almost certainly dead. When I returned home after seeing you, I wrote this letter and left it with Aaron, my father, in case the worst should happen. Going to Nazareth will be dangerous for me because I have Zealot enemies there who have already destroyed my reputation.

After our meeting I said I had told you all that I know. That was not quite true. In fact, I kept back the information I knew you would value most highly, namely the new identity and location of the Zealot leader known to you as Eli bar Abbas. I came by this information when some of those murderous, silent warriors called 'Shadows' by the Zealots visited Joseph, leader of the Nazareth Council of Elders recently. As usual I was forgotten as a non-person while working in the office next to Joseph's so the connecting door was left open. There was much talk about the Zealot treasury which I could not hear clearly, but I stopped working and listened more carefully when I heard Joseph ask how he could contact the Zealot leader.

Just before someone closed the connecting door between our two offices, I heard a voice answer Joseph's question. It seems that bar Abbas has changed his name to bar Ezra and lives in a hamlet too small to have a name, which is about a mile from Bethlehem along the Jerusalem road. This is a closely guarded secret. Contrary to what you may have heard, the

Zealots have not given up the armed struggle against Rome. They are simply biding their time and building up their strength for the moment when the Messiah declares himself. Then the whole of Judea, Idumea and Antipas' tetrarchy will go up in flames in yet another useless bloodbath.

High priest, you now know everything. I am holding nothing back. I am sure you will use this information well. This gives me comfort for although I shall not see it, I can now face whatever fate has in store for me knowing I have made a difference.

May God protect and keep you safe,

Ehud bar Aaron.

Caiaphas rolled up the scroll and leaned back on his chair. This letter from the grave, for that was what it really was, would change history if Ananas used it wisely. The high priest would have within his power the ability to crush the Zealot sect and set Judea and the Jerusalem temple on a course for unparalleled prosperity. He would be remembered as the greatest high priest of all. Then a little voice in the back of Caiaphas' mind whispered, 'Why should this be so? You will soon be the high priest and surely the credit for this success should belong to Joseph Caiaphas?' He tried to dismiss the thought, but it kept returning, 'Why Ananas? Why not Caiaphas?'

Ananas had promised him the succession though the final decision would be made by the Roman prefect, but the Romans just wanted taxes and a quiet life so a recommendation from a successful high priest was almost certain to be accepted. Yet Ananas had shown no desire to retire from his exalted status and might remain high priest for many years to come, especially if he took the credit for destroying the Zealot sect. Suddenly the confusion in Caiaphas' mind cleared. God favoured the bold, not the weak. Once more he looked at the scroll containing Ehud's letter then, instead of placing it in the box for the high priest's attention, he hid it away amongst his own private correspondence where it would remain until the time was right to use it. Aaron would never know and Ehud must now be dead.

Having made his fateful decision, Caiaphas could plan for the future. Alone amongst the temple hierarchy, he knew the new name and location of the Zealot leader. He decided to go to Bethlehem immediately himself and covertly verify the facts as stated in Ehud's letter. Then he would wait patiently until the Messiah declared himself knowing he could snuff out bar Abbas whenever he chose and, by cutting off the head of the Zealot sect, the Messiah would be alone and at the mercy of the high priest whoever that might be. He was determined to be that high priest. What power! It might take many years but with patience, Joseph Caiaphas would become the most celebrated high priest in Jewish history!

***

III

Judas spent the Passover celebrations at Qumran in a black depression knowing his influence over the Messiah was rapidly waning. Matters were made worse because Reuben had left and been replaced by another Shadow, Joab from Beth Shan, who was a much quieter, more self-contained character. At least Joab and Judas had met before during the raid on Herod's armoury at Sepphoris, so there was some affinity between them.

On Passover morning, Judas saw Jesus leaving the house of Judah who, despite his advanced years, was still the Teacher of Righteousness amongst the Essene community. He had also, in Judas' mind at least, replaced him as mentor of the Messiah so he took the opportunity to intercept Jesus before he reached his quarters in the desert town.

Judas called out, "Happy Passover to you Jesus! Come and walk with me for a while. I am going down to the Great Salt Sea for some exercise. Life in Qumran is rather too sedentary for me."

"A good idea Judas," replied Jesus, "And the walk will improve our appetites for this evening's feast." Jesus was at the stage between boyhood and adolescent man. Although now taller than Judas, who was himself tall for a Jew, his beard was slow to grow, a feature made all the more obvious because it was not the usual pitch-black Jewish colour. Judas decided to use the beard as a lightweight start to what he felt might become a heavyweight conversation. "Your beard is developing an interesting colour, brown with tinges of red and copper."

"Yes, it seems to be struggling to decide what colour it wants to be. When I asked my mother about this, she told me that her family on her mother's side had received an input of northern blood when, many generations ago, a Hittite mercenary from Carcemish fell in love with one of our ancestors and accepted the Jewish faith so that he could marry her."

"Ah, the much vaunted, blue-eyed Hittites! That explains why you are growing so tall, and your eyes are green instead of the usual dark brown."

"Yes, though strangely those features do not seem to have been passed on to my brothers."

Once again, a momentary sense of unease pulsed through Judas but he quickly banished it to the back of his mind. "Jesus, I have seen very little of you lately. Have I said or done something to trouble you?"

"Of course not! What a preposterous thought! I always enjoy your company."

"I am indeed grateful to hear that, but I have noticed you do not speak to me about your revelations anymore."

Jesus did not immediately respond, so they walked together in silence for a while. Eventually Judas could not prevent himself from asking again. "Is it that you are no longer receiving revelations or are you reporting them to Judah instead of me?"

"I don't think you would like the revelations I am receiving now."

"Why not? You cannot control the content of your revelations so why should I not like them?"

"Because you are a Zealot. My revelations conflict with the

hopes and aspirations of the Zealot sect. They would also be regarded as blasphemous by the Pharisees and the Sadducees."

"But acceptable to the Essenes?"

"Judah listens and occasionally comments but he does not judge."

"Jesus, you are the Messiah. No-one will judge you, least of all me. Will you not share your revelations with me like you used to? I love you as if you were my own son. I earnestly want us to become close again as we once were."

By now they were close to the edge of the Great Salt Sea. Jesus stopped and looked across the vivid, blue water that stretched out for many miles ahead of them. Judas could see he was deeply troubled but now he remained silent giving Jesus time to gather his thoughts and prepare his response in his own way. "Very well, I will try and explain what has happened, but I am still confused about some of the things I have seen and await further clarification before I can understand fully what is expected of me."

"That is the nature of revelation. You must accept it in small, gradual doses. Too much at one time would destroy your mind."

Jesus smiled. "Well, that is comforting. That's exactly what Judah says."

Judas was not especially pleased to be compared to Judah in that way, but he said nothing and waited for Jesus to speak again.

"Jehovah created this world and all that exists in it." Judas nodded approvingly – so far so good. "But he is not the creator of all things. In fact, he is just one of the creations of the supreme spirit whose name is Barbelo. Jehovah is not God as you mean the word but a powerful archangel. His true name is

Yaldaboath. Barbelo gave Yaldaboath and others like him the power to create life in worlds of their own, but Yaldaboath performed poorly at this because he wanted his creatures to think he is the supreme being. Did he not tell us that we must have no false gods to worship, but just him alone because he is a jealous god? If he really is the supreme spirit he would have no need to be jealous but he is not."

Judas drew breath to argue against such heresy but Jesus held up his hand and said, "I told you this would be difficult and you would not like it but please hear me out before you say anything. There are many other powerful archangels like Yaldaboath who have created life in their worlds, but only our angel has corrupted his world by claiming to be the supreme spirit. It is Yaldaboath, or Jehovah as you call him, who is the fallen angel, not Lucifer who is merely an invention from Yaldaboath's own mind."

Judas could restrain himself no longer. "But this contravenes everything we have been taught. Are we not God's Chosen Race?"

"No, we are not. We are only Yaldaboath's Chosen Race. Barbelo chooses his companions for their merits not their race. He offers eternal life after death for those who follow his principles in this life."

"Which are?" demanded an increasingly frustrated Judas.

"Truth, knowledge, tolerance and respect, but above all love for our fellow human beings."

"And what of those who do not follow Barbelo's principles?"

"They will die with their bodies. There is no Hell or Hades, just oblivion for them. But those who do not know Barbelo but still live by his principles will also be rewarded with eternal life."

"But surely Jehovah's commandments are sufficient for the Jews?"

"They should be, but Yaldaboath does not even abide by his own commandments. How do you explain his orders to the patriarch Joshua to exterminate the Canaanites, every man, woman, child and even their animals so that the Promised Land should be cleansed to make way for his Chosen Race? That is plain murder on a grand scale yet that is the god you worship!"

Judas had no immediate answer to that so he changed the nature of what was fast becoming a fraught debate. "Even if what you say is true, how are you going to persuade a deeply religious people like the Jews that they have been worshipping a mass murderer for the last two thousand years!"

"I do not know. That has not yet been revealed to me."

"But as the Messiah you will need an answer to that question before you lead the Jews to victory over Rome."

Jesus sighed. "Judas, you have not really understood. I know I cannot expect that yet, but put simply, I will never sanction the shedding of human blood."

"The Essene philosophy! Judah has contaminated you! You are the long-awaited Messiah yet you will allow the Jews to be subjugated by a pagan empire forever!"

"I did not say that; there is another more effective and less costly way. The pagan empire you speak of is Rome. What if it were not pagan?"

"I don't understand."

"I shall take my message to the ordinary Jewish people first, then the temple hierarchy in Jerusalem, and finally the emperor and senate in Rome. When the Romans and Jews worship Barbelo together, the distinction between conqueror and conquered will vanish. We shall become one people. Then, as the empire extends its boundaries further still, as it surely will, the gift of peace will follow in its wake. Surely that is something worth fighting for, if fight we must."

"But you just said you will never sanction the shedding of human blood!"

"I know I am still young and unworldly. I should have said 'human blood within the empire'. I realise the imperial boundaries will not be extended without fighting but the bringing of permanent peace would be worth fighting for would it not?"

"Certainly, but such a thing can never be achieved."

"Why not?"

Once more, Judas did not have a ready answer. It was true Jesus was still young, not yet fifteen years old, but he was already debating with the authority of an elder. Judas could not help admiring his erstwhile student and hoped that some of his maturity was due to himself as his teacher and mentor. "Jesus, listen to me. There can be no doubt you are receiving extraordinary messages within your revelations. I know you speak only the truth, so it may be that through you we Jews can begin to understand why the great empire you speak of is Roman and not Jewish. But how are you going to deliver this message to a people who are mostly illiterate and have been inculcated since childhood to believe that they are not only special but God's Chosen Race?"

Jesus bent down, picked up a hand-sized rock and threw it into the blue water of the Great Salt Sea. From the splash, ripples flowed outwards in concentric circles. "It will be difficult. My revelations have not yet completed giving me the message in full, but when they have, I sincerely hope they will also show me how all this is to be done. All I can tell you at this moment is that the knowledge I have been given will spread outwards like those ripples in the blue water yonder. The promise of eternal life after death on this earth will be the driving force behind the success of Barbelo's message."

"But surely our people will need some sort of physical proof to support the idea of life after death?"

"Of course they will and that troubles me, but having taken me this far, I am sure my revelations will provide me with the answers I shall need."

That reply troubled Judas too, for he sensed an inevitable approaching tragedy, but now he just needed time to think. "Enough talk for now," he said. "Let us return to Qumran and prepare for the Passover feast."

***

IV

The Passover celebrations were now almost two weeks in the past. With Jesus safe under the watchful eyes of Joab, Judas felt confident enough to leave him at Qumran for a few days while he made the three-day journey south to visit bar Abbas in Bethlehem. He arrived at the house of Ezra on the eleventh day of Nisan (April) tired but happy with the anticipation of seeing his old friend again after fourteen years, but at the same time he was anxious about the message he was bringing concerning Jesus. The house had not changed much since that terrible day when King Herod sent out his Galatian guards to slaughter all the male babies of Bethlehem, but the outhouse where Jesus was born had been turned into an extension of the main house. Two young boys were playing near the well in the courtyard but were too engrossed in their game to notice the arrival of a stranger.

"I am looking for Eli bar Ezra," said Judas. "I believe he lives here."

The elder of the two boys, who looked to be about eleven years old, had been well schooled in manners and replied confidently, "He is our father sir and is in the house. Who shall I say wishes to see him?"

"Judas Sicariot."

The boy and his brother went into the house. A few moments later, a man Judas did not recognise came out and smiled warmly. "Judas my friend, what a pleasant surprise to see you after all this time. Come inside and meet my wife." It was only by the clear, almost metallic voice that Judas recognised bar Abbas. His lean, cadaverous frame was now well rounded, his hair and beard were more grey than black and his eyebrows had become bushy. Bar Abbas saw Judas staring and laughed, "Yes, married life has changed my appearance, that's contentment for you, but my dedication to the Zealot cause remains as fervent as ever. You, however, have hardly altered at all!"

"That's stress for you! But it's good to see you, Eli. However, the reason I have come here is because our cause may be in jeopardy."

The smile left bar Abbas' face. "Then come in and once you are rested and refreshed from your long journey we shall talk."

By the time Judas had washed and eaten and had met Sarah, bar Abbas' charming wife and their children, the sun had set and the braziers had been lit. At last, they were alone and Judas could pour out his torrent of concern about Jesus.

Bar Abbas listened in silence saying nothing until Judas had finished. "How confident are you that these dreams the Messiah has been having really are revelations? Jesus is not yet fifteen years old. I never heard of a child having revelations."

"He is not a child Eli. On the contrary, he is mature for his age. I cannot be sure about the revelations because I have never been blessed with one, but the descriptions Jesus gives of them match very closely to those your own father described to me when we shared a prison cell together in King Herod's castle fifteen years ago. I am as certain as I can be that the revelations are genuine."

"It sounds to me that Judah, the Teacher of Righteousness, has got to him."

"But Jesus started having revelations before he met Judah. I even witnessed one of them."

"Perhaps, but apart from turning the Romans away from their pagan gods, Jesus is extolling pure Essene philosophy."

"I know, I just don't understand how this has happened."

"Well, we could live with much of it but the commitment to non-violence makes a mockery of our sect. Can you imagine the Romans ever treating us as equals?"

"Jesus would say it must be the Jews who treat the Romans as equals!"

Bar Abbas pondered for a moment. "Mmmm, a Messiah the anointed King of the Jews who is not prepared to fight for his throne or for his people. It makes no sense. Judas, how could you allow this to happen? He was under your stewardship all the time."

"It would have happened whether I was there or not. It came from revelations."

"So you say. Reuben said nothing of this."

"It did not happen in his presence. The only comfort I can offer is that Jesus is still young and said himself that the revelations are not yet complete. He is highly intelligent and will come of age early. By then we should know the full meaning of what his revelations are telling him. Maybe they won't be as bad as they seem to be now, perhaps it may turn out that he is misinterpreting the meaning of some of them, but I could not wait until then before speaking to you."

"My friend, you did the right thing by informing me. If anything, you left it too long but we still have time to formulate a strategy in case the worst should happen."

"The worst?"

"The Messiah fails his people. I can hardly believe I've just uttered those five words, but from what you have said we must be ready in case it happens."

"If it really does happen, then key articles of our faith will be shattered. Has God's anointed one been corrupted? Is God's anointment of no value? If so, is Jehovah really all powerful or is he lying to us? I could go on!"

"Judas, the first thing we must do is to re-check the ancestry of our Messiah. There may have been an error."

"But Eli, the records are locked away in the temple."

"It can be done with care. We have agents there. I will give the order and let you know the result as soon as I have it. Meanwhile enjoy my hospitality tonight. Tomorrow you shall begin your journey back to our safe house in Nazareth. You still have your essential duties managing our treasury there."

"I thought the treasury was going to be moved?"

"That plan has not yet been carried out. Now it no longer needs to be. Joshua the Messenger is our temporary custodian there so you will have protection when you return because he has advanced within our sect to become one of Isaac's Shadows."

"What of Jesus?"

"He still has Joab's protection and will be safe amongst Judah and the Essenes. I think he is beyond your mentoring now or anyone else's for that matter. The Teacher of Righteousness can take care of his education for the time being. He can't do any more damage than he already has done. I will leave you now so you can get some sleep before tomorrow's journey."

"Eli, before you go can you tell me what happened to

Ezra?"

"Certainly! At least that story has a happy ending. As I think you know, his wife had died not long before Joseph and his family arrived unexpectedly on that cold winter night more than fourteen years ago when Jesus was born. You will certainly recall Ezra's forbidding appearance which masked a kind and gentle nature. A year later, he welcomed me into his house as his supposedly illegitimate son. When I married Sarah, we soon had children and Ezra changed from a wizened old man into a delightful adoptive grandfather. He and his wife were not blessed with children and he always maintained that his old age was the most rewarding time of his life. The boys wept bitterly when he died last year aged ninety-one. We all miss him."

Judas was ready to leave early next day and bade farewell to bar Abbas, Sarah and their two sons Jacob and Ahab. Bar Abbas and Sarah walked with him to the gate which divided their front courtyard from the Jerusalem road but, as he opened the gate, Judas stopped and said, "Eli, I would like your consent to visit Qumran on my way back to Nazareth to explain to Jesus why I shall no longer be teaching him, otherwise he may feel I have deserted him."

"Of course you may, Judas and as soon as it is safe to do so he will return to Nazareth to re-join his family."

"Thank you. And now I will bid you farewell—"

"Just a moment," interrupted Sarah. Both men looked at her, astonished that a Jewish wife should interrupt a conversation between her husband and another man. A similarity to the Messiah's mother, Mary, flashed through Judas' mind. He had hardly noticed her the previous evening when they had dined together, but now her inner strength and love for her husband showed in the fire in her eyes.

An embarrassed bar Abbas said, "Judas, I apologise—"

"But there is nothing to apologise for. Sarah is your guardian as well as your wife. You are a fortunate man. We must both listen to her."

Bar Abbas nodded his approval and Sarah gripped his hand. "Husband, have you spoken to Judas about your concerns during the last few days?"

"What concerns My Dear?"

"You know very well; your concerns about being watched."

"No, but I don't think that should involve Judas."

"Well, I do." And without further consultation with her husband, Sarah addressed Judas directly. "For the last week or so, Eli has sensed he's been under observation by a man who lingers near here but quickly disappears into the city when Eli approaches him. It may be nothing of course but the man who leads the Zealot sect should take no chances. Is that not so?"

"Indeed, you are right," agreed Judas. "Your husband is far too valuable to our cause to ignore even the most insignificant threat."

Then turning to her husband, Sarah said, "Please speak to Judas."

Quietly proud of his wife's uncompromising support, bar Abbas smiled, "A few days ago I noticed a man standing beside an acacia tree looking at our dwelling. I thought nothing of it at the time, but when I left to go to the marketplace in Bethlehem I sensed I was being followed. Just as I reached a sharp bend in the road, I turned round suddenly just in time to see the same man duck down behind some bushes clearly wishing to hide from me. I did not see him again for the rest of the day, but on the following morning I thought I saw him in Bethlehem again but I cannot be sure. That is all."

"That is enough," replied Judas. "You did not recognise him?"

"No, but if he confronts me, I am sure I can deal with him."

"So am I, but I doubt he is a common thief. He could be an agent of our enemies."

"Who do you mean?"

"The temple. The priests there hate us more than the Romans!"

Bar Abbas laughed heartily. "Judas, the man I saw was a bumbling fool. A temple agent would have made a far better job of surveillance."

"Sarah," said Judas. "I think your husband is right about that. It was probably just a part time, opportunistic thief but, as I said before, we should take no chances." Then turning to bar Abbas again, he said, "Eli, to the Zealot sect your safety is second only to the Messiah's in importance, therefore I ask your permission to visit Isaac on my return journey with a request to send a Shadow to watch over you for the next few weeks. That is the best way to make certain we are not dealing with a real threat to your safety."

Bar Abbas put his arm round his wife, kissed her on the forehead and replied, "I am blessed to have Sarah to take care of me. Please go to Isaac with your request."

Caiaphas returned to the temple, well pleased with his first attempt at surveillance. He had no idea it was his incompetence that had resulted in his success. At first, he was worried because he had only met bar Abbas once before during the great rebellion that followed Herod's death. That was nearly fifteen years ago, but the man living near Bethlehem as bar Ezra did not really resemble the slim, wolf-like man he recalled. But when he heard him speak in the marketplace, his thin, precise voice was unmistakable. Now he was certain of the identity and location of the leader of the Zealot sect. He possessed a secret of priceless value and would keep it safely hidden until the moment came to strike. And when that moment came the credit would go to Joseph Caiaphas and him alone!

By the time Isaac's Shadow took up his observation position to watch over bar Abbas' house, Caiaphas was safely back in the temple blissfully unaware of his lucky escape.

***

V

By the time spring moved into early summer, Judas had returned to the Zealot safe house in Nazareth where he could resume managing the Zealot treasury. Every day he thought about his time with Jesus, wondering if there was something more he could have done to prevent, or at least reduce, the influence of the Teacher of Righteousness. But at least there was some compensation in the form of his new Shadow guardian, Joshua the Messenger, whose company he enjoyed even though he had lost his youthful exuberance since becoming a Shadow.

Judas now concentrated his energy on managing and developing the Zealot treasury which was becoming richer almost daily from more and more donations. Despite his disappointment with the Messiah, life could be a lot worse.

Meanwhile, in Joseph's household, there was concern about Ruth. On a sunny Iyar (May) morning, Joseph and Mary sat down together for breakfast as usual. "Mary, I'm worried about Ruth. She hardly leaves her room these days except for meals and collecting the rent for her house. Is there anything that can be done?"

"Since the news of the Germania disaster she has become a different woman. Sad and quiet, she seems to have lost her zest for life. I try speaking to her and, occasionally, she comes to the market with me, but she does not engage in conversation with me or anyone else. There was a time when I could not stop her talking and she was popular with other women, but now they avoid her."

"It's a beautiful morning today. Perhaps she would like to work with you in the garden?"

"She certainly needs to get out more. I'll take her with me to the marketplace. The cloth merchants will be there today, and we need more material to re-line some of our furniture. She always used to enjoy bargaining with them so perhaps that will bring her out of her depression a little bit."

After some serious exhortation, Mary managed to prise her friend out of her private lair and, as they walked towards the marketplace, the beautiful spring morning began to have a beneficial effect on Ruth. She even smiled when she saw the cloth merchants' stalls and began to examine the quality and price of their goods with some of her old gusto. Mary stood back, delighted to see her best friend beginning to take some interest in life again and looked at the bustling activity in the market. Although only a small town, Nazareth's market had a good reputation in central Galilee and attracted a fascinating variety of traders. Mary glanced up the hill, which marked the high point of the town, then looked back at the traders again. Suddenly she realised something was wrong. She looked back up the hill once more but more intently this time and saw a Roman soldier looking back at her. She nudged Ruth who was busy examining a bale of cloth on one of the stalls and pointed to the soldier. "Look! That Roman seems to be staring at us!"

Ruth sniffed, "Probably a deserter. Best leave him be."
"But Ruth, look again."

Ruth put down the bale of cloth and shaded her eyes with her left hand against the morning sun. Then she frowned and took a few steps which took her past the cloth merchants' stalls and stopped. Then she walked slowly beyond the market and stopped again. Now Mary began to follow her but before she could catch up, Ruth started walking again but more quickly this time. Mary increased her pace too but by now Ruth had accelerated into a steady trot in the direction of the Roman soldier. When she was about forty paces from him he opened his arms to greet her. She dropped the little bag she was carrying and ran faster and faster until she was sprinting over the rough scree like a mountain gazelle. Then, without slowing down she threw herself into my arms!

"Lucius! Lucius! My love! I thought you were dead!"

"I nearly was, quite a few times, but somehow I struggled through."

She wept huge tears of joy, soaking my shoulder in warm, salty water. She clasped me so tightly I could hardly breathe but I did not care. This was all that I could have hoped for. I managed to gasp, "Is that Mary coming up the hill behind you?"

She suddenly released me and whispered, "Yes, what of Caius?"

"He was with me all the time and got through without a scratch."

She released me and ran back down the hill to Mary. After a few words they hugged each other and came to join me.

Mary asked, "Is Caius with you?"

"Sadly no, but he is well and has been promoted to a centurion in the Praetorian Guard." From the eagerness in Mary's beautiful face I had no difficulty in passing on Caius' message. "Mary, he sends you his love and regrets he cannot be here to tell you himself."

Mary's large eyes moistened and it was only then I realised it was possible to look happy and sad at the same time. Then, as

Ruth nestled herself into my arms, Mary smiled a smile that would have melted the hardest man's heart. "Well, at least you are here Lucius, and you are most welcome."

Ruth asked, "How long for this time?"

Now was not the moment to mention Germanicus' condition which accompanied my early discharge from the legions, so I simply said, "I have been honourably discharged on full centurion's benefits. I am here to stay!"

A howl of joy presaged another crushing embrace from Ruth as the darkness of her world was banished by hope once more.

And so, five blissful years in our lives began. We were married in the Roman rite and set up home near Sepphoris where I could easily attend on Antipas when needed, which was not often, and Ruth and Mary could see each other whenever they wanted. Children soon followed, a boy and two girls. I had never known such happiness but, as Caius had predicted, Germanicus did not forget me and eventually I was summoned back to re-join the eagles for the final battle in Germania.

END OF PART TWO

CAST OF MAIN CHARACTERS – PART TWO * = Nonfictional

Narrator Lucius Veranius centurion 3rd century 5th cohort 3rd legion (Gallica)

The Jews

Ananas* – High priest.
Antipas* – son of Herod and Tetrarch of Galilee and Perea.
Archelaus* – son of Herod and Ethnarch of Judea, Idumea and Samaria.
Arethus – house slave of Menahem.
Ariel bar Eleazar – Zealot commander.
Asher – brother of Achiab and commander in the Jewish army.
Caiaphas* – chief secretary to Ananas.
Deborah – servant in Joseph's household.
Ehud – contract manager for Joseph.
Elijah bar Abbas – leader of the Zealot sect.
Ezra - owner of the outhouse in which Jesus was born.
Isaac – commander of the Shadows.
Jesus* – Messiah and King of the Jews.
Joazar* – high priest.
Joab – a Shadow from Beth Shan.
Joachim* – father of Mary and grandfather of Jesus.
John* – an Essene and cousin of Jesus.
Joseph bar Jacob* – husband of Mary.

Joshua the Messenger – friend of Judas and Zealot warrior.
Judah, Teacher of Righteousness* – leader of the Essene sect.
Judas Sicariot* (biblical Iscariot) also bar Menahem – teacher and mentor to Jesus.
Judas the Galilean* – a false messiah.
Mary Magdalene* – daughter of a priestess of Artemis who converted to the Essene sect.
Mary* – mother of Jesus.
Menahem – father of Judas Sicariot.
Philip* – son of Herod and Tetrarch of Gaulantis and Trachontis.
Rachel – Menahem's second wife and step-mother of Judas.
Reuben – Zealot bodyguard.
Ruth – companion of Mary and lover of Lucius Veranius.

The Gentiles

Aelius Sejanus* – tribune and son of the prefect of Praetorian Guard.
Allix – commander of Belgian auxiliary cohort.
Arminius* – adjutant German auxiliary cohort.
Attalus – commander of Herod's Galatian bodyguard.
Brasidas – slave and personal secretary to Varus.
Caius Pantera – father of Jesus and centurion 5th century, 5th cohort, 3rd legion (Gallica).
Caidicius* – Roman commander at Aliso.
Eumenes – deputy commander Galatian bodyguard.
Friedrich von Vechten – commander of Batavian auxiliary cohort.
Galerius – file leader 3rd century, 5th cohort, 3rd legion (Gallica).
Germanicus* – nephew of Tiberius and future commander of

Roman forces on the Rhine.
Gnaeus Servilius – centurion 2nd century, 5th cohort, 3rd legion (Gallica).
Juba – commander of Numidian cohort.
Licinius Piso – tribune and commander of 5th cohort, 3rd legion (Gallica).
Lucius Eggius* – commander of Roman army in Germania Magna after Varus dies.
Lucius Veranius – centurion 3rd century, 5th cohort, 3rd legion (Gallica).
Marcus Aius – centurion 4th century, 5th cohort, 3rd legion (Gallica).
Marcus Sempronius – centurion 1st century, 5th cohort, 3rd legion (Gallica).
Marcus Tullius – legate 3rd legion (Gallica).
Publius Quinctilius Varus* – Governor of Germania Magna.
Quintus Paterculus – decurion, 5th cohort, 3rd legion (Gallica).
Rufio – file leader 3rd century, 5th cohort, 3rd legion (Gallica).
Septimus Nasicus – centurion 6th century, 5th cohort, 3rd legion (Gallica).
Tiberius* – nephew of Augustus Caesar and imperial heir apparent.
Zenub – Felicifer (bringer of happiness) Third Legion Gallica and lover of Lucius Veranius.